Love and Lies

Loren Dempsey

Contents

Prologue

♥

She should have known.

The chaos in the sky had been a warning, a premonition of the tragedy about unfolding. The clouds churned and writhed like the ocean during a storm, and the emptiness in her chest matched the hollowness of the sky.

But Fatimè ignored the signs. Today was supposed to be the happiest day of her life, the day she would marry the man she loved more than anything in the world. She had no time for jitters or omens of doom.

Everything changed when her father appeared in the doorway. His face was ashen, his eyes brimming with tears. The sight of him made her heart race and her stomach drop.

He cleared his throat, and every sound in the room became amplified, the rustle of his crisp babbar riga, the creak of the bed as he sat down beside her. He took a deep breath as if summoning the strength to deliver the news.

And then he spoke.

"Fatimè, there's been an accident..."

Those words echoed in her head, drowning out everything else. She wanted to scream, to deny the reality of what she had just heard. She clung to her father's arm, seeking comfort, but he seemed far away as if he were delivering the news from another world.

"I am sorry," he whispered.

The tears came, hot and fierce, and she wondered if she could ever stop crying. The words that kept ringing in her head were "in an accident," "he's no more," and "I am sorry."

This had to be a bad dream. She would go with that.

"Is she going to be okay?" her mother asked.

She was tempted to laugh out loud at the question.

"Okay?" After this, how would she be okay?

She should have known there was nothing good about chaos in the sky.

Chapter 1

♥

Abuja, Nigeria.

7th December 2016.

Kamal stood in the middle of the restroom, rubbing his chin, lost in his thoughts. As he contemplated his next move, his phone buzzed insistently in his pocket. He initially considered ignoring it, frustrated with the incessant interruptions. But when the phone announced the caller, he quickly changed his mind and hastily left the restroom.

Outside, he pressed the answer button, and Abdul's voice boomed through the speaker. Kamal's irritation was palpable as he responded, "Abdul? Haba, now I have been following you for months let's seal this deal but all I get are excuses and more excuses."

Kamal had known Abdul for years and his lack of commitment, respect, and disregard for time was not new. The deal they were working on involved handling the logistics of medical supplies for a pharmaceutical company, a significant partnership that could elevate his business to new heights. Kamal had invested time, resources, and his reputation into securing this contract, but Abdul's constant delays were testing his patience.

"I'm sorry, man," Abdul apologized. "I have to accompany Mama to an important family engagement."

Kamal let out a weary sigh, running his hands through his hair. He knew he was at a crossroads. He could either cut ties with Abdul or find another solution, or he could reluctantly agree to Abdul's proposal. Deep down, he knew Abdul was the best man for the job, and finding a replacement would only lead to further delays and setbacks.

"Okay, let's do it this way," Abdul said. "We'll attend the event and seal the deal. What do you think?"

Abdul's suggestion wasn't ideal, but Kamal had no choice if he wanted to seize this opportunity. He needed Abdul's expertise and connections to make this project a success.

"Fine, send me the location," Kamal replied briefly before ending the call. Moments later, a message from Abdul with the details appeared on his phone screen. Kamal couldn't help but exclaim, "What?" in frustration.

Did Abdul expect him to travel to Gombe? It was inconvenient and would disrupt his carefully crafted plans. Kamal groaned, knowing that this was going to be a significant inconvenience.

With a resigned sigh, Kamal pocketed his phone and made his way back to the restroom. However, upon his return, he was met with an empty stall, exacerbating his frustration.

"Shit," he cursed under his breath, realizing that he would have to wait a little longer. Little did he know that this unexpected delay would set in motion a series of events that would change his life forever.

Fatimè plopped down onto a seat next to her cousin Madina, letting out a deep sigh. Madina turned to her, scoffing at her dramatic demeanor. "Walahi, you are funny," she said, rolling her eyes.

Fatimè ignored Madina's comment and pulled out her phone from her bag, seeking solace in the digital world. "And why do you look like you're going to a funeral?" Madina asked, taking a good look at her cousin.

Fatimè was dressed in all-black, from her abaya to her shoes and even her suitcase. On the other hand, Madina looked ready for a day out, wearing a vibrant floral gown with a turban and her signature red lipstick. Fatimè let out an exasperated sigh, "I'm in zombie mode here, please. And why on earth did you book us a morning flight?"

Fatimè was not a morning person at all. Left to her, she would start her day at noon. "Oh come on, Tims, how else do you expect us to get good lalle if we don't get there early? Besides, we've already missed the bridal shower, and Mufida is not happy about that."

"The whole idea of a wedding is ridiculous," Fatimè muttered, her voice tinged with bitterness.

Madina rolled her eyes. "What's ridiculous about free food, fancy outfits, and fine boys in kaftans?"

"Well, I hope this is the last wedding I have to attend. I am T for tired," Fatimè replied, her weariness evident in her tone.

"Knowing our family, I'll advise you to forget about that wish. Not happening," Madina remarked knowingly.

There was no need to argue because Madina was right. Someone was always getting married in their family - a cousin, an aunt, or an uncle. With the extensive network of relatives, it was best for Fatimè to let go of that wish.

It had been nearly two years since she had attended a wedding. The mere thought of those joyous occasions stirred up a well of emotions she had become adept at hiding. Attending weddings reminded her of her painful loss.

The memories rushed back vividly, like a haunting melody she couldn't escape. The preparations, the excitement, and the anticipation for a future filled with love and happiness—it had all turned into a devastating tragedy. Fate had indeed, dealt her a cruel hand

The lounge in the airport was eerily quiet, with only a few passengers scattered about. Fatimè welcomed the silence, as any additional noise would only worsen her existing headache. Madina got up to answer a call, complaining about the lounge's bad network, while Fatimè busied herself with a game of 'candy crush' on her phone.

Suddenly, she heard someone approach and assumed it was Madina returning. But when she looked up, she saw the most adorable little boy standing in front of her, his hands hidden behind his back. Judging by his 'PJ Masks' hoodie, she guessed he was about three years old. Every three-year-old seemed to be obsessed with that cartoon.

"Hello, cutie," she said with a warm smile, unable to resist the charm of the child.

As Madina ended her phone call and returned, she was surprised to find her cousin accompanied by a little boy. "Dume fe'ata?" she asked, confused.

"I think he's lost," Fatimè replied, crouching down to the boy's level and gently taking his hand. "What is your name, cutie?"

"Aaa-dil," the boy answered with a squeaky voice, his eyes darting around anxiously.

"Okay, Adil. Who are you here with? Where is your mommy?" Fatimè asked, her heart going out to the young boy.

The boy pointed upwards, indicating his mother was somewhere above them. Fatimè couldn't help but feel a pang of sadness for the boy. "And your daddy?" Madina quickly added, hoping to find someone responsible for the child. The boy shrugged, indicating he had no idea where his father was.

"Don't you think we should take him to the authorities or something?" Madina suggested, her concern evident.

Adil looked like he was about to burst into tears, clutching onto Fatimè's hand tightly. "There, there," Fatimè comforted him, picking him up gently. "Don't cry. We'll take you to your daddy, okay?" She glanced around, searching for any signs of a frantic father searching for his son, but found none.

"We need to report this immediately," Madina said, concerned about potential accusations of kidnapping.

Fatimè agreed with Madina, realizing the urgency of the situation. However, she also wanted to gather more information about the child's parents and their actions. She couldn't fathom how any parent could allow such a young and adorable boy to wander alone in such a vast and busy airport. While she understood that kids had a knack for running around, it was no excuse for neglecting their safety. Fatimè was determined to give the parents an earful when she found them.

After waiting a few more minutes, Fatimè made a decision. "Okay, let's go find your daddy," she said to Adil, lifting him into her arms. She noticed Madina still sitting, showing no intention of assisting her in the search.

"Madina?!" Fatimè called out, surprised by her cousin's lack of support.

"What?" Madina replied nonchalantly, engrossed in her phone.

"Are you not coming with us?" Fatimè asked, raising an eyebrow in disbelief.

"Someone needs to look after our bags, and besides, you've got this under control," Madina responded, waving her hands dismissively and returning her attention to her phone.

Fatimè didn't need to move an inch because as she turned, she locked eyes with a man clad in a sky-blue kaftan and matching cap. She recognized the familiar earthy scent of 'black afgano' lingering in the air, one of her father's favorite fragrances. The resemblance between the man and Adil was uncanny, and it became apparent that he was the boy's father as Adil reached out to him. The man collected his son and breathed a sigh of relief, expressing gratitude, "Alhamdulillah."

He then turned to Adil, pulling playfully at his nose. "How many times have I told you not to run off like that, huh? You almost gave me a heart attack when I turned around and didn't see you. Please don't do that again, okay?" Adil nodded earnestly and snuggled up to his father.

Fatimè stood there, watching the heartwarming scene unfold. Her initial frustration and scolding intentions melted away as she witnessed the genuine concern and love between them.

He turned to Fatimè, smiling apologetically. "Forgive my manners," he said. "I was just thrilled to find him. I'm so sorry he disturbed you. Adil loves running around."

"Oh, I am sorry about that. I'm just glad he is back with you, and a cutie like this can never be a bother," she replied warmly.

Kamal's gratitude was evident as he smiled gratefully. "Very well then. Thank you again; we'll be leaving. Safe flight," he said, turning to walk away with Adil in his arms.

Fatimè watched them leave and turned to see Madina giving her a disappointed look. Fatimè shrugged and returned to her seat, choosing to ignore her cousin.

Madina sighed loudly, unable to contain her frustration any longer. "Dun hanjun fu? THAT IS ALL?" she exclaimed, slapping her forehead in disbelief. Fatimè furrowed her brows, puzzled by her cousin's outburst.

"What?" Fatimè snapped, slightly annoyed by Madina's persistent reaction.

"Come on," Madina pleaded. "Him losing his kid, and you finding him? Don't you think that is a sign or something? Like the beginning of a beautiful romantic story."

Fatimè let out a low hiss, growing exasperated. "Have I not told you to stop reading all these lovey-dovey books that put nonsense ideas in your head? It's not only a romantic story."

Madina's excitement didn't wane. "How can you let a fine guy like that slip away? I know I would have at least gotten his number," she said, undeterred by Fatimè's dismissal.

Fatimè sighed, shaking her head. It seemed highly unlikely that she would meet the man again, considering they hadn't exchanged any contact information. Why was she even entertaining the thought?

"Yan dillu," Fatimè said, dragging her trolley along as their flight was announced, leaving Madina to ramble on about how good-looking the man was and how they would be perfect for each other.

Fatimè shook off any lingering thoughts about a potential romantic encounter as they boarded the plane. She couldn't let her imagination run wild with such fantasies. After all, they were both strangers, and their lives were headed in different directions.

Gombe, Nigeria.

The warm breeze brushed against their skin as they drove through the streets of Gombe with the windows down, carrying with it the familiar scent of spices that wafted from nearby food stalls. People hurried along the bustling streets, going about their daily activities.

The Ardo family was renowned for their love of grand affairs, and the atmosphere at their grandfather's mansion was enough evidence.

The sprawling estate was packed with guests enjoying the lavish spread of food and drinks. After enduring over a million 'yan nyalli jams' Fatimè and Madina managed to escape to one of their aunt's houses down the street, where the bride, Mufida, was staying.

It was a large estate, and all of Fatimè's family lived nearby. Her grandfather had always emphasized the importance of fostering unity and ties of kinship, but unfortunately, some of her aunts had taken that to mean that they had the right to be nosy and gossip about everyone's business.

All Fatimè wanted was to take a power nap and sleep away her exhaustion, but she knew that Mufida would not take kindly to any delays. Their cousin, Intisar, had already left them a bunch of missed calls and a single message, which meant that they needed to hurry and get there as soon as possible.

When they finally arrived, they made their way straight to the back of the house, where the henna party was taking place. It was an outdoor garden-themed event, with lush pillows and carpets scattered across the ground. The decorator had done an excellent job of transforming their aunt's carport into a picturesque setting for the henna party.

Fatimè and Madina marveled at the beautiful decorations, as colorful flowers adorned the area, adding a touch of elegance and freshness. The air was filled with the scent of lalle, a mixture of henna and essential oils, creating a fragrant and soothing atmosphere. Soft music played in the background, adding to the serene ambiance.

The women gathered around Mufida, seated on a large pillow, as a skilled henna artist delicately designed intricate patterns on her hands and feet.

As they settled in and got comfortable on the cushions, they were enveloped by the joyful chatter and laughter of their cousins and Mufida's friends. Everyone was dressed in their colorful anko, which added to the vibrant atmosphere, creating a visual feast of hues and patterns.

Madina's infectious energy filled the air as she engaged in playful banter with Intisar and other cousins.

Five minutes had passed, and Madina was already in the midst of an argument with Intisar about whose hands should be designed first. "Keh. Keh. When did you arrive that you want to overtake huh?" Intisar stood with her hands on her hips, looking down at Madina as she took off her wristwatch so the henna artist could get to work.

Fatimè shook her head as she watched the two women go at it. Madina and Intisar were like cat and mouse, always bickering over one thing or another. She didn't make any move to settle them down because it was a waste of time. They made up as quickly as they fought.

"Who asked you to go sit inside then?" Madina shot back.

"I went to pee joor, and now I am back, so scoot," Intisar said.

"I am not moving from here o. you just have to be patient," Madina replied.

The henna artist watched on helplessly as they argued about who was going first.

Fatimè moved closer to Mufida, admiring her henna designs. The deep maroon color contrasted beautifully against her fair skin, enhancing her natural beauty. "a jamo?" Fatimè asked.

Mufida let out a contented sigh. "Tired? Annoyed? Overwhelmed? I am just so over the singing about responsibility and being a good wife. Honestly, everything and everyone is just so annoying."

Fatimè raised an eyebrow. "Even Mahmud?"

"Yes! Sometimes I feel like smacking his head shima."

"Aww." Fatimè adjusted her veil, which was getting displaced by the gentle breeze. "I'm sorry you feel this way; whatever it is, it's valid and normal. But then again, I need you to relax and not let them consume you, okay? Take it one step at a time. This is your wedding, enjoy it, and look at the bright side, you're getting married to the man you love."

Mufida couldn't help but smile at Fatimè's words. "Well, I must admit, I love the annoying guy."

"There you go." Fatimè chuckled, recalling a bittersweet memory but decided now wasn't the time to mention it.

"Look at your cousins." Mufida laughed, pointing at Intisar and Madina, who were huddled up together, giggling over something on their phones.

"Ahaps! Those two have issues," Fatimè replied laughing.

With their lalle done, they went to prepare for the kamu event that would take place later that night.

9th December 2016

The mosque located in the Ardo estate was packed to capacity with guests gathered to witness the wedding of Fatiha of Mufida and Mahmud. As the groom had a photo session with his groomsmen, the elders engaged in conversations and congratulated the father of the groom. Alhaji Faruk, one of the elders, shook hands with his cousin Alhaji Muhammad, "Miyatti. Allah hokkabe jode jam." He said.

Alhaji Faruk's phone rang, and he stepped aside to answer the call. Upon completing the call, he felt a sharp pain in his leg, which was not surprising, considering his previous accident. His doctor had advised him against standing or walking for extended periods, but he had ignored the advice due to the wedding preparations and farm visits. Jidda had warned him to let Hammadi handle everything, but he insisted on going too. Knowing that walking home in this state was not ideal, he attempted to call Mubarak to come to take him home. However, he hesitated, realizing that his son was busy being a groomsman, so he called Hammadi instead.

"Adon toye?" he asked as Hammadi answered the phone.

"Just outside the mosque, Baaba. By the other side," Hammadi replied.

"All right, get the car and come take me home. I'm at the parking lot," Alhaji Faruk instructed.

"Midon wara joni," Hammadi said and cut the call.

As soon as he arrived, Hammadi noticed his father was in pain and asked, "Baaba, are you okay? What's wrong?"

"Just a little pain. Can we go now?" Alhaji Faruk replied, trying to hide his discomfort.

Suddenly, a man in an ash kaftan approached them and greeted them, "Salaam Alaikum."

"Walaikumul Salaam," they responded, confused as to who he was.

Hammadi assessed the man, noting the classic 'Sheffield Daniel Wellington' watch adorning his wrist, a subtle sign of his affluence. The stranger expressed a desire to speak privately about Alhaji Faruk's daughter, Fatimè. Curiosity piqued, Alhaji Faruk agreed to hear him out, while Hammadi remained skeptical and interjected, "And what about my sister?"

"Please, let the young man speak," Alhaji Faruk chastised his son, acknowledging the stranger's request for privacy. Sensing a more convenient location for the conversation, the stranger proposed discussing matters at Alhaji Faruk's home. After a brief consideration, Alhaji Faruk consented to hosting the man, and the three of them departed together, leaving the mosque and the wedding behind temporarily.

After adjusting her head tie, Fatimè stood up and smoothed out her pale pink lace komole dress. Today, she had chosen to keep her look simple, emphasizing her captivating features which exuded a sense of calm and grace, reminiscent of her mother's elegance. Fatimè had inherited her mother's striking beauty, and she knew how to enhance it with subtle makeup that accentuated her best features.

Just as she was about to leave, the door swung open, revealing her mother's entrance. Hajiya Hauwa, a traditional woman with a regal air, was dressed in a simple yet elegant lafayya and adorned with gold jewelry, showcasing her opulence. Her glasses, a reflection of astigmatism she had passed down to her daughter, perched on her nose.

"Mami," Fatimè greeted, acknowledging her mother's presence.

"A taski?" her mother asked, concern lining her features. "I have been trying to reach you. Didn't you see my missed calls?"

Fatimè reached into her bag and realized she had forgotten to take her phone off do not disturb mode. "Wadu munyel," she apologized. "Did you need me to do something for you?"

"Yes, I wanted to introduce you to someone," her mother replied, sitting on the bed.

Fatimè sighed and rubbed her temples. She had grown tired of her mother's persistent attempts to set her up with potential suitors. This had become an all-too-familiar refrain in the past few months. When would her mother understand that she wasn't ready for a relationship?

"He's Hajiya Balaraba's son," her mother continued, oblivious to Fatimè's lack of interest. "He just completed his Ph.D. program from..."

Fatimè tried to listen, but she couldn't care less about his academic qualifications. She found academic people boring and the fact that most of them never spoke simple English, always trying to stress her brain with cumbersome words.

"The two of you would make a great match," her mother added, her eyes shining with hope.

Fatimè knew deep down they wouldn't. She despised emotional manipulation and wasn't prepared to dive into a relationship for the sake of pleasing others. "Mami," she interjected, trying to be firm. "I don't think I'm ready for any relationship at the moment."

"He is a decent man, Fatimè," her mother pleaded. "Just give him a chance. It might work. I mean, look at your cousins. Everyone is settling down."

"Mami. Mami," Fatimè interrupted. "My cousins are settling down because it is their time, and you know very well why I am hesitant about..."

Before Fatimè could finish her sentence, her phone began to ring. "Madina is calling," she announced, grateful for the interruption. "I have to go. We'll talk about this later."

Without waiting for her mother's response, Fatimè hastily left the room, desperate to escape the constant pressure and nagging. In her hurry, she accidentally collided with someone in the corridor. "Whoa, whoa," the person exclaimed, reaching out to steady her. She looked up and saw Fahad, her cousin.

"Fahad, whew! Great timing. Let's go out... hurry, hurry," she exclaimed, pulling him towards his car parked outside.

Once inside the car, Fahad leaned back in his seat, trying to catch his breath. "Butterfly, who's chasing you?" he asked, concerned.

"No one, fa. I was escaping from Mami," she replied, exasperated.

"Who is it this time around?" he probed.

"Some guy with a Ph.D. I didn't care to listen to the other details," she answered, clearly annoyed.

Fahad scoffed and switched on the air conditioner to cool them down, providing a moment of respite from the tension.

"If I hear one more 'I want to introduce you to someone' from Mami, I might just explode," she said.

"Relax, Butterfly. Don't let it get to you, okay?" he offered, trying to calm her down.

"Easier said than done, you know. It's only been three years, and she's already bugging me," Fatimè said, trying to hold back tears, but they started to fall anyway.

Fahad handed her some tissues and let her cry for a bit before speaking again. "Here, don't ruin your makeup."

In moments like these, Fahad knew that words would never be enough.

Intisar turned to Madina, who was engaged in conversation with a photographer, and asked, "Wai where is Tims ne?"

"She said she was on her way. I don't know what is taking her so long to get here," Madina replied, a hint of impatience in her voice.

Madina and Intisar, both looking stunning in their pale pink lace anko outfits were at the event center, trying to get everything in order before the bride arrived. Their outfits hugged their figures flawlessly - Madina's fitted gown accentuating her elegant stature, while Intisar's peplum top and six-piece skirt displayed her petite frame with grace.

"Abdul just texted me that they're on their way, and we can't go in without Tims. Call her again, Dan Allah," Intisar urged

Just then, Madina spotted Fahad's car. She hissed, "Look at whom we are waiting for. She was busy with Fahad." The two stood with their arms crossed, their facial expressions revealing their annoyance as they awaited the arrival of Fatimè and Fahad.

"Damn," Fahad chuckled as they finally approached. "If looks could kill... You guys look like the 'avengers' getting ready for battle."

He couldn't help but find the situation amusing, but a stern glance from Intisar quickly wiped the smile off his face.

"Do you know how long we have been waiting for her? We are supposed to help out before the bride gets here," Intisar said, exasperated.

"Intisar," Fatimè cut her off. "It's not his fault I'm late. Cut it out."

"Oh yeah?" Madina said with a smirk. "We all know he cannot stay away from you. At this point, we think the next wedding should be yours and his."

Fatimè rolled her eyes at the statement. She didn't have time for Madina's teasing. She turned to Fahad and said, "I'm sorry. See you later?"

He nodded, a fond smile on his lips. "Anytime, butterfly. See you later, ladies." He waved before taking off.

"What were you guys up to anyway?" Intisar asked after he left.

"Nothing. Can we just finish off before Mufida gets here?" Fatimè replied, eager to get to work.

Madina silently walked away, leaving them standing there. Intisar couldn't help but notice the slight disappointment in her cousin's eyes

"What's with her?" Intisar asked, puzzled.

"I don't know," Fatimè said, shaking her head. "Let's just go." She pulled Intisar towards the event center.

The loud music at the wedding was starting to make Fatimè feel dizzy. This was reason #599 why she did not like weddings. She had been standing for almost two hours now, and everything was going according to plan, so she decided to find a place to sit. But first, she needed to take off her shoes.

Thankfully, her slippers were in Madina's car, but the problem was the key. Madina had it, and she was busy busting some moves on the dance floor. Fatimè groaned as she walked towards Madina to collect the key.

Finally, she got the key and headed toward the parking lot. She retrieved her shoes and was about to head back inside when someone blocked her.

"Hi," he said with a smile.

Chapter 2

♥

Gombe, Nigeria.

9th December 2016

Fatimè gazed at him, her face etched with confusion at his sudden presence. She couldn't help but notice his tall, dark-skinned figure, radiating a handsome charm. His eyes, the most striking feature on his face, held a depth that intrigued her. Dressed in a well-tailored light brown kaftan, with the tangaran cap sitting beautifully on his head, he exuded an air of elegance, complemented by the subtle woody scent of 'Maison Margiela'. His wristwatch, glinting in the light, added a touch of sophistication to his attire.

What are you doing here?" Fatimè asked.

He replied, "I have a business meeting."

She couldn't fathom why he would have a business meeting at a wedding.

Sensing her confusion, he quickly added "It's the only place I could reach the client," "What about you?" He asked, genuinely interested in her presence.

"Bride and groom. They're both my cousins," Fatimè replied, subtly mentioning her familial connection to the event.

He then felt the need to address any concerns she might have, he said, "My son is safe at home. It was a one-time incident. I'm not careless with my child."

"I'm glad to hear that," Fatimè smiled, appreciating his reassurance. "I'm heading back inside now, so..."

"Oh, right, me too. After you," He gestured, inviting her to lead the way.

She glanced around as they returned to the bustling wedding hall and was relieved to see that most of the guests had left. She didn't want to draw any unnecessary attention or field any nosy questions from her relatives about the young man accompanying her.

They sat at a nearby table in silence, Fatimè tapping away on her phone to occupy herself. When the DJ lowered the volume for the couple's first dance, Kamal seized the opportunity to initiate a conversation, "What do you like to do?"

Without looking up from her phone, she replied with all seriousness, "Sleep."

He was taken aback by her response, finding it both amusing and intriguing. To him, sleep was merely a necessity, so he couldn't fathom someone viewing it as a hobby.

"And what's your favorite brand of toothpaste?" He continued.

Fatimè burst out laughing, finding the question rather unconventional. "What kind of silly question is that?"

"Okay, let me ask a more serious one,"

Fatimè took a sip of water from the bottle on the table.

"Will you marry me?" He blurted out.

She choked on the water, coughing and sputtering in surprise. "What the hell?" she gasped, her physical reaction mirroring the shock and confusion that surged within her. Quickly regaining her composure, Fatimè stood up from the table and walked away, leaving him perplexed, wondering what he had done wrong.

Fahad let out a yawn for the nth time. The girl seated next to him just wasn't getting it at all. Her incessant chatter was starting to wear him down, and he couldn't help but wonder why his mother insisted on sending girls his way. While he acknowledged that the girl seated beside him was undeniably pretty, her non-stop talking was becoming unbearable.

He was also exhausted from last night's sotol event. It was a small event for the groom where he comes before his mother for blessings and prayers. He is then showered with gifts and his cousins have to give him a new name. one of their cousins, Mukhtar suggested the name, 'basir' prompting Mahmud's friends to pay for a 'ransom' so the name could be changed.

The event center was adorned with elegant decorations, casting a warm and inviting ambiance. Soft lighting created an enchanting atmosphere, and the lively music filled the air, punctuated by bursts of laughter and conversation. It was a grand affair, befitting the joyous celebration of Mahmud and Mufida's wedding.

Fahad's rugged handsomeness had caught the girl's attention from the moment they sat down together. His striking features and tall stature made him stand out in a crowd. Coupled with his charismatic charm and easy smile, he was used to attracting attention. However, he wished this particular girl would take the hint and give him some peace.

"So do you like bread?" she asked again. "I love bread! I can eat it all day. There's a bakery near our house, and because of my..."

As the girl continued to prattle on, Fahad's attention shifted to his surroundings. He spotted Madina and Intisar approaching, their faces flushed from dancing and panting for breath. Madina took the seat beside him, and Intisar settled down next to the talkative girl, reaching for a bottle of water.

"Whew, I am E for exhausted," Intisar exclaimed, expressing her fatigue from all the dancing.

The talkative girl fell silent, clearly annoyed by the interruption. Fahad silently mouthed a 'thank you' at both Madina and Intisar, grateful for their timely arrival. Madina, sensing his gratitude, let out a small laugh.

"Have you seen Tims anywhere?" Madina asked, "She said she was going to change her shoes or something."

Fahad shook his head, his gaze scanning the room. "She's probably outside. Let's go check," he suggested, eager for a chance to escape the girl's relentless chatter.

"I could do with some fresh air anyway," Intisar added, seizing the opportunity for a respite.

"Yeah, me too," Fahad agreed. He turned to the talkative girl and said, "Bye, Khadija."

"It's Kauthar, not Khadija," she corrected with a roll of her eyes, clearly annoyed by his lack of attention.

"Baby am!" Fatimè greeted Khalid enthusiastically over the phone, her voice filled with warmth and affection. "How was your trip? Did you meet everyone well? How's the weather over there? Have you eaten....?"

Khalid struggled to suppress a chuckle at her stream of questions. He always wondered how she managed to talk so much, but he let her finish before responding. "Bunny, bunny. Relax. One at a time," he teased. "My trip was fine. Everyone is all right, Alhamdulillah. The weather is great, and yes, I've been stuffed to the brim by Mama, who can't help but dote on her favorite son."

"You wish," Fatimè retorted. "We all know who Mama's favorite is, and it's not you, old man."

"Whatever. This old man is the love of your life, and that's a fact," Khalid declared with a grin.

Fatimè rolled over to the other side of the bed, smiling and agreeing with him.

"This one that you called as if you were timing my arrival, are you missing me that much?" he asked playfully.

"Of course not," she replied with a scoff, attempting to hide her true feelings "I just wanted to know how my dear Mama is doing."

"I see. Very well, then," he said, faking indifference. "Let me call someone else who misses me."

"Ahn ahn. Small play," Fatimè chuckled.

"Ah, toh, if you don't care about me anymore... I can...," Khalid trailed off.

"Oh, shut up. Afterward, you'll say I am the dramatic one. You know I miss you. It has been a few hours, but I miss you like crazy. Ever since you went away, every hour of every day...."

"Broooo. 'Natalie Cole' must be rolling at wherever she is right now. Is that how you plan on destroying my eardrums when we get married?" Khalid joked.

Fatimè clicked her tongue, playfully challenging him. "Your loss, mister, because I've changed my mind about the marriage. You can as well begin your search for another bunny."

"There can only be one bunny, and that's you. Today, tomorrow, and forever. The only one that makes my heart leap, jump, summ ersault...," Khalid professed.

Fatimè's voice dropped to a whisper. She knew how much his words affected her, making her weak in the knees and sending her stomach aflutter. Everything else faded away, and the only thing that mattered was him. "Khaliddddd," she breathed.

"I never want you to doubt my love for you," Khalid continued, "even for a second."

Fatimè nodded, silently affirming what they both knew. There was never any doubt in her mind about Khalid's love for her. His words were always backed up by actions.

"I should go pray," Khalid said when he heard the call for Asr.

The air around him felt strange, and the street was unusually quiet, devoid of people. He briefly considered going back to ask his brother to come with him but decided against it as he was already close to the mosque.

"Let me go pray too. I love you," Fatimè said.

"I love you too," Khalid replied before ending the call.

As they searched outside, their worries grew, and a sense of unease settled over them. Each passing moment without finding Fatimè only intensified their concerns. Their calls to her went unanswered, deepening the fear that something might have happened to her. Intisar's voice trembled with worry, and Madina's eyes welled up with tears that threatened to spill over.

Fahad attempted to calm their fears, his voice filled with reassurance. "Relax, she's fine, in sha Allah. Let's check the parking lot," he suggested, hoping to find some trace of Fatimè. However, when they reached the crowded parking lot, their search seemed futile. The sea of cars seemed to swallow any clue of her whereabouts, causing a surge of panic within them. At that moment, they decided to split up and intensify their search efforts.

It didn't take long before Intisar's voice pierced through the tension, bringing them back together. "She's here! I found her."

They hurried to where Intisar had discovered Fatimè, finding her seated on the pavement between two cars, her body curled up, hugging her knees tightly. She rocked back and forth, her distress evident. The sight of her in such anguish struck a chord within Madina and Intisar, who moved closer to her, gently rubbing her back.

"Tims," Madina called softly, "A jamo?"

Fahad stood nearby, a concerned and watchful presence. They had witnessed Fatimè in similar states before, knowing the depths of her struggles all too well, but she found solace in their presence, her breathing gradually steadying.

Fahad handed her a tissue from his pocket, his eyes filled with empathy. Madina and Intisar exchanged worried glances, silently communicating their shared concern. He then took charge, his voice gentle yet firm. "Ko fe'i?"

Fatimè shook her head, unable to find the words to express her inner turmoil. Her head throbbed, a physical manifestation of the emotional weight she carried. All she wanted was to find respite, to lay down her burdens.

Intisar offered a suggestion, concern lacing her words. "Maybe you should go home."

Madina, ever supportive, added, "I'll come with you."

Fatimè hesitated, "No, no. I'll be fine," she finally replied, her voice tinged with a mix of gratitude and stubbornness. "Just stay here in case Mufida needs something."

Fahad, understanding her need for space, offered to drive her home. With a nod of agreement, Fatimè bid farewell to the girls.

The car ride was enveloped in silence, Fahad respecting her need for solitude. He knew that Fatimè would open up in her own time and that forcing her to speak would only hinder the healing process.

Sani Abacha International Airport.

Gombe, Nigeria.

11th December 2016.

"Tims, you won't even extend your stay for at least a day? Haba now..." Fatimè's sister-in-law, Fa'iza, pleaded, her hands clasped together.

Fatimè looked into Fa'iza's eyes, seeing not just a sister-in-law but an elder sister. Fa'iza had a way of filling the void left by Furaira, Fatimè's late sister. Her presence brought a sense of comfort and familiarity. It was as if Fa'iza had taken it upon herself to step into Furaira's shoes, offering a sense of continuity and support that Fatimè sorely needed.

"Adda Fa'i. I don't want to go too, but I have some work to finish up," Fatimè replied, with a tinge of regret in her voice.

Fa'iza crossed her arms and pushed her lips in disapproval. Gombe was getting too boring for her, and she needed company.

"Just pray you don't wake up one day with your mouth looking like that permanently,"

Fatimè turned to see her brother, Hammadi, walking towards them with two trolleys.

His tall stature made him a commanding presence which exuded an air of structure and discipline that was comforting to Fatimè.

Fa'iza eyed him when he got to her side. Fatime laughed, "Hamma, please leave my Adda alone. She can push her mouth all she wants."

"Ah okay o," he raised his hands in surrender. "Wala ko a wawi sai tubbuki honduko."

"I'll just go talk to Baaba. You are annoying," Fa'iza said, stalking off to meet her father-in-law who was seated next to Fatimè's younger brother, Khalifa.

Their father was engrossed in a CSI show on his iPad, and Khalifa's attention was on his PSP. They still had thirty minutes before boarding, and Fatimè was glad her mother was not coming with them and had opted to return the following week. That meant she was going to catch a break. She knew the conversation they had that day was far from over.

"Can we talk?" Hammadi asked, his gaze fixed on Fatimè, his concern evident in his eyes. The genuine worry in his voice made her appreciate the depth of their bond even more. They moved away from the bustling crowd, finding solace in a quiet corner of the lounge where their words could be shared without interruption.

"A Jamo?" he asked.

Fatimè adjusted her glasses, meeting his gaze, "Yes, Hamma. I am fine. Is everything all right?" She was wondering what prompted the question.

"Hmm. Are you sure?"

She gave him a faint smile. "You worry about me too much. I am fine." The last sentence was a blatant lie. She just was not ready to have the conversation or burden anyone with the turmoil that was going on in her life.

"You're my sister; I have to worry about you," Hammadi declared, pulling her into a warm embrace. His familiar scent of Al-Haramain filled her nose, offering solace and comfort. Hammadi pondered telling her about the stranger but decided against it. It was between her and Baaba.

"Take care of yourself, okay?"

She nodded.

"And Baaba too."

Fatimè raised her head in question.

"His leg," Hammadi said. "He complained about it, although he keeps saying it's not that serious. You know Baaba."

Their father was like that. He'd die before admitting anything was seriously wrong with him. "I asked Dr. Aminu to drop by tomorrow and check, just to be sure it's nothing serious." And that was Hamma, making sure everything was in order.

Their flight was soon announced, and Fa'iza grumbled about how she was already enjoying the series with Baaba. They all laughed when Hammadi suggested she go with them, and she declined by moving to his side.

Fatimè couldn't wait to go home and bury herself in her drawings. It was all she needed to forget that encounter.

After a quick lunch of rice and stew when they got home, Fatimè headed to the study to work on her project. She needed silence and light to draw, knowing that the creative process demanded her utmost focus. Placing her phone on Do Not Disturb mode to avoid distractions, she switched on her "drawing playlist" and immersed herself in her work. The study provided her with the perfect environment, with its large windows allowing natural light to flood the room, illuminating her sketches and drawings.

As Fatimè poured her heart and soul into her architectural masterpiece, time seemed to slip away. Five hours and five cups of tea later, she finally concluded her drawing and admired the intricate details and precision of her creation.

Feeling a wave of exhaustion wash over her, she flopped onto the beanbag on the floor, letting out a tired yawn. She was spent after pouring her energy into the project. However, her tranquility was short-lived as she heard a gentle knock on the door, followed by her brother, Khalifa's voice calling out to her.

"Adda," he called, "Are you done?"

"Yeah. Ko fe'i?" she replied.

His eyes caught the render on her laptop, and he moved closer to get a better look. "Damn. This looks dooooupe."

Fatimè laughed at his playful imitation of one of their mother's friends, who had praised Fatimè's room renovations with the word "dooooupe."

"They better give you a raise. You are so good at this."

"I know, right? With that, we can afford those tickets." Fatimè mused, referring to their shared dream of attending the 'UEFA Champions League final'. They had been saving up for months, but their parents had been hesitant to indulge them in their extravagant desires.

"Why then do I pay for DSTV?" Their father had responded in disbelief at their desire to spend exorbitantly for the sake of watching a football match live.

"In sha Allah," Khalifa added, a glimmer of hope in his eyes. He then remembered their father's errand and said, "Baaba's calling you."

Fatimè's eyes met Khalifa's, and she couldn't help but raise an eyebrow in question. "How serious? Scale of 1 to 10?"

Khalifa paused for a moment, considering the seriousness of their father's request. "Five," he replied, hoping to alleviate some of Fatimè's anxiety.

Taking a deep breath, Fatimè cleared the study and made her way upstairs to her parents' sitting room.

The sitting room displayed a simple and elegant style, showcasing her mother's appreciation for the finer things in life. The tastefully arranged furniture, adorned with intricate designs and plush cushions, created an inviting atmosphere with a bookshelf neatly organized with volumes on various subjects, a symbol of her father's thirst for knowledge.

Fatimè found her father with a tray containing a teapot, mug, and a pack of Twining's tea bags—Earl Grey, to be specific. The CSI show played on the television, paused as her father answered a phone call. She marveled at how her father never seemed to tire of watching the same show for years, appreciating his unwavering dedication and routine.

Spotting Fatimè's entrance, her father gestured for her to wait, "Yes, in sha Allah, and I apologize for the delay. We had some unexpected issues that slowed down our production and caused some delays with our deliveries but we expect to have your produce ready within the next two days." There was a pause before he added, "Thank you very much for your understanding," he said, ending the call and turning to face her. "Our cheese is packaged and ready for delivery finally. That thing gave Hamma and i a hard time," he added, a look of glee on his face.

Fatimè knew that her father found immense joy and satisfaction in his farm, finding solace in the land and the fruits it bore. They had been working on cheese production for a long while now. "Ma sha Allah Baaba," she said warmly, her smile reflecting her genuine happiness. "Allah wadika wadanki dun barka."

"Amin Fatimè am," he replied, offering her a cup of tea. Despite having already consumed five cups downstairs, she couldn't resist her father's offer. Tea had become a tradition and a symbol of their conversations. It provided a comforting backdrop to the important discussions they often had.

Accepting the cup, Fatimè settled on the couch beside her father and took a sip, savoring the familiar taste.

"You called for me, Baaba?" she asked, her voice filled with both curiosity and anticipation.

Her father set his cup down, clearing his throat before answering, "Yes, I did. Do you have something to tell me?"

She shook her head, a hint of anxiety creeping in. "No, Baaba. Is there something you think I have to tell you?"

His question bore weight, and Fatimè recognized it as the platform he provided for them to confess their mistakes willingly, saving them from harsher consequences.

"Hmm," he replied, confusion flickering across his face as he pondered her response. "Someone came to see me regarding you."

Fatimè shifted uncomfortably, her mind racing to decipher his words.

"Baaba, I'm a bit lost. I don't understand," she said, her stomach knotting with unease.

"At the mosque, after your cousin's wedding Fatiha, Hamma, and I were about to head home when a fine young man approached us and requested to see me. I granted him an audience, and he asked for your hand in marriage."

The shock of his words threatened to make her spit out her tea. "What?" she almost yelled, her voice barely restrained.

"Yes, I was wondering if you had sent him to me," her father clarified, his voice calm and composed.

"I did not. I promise. I'm not even seeing anyone at the moment," she replied, cursing silently. If this was one of her mother's schemes, then there was going to be a huge problem.

Concerned, Fatimè inquired, "What did you tell him, Baaba?"

"I told him to hold on until I had spoken to you about it," he responded, his tone reflecting his unwavering respect for her autonomy in making such important life decisions.

Relieved, Fatimè let out a sigh, grateful for her father's understanding. She couldn't help but wonder who it was that dared to approach her father without her consent. A thought crossed her mind, but she dismissed it. He wouldn't dare.

Her father reached for something on the coffee table, extending it toward her. "He gave me his card. Perhaps you would like to speak to him?"

"Oh, I'll be speaking to him," She muttered silently.

Examining the card, it had, "Kamal Hussein Maitambari" prominently displayed with 'CEO Stride Logistics.' His phone number and address in Lagos was written beneath his name.

The call to Magrib was made, and she excused herself to pray. She would deal with whomever the hell this Kamal was later.

Fatimè was in the middle of her Adkhar when the sound of her phone interrupted her prayers. With a deep breath, she set the tasbih aside and reached for her phone on the nightstand. The caller ID displayed an unfamiliar number. She hesitated for a moment before answering.

"Hello?" she answered, unsure of who might be on the other end of the line.

"Assalamu Alaikum," the voice said.

"Alaikum Salam," she replied, recognizing the voice but not wanting to believe it was who she thought it was.

"Oh my God!" she yelled in disbelief, her temper beginning to rise.

She grabbed the card with Kamal Hussein Maitambari's name and number from the bed, quickly comparing the phone number to the one on the screen. It was him, the audacious man who had the nerve to ask for her hand in marriage without her knowledge or consent.

"You!" she screamed, her voice shaking with anger. "How dare you?!"

Chapter 3

♥

Abuja, Nigeria.

11th December, 2016.

Kamal's unwavering determination to pursue Fatimè was evident as he remained unfazed by her response. "I take it that you received my message," he said calmly.

"Yes," Fatimè replied curtly, "and you must be out of your mind to think that going to my father would make me say yes. What is your problem?"

Kamal listened attentively, understanding the depth of Fatimè's anger. He wanted to explain himself, to make her see his perspective, "I am sorry," he began, his voice tinged with regret, "I just wanted to..."

"Listen and listen well," Fatimè cut him off, her voice laced with anger. "Stay away from me. I don't know who you are, and I don't bloody care. It would do you good to stay away from me and my family! Do not ever call me again!" she exclaimed, her tone leaving no room for argument.

Without waiting for Kamal's response, Fatimè ended the call, her finger hovering over the disconnect button. Kamal's words had only made things worse. How did he even get her number? Fatimè wondered as she threw her phone on the bed, trying to calm her frayed nerves.

Gombe, Nigeria.

Madina emerged from the bathroom, adjusting the towel on her head. The soft hues and clean lines of her room provided a quiet atmosphere, complementing her need for serenity after the exhausting wedding events. She thought about how hot showers were truly a blessing to mankind.

Lying on her back, Madina let out a deep sigh of relief, the coolness of the air hinted at the arrival of the harmattan season, adding a slight chill to the atmosphere.

Just as she was about to fully immerse herself in her thoughts, her phone rang, interrupting her moment of solitude. A groan escaped her mouth, signaling her lack of interest in any conversation at the moment. Nevertheless, she reached for the phone, knowing it was Fatimè on the other end. "Good timing," Madina thought to herself, realizing she had been planning to call her cousin anyway.

"Madina! What the hell?" Fatimè exclaimed as soon as Madina picked up. The intensity of her cousin's voice immediately caught her attention. "Why did you give him my number?"

Fatimè sounded angry, and Madina had to pause to register whatever it was that she was saying.

"What number? What are you talking about?" Madina asked, genuinely confused.

"Cut the crap. Airport guy? How did he get my number?" Fatimè snapped back, her frustration evident.

"Whoa, whoa. Hold up. He called? Sleek!" Madina exclaimed, trying to contain her laughter, though she understood the seriousness of the situation.

"Madina Hamidu! I am not in the mood for your games," Fatimè retorted, her tone still laced with irritation.

Realizing the need to assure Fatimè of her innocence, Madina composed herself and replied, "Okay, okay. Calm down, Tims. Walahi, I did not share your contact with him."

Fatimè's anger seemed to simmer down slightly at Madina's reassurance. "And why would you even think I did? Last time I checked, you were the one who had a conversation with him at the airport. Not me."

Fatimè let out the details of the encounter and Madina squealed when she learned that Kamal had met with Baaba, her excitement mixed with disbelief. "Nah, this man has got some balls," she exclaimed, unable to contain her amusement.

Fatimè nodded, her weariness apparent. "Uhm, that was after he had asked me at the wedding..."

"Wait, wait," Madina interrupted, her curiosity piqued. "He was at the wedding?"

"Yes. He said he was there to meet a client... ugh, you know what? I do not even care. He had the effrontery to call me after the stunt he pulled. I am just confused as to who gave him my number."

Madina, pondering the situation, offered a plausible explanation. "Come on. Did you not say he met with a client there? The client could have been anyone, maybe one of our cousins, and they might have given it to him."

Fatimè rubbed her temples, considering Madina's theory. Maybe there was some truth to it.

"So what did you say when he called?" Madina inquired.

"What else? I told him to fuck off," Fatimè replied.

Madina chuckled at Fatimè's straightforwardness. "Of course. I'd expect something like that from you." She switched the call to speaker, allowing her to continue the conversation while searching for something to wear for the chilly weather.

"Listen, Tims, just relax. We'll figure this out when I get back," Madina reassured her cousin,

"Sure, sure. Till you get back, bye," Fatimè said.

As Madina got dressed, she couldn't help but look forward to the deep tissue massage she was going to get when she got back. But the next thing on her mind was the drama that was about to unfold and if there was anything she loved, it was drama.

Abuja, Nigeria.

12th December 2016

The only sound that filled the dining room was the clanking of metal against plates as Kamal and his mother enjoyed their meal. The room exuded an aura of elegance, with beautiful furniture and the soft, ambient lighting illuminated the space, adding to the tranquil atmosphere.

Kamal's mother, Hajiya Hillu, radiated a calm and peaceful demeanor, her beauty and poise apparent in the way she carried herself. She was known for her flowing dresses that covered her modestly, reflecting her traditional values. As she paused mid-bite, her eyes fixed on Kamal, her love and concern for her son were evident.

"So what are your plans?" she asked, her voice gentle yet filled with underlying intent. Kamal took a sip of water, placing his glass back down, aware that his mother wasn't referring to work matters.

"The expansion? I'm still waiting for feedback from Sa'ad," Kamal responded, trying to divert the conversation.

She pursed her lips, "You know I'm not asking about work," she pressed on, her concern evident. "Your plans with Rukayya. Have you talked to her about reconciliation? You can still bring her back. Your son should not grow up like this."

"Maa, can you please stop?" Kamal replied, frustration seeping into his voice. This topic always hit a nerve, even after four years. "Rukayya and I are done, and you know it. I've told her if she's found a man to marry, she can go ahead. I won't be a hindrance."

His mother's gaze softened, but her worry remained. "But... okay, fine. What about someone else? You're not getting any younger," she prodded, desperate to see her son find happiness.

"But nothing, Maa. Can we please not talk about this? It's honestly draining," Kamal replied, feeling the weight of the conversation bearing down on him. He regretted leaving his meal unfinished, a reflection of how he hated wasting food. "If you'll excuse me, I think I've lost my appetite."

Hajiya Hillu didn't utter a word, understanding the futility of convincing him further. She had come to accept that her son was just as hardheaded as his father.

"I'm leaving," Kamal announced upon his return from the kitchen, the tension still lingering in the air.

"You won't wait for your father? I asked them to clean your room," his mother said, her desperation evident in her eyes, wishing he would stay.

"Adil can stay back for a few days before he leaves; also tell Hafsah I'll call her," Kamal assured his mother.

"Okay," his mother nodded, a touch of sadness in her eyes as he kissed her forehead and walked out, leaving her sighing in the wake of his departure.

Five minutes into his drive, his phone beeped, indicating an incoming call from Aziz, his trusted assistant. It was precisely whom he needed to talk to at that moment.

"Aziz," Kamal answered.

"Yes, boss. Everything is set, and I've sent the details to your email," Aziz responded.

"Very good. Thank you," Kamal acknowledged, ending the call with a sense of relief.

13th December 2016.

The office hummed with the usual activity of a bustling architectural firm with sunlight streaming through the large windows, casting a warm glow on the sleek desks and ergonomic chairs that filled the workspace.

Rahila leaned over Fatimè's desk, her disappointment was evident as she discussed the upcoming training. "I had plans for next month, and now my detty December plans have been ruined. What kind of wahala is this?"

Fatimè, however, seemed distant, her mind preoccupied with the events of the previous night that had left her restless and sleep-deprived.

"Are you even listening to me?" Rahila tapped Fatimè on the shoulder, drawing her attention away from her troubled thoughts.

"Sorry, I'm just tired. What were you saying again?" Fatimè sighed, her voice tinged with fatigue. The lack of sleep weighed heavily on her, making her feel detached from the energetic ambiance of the office. Tardiness was not a trait she typically exhibited, but today was an exception.

As they conversed, a knock on the door interrupted their discussion, and Ezekiel, one of the office cleaners, entered with a bouquet and a gift basket. The aroma of freshly brewed coffee wafted through the air, mingling with the scent of the flowers.

Rahila couldn't resist teasing Ezekiel, her playful tone echoing in the vibrant space. "Ah, Ezekiel! Valentine's Day is still two months away oo," she exclaimed, drawing laughter from nearby colleagues.

Ezekiel chuckled, "Madam, no oo. It's not from me," he clarified, a smile playing on his lips. "I was asked to deliver this to Miss Fatimè."

Fatimè's attention was now fully focused on Ezekiel, her tired eyes seeking answers, "Me? From whom?"

Rahila's excitement peaked as she collected the gift basket, "You went to Gombe and came back with a new beau, and you did not tell me? Is that what friendship is?"

Fatimè rolled her eyes at the accusation, "I don't even know who that is from."

Rahila shrugged, he had become accustomed to Fatimè's dismissive response to romantic interests. It seemed that every proposal or advance made toward her was met with rejection.

Well, let's find out then," Rahila said, handing the card she had found in the basket to Fatimè. The soft rustling of the card mingled with the sounds of activity in the office, creating a moment of quiet anticipation.

"Hope you'll unblock my number now." The words on the card resonated with her, evoking frustration and a sense of powerlessness. With a swift motion, she tore the card into pieces and discarded it.

The nerve of this guy!" Fatimè exclaimed.

"Kai kai, relax. Who sent it?" Rahila asked, taken aback by Fatimè's intense reaction.

Some guy I met at the airport that won't leave my life alone," Fatimè replied, her voice carrying a mixture of annoyance and exasperation.

Rahila, however, couldn't help but remark on the thoughtful selection of gifts. "Ah, but these things are nice o. He even got you your favorite. Peanut butter and apples."

Fatimè hissed. "Please take these things away. I do not want to see them."

Rahila sensed the intensity of Fatimè's reaction and wisely refrained from pressing further. She hugged the flowers to her chest, acknowledging that they were not to Fatimè's liking. The contrast between Fatimè's love for apples and peanut butter and her disdain for the gifts was stark.

As Fatimè arrived home, she noticed an unfamiliar car parked in the driveway. The driveway itself was simple and unassuming, leading up to their modest yet comfortable home. She assumed the car belonged to one of her mother's numerous friends who often stopped by for visits.

The women were always coming over, either to pitch their sons as potential suitors, advertise household items for Fatimè's future marriage, or simply engage in gossip. It had become a regular occurrence, and Fatimè had grown accustomed to the constant flow of visitors

To Fatimè's surprise, the house was unusually quiet, contrary to the usual lively chatter of her mother's friends. Then, she heard a man's voice, followed by her mother's eerie laughter. The voice certainly did not belong to her father or any of her brothers, leaving

Fatimè curious about the identity of the person responsible for her mother's cheerful mood.

As she stepped into the living room, the scent of halut filled the air, creating a pleasant and inviting atmosphere in the living room. The room itself was elegant, boasting a palette of soothing grays and whites, with sleek, low-profile furniture and large windows that framed breathtaking views.

"Oh, for God's sake, what are you doing here?" Fatimè exclaimed as she spotted him, her eyes scanning his classic kaftan and the matching cap he wore. He stood out in the living room, a stark contrast to the modest atampa sewn into a simple style that her mother was wearing.

"Fatimè," her mother gave her a warning smile, "Renu hore mada,"

Fatimè restrained herself due to her mother's presence and spoke calmly this time, "What are you doing here? How did you even get my home address?"

"I invited him over," her mother answered matter-of-factly, her voice hinting at her meddling nature. "Your father informed me about what happened, and I was lucky to find the card lying in your room, so I called him."

What?" Fatimè's disbelief filled the room. She knew her mother had not merely stumbled upon the card; she had actively searched for it.

"Mami? Seriously? Fatimè exclaimed, her voice carrying a mix of shock and indignation.

"What?" Her mother responded as if her actions were perfectly normal, her eyes betraying a hint of disapproval at Fatimè's reaction.

Kamal, sensing the escalating tension, realized that he had unknowingly walked into a volatile situation. If he had known, he would not have honored her invitation. This was not how he wanted things to go.

"Thank you for your time. It was wonderful. I'll take my leave now," Kamal said to her mother.

Fatimè looked at him in disbelief, her frustration lingering in the air. "I think it's time we have a heart-to-heart."

"I'll excuse you," her mother said, making a move to leave the room. "Nice to meet you, Kamal."

As soon as her mother left, Fatimè shot him a deathly glare. "What do you want from me?"

"Nothing," he shrugged. "What do you think I want from you?"

"You do not get to answer my question with another question, dammit."

"Relax, Fatimè," he said, his voice soothing like a bottle of chilled water after a 100m race. Her tension eased for a moment, only to be reminded that he was the source of her frustration.

"Let's get things straight here, airport guy..." Fatimè began, her annoyance returning in full force.

"The name's Kamal," he interjected, his voice calm but firm.

"I do not care about your name, okay? I just want you to stay the hell away from me."

He tried to say something, but she cut him off.

"Stay away from our house, my parents, and how the heck do you even know where I work?" she demanded, her voice echoing her frustration.

He only smiled before finally leaving the room.

Fatimè couldn't care less as she dropped onto the couch and unhooked her bra. Nothing beats the feeling of taking it off after a hectic day.

"What was that?" Fatimè's mother asked, entering the sitting room with a concerned expression on her face.

"Mami, can we please not talk about this?" Fatimè responded, her tone indicating that she did not want to discuss the matter further.

Her mother frowned. "Yes, of course," she said, her voice tinged with disapproval. "You don't want to talk about how you were being rude to a guest. I raised you better than this. So what if you're not interested in him? Couldn't you have let him down more politely? It wouldn't have hurt you to be more considerate. He deserves an apology."

Fatimè's eyes widened in shock. Her mother expected her to apologize to this guy. Over her dead body! She was the one whose privacy had been invaded by a guy she had run into at the airport. The only thing he deserved was a knock on that big head of his. Nevertheless, she forced herself to mumble something about an apology and left the sitting room, knowing that it was the only way her mother would leave her alone.

As Fatimè prepared to retire for the night, she found solace in her room, a space that reflected her eclectic interests and personal style.

Subtle accents completed the aesthetic, a striking hokage-style wallpaper adorned the wall reflecting her love for the popular 'Naruto' anime and a crafted kunai-shaped bookshelf held a collection of manga volumes and most of her prized possessions. A potted plant sat on a windowsill, its vibrant green leaves adding a touch of nature and life to the space.

Her wish for privacy was short-lived as her mother entered the room unannounced. Fatimè sighed, knowing that Hajiya Hauwa's concern for her well-being often superseded boundaries. "Mami? I thought you had gone to bed," she murmured, a hint of weariness in her voice.

Ignoring Fatimè's question, her mother settled onto the bed and patted the space next to her, motioning for Fatimè to join her. "You know how much I love and want the best for you, right?" she began, her voice laced with genuine concern.

Fatimè braced herself, knowing that this conversation would lead to a topic she had been avoiding. "I know it's hard getting over someone you loved, but don't you think it's time to move on?" her mother continued gently.

"What do you mean, Mami?" Fatimè asked, her voice trembling.

"It's been three years since Khalid's demise. May his soul rest in Jannatul Firdaus," her mother said solemnly.

Fatimè closed her eyes, saying a silent prayer for Khalid as tears welled up in her eyes. Yes, it had been three years since his passing, but the pain of losing him still reverberated through her heart. Khalid was her first love, her soul mate, and no one could replace him. Her mother had no idea what Khalid meant to her and how his loss had shattered her world.

"Everything reminds me of him," Fatimè said softly.

Her mother nodded sympathetically, her concern evident. "I understand, but you need to move on. So many men are interested in you because you're beautiful and talented. You are young and you have your whole life ahead of you. Give someone else a chance."

"Mami, I'm not interested in anyone else," Fatimè said firmly. "None of those men appeal to me. They're not Khalid."

"Of course not, because you keep comparing them to Khalid," her mother said, exasperated. "He's gone forever, Fatimè. He's never coming back."

Fatimè felt a sharp pain in her chest as if a knife had pierced her heart. "Mami, please," she pleaded, her voice filled with tears. "Can we not do this?"

"I'm sorry, Fatimè. I just had to be honest with you. I want the best for you," her mother said, standing up to leave. "Get some sleep. Goodnight."

As her mother left the room, Fatimè clutched her blanket tightly, seeking comfort in its familiar scent. Closing her eyes, she allowed herself to release the floodgates of grief, letting the tears flow freely.

Losing two important people within six years had left an indelible mark on her heart. Despite the passage of time, she questioned the notion that it could truly heal all wounds. The pain of losing someone she loved wholeheartedly was a unique kind of heartbreak that lingered, refusing to dissipate.

Grief is the toughest punctuation mark that exists. It doesn't allow you to move on to the next line after taking a breath. It doesn't appear on the page in a gentle poetic way. Instead, amid everything, it suddenly appears and commands you to stop, and you have no choice but to obey. Then, there's emptiness, the part where you face grief and dwell in its void.

Every day, Fatimè experienced the agony of losing fragments of Khalid - his laughter, his passions, his essence. It was the hardest part of grieving, having to let go of him repeatedly, day after day.

Kaduna, Nigeria,

14th December 2016.

Fahad had just stepped out of the shower when he heard the familiar ringtone of his phone. He quickly wrapped a towel around his waist and scanned the room for the ringing device. Amidst the usual messiness that reflected his busy and active lifestyle, one thing stood out on a shelf against the wall — his collection of Marvel superhero figures.

With water dripping from his hair, Fahad finally located his phone among the scattered clothes and belongings. As he listened to the voice on the other end, his expression changed, and without hesitation, he quickly got dressed, grabbed his car keys, and hurriedly left the house. Instructing the help to inform his mother of his whereabouts and not to wake her.

Driving to the train station, Fahad couldn't shake off his curiosity. He parked his car under a tree in the parking lot and spent the time playing 'Candy Crush' on his phone while waiting for her arrival. When his phone beeped, indicating her presence, Fahad easily spotted her among the bustling crowd. She was in a black abaya adorned with delicately embroidered red flowers at the edges, dragging a mini silver suitcase behind her. She waved at him.

"You are living up to this butterfly name." Fahad chuckled as he collected her suitcase. "Running away again?"

This was not the first time Fatimè had come to Kaduna when something was bothering her.

"No, I'm not. I just needed some fresh air," she said.

"With this weather, I doubt you'd be getting any of that. It's like a hundred degrees out here," Fahad quipped, opening the back door of his car and stowing away her suitcase.

Seeking solace in silence, Fatimè stared out of the car window, not yet ready to engage in the conversation he prodded her with. She simply longed to be in the comforting embrace of her aunt's house and enjoy a refreshing glass of water.

Fahad understood her need for space and didn't press her for answers. He knew she would confide in him when she was ready.

During the drive back from the train station, Fahad couldn't help but notice the dark circles under Fatimè's eyes, evidence of her sleepless nights. He wished he could take away her pain, saddened to witness the once vibrant and bubbly Fatimè gradually fade into a shadow of her former self. It wasn't until Fahad clapped his hands in front of her face that she snapped out of her reverie.

"Hey, you. We're here. Come on, I'm sure Ammi would be delighted to see you," he said.

Nodding, Fatimè stepped out of the car, gracefully greeting everyone with the salaam as she entered her aunt's house. It retained the familiar warmth, with only a few minor changes. The curtains had been replaced, and a new, larger TV now occupied the room. Her Aunt Zainabu had complained incessantly about the previous one, claiming it strained her eyes. Fatimè couldn't help but feel a sense of joy for her aunt's small pleasures.

Flopping onto a chair with a sigh, Fatimè found herself immersed in the quietude of the house, save for the sound of the TV tuned to Zee World, playing its low-budget dramas. She shook her head, pondering what her aunt found so captivating about the exaggerated tales unfolding onscreen.

Just then, her aunt entered the room from the kitchen, her eyes lighting up at the sight of Fatimè. "Mamana!" she exclaimed, moving in to hug her tightly... "deye ayottake? I'm so happy to see you!"

Their embrace was interrupted by Fahad's entrance, carrying Fatimè's suitcase. Zainabu turned to him, slightly reproachful, and asked, "Why didn't you tell me she was coming?"

"Oh, Ammi, don't blame him. He didn't know either. I wanted to surprise you," Fatimè interjected, a mischievous smile gracing her face.

"Very well, then. It was a wonderful surprise. How was your trip? Have you eaten? You must be really tired. Do you want to eat or freshen up first?" Zainabu's questions flowed effortlessly, a testament to her boundless love and concern.

Fatimè grinned, appreciating her aunt's eagerness, while Fahad rolled his eyes playfully. "Won't you ask if I'm hungry too?" he interjected, feigning offense.

"Dun bo an dun wanni," Mummy replied, playfully pulling Fatimè's hand toward the kitchen, continuing their exchange.

Fahad shook his head, taking a seat on the couch. He was no stranger to the close bond between his mother and cousin.

As Fatimè and her 17-year-old cousin Fadila sat in the living room, engrossed in an episode of 'Riverdale', Fahad entered the room after returning from the mosque.

"Hamma Fahad!" Fadila beamed, clearly excited to see him. "Thank God you're here. I've been waiting for you."

Fatimè smiled, adjusting her scarf. "Hey, how was your day?"

"Bleh," he replied dismissively, turning to Fadila and pinching her cheeks. "Why are you looking for me?"

"Pringles now. You promised," Fadila pleaded.

"Not now. I'm tired," Fahad replied, sounding weary.

"Please now. Hamma Fahad. Useni," Fadila whispered, seeking Fatimè's help.

"Useni, Hamma Fahad," Fatimè chimed in, joining her cousin's plea.

"Fine, fine, but only on one condition: Butterfly, you're coming with me," Fahad declared.

"But..." Fatimè began to protest.

"But nothing. We need to talk anyway," Fahad insisted.

Abuja, Nigeria.

The couple sat in their bedroom which was enveloped in a warm ambiance. Soft lighting from a bedside lamp casts a gentle glow, creating a peaceful atmosphere.

"Are you not going to say anything?" Hajiya Hauwa demanded. The soft fabric of her loose-fitting silk pajama set was draped gently over her frame. Her hair was loosely tied back, and she had removed her jewelry, allowing her to fully embrace the comfort of her night-time attire.

Alhaji Faruk continued reading his copy of 'After Dark', trying to maintain a sense of calm. "What do you want me to say, Jiddu?"

Hajiya Hauwa was livid with both her husband and daughter. It seemed like they were making a concerted effort to stress her out. Upon arriving home, she learned that Fatimè had once again traveled to Kaduna with her father's approval. "You cannot keep indulging this girl. We had a small misunderstanding and she packed her bags off to Zainabu's. Who does that?"

Alhaji Faruk sighed, closing his book and setting it aside. "Don't you understand that the girl is upset and needs some space? What you did was not okay. At all," he said, his voice tinged with disappointment.

"And what did I do?" Hajiya Hauwa retorted. "I am trying to see how our daughter will settle down, and you are complaining."

Alhaji Faruk's face softened, and he reached out to hold Hajiya Hauwa's hand gently. "Jiddu, Jiddu... how many times have I told you that is not how it works? You do not pressure anyone into settling down," he explained, his voice filled with empathy. "It is something that happens when it is meant to happen. Wasn't she supposed to get married three years ago? But Allah took him away because it wasn't meant to be. Why don't you focus on other things, like your business or the fact that our children are alive, healthy, and doing well?"

Hajiya Hauwa scoffed at his statement, feeling even more agitated as she stood up and left the room, frustration etched on her face.

Alhaji Faruk shook his head in sadness. He felt sorry for his daughter and the losses she had endured. He had witnessed her decline, and it was as though a part of her was missing. There was no longer a radiance on her face. He missed his two daughters, but the difference was that one was truly gone, and the other was slowly dying inside.

Kaduna, Nigeria.

Fatimè expressed her disappointment when Fahad pulled up in front of a restaurant, "I thought we were going to get Pringles," she said.

"We'll get it on our way back. Now it's time to talk," Fahad replied. Fatimè knew how persistent he could be, so she did not protest. She got out of the car and walked with him into the restaurant, which was cozy and quiet, with only two people seated inside.

They took a booth at the far end corner of the restaurant, and Fahad ordered chapman for them. "So what was it this time around?" he asked, looking at her.

Fatimè let out a long sigh and shook her head. "The usual, settling down. I'm appalled at how Mami just doesn't understand my situation. The only person I planned to spend my whole life with was gone. Does she think it is easy to pick up those pieces and just move on?"

"Okay, okay. Calm down, butterfly," Fahad said.

"No, Fahad, you don't understand how frustrating it is. Everything is still fresh, and there are so many things on my mind, I feel like exploding." She rubbed her temples and continued, "Work has gotten more hectic, I'm trying so hard to focus, and then there's that damn airport guy that keeps appearing from nowhere."

"The airport guy? Who is he?" Fahad asked, intrigued.

"One guy that I met at the airport."

Fahad laughed. "Of course, you met him at the airport. What else?"

Fatimè shrugged. "He went to ask Baaba for my hand in marriage? I was like what the hell? I barely even know you, and then went ahead to send gifts to my office"

"Damn. I like his courage," Fahad said.

She rolled her eyes.

"Dume?" Fahad laughed, "He was just shooting his shot."

"I told him to get lost. This guy didn't even stop there. Do you know Mami invited him over, and he came? Why would she even do that? It was like she was desperate to hand me off to whoever was interested."

Fahad let out a sigh and said calmly, "Butterfly, I need you to relax and take a deep breath, okay? You need to understand Mami; she's just looking out for you. She wants you to be happy, you know, the happy-go-lucky Fatimè that everyone is used to. We just want you to get better. We might not understand how you feel, but we know how important Khalid was to you, and best believe no one is taking that away from you. Mami needs to be more patient and take things one at a time. Perhaps you should talk to her."

She rolled her eyes. "As if she would listen to me."

"You see," Fahad said, taking another sip of his drink. "You have already concluded it without trying. Give it a try, have a heart-to-heart conversation."

She nodded and resolved to talk with her mother as soon as she got back. "And for the 'airport guy,' you really shouldn't blame him. It's hard not to go crazy for someone as charming and beautiful as you."

"Dalu," Fatimè replied.

"Dume? Just spitting pure facts. Anyways, we should get going; it's getting late. Plus, if I don't get those Pringles for Fadila, I doubt I'll be getting any sleep tonight.

"We." She corrected and grabbed her bag as Fahad paid for the drink.

She felt relatively better after talking to him. Fahad was everything she could ever wish for in a cousin. He was a great listener, gave the best advice, and also taught her a lot.

Whoever ended up with him was going to be lucky.

"Thank you." She said as they got into the car.

"Anytime butterfly. I got you okay?" He smiled at her. "Now let's go get some hot and spicy."

Abuja, Nigeria.

15th December 2017

Madina sat in her slightly messy room, the shelves lined with books filled with romantic novels, a reflection of her love for captivating stories. The room had a girly touch with clothes strewn across the bed and a mirror stood on the dressing table, reflecting her casual attire and slightly disheveled hair,

"It's not going to be a problem, I promise. I'll handle it," Madina said into the phone.

As she spoke on the phone, her attention was abruptly interrupted by her mother's entrance into the room. Hajiya Asiya was a petite and dark-skinned woman who oozed an air of both beauty and intimidation.

"What are you going to handle?" Umma inquired, her tone filled with curiosity and concern.

Madina swiftly ended the call, her voice slightly tense as she responded, "Nothing, Umma. Work-related issues."

Umma's eyes narrowed slightly, sensing that there was more to the conversation. "I hope everything is okay. Did you speak to your cousin? Your aunt is really worried."

Madina let out a sigh, feeling the weight of the situation. "Umma, I've told you and Anty Jidda to stop getting worked up over Fatimè. She just needs some time alone. She's going through a lot."

The concern in Umma's eyes was evident. "Yes, and that's why we're all worried. She can't keep running away from home over the slightest issue."

Madina's voice softened as she tried to reassure her mother. "Technically, she didn't run away. She just went to Anty Zainabu's house for a while to clear her head. She will be back in no time."

Umma's gaze held a mix of understanding and worry. "So, what is this I am hearing about an airport guy?"

Madina chuckled, the tension momentarily easing. "Umma, he is just some guy we met at the airport. I think he likes Fatimè. He even asked her to marry him."

Umma expressed her disbelief, shaking her head. "Ahn. Straight to the point kawai?"

Madina nodded in agreement. "That is what I said too. Maybe if he had taken things slowly, she would have listened to him, but with Fatimè, that would be a hard nut to crack. Khalid is still fresh in her mind.

Umma's voice softened her concern for her niece apparent. "Of course, losing someone you love is one of the hardest things. Moving on is even harder. Like I told Jidda, she needs to be patient with her. She will come around."

"Exactly. I will talk to her too, In Sha Allah. Everything will be all right."

Umma nodded, her thoughts momentarily shifting. "I hope so. Let me get some sleep. Your father and I are traveling to Kano tomorrow for that wedding."

"Okay. Goodnight, Umma,"

"Goodnight," Umma replied, leaving the room.

Abuja, Nigeria.

16th December 2017.

Kamal raised an eyebrow, looking at his friend with a mix of incredulity and amusement. "Come on Nabila, I don't even know what's funny," he remarked.

She couldn't contain her laughter as she replied, "What's funny is the fact that you are crazy, M.K."

The atmosphere in the café was cozy and intimate, reflecting the warmth of their conversation. Nabila, always the fashionista, oozed an air of class, her impeccable sense of style evident in her attire. Though she considered herself average-looking, her self-assured demeanor added an extra touch of appeal.

Kamal crossed his arms, a challenge in his eyes. "Tell me one crazy thing I did, please."

"M.K, you cannot be serious. Everything you did was crazy," Nabila exclaimed between fits of laughter. "From asking her to marry you after talking to her for just ten minutes, to meeting her dad, sending gifts to her office, and even honoring her mom's invitation. Nothing about it is normal. I mean, I know you have a few knots loose in your brain, but I had no idea it was THIS bad."

Kamal patiently waited for her laughter to subside before he spoke up, a determined expression on his face. "I met her dad because it was the right thing to do. If you develop an interest in someone, you meet their parents so everything can be halal."

Nabila scoffed, still struggling to contain her amusement. "Did you not tell me you met this girl just last week at the airport? Is that not too short, you know?"

"You've never heard about love at first sight? You have no idea how I feel about this girl," Kamal retorted, his voice filled with conviction.

Nabila observed him closely, noticing an expression she hadn't seen in a very long time. The intensity in his eyes mirrored the way he used to talk about Piya, the only girl who had ever stirred such passion within him. She recalled the dark era when he lost Piya, and how she had felt helpless in consoling him. The pain had been so deep that she had feared he might even contemplate taking his own life.

Wow, M.K. Are you sure about this? You don't even know her," Nabila expressed her concern.

Kamal understood that no one would truly comprehend his feelings. He sighed, a mixture of frustration and longing.

"And Rukayya?" Nabila asked.

He rolled his eyes. "You know it was over even before it began."

Nabila nodded, remembering how Rukayya had stood no chance against Piya. "So this girl... who is she, and how do you plan on getting her? I know she told you to fuck off, but omo from the look in your eyes, you do not plan on listening."

"That's why I came to you, dummy. How can I convince her? I like her," Kamal sought Nabila's guidance.

Nabila mused for a moment, her mind racing with thoughts.

"Her name is so beautiful. Fatimè. Just like her smile too. The world stops when she talks, just like my heart. I can see myself with her," Kamal said, lost in his world.

Nabila clapped her hands dramatically, a mischievous glint in her eyes. "Omo, what is this? I don't believe it. Hard guy, hard guy, but you are catching feelings."

Kamal discharged her response with a dismissive gesture. "Don't be so dramatic."

Curiosity piqued, Nabila couldn't help but probe further. "Does this mean you are over Piya?"

His eyes shut briefly, the pain of the past resurfacing. "I'm not over her, and I don't think I'll ever be. It's just... I know she's never coming back. Maybe it's time I give love another chance."

Nabila, understanding the weight of his words, nodded empathetically. Their bond as friends ran deep, and she had witnessed the complexities of his past relationships. She remembered Rukayya, and how he had walked away from that situation.

"You never gave others this chance, even the mother of your child. Why is this one different?" Nabila asked, her curiosity tinged with concern.

Kamal let out a sigh, his eyes reflecting both hope and uncertainty. "You know how it was with Rukayya, and I do not need to go into details. I cannot explain why it's different with Fatimè; it's just how I feel."

After their heartfelt conversation, Kamal checked his watch, realizing that he needed to leave soon. "I have to go. I'm picking up Adil from Maa's; he's leaving tomorrow with his aunt."

Nabila's disappointment was evident. "Aww, I didn't even get to see him. You are making me look like a bad godmother."

"I'm sorry. When he comes over next time, I promise. Anyways, you're the one who's always busy with work," Kamal playfully teased.

"Bro, it's not easy being a doctor," Nabila shot back with a smile. "You wouldn't know, sha, since you dumped us."

"Whatever," Kamal replied, signaling the waiter for the bill. After paying, he turned to Nabila. "I'll see you when I see you. Take care of yourself."

Nabila watched him leave, sipping her drink in silence. She replayed their conversation in her mind, reflecting on Kamal's intense feelings for Fatimè. Just as she immersed herself in her thoughts, her phone beeped, alerting her to a message from Kamal. Curiosity piqued, she opened the message and was greeted with an image. "What?!" she exclaimed, causing heads to turn in the restaurant. Ignoring the curious gazes, she looked at the picture again.

Nabila's eyes widened, and a sense of urgency washed over her. She swiftly finished her drink and hurriedly left the café. There was something she needed to take care of immediately.

Chapter 4

♥

Abuja, Nigeria

17th December 2016.

Fatimè couldn't help but smile as the wind blew her green scarf into her face. She was glad that the weather was a bit manageable for today. All she wanted was to cuddle up in her bed and watch sappy romantic shows with some packs of purebliss. After her three-day fresh air break, she was feeling a whole lot better. A talk with Fahad, hanging out with her aunt and family, and some 'dalema' fudge cake had been therapeutic. She didn't want to leave but realized that running away from her problems was not the solution.

The train station buzzed with noise, and a multitude of cab drivers approached her, eager to offer their services. Politely declining, she noticed her brother, Mubarak's red car parked at the far end of the bustling parking lot and made her way towards it.

Mubarak bore a striking resemblance to their father in both appearance and mannerisms, although, he was a more playful version of him.

Fatimè's attire for the day was her signature style of a casual abaya, with subtle embroidered details and a comfortable fit. The loose folds of her abaya swayed gracefully with the breeze as she walked

"Aye." He opened his arms to hug her. "The prodigal daughter is back!"

Fatimè embraced him tightly, savoring the warmth of their reunion. "I missed you too," she said, finally releasing him

Why do you look like a groom?" she teased, noticing his attire consisting of a white kaftan and Zanna Bukar cap. It was unusual for her brother to go full kaftan mode.

"Because I am coming from a wedding, dummy."

"You have finally decided to settle down kenan? Ma Sha Allah. Mami must be very happy. So who is the lucky girl, or should I say, who are you lucky to have?"

"Shut up," he chuckled. "I meant a friend's wedding. As for me, I'm still searching for someone who can handle this package." He flexed his muscles playfully, eliciting laughter from Fatimè.

"Package indeed."

"Come on, yan dillu," Mubarak urged. "Mami is dying to see her prodigal daughter."

Sensing her unease, Mubarak gently lifted her face with his finger, ensuring she looked at him. "Relax, I'm sure everything is calm now. You can talk to Mami and sort it out. Stop beating yourself up about it. All she does is from a place of love, it's just, you know, different, more like the millennial way."

Fatimè laughed. "Don't let her hear you calling her a millennial, or else you'll be moving out permanently."

"That's the plan, mumu. Vex her so she kicks me out, and I don't get to hear her yap about how it's her house yen yen yen."

If Fatimè had a dollar for every time her mother mentioned the statement "this is my house," she'd be richer than "Jeff Bezos'.

"Maybe you should get married then," she suggested.

"Now you sound like Mami. Please yan dillu, this sun is killing me." Mubarak complained, shielding his eyes from the blazing sun.

"Branch 'Yogurberry'?" Fatimè begged with the biggest grin she could muster.

"One of these days, you'll be peeing frozen yogurt."

She knew it was a yes and got into the car, thinking about how the blueberry flavor was going to melt in her mouth.

Dublin, Ireland

17th December 2016

Rukayya's hands were covered in flour from her culinary endeavors and quickly wiped them on her apron before removing it altogether. As she rushed to answer the door, the aroma of incense wafted through the house, filling the air with a pleasant and inviting fragrance.

As December approached, the weather in Ireland turned colder, with occasional gusts of wind and a constant chill in the air. Even after spending two years here with the intention of furthering her studies, she was still getting used to the weather.

She had been eagerly anticipating the arrival of her sister Raliya who was also schooling here and her son Adil all day. As soon as she swung the door open, Adil burst out of his aunt's grasp and threw himself into his mother's arms. They held each other tightly for almost five minutes, relishing the long-awaited reunion.

Interrupting their embrace, Raliya cleared her throat and gestured towards the boxes they had brought with them. "Hellooooo...

need some help over here," she teased. "You can continue your mama and son bonding later."

Reluctantly releasing Adil, who eagerly ran inside the house, Rukayya turned to her sister, embracing her warmly, "I missed you too, dumb dumb. How was your flight?" she inquired, genuine concern etched on her face.

"Meh..." Raliya shrugged, visibly exhausted. "Slept all through it."

Helping Raliya carry the boxes inside, Rukayya couldn't contain her excitement. "Oya, where's my tsaraba?" she asked, playfully dragging one of the trolleys.

"I can't believe you made me package kilishi from Nigeria," Raliya remarked, rising from the couch and opening one of the boxes.

Peering into the box, Rukayya let out a joyful squeal. "Oh, mummy! Even 'indomie!' Her mother truly was the best. While she had only requested kilishi, her mother had gone above and beyond, including an assortment of her favorite goodies. "You wouldn't believe she wanted to add daddawa too. She thought we were looking too skinny and needed some tuwo and miya.

"Kai," Rukayya chuckled, "Daddawa that can be smelled from a mile away? I can only imagine the reactions at the airport."

"I had to beg her not to include it. It's not me who would be embarrassed," Raliya sighed, stifling a yawn. "I'll leave you to the unpacking. This girl here needs a hot shower and some beauty sleep so I can properly catch up with you later."

"I should bathe Adil too. Where is he?" Rukayya looked around the house, hoping her mischievous son hadn't caused any trouble in their absence.

Inside Adil's room, a typical haven for a three-year-old, the walls were adorned with colorful posters of dinosaurs, showcasing his fascination with the prehistoric creatures. A small desk stood against one wall, cluttered with coloring books and crayons, evidence of his creative endeavors. On the floor, scattered toys created a cheerful mess.

Adil, who was a carbon copy of his father but had taken his mother's light-skinned complexion, sat on the bed, engrossed in game on his iPad, his features reflecting a hint of disappointment. Rukayya, concerned by his sullen expression, approached him gently, trying to understand his mood.

Adil?" Rukayya asked, her voice tinged with care. She sat down beside him, her eyes filled with affection. "Are you okay? Don't you want to tell mummy about your trip? How was it? Did you have fun?"

Adil, still captivated by the television screen, shrugged nonchalantly. "It was nice," he replied, his attention seemingly elsewhere.

Confused by his subdued response, Rukayya persisted, "You were with Aunt Hafsah, right? Did you go to the movies and the park like you planned? I'm sure she taught you some cool things."

Adil's disappointment became more apparent as he replied, "Yeah. Daddy was busy."

Rukayya's heart sank as she struggled to fathom what could be so pressing for Kamal that he couldn't spare time for their son. The dedication he had shown in maintaining their relationship made this absence all the more bewildering.

"Mummy, when are you going to daddy's house?" Adil's innocent question hung in the air, his furrowed brow revealing his confusion.

Rukayya, bracing herself for this conversation, knelt next to him, her touch gentle as she placed a hand on his shoulder. "Well, sweetheart, not anytime soon because Daddy and I aren't married," she explained delicately, aware of the difficulty Adil might face in understanding the situation.

Adil's young mind struggled to process the information, his innocent eyes searching for clarity. "Why?" he asked, his voice tinged with concern.

"It's just that sometimes grown-ups have issues, and we decided it was best if we separated." Rukayya reassured him, her voice filled with warmth and sincerity.

Adil's face reflected a mixture of comprehension and sadness as the reality settled in. "Oh, okay." he responded quietly.

Rukayya wanted to ensure Adil knew their love for him remained unwavering. She looked deeply into his eyes, her gaze filled with love and assurance. "But I want you to know that your daddy and I love you very much, and that will never change," she emphasized. "You are the most important thing to us, and you will always come first."

Adil's face lit up, and he threw his arms around his mother in a tight hug, holding onto her tightly. "I love you too, mummy," he whispered.

Rukayya smiled, ruffling his hair playfully. "Now, let's go take a bath. You smell like airports."

Abuja, Nigeria.

The home study radiated an air of warmth and familiarity with the room adorned with shelves, filled to the brim with books on various subjects. Soft ambient light cascaded from a beautiful pendant lamp, casting a gentle glow on Hajiya Hauwa.

She shut down the computer on her desk and leaned back on her chair, deep in thought. Being an entrepreneur was not an easy job, especially when you had to find a new assistant ASAP.

She sighed, reminiscing about her former assistant, who had to relocate after getting married. Finding a replacement had proven difficult, and all the applicants she had met so far were not even close to being efficient.

Her gaze shifted to the framed picture of her late daughter, Furaira. The photograph captured the vibrant spirit and infectious smile that had been a constant presence in their lives. Memories flooded back, and Hajiya Hauwa's heart ached with the void that Furaira's absence had left behind.

It was moments like these that made her wish she could bring her daughter back. The one who was always on top of things. She smiled at the thought of her daughter's confidence, always assuring her, "Don't worry Mami, I got it covered."

She reached out for the framed picture on her desk and ran her fingers over it, feeling the pain in her chest constricting her breathing. The loss was still fresh, and anytime she thought about it, she felt like her heart broke into pieces. The doctor's words still echoed in her head, "I'm sorry, we lost her."

"I miss her too," Fatimè's voice resonated, breaking the weight of silence that enveloped the room. She moved closer, placing a comforting hand on her mother's shoulder.

Hajiya Hauwa, still wiping away a tear, tried to regain her composure. She welcomed the embrace of her daughter, finding solace in their shared grief.

Fatimè knew how much her mother was affected by her sister's death. She always dismissed their closeness as Furaira being the first girl and was never bothered about it. But for her mother, it was a deafening blow that almost broke her. At some point, everyone was scared that she would leave them too because of how sick she had gotten.

It took her more than a month to leave Furaira's room and almost a year before she could mention her name without crying. For Fatimè, it was numbness; she could not shed a tear and felt responsible for whatever had happened.

Fatimè felt a pang of guilt as she sat in her room, thinking about the deteriorating relationship with her mother. She couldn't help but think that her sister was the glue holding them together, and now that she was gone, everything had changed. For as long as she could remember, she had relied on her sister to solve every problem, whether it was with their mother or her life issues. However, she knew that she needed to grow up and take responsibility for her actions, especially with her mother.

"I'm sorry for leaving like that earlier. I feel like you misunderstand me a lot, and everything is so overwhelming. I wish you would just make things a bit easier for me," Fatimè spoke softly.

Mami looked at her with a mixture of hurt and understanding flashing across her face. She took a deep breath, struggling to find the right words. "How am I supposed to understand you when you never let me in? You always run to your father or your aunt instead of talking to me."

Fatimè's expression softened, realizing the impact her actions had on her mother. "I'm sorry, Mami. Sometimes, I feel like you don't know me at all."

Her mother shook her head in disbelief. "That's not true. I just want the best for you. It's just that you think you know better than me, and that you don't need my help."

Fatimè felt a lump in her throat. "I don't mean to make you feel that way, Mami. I wish you would listen to me and allow me to make my own decisions."

Hajiya Hauwa let out a weary sigh, her eyes filled with a mix of sorrow and love. "Things were easier with your sister. She never questioned my decisions or stressed me out. But you, you're always pushing back and making things difficult."

Fatimè's heart sank as her mother's words pierced through her. "I'm sorry, Mami. I know I'm not Adda and I can't be her. But I'm my person, and I hope you can accept that."

Silence enveloped the room, their words lingering in the air like fragile threads of hope. The call to prayer sounded, a gentle interruption that broke the heaviness of the moment.

When Fatimè finished praying, she found a tray adorned with a steaming teapot, delicate cup, and an assortment of snacks. Hajiya Hauwa had prepared the tray, her gesture serving as an unspoken apology.

21st December, 2016.

Fatimè entered her boss's office, clutching the report she had meticulously prepared for their meeting. Mr. Williams engrossed in reviewing the documents on his desk, looked up as she entered.

"Do you have any other suggestions, Fatimè?" Mr. Williams asked after looking through the report.

Fatimè shook her head, "No, everything looks perfect."

"Very well then, I would be expecting the complete project after the holidays," Mr. Williams stated, closing the file and signaling the end of their discussion.

"Okay, sir," Fatimè replied, a sense of relief washing over her. She gathered her belongings, eager to escape the confines of her office. The past week had been exceptionally demanding, and her head was throbbing with exhaustion. The thought of a few days of rest during the upcoming holiday break brought her much-needed solace.

As she made her way outside, hoping to evade the notorious Lokogoma traffic, she ran into Lolade, one of her colleagues who was also preparing to head home.

"Yo girl!" Lolade called out, catching Fatimè's attention. "Where have you been? I've been trying to catch up with you."

Fatimè sighed, her fatigue evident. "Buried under work," she lamented. "I've wanted to check up on you too, but my schedule has been a mess."

Lolade empathized with her, understanding the demands of their profession. "Believe me, sis, I get it. How about we grab some lunch tomorrow? My treat," Lolade offered.

Fatimè managed a smile. "Sure. See you tomorrow then."

Approaching her car, Fatimè noticed it was empty, wondering where their driver, Sule, had disappeared to. Frustration crept in as her weariness intensified. Just then, her attention was captured by an unwelcome presence standing in her path. It was Kamal.

"You again? When will you leave me alone?"

Kamal, undeterred, pleaded with her, his voice filled with genuine remorse. "Fatimè, please. Just five minutes of your time. Just five," he implored.

Reluctantly, Fatimè agreed, deciding that perhaps listening to him might finally lead to some respite from his persistent pursuit.

"First of all," Kamal began, his tone sincere, "I want to apologize for bothering you. I am truly sorry. It was never my intention to upset you. Since I saw you at the airport, I couldn't stop thinking about you. I've never been drawn to anyone like I am to you. Call me crazy, but that's how I feel."

Fatimè pursed her lips, her guard still up, but she allowed him to continue, intrigued by his earnestness.

"I admit my approach has been weird and invasive, but I genuinely apologize and would like to beg you for another chance to prove myself. In other words, a fresh start as friends. That's if you agree," Kamal pleaded.

She remained silent, carefully observing him. His eyes held a sincerity she hadn't seen before, and a part of her wondered if it would be worth giving him a chance, even if it was just as friends.

"Hm," was all she could muster, unsure of how to respond?

"You don't have to give me an answer right away. Take all the time you need. No pressure. I promise you that if you don't want this, I will never bother you again," Kamal assured her.

"Okay," Fatimè replied, a small smile gracing her lips.

"You should do that more often," Kamal remarked. "Your smile is beautiful."

Just then, Sule arrived, interrupting their conversation. "I'm sorry," he apologized. "I went to use the toilet."

Fatimè turned to Kamal. "I have to go now. Excuse me," she said, walking away, leaving Kamal with a grin on his face.

Fatimè arrived home earlier than expected, grateful for the light traffic that allowed her to escape the usual Lokogoma gridlock. After helping her mother with dinner and bidding farewell to her brother who was heading to Lagos, she retreated to her room.

As she began reciting her adkhar, seeking solace in her prayers, her sanctuary was abruptly invaded by the energetic entrance of her cousin, Madina.

Hey, coz!" Madina exclaimed, flopping onto Fatimè's bed. "Noi kadi?"

Fatimè couldn't help but let out a small sigh. "No Salama, no nothing. When will you grow up, Madina?" she teased, feigning annoyance.

Madina rolled her eyes, dismissing the remark. "Yen yen," she retorted. "You promised to stop by today, but since you didn't, I decided to pay you a visit instead."

"I'm sorry," Fatimè apologized sincerely. "It was a hectic day at work."

She stood up, neatly folding her hijab and prayer mat, then switched on the air conditioner to cool down the room.

Madina reached over and grabbed the basketball sitting in the corner, its worn out exterior, a testament of Fatimè's love for the sport.

"How come Abba allowed you to drive at night?" Fatimè asked, curious about Madina's unexpected visit.

"I'm here with Umma. Ya Mujahid is getting married, so she came to discuss some things with Mami," Madina explained casually, her attention still drawn to the basketball in her hands.

Fatimè's eyes sparkled with excitement. "Ah, Ma Sha Allah. Kai, I'm so happy for him," she exclaimed

Madina, however, dismissed the topic, her focus now fixated on Fatimè, "Me I'm here for gossip. What's up with 'airport guy'?

Fatimè couldn't help but smile, trying to hide her amusement. "And what's up with him?" she retorted, playing along.

"I mean, has he contacted you again?" Madina probed, eagerly awaiting the details.

Knowing that hiding the truth from Madina was futile, Fatimè decided to be honest. "Yeah. He stopped by my office today," she admitted.

Madina leaned in, eagerly anticipating more information. Fatimè, however, ignored her curiosity and picked up her phone, diverting her attention.

"And?" Madina clapped her hands impatiently, urging her cousin to continue.

"And nothing," Fatimè replied casually, trying to downplay the significance. "He just apologized, that's all."

Madina squinted her eyes suspiciously, sensing that Fatimè wasn't revealing everything. "I feel like there's something you're not telling me, but oh well, I'll find out eventually."

"Toh FBI," Fatimè teased, playfully pulling Madina up from the bed. "Come on, I want to say hi to Umma."

Madina and her mother finally left past 9 PM, leaving Fatimè alone in her bedroom. She decided to unwind by watching an episode of 'One Piece' when she noticed an email notification on her phone.

From: Kamal Maitambari

Subject: Safety

Date: December 21, 2016. 21:00

To: Fatimè Ardo

Since you have blocked me from calling or texting, I had to resort to this. I hope you arrived home safely?

K.

She smiled and proceeded to reply.

From: Fatimè Ardo

Subject: Re: Safety

Date: December 21, 2016. 21:48

To: Kamal Maitambari

You deserved it, work hard and you might get unblocked. Yes, I got home safe and sound, what about you?

F.

Almost instantaneously, there was a response.

From: Kamal Maitambari

Subject: Re: Safety

Date: December 21, 2016. 21:50

To: Fatimè Ardo

Hard worker is my middle name, I would work towards that in sha Allah. I didn't think you'd reply and yes I arrived home safely.

K.

She shook her head and typed a quick reply.

From: Fatimè Ardo

Subject: I am a nice person

Date: December 21, 2016. 21:53

To: Kamal Maitambari

We'll see if you can live up to that name. Of course, I would, friends reply to emails and it is nice of you to check up on my safety. I appreciate that.

F.

She didn't wait another minute before she heard the beep again. He was a fast typer.

From: Kamal Maitambari

Subject: Friendly Question

Date: December 21, 2016. 21:54

To: Fatimè Ardo

Are you free this weekend?

K.

She wondered what he was up to and contemplated saying yes or no.

From: Fatimè Ardo

Subject: Friendly Answer

Date: December 21, 2016. 21:58

To: Kamal Maitambari

It depends, why?

F.

His reply was again instant.

From: Kamal Maitambari

Subject: Friendly Question (Again)

Date: December 21, 2016. 22:00

To: Fatimè Ardo

On? I was wondering if we could go somewhere. As friends though.

K.

She was feeling sleepy so decided to wrap up the conversation.

From: Fatimè Ardo

Subject: Friendly Answer (Again)

Date: December 21, 2016. 22:03

To: Kamal Maitambari

When I think about it. I have to go now. Goodnight Kamal.

F.

She had already switched off her lights when she got his reply.

From: Kamal Maitambari

Subject: Hope

Date: December 21, 2017. 22:05

To: Fatimè Ardo

I will be looking forward to your reply. Goodnight Fatimè. Sleep well.

K.

Fatimè switched off her data and went to sleep. Kamal, on the other end, had already dialed Aziz's number. Despite the late hour, Aziz knew the stakes and picked up on the third ring. "Boss?" he said.

"Yes, Aziz. Book a flight to Abuja for this weekend and get that thing ready. No mistakes, please," Kamal instructed.

"Got it," Aziz replied.

24th December 2016

Fatimè stood before her closet, carefully surveying the neatly folded garments. The variety of clothing options displayed her chic and simple style. Among them, she noticed a collection of elegant abayas, but decided against them, opting for a more casual attire as Kamal had hinted at an activity date. Her eyes then settled on a blue-back knee-length flannel shirt, beckoning her to choose it.

Her gaze shifted to a row of meticulously folded jeans, offering both comfort and style. She selected the second pair, confident that they would strike the perfect balance for the evening. Instead of her beloved white 'converse all-stars,' she opted for a pair of blue 'vans'.

Fatimè turned her attention to the assortment of bags neatly arranged on the shelf. She reached for a small blue 'chanel' cross body bag, perfectly sized to hold her essential items for the day—lip gloss, wallet, sunglasses, pocket perfume, chewing gum, pen, sticky notes, and two bars of Snickers chocolate.

With her outfit now finalized, Fatimè turned her attention back to her reflection in the mirror. She quickly lined her eyes with kohl, enhancing her features, and applied a light dusting of powder to her face for a polished look. A swipe of lip gloss added a touch of color and she spritzed some perfume.

Fatimè emerged from her closet and found Khalifa sitting on her bed, munching on some 'famous amos' cookies while engrossed in a football match blaring from the TV. The room was filled with the excitement of the 'Manchester City vs. Bournemouth' match. Annoyed by the crumbs scattered on her bed sheet, Fatimè swiftly grabbed a pillow and playfully threw it at Khalifa, prompting him to groan in response.

"Ouch! What was that for?" he said standing up, while cookie crumbs lingered on his Real Madrid jersey that displayed his unwavering support for the club.

Khalifa's tall frame towered over Fatimè, despite her being five years older than him. They both shared their mother's astigmatism, and their glasses hinted at their reliance on vision aids.

Khalifa raised an eyebrow when he noticed how dressed up she was looking. "Where are you going to?"

"To the island of noneya, none of ya business. Now I need you out of my room," Fatimè retorted, snapping her fingers as she reached for the TV remote "And don't you have practice or something?" Fatimè inquired, her eyes missing Khalifa's bandaged ankle, indicating yet another injury.

"Injury, madam," Khalifa replied, a mixture of annoyance and amusement in his voice.

"Again? At this rate, your footballing career has ended even before it started. I'm not sure any club would be willing to sign a low-budget Dembele, she teased, a mischievous grin appearing on her face.

Khalifa scoffed, knowing his sister's playful jabs all too well. He was about to leave when Fatimè's phone beeped, signaling an incoming email. It was from Kamal, notifying her of his arrival.

Fatimè smiled as she turned to Khalifa. Sensing what was coming, he quickly interjected, "Oh oh, the answer is no."

"Khalifa, please, I just need you to let him in while I handle Mami. Useni Mana. Do it for me," she pleaded, pulling him into a side hug, "As your only sister and you, my favorite brother..."

"Ah, ah, Adda, we know your choice of favorite brother changes every day. You'll be moving around like Prime Rivaldo. Change tactics," he joked, flashing a playful grin.

Fatimè couldn't help but burst into laughter. "Fine, just do it, and we'll talk later?"

Satisfied with his sister's request, Khalifa returned her smile and confidently walked out of the room.

She stood nervously in the doorway of the sitting room, her eyes fixated on her mother, who was seated one of the armchairs. Hajiya Hauwa looked effortlessly elegant in a simple dress, her hair neatly tied into a bun, highlighting her natural beauty even in the comfort of their home. Surrounding her were stacks of fabrics, as she diligently took inventory of the new designs that had been brought to her. The sweet aroma of sandal flakes wafted through the room, emanating from a kasko resting in the corner, creating a serene ambiance.

"Mami?" Fatimè said softly, breaking the silence that enveloped the room.

Hajiya Hauwa paused her typing and glanced up, her gaze meeting Fatimè's. She peered over the rim of her glasses, her expression a mix of curiosity and anticipation. "Yes, what is it?" she inquired.

Fatimè's heart raced as she nervously scratched the back of her neck, trying to gather her thoughts. "Um, it's just that Kamal is here, and he wants us to go somewhere," she began, her voice filled with a mixture of apprehension and hope. "We'll be back before Magrib, I promise."

Her mother raised an eyebrow, her gaze discerning as she carefully considered her Fatimè's words.

"We're just friends, Mami. Nothing more," Fatimè replied earnestly, desperately hoping to allay her mother's suspicions.

Hajiya Hauwa let out a small sigh, nodding her approval, she offered a small smile. "All right, you may go. But you better be back in time for Magrib prayers," she cautioned, her motherly concern evident in her voice.

Relief washed over Fatimè as she thanked her mother and hurriedly left the room to meet Kamal downstairs.

Hajiya Hauwa couldn't resist the urge to share the news with her sister, Asiya. Picking up her phone, she dialed Ammatullah's number, eager to divulge the exciting development.

"Amma, I have good news," Hajiya Hauwa exclaimed, her voice brimming with excitement. "With the way things are going, we might have a wedding next year!"

Asiya's curiosity piqued, she leaned in closer to the phone. "Oh really? Ko fe'i?" she urged, her anticipation evident.

Pushing her work aside, Hajiya Hauwa's attention was fully on her sister. "Well, Kamal is here with Fatimè right now. They're just friends, but who knows? Maybe things will progress from there," she shared, a spark of hope igniting in her heart as she envisioned a future wedding

Fatimè descended the stairs, her footsteps echoing in the spacious hallway. As she reached the sitting room, she found Kamal and Khalifa engrossed in conversation, their voices blending with the soft hum of the TV. The room radiated a sense of comfort, cooled by the gentle breeze from the air conditioning. A hint of oud wafted in the air, adding a touch of warmth to the atmosphere.

Kamal and Khalifa seemed to be hitting it off, their friendliness evident in their animated gestures and shared laughter..

"Hey" Kamal's voice rang out as he caught sight of Fatimè. His eyes lit up as he took in her appearance.

She returned the smile, however, she was mindful of Khalifa's presence and didn't want to give him any more ammunition for teasing. He got up from his seat, turning to face Kamal. "It was nice meeting you," he said, extending a hand.

Kamal shook Khalifa's hand warmly. "Same here," he replied, his easygoing nature evident in his demeanor. Fatimè watched as they exchanged a few friendly words, their conversation flowing effortlessly. It was as if they had known each other for years, which surprised her, considering how reserved her brothers usually were.

As Khalifa stepped closer to her, he leaned in and whispered in her ear, "He's a Real Madrid fan. A boost to your mid-life. Hold him tight." Fatimè couldn't help but swat at him playfully, a mixture of annoyance and amusement etched on her face. Khalifa, with a smug smile on his face, sauntered away, satisfied with his teasing.

Shall we?" Kamal said, standing up.

She nodded, feeling a mix of excitement and apprehension as they left the sitting room. As they stepped into Kamal's car, Fatimè couldn't help but notice his casual yet refined attire—a plain white t-shirt paired with black khaki pants. The simplicity of his outfit accentuated his natural charm. A faint whiff of his pleasant cologne, mingled with the scent of sandalwood, greeted her senses.

"So..." they both started.

Kamal laughed. "You first."

"So where are you taking me?"

"You just have to be a bit more patient. You'll find out soon."

Fatimè's eyebrows furrowed slightly. She wasn't particularly fond of surprises and preferred having some control over her plans. She sighed, looking out the window.

Inside the car, the scent of sandalwood enveloped her with the soft melody of James Arthur's "Naked" playing softly, creating a gentle ambiance.

Finally, they arrived at their destination—an open sports arena with a football pitch and a basketball court. Fatimè took in the familiar surroundings, the sights and sounds of a typical arena where people came to enjoy their favorite sports. Kamal wore a boyish grin on his face as he led the way toward the turf. The football pitch was occupied by a group of boys engaged in a spirited game, while the basketball court stood empty, waiting for action.

As Fatimè stepped out of the car, Kamal swiftly made his way to someone nearby, appearing to hold some authority at the arena.

While waiting for Kamal's return, Fatimè received a message from Madina, inquiring about their plans. She quickly responded, sharing her location. It was a precaution she deemed necessary, given the circumstances.

Soon enough, Kamal reappeared, a basketball in hand. Fatimè couldn't help but burst into laughter at the unexpected turn of events. "Basketball? Normal people go out for movies or dinner on their first outing, you know," she playfully teased him, her curiosity growing.

With a smirk, Kamal retorted, "Well, who said I was normal?" His response intrigued Fatimè, and she wondered how he had learned about her love for basketball.

"There's so much you can find out from one's 'Twitter' account, you know?" he remarked, a mischievous glint in his eyes. "Plus, it's hard not to notice that award in your hallway for basketball champion of the year. It was quite obvious."

Fatimè adjusted her glasses, momentarily concealing the sadness in her eyes. "That was me years ago. I don't play anymore," she confessed.

Undeterred by her admission, Kamal persisted. "Come on," he urged. "I know you want to. You look stressed, and what better way to relax than a game of basketball?" He skillfully used her own words against her, reminding her of the pinned tweet that had hinted at her love for the sport.

Fatimè hesitated for a moment, contemplating Kamal's proposition. With a determined smile, she accepted the challenge. "Fine. Just one game,"

With the ball in her hands, Fatimè made her way toward the court, removing the abaya on top of her outfit and securing her scarf with a pin, embracing the comfort of her outfit. The boys had already departed, leaving only Kamal and her standing there.

"Let's see if I've still got it in me," she mused.

Kamal smiled, a glimmer of determination in his eyes. "Loser buys dinner for the winner. Deal?" he proposed.

"Deal."

Sumayya tapped her foot impatiently, her frustration mounting as she repeatedly dialed her brother's number. She was beyond irritated with Suleiman.

Dressed in her gym outfit, ready for a workout, Sumayya had searched for her missing earpiece. It didn't take long for her suspicions to fall on her brother, especially when he deliberately ignored her calls. Too bad for him, she knew his routine all too well, and she was certain she'd find him playing football here.

Letting out a frustrated hiss, she stepped out of her car and made her way toward the pitch with determination. Suleiman was about to face her wrath today, and she couldn't care less if she embarrassed him in front of his friends.

As she approached the football field, her eyes scanned the area, but to her surprise, it was empty. A puzzled frown creased her forehead. Where on earth had he disappeared to? She decided to venture further, her steps leading her toward the nearby basketball court. Little did she know that she was about to stumble upon something even more intriguing.

Her eyes widened, and a mischievous grin spread across her face. "Wow. Wow. Wow," she muttered to herself, unable to contain her excitement. Quickly reaching for her phone, she dialed the number of the first person who needed to hear this juicy piece of news.

Chapter 5

♥

An hour had passed since the start of the game, and Fatimè was leading by ten points. As the game had reached its conclusion, they decided to call it a day. Panting, Fatimè sat down on the floor to catch her breath.

"Okay, that was refreshing," she said, taking a deep breath.

The evening sun casts a warm golden glow over the basketball court, painting the surroundings with a soft, tranquil hue. A gentle breeze rustled the leaves of nearby trees, providing a soothing respite from the intense physical activity

Kamal, who had left to fetch some water, returned and handed her a bottle. "You deserve that award. You are that good."

Fatimè took a sip of water and sat back to relax.

"Now I owe you a lunch date," he said with a smile.

Fatimè smirked, "Did you lose on purpose so you could take me out again?"

Kamal chuckled, "Nope, you are just that good."

"There's no way I am going out with you again if all I know is your name and also the fact that you like to appear and disappear."

Kamal laughed, "Fact number one about me: I love to travel. In my 33 years on this earth, I have gone around this whole country."

"What?" Fatimè looked surprised. "How is that even possible?"

Kamal grinned, "Yep, I have been to all 36 states in Nigeria. As for the countries in the world, I'm still on that, but I hope to visit at least a hundred."

"Wow, you love traveling," Fatimè remarked with genuine curiosity, "What kind of work do you do that gives you all this free time? Or are you a pilot?"

Kamal smiled at the question. "No, I'm not a pilot. My father planted the love for traveling in me. He's a retired soldier, so we moved from state to state and I always looked forward to it. I own a haulage and logistics company with a side of drop-shipping."

Fatimè let out a scoff. "That's it? Come on, I do details."

Kamal chuckled, "Fine. We transport goods and services from one place to another. We also move goods from the ports to the warehouses and stores across the country but that's not all, we also partner with suppliers and directly ship products to customers."

"That's drop-shipping?" Fatimè asked.

"Yes. When a customer places an order for a product, we contact our suppliers and we drop ship it. We coordinate the delivery from the supplier to the customer using our services. I have been thinking about expanding though."

"Oh?"

"A taxi-hailing company. We already have the infrastructure in place." Kamal explained, "So we are using our existing fleet of vehicles to offer rides to customers.

"So who does all the work while you travel about?" Fatimè inquired.

"When I started, it was just me, myself, and I. But with time, I trained and built a very efficient team that could handle everything.

Now, I can travel as much as I want, although I have to supervise and all that," Kamal explained.

Fatimè was impressed. Seeing people achieve so much at such a young age always wowed her.

"So besides traveling, what else do you do?" Fatimè asked.

"Photography. I love taking pictures. I also enjoy coding, cooking too; trying out new recipes from cookbooks. Sometimes, I imagine if I did not love my job so much, I'd probably be a chef. Oh, and I like to draw too whenever I get the chance. It helps me de-stress," Kamal replied.

Fatimè was surprised to hear about Kamal's interest in cooking. He certainly did not look like someone who knew how to boil an egg. She imagined him in the kitchen making her breakfast and quickly shoved the thought out of her mind. That was not going to happen.

"So, Mr. Chef, 'Indomie Chicken or Indomie Onion?" Fatimè asked mischievously.

Kamal looked at her, a bit confused. "So this is payback for the toothpaste question?"

"No," Fatimè replied with a serious expression. "This is a very important and serious question; it can change the dynamics of this friendship and also if I would go out with you again, so think carefully."

"Really?" Kamal asked, surprised at the gravity of the situation. "Our friendship depends on Indomie? Subhanallah."

He couldn't help but find it ridiculous.

As if she knew what he was thinking, Fatimè said, "Yes, I love Indomie that much."

Kamal paused for a moment, then confidently answered, "Indomie Chicken."

Fatimè's expression was initially a frown, but it quickly turned into a smile. "We're still friends," she said.

Kamal shook his head, a look of relief spreading across his face. "For a minute there, I thought I was going to have to get down on my knees this time around."

"You're not serious," Fatimè said, pushing her glasses up slightly.

"I've never been more serious in my entire life, Fatimè. If that's what it takes for me to be a part of your life, then I won't hesitate to do it," Kamal said, turning to face her. "Ever since our eyes met, I haven't been able to forget you. I've never seen anything like it."

Fatimè was now overwhelmed. This wasn't how she imagined the conversation would go. "But you don't even know me," she said, getting up from her seat. "How can you feel all of this about someone you just met?"

"That's why I'm asking for a chance to get to know you," Kamal replied calmly. "You don't have to say yes right away. Take all the time you need."

Fatimè sighed. She needed time to process everything. "It's getting late. Let's go," she said, walking away.

As they drove home, Lorde's album "Melodrama" played softly in the background. Kamal contemplated saying something, but he decided against it. With the way Fatimè was looking out the window, it wasn't a good idea.

"We're here," Kamal said as he pulled over in front of her house.

Fatimè had already reached for the door handle when Kamal asked her to wait. He reached for something in the backseat and handed it to her.

"What's this?" she asked.

"Just a small gift," Kamal said.

"Why? You don't have to give me a gift just because we hung out, you know."

"Please, just take it," Kamal pleaded. "And I'm sorry I ruined our date."

"Friendly outing," Fatimè corrected. "It is fine, and I had a nice time."

She didn't want to argue with him anymore, so she just collected the gift and said goodbye with a smile.

Just as he was about to start the car, his phone beeped, signaling an incoming call. With a deep sigh, Kamal glanced at the caller ID, recognizing the number of someone he did not want to speak to. He knew that if he didn't answer, she would just keep calling, so he reluctantly answered the call.

"What do you want?" he snapped, his frustration clear in his tone.

"Easy tiger," the voice on the other end replied. "I just called to check up on you and, you know, ask how your 'date' went?"

Kamal rolled his eyes, already feeling his irritation mounting. "I don't think that's any of your business," he said briefly, gripping the steering wheel to prevent himself from yelling.

"You need to accept that we'll always be in each other's business," she continued, undeterred. "And with the way you sound, it means you didn't take my advice."

"And I want you to understand that I don't need it," Kamal shot back, his patience wearing thin. Without waiting for a reply, he hung up the phone, feeling a sense of relief wash over him as the call disconnected.

As he drove home, Kamal couldn't shake the feeling of frustration that lingered from the call. He was still annoyed, but his thoughts quickly turned to Fatimè. The only thing that mattered to him now was fixing things with her.

On the other end of the line, the caller wasn't surprised that Kamal had hung up on her. She was expecting it. She knew him well enough to know that he always came back, no matter how frustrated he got with her.

Fatimè's surprise was evident when she saw her father sitting on the front porch, sipping his tea. She thought he was scheduled to return the following day.

"Baaba, I didn't know you were coming back today," she said, placing the gift bag on the table and sitting beside him.

"Something came up at the office, I need to go in," he explained.

Occasionally, she overlooked the fact that her father possessed an architectural firm. Despite delegating most of the responsibilities to one of her uncles, a partner in the company, he retained a significant stake in its operations.

Fatimè asked how everything was at the farm and if he managed to fix the problem.

"Yes, everything is in order now but there are a few technicalities left, and Hamma can handle that," he replied before studying her intently.

Fatimè knew what that meant; 'explain yourself before I ask' but she tried to avoid the topic by pouring herself a cup of tea.

"So I see you're getting along with the airport guy. Even going on dates..." he remarked, with a hint of amusement.

Madina had successfully labeled Kamal 'airport guy,' and it was now looking like everyone had caught on.

"Baaba, it was not a date. Just a friendly outing. As friends," Fatimè emphasized the word 'friend.'

"Ati am," he called in the pet name he reserved for her, "I know what a friendly outing is," he chuckled. "Well, I'm happy you're going out more and enjoying yourself."

However, the call to Isha's prayer interrupted their conversation, and she made her exit, bumping into her brother on his way out.

She had promised him a 'token,' and he was quick to remind her. She told him to return from the mosque first and breathed a sigh of relief when she didn't find her mother in the sitting room.

After taking a shower, she felt refreshed and relieved. As she finished her prayers, Khalifa appeared.

"Before I start, let's talk about this guy..." he said.

Fatimè rolled her eyes. "My problem with you is you like amebo."

"Wanting to know whom my sister is going out with is now amebo. Ah. So much for trying to be a good brother," he teased.

"Well, you can start by getting your feet off my bed," she retorted, pushing his feet away. "We're not going out. He's just my friend, okay? Don't start getting any ideas."

"I see. Just friends," Khalifa smirked. "We'll see about that."

"Now I need you to continue being a good brother by letting me get some sleep. I am E for exhausted," she pleaded.

"Not until you grease my palms," he demanded, extending his hand.

She transferred some money to him, and he left with a grin.

Fatimè sighed, knowing that he had no idea that he had received his birthday gift in advance.

As she prepared for bed, she saw a paper bag on the bedside drawer that she had forgotten about. She opened it with excitement, revealing a mini basketball hoop and a small ball inside. The accompanying card read:

"I know it's not as big as your regular hoop, but it should serve its purpose of making you want to play again."

She couldn't deny that Kamal was thoughtful, but it wasn't what she needed right now.

Dublin, Ireland,

26th December 2016

Rukayya lay in bed regretting the phone call she had answered. She couldn't believe that things still affected her this way even after moving away to start a new life. She tossed and turned, and as she tried to get comfortable, she remembered one of the reasons why she left Nigeria.

Lagos, Nigeria

January, 2013.

Rukayya had just finished speaking to her mother. She did not like lying to her, but she reassured herself that it wasn't a complete lie. She was tired of everything, and a whole year had gone by without anything changing. She looked at herself in the mirror and realized that her mother was right; she looked different. Her eyes looked sad, and she had lost a lot of weight. This was not the life she wanted for herself, but she was still holding back, hoping that things would eventually work out. It was like being in a bubble, and not seeing the reality of things.

As she walked to his room to find some pain relievers, she thought back to the last time she had been there. The night she thought things would have changed but alas, the next day, it was like it never happened. He had come home with a different demeanor, talking about fixing things and it looked real until after receiving a phone call and then it was back to square one.

She searched through his drawers and closets, but she couldn't find what she was looking for. She reached for a medicine box on the top shelf and accidentally knocked over a shoebox. The contents spilled out, and Rukayya was shocked by what she saw. She sat there for thirty minutes, staring at her discovery.

Suddenly, she heard the door open, and she knew it was him. She could smell his fragrance from the doorway. She didn't feel like getting up because what she had seen had left her feeling grounded. As soon as he entered, he sensed that something was wrong. His bedside drawer wasn't closed properly, and he could smell a floral scent in the air. "What are you doing?" he asked.

Abuja, Nigeria

2nd January 2017

Fatimè chuckled to herself as she watched her cousins dance. They were at Mufida's house to spend the day, and Intisar was the only one missing from their quad meet. Fatimè and her cousins referred to themselves as the "quad," with them being born days apart from each other.

This eclectic quartet, bonded by an unbreakable friendship, constitutes a dynamic tapestry of personalities. Madina was the group's vibrant nucleus with a gift for conversation. She possessed a sharp wit that came with clever banter and a sprinkle of 'lawyering', she was mostly dressed in impeccable style which intertwined effortlessly with her love for romance. Intisar on the other hand was the quad's vivacious baker who infused all their gatherings with her infectious bubbly energy and a dash of sarcasm even though she was a bookworm at heart. Mufida, the reserved pharmacist, often stood as the voice of reason with an unrivaled sense of discipline. Always well-behaved, she added a touch of calm to the group's dynamic. Lastly, Fatimè served as the powerhouse of assertiveness and quiet strength, bringing a straightforward demeanor to the mix. Her love for sports and TV, coupled with her classy disposition, completed the mosaic of this distinctive and inseparable group.

"Tims!" Mufida yelled over the sound of the music. "Come on, join us."

Fatimè nodded and got up from the bed. There was more dancing and whining until Madina almost twisted her ankle, and they decided to call it a day. They lay on the plush carpet in the middle of the room trying to catch their breath when Mufida said, "I miss Intee. She would have taught us some new dance moves."

Yes, Intisar was the quiet bookworm, but one thing she was not shy about was dancing. She was an A in that aspect, and there was no dance move she was not familiar with.

"Oh well, she's over there in Dubai shopping to her heart's content and possibly dreaming about her and Al-Qasim doing it," Madina said.

"Madina!" Fatimè and Mufida both yelled.

"What?!" Madina shot back. "They are getting married in two months, of course, she's thinking about it."

Fatimè shook her head at her cousin's shamelessness. If only Intisar were here, she would have given her the perfect answer.

"I'm hungry," Mufida said, changing the topic.

Madina turned to Fatimè, "Help us with your fried indomie abeg."

"Only if you'll blend the pepper and onions."

"I have shrimps," Mufida suggested.

Madina squealed, "I love shrimps!"

"Is there any food you do not love?" Fatimè said.

They all got up and headed to the kitchen. Mufida's kitchen still looked the same way they had arranged it weeks before the wedding. Fatimè took a trip down memory lane as she thought about when she and Khalid were about to get married. They had beaten down their legs and asked their parents to let them renovate and furnish their house themselves. Khalid's father had left him a three-bed-room bungalow as part of his inheritance, and with that, the archi-tect and engineer couple had gotten to work. They were able to turn it into what they wanted. From the color of the paint to the furniture in the house, they had chosen it together and everything had gone according to plan until everything came crashing down.

It took Fatimè a while to register that Khalid was gone. She could not speak for days and watched her phone like a hawk, hoping he would call and she would hear him call her bunny one last time. She lost interest in everything, zoned out a lot, and then there were nightmares, and she could not stop crying. Her parents got her a therapist, but even then, there was nothing much Dr. Alaba could do for her. A part of her life was dead and it was never going to come back. She had given her whole heart to him; everything revolved around Khalid Dambo, and now her everything was gone.

"Tims! Tims!" Madina and Mufida both yelled, startling her so much she dropped the packs of indomie she was holding.

"What are you thinking about?" Mufida asked, picking up the packs Fatimè had dropped.

"Not what. Who. Who is she thinking about?" Madina said, butting in.

Mufida wondered if Madina was referring to Khalid, but she did not ask. She knew the Khalid topic was a sore one, and she did not want to make her cousin sad.

Fatimè's phone started to ring, and with the look, she was getting from Madina and Mufida, she regretted having set it to announce phone calls. She had set it that way so that anytime her phone was out of reach and someone she did not want to talk to was calling, she would not waste her time getting up.

"This is the 'who' she is thinking about. Her airport boyfriend," Madina said.

"How many times do I have to tell you, we are just friends, Madina?" Fatimè warned, clearly annoyed, but Madina refused to budge.

"Yeah, yeah, that is what everyone says, 'just friends,' and before you know it, you guys are married and expecting a baby..." Madina then turned to Mufida who was still holding the packs of indomie, "Mufida here is a perfect case study."

Fatimè remembered how Mufida kept insisting Mahmud and her were just friends, and before you knew it, a wedding date had been set.

"Just friends are not supposed to call more than once sha," Madina said when the phone rang again.

Fatimè rolled her eyes and grabbed the phone, leaving it in the kitchen.

She would deal with her cousin later.

"What airport boyfriend?" Mufida asked after Fatimè had left, "When did this one happen?"

"The week of your wedding." Madina replied, "They met at the airport when he lost his son and Tims found him, we thought that was it, well Tims thought, as for me, I knew they were going to meet again. Sha, boom there he was at your wedding and had even asked Baaba for her hand in marriage. Classic romance story I tell ya."

"Wait what? Is he crazy?" Mufida said laughing, "I'm surprised he is still alive and she is talking to him."

"Well, apparently he apologized and they are now on good terms."

"He has a son you said?" Mufida asked

Fatimè returned at that moment and answered Mufida's question, "Yes, he has a son."

"With his ex-wife." She added when she noticed the lost expression on Mufida's face.

"You still have not told me why they got divorced you know. " Madina said.

Fatimè let out a frustrated sigh, sometimes, Madina could be very annoying. "Because it is none of my business but you can go ask him since you care so much."

Madina was about to reply when Mufida cut her short, "What about you Madee? You never talk about any guy."

Fatimè was glad the conversation had moved away from her.

"There's no guy." Madina said, "Well, there was one but he does not feel the same way, so I am done. Pass me the peppers please."

Madina's tone was now scary. She sounded so hurt.

Fatimè looked at Mufida and she shot her an 'I don't know too' look.

"Come on, I'm hungry, let's cook," Madina said with a huge smile, but Fatimè did not buy it.

She was going to find out about this guy soon.

Minna, Nigeria.

July, 2009.

Madina struggled to walk in her extra-long dress. She had complained to her mother about it, but her mother insisted that it looked better that way and all she needed was to put on some heels. After collecting her certificate, Madina had taken off the heels and was now in her favorite Nike slides. Today was graduation day from secondary school and the ceremony had just ended. Outside, everyone was taking pictures or saying goodbye to their classmates. Madina had been with her cousins, Fatimè, Mufida, and Intisar until she excused herself to use the restroom. When she returned, they were nowhere to be found. Thankfully, Madina had her mother's phone to take some pictures, so she called one of her aunts to ask where everyone was. Her aunt told her that everyone was at the basketball court and she hoped everyone, including him. Madina could not wait to see him and was super glad she was done with this whole boarding school thing and did not have to wait for a holiday to see him again.

She took a shorter route to avoid running into too many people and wasting time saying hello and hi. The shorter route involved passing by the classrooms at the back, and if Madina had known what she was going to find, it would have saved her the trouble. Inside one of the classrooms, through the window, she caught a glimpse of him. At first, she did not want to believe it was him, but she needed to be sure, so she moved a bit closer and stood behind the window. She prayed to God that no one would come walking past because she had no idea how to start explaining what she was doing there. Madina could only see the back of his head from where she was standing; he was with someone, a girl who was sitting next to him at a desk. She had crammed all his features not to know it was him: the curls on his head and the broad shoulders. And when she heard his voice, she knew. It was so distinct and profound; unarguably her best sound to hear.

"You did not have to get me anything, you know," the girl said.

"Well, I did. You deserve it. You know how much I love to see you win, so this is me saying congratulations to you," he replied.

"Thank you. Thank you so much," the girl said.

"You're welcome. Go ahead, and open it," he said.

Madina could see what it was as the girl lifted it. It was a necklace.

"Wow. This is so beautiful," the girl said, handing it over to him. "Help me put it on."

Madina watched sadly as he put on the necklace for her. The girl turned and gave him a huge smile. "I love it. It is so beautiful."

"Just like you..." he said.

Madina did not even wait for him to finish as she left abruptly. She was not going to stay back and watch the love of her life with another girl. It hurt a lot. It did.

Chapter 6

♥

Abuja, Nigeria.

26th February, 2017.

Jiddu, I don't think your daughter would be happy if she finds out you are spying on her." The deep resonance of Alhaji Faruk's voice startled Hajiya Hauwa, and she instinctively rolled down the blinds. The living room, adorned with intricate patterns of earth-toned rugs and plush cushions, offered a discreet vantage point to observe the garden outside.

Peeping from the window, Hajiya Hauwa caught glimpses of the well-tended garden bathed in the warm glow of the evening sun. Lush greenery, vibrant flowers, and the gentle rustle of leaves provided the backdrop for the unfolding drama. The ambient sounds of chirping birds added to the tranquility of their upscale suburban home.

"I was not spying," she said defensively, her eyes still fixated on the garden. "Just wanted to check if they were okay."

He shook his head, his disapproval evident, and moved to switch on the sleek flat-screen TV mounted on the wall. Hajiya Hauwa knew that convincing him otherwise was futile. Of course, she would not confess to spying on Fatimè and Kamal.

Tuning into NCIS: NY, Alhaji Faruk settled back down on the plush leather sofa, the rich aroma of incense lingering in the air. Hajiya Hauwa, seizing the opportunity, moved close to him and gracefully took a seat on the intricately designed divan. "Faruku, we need to talk. It is very important."

He braced himself, knowing that the phrase "We need to talk" rarely heralded good news. "I'm listening..." he said.

"Don't you think it is time for this relationship to move forward? You know, to the next stage?"

"Next stage? Aren't we like married?"

Hajiya Hauwa rolled her eyes at his response, "I'm talking about Kamal and Fatimè. They've been seeing each other for two months now. It's time to know where they're headed."

"And Fatimè has repeated several times that they're just friends. If they were moving to the next stage, I'm pretty sure she would not hesitate to inform us. Why are you in such a rush anyway?"

"Ehn ehn, don't give me that friendship story..." she protested. "What kind of friendship lingers on for this long? They should better come and get married; people are already talking..."

He cut her short, his annoyance evident. "If by people you mean those group of minions you call your friends, then I'd suggest... no, I want you to pass this message to them; my daughter's life is none of their business."

"Yide am," she started, this time calmly, "You don't understand; time is not really on her side..."

"And what do you mean by that?" he questioned. "She is just 24."

"I was already pregnant with our second child at that age."

He let out an exasperated sigh, "You are going to compare your-self to our daughter? It was your time; Allah had already ordained it for you. Everyone has his/her destiny. That is why you are Hauwa and she is Fatimè. Clear difference."

"Destiny plays a big role, but she's not helping matters with the way she keeps rejecting suitors. You need to understand...."

He rose abruptly from his seat, the chair scraping against the tiled floor, the sharp noise cutting through the tense atmosphere. The frustration etched on his face was evident, his brows furrowed and jaw clenched. Hajiya Hauwa, for a fleeting moment, sensed a tinge of fear creeping over her. Her husband rarely allowed his emotions to surface in such a raw manner, and the intensity of his reaction made her pause.

In the silence that followed, his anger lingered palpably in the air, each word carrying the weight of his displeasure. "No, you are the one here who needs to understand that no one has any right to force her to accept anyone in her life. If she's not ready, she's not ready." His tone was firm, a testament to the depth of his conviction.

His gaze bore into her, a stern expression emphasizing his point. "The people who are talking should learn to focus on their own families and leave mine alone."

"I don't go around asking them what they are up to, so I see no reason why mine should be a topic of discussion." The words were laden with a sense of boundary, a clear delineation between their private matters and the intrusive opinions of others.

"Anyways..." he added, a touch of weariness entering his voice, "I blame you for giving them the platform to talk."

"Now, if you'd excuse me, I'd be going to bed. You have ruined my night already." With those words, he retrieved his phone and left the sitting room, the door closing behind him, leaving Hajiya Hauwa alone with the weight of his disappointment and the consequences of her meddling.

Abuja, Nigeria.

September 2005.

"Hey, nice moves!" a voice called out from the stands, causing Fatimè to turn around in surprise. Accustomed to practicing alone, she wasn't accustomed to an audience, especially at this hour. The basketball court, usually her solitary refuge after extra lessons, now felt exposed.

To her surprise, a guy was walking towards her. His senior tie and the prefect's badge on his blazer identified him. A grin stretched across his face, revealing a dimple on his left cheek. Standing next to him, she looked short despite being the tallest in her class.

"Hiii!" he beamed, his enthusiasm palpable. Fatimè couldn't help but smile back, her curiosity piqued.

"Hello," she replied, unsure of what he wanted.

"Are you on the basketball team?" he asked, his eyes sparkling with genuine interest.

"No," she answered, a hint of confusion in her tone.

"Why not?!" he exclaimed, his smile fading into shock. "You should be on the team. Nooo... You NEED to be on the team."

His fervor caught her off guard. Just a few shots, and he was already acting like her biggest fan?

"Uh, thank you, but tryouts were held last week," she explained, cautious not to let her hopes rise.

"I think the coach would make an exception," he said, rubbing his chin thoughtfully. "I'm the captain of the boys' team. What class are you in?"

"Js3," she replied.

"Perfect! We need more juniors on the girls' team," he said confidently.

"No, uhh," Fatimè started to protest, but he cut her short.

"No buts. I'll speak to the coach, and we'll see," he declared.

Fatimè glanced at her watch, realizing it was already 4:30. Abba, her driver, would be waiting for her outside the gate.

Realizing she had to leave, she picked up her bag, and as she told him she had to go, Khalid called out, stopping her. "Wait," he said. "You did not tell me your name?"

"Fatimè... Fatimè Faruk Ardo," she replied.

"I'm Khalid Dambo," he introduced himself, extending his hand for her to shake

Abuja, Nigeria

11th March 2017

Fatimè stirred from her sleep at the intrusive melody of her phone, and she let out a groan. The duvet tangled around her legs as she fumbled for her glasses in the dim morning light. The room felt hazy, and her hand searched the bedside drawer, eventually retrieving the elusive phone.

Hammadi, her brother, greeted her with his usual exuberance, his cheerful voice singing a birthday song through the receiver. Fatimè smiled at the unexpected wake-up call, realizing she had completely forgotten that today was her birthday.

"Miyatti," she said quietly, still groggy.

"I am guessing you just woke up, A jamo?"

"Yes," she laughed, "I am okay, and you? Adda Fa'i? How's the village life?" she asked, grateful for the distraction from her thoughts.

"Look at you shitting on your history and lineage, now what a shame..." Hammadi responded, his voice tinged with amusement. She loved their banter about Gombe, finding it amusing how he defended their hometown so passionately.

"Whatever though," he continued, "My baby girl makes this place a hundred times better."

"Ahn ahn. Lover boy!" Fatimè teased.

"Get out abeg. I just called to wish you a happy birthday and to remind you about the game," he said, chuckling. They had made it a habit to 'Facetime' over basketball games, and Fatimè was looking forward to their usual ritual.

"Sure. I'll call you. Thank you, Hamma," she said, ending the call.

A few minutes later, her phone beeped, indicating a credit alert text message. Hammadi had sent her a little something to spoil herself on her special day. She was elated and almost jumped off the bed in excitement.

Quickly sending a thank-you message to her brother, Fatimè walked into the bathroom to freshen up. The room was now filled with the soft morning light, casting a warm glow.

Fatimè had just finished dressing up when she heard a knock on her door. "Come in," she said, and the door opened with her brother Khalifa holding a small birthday cake with a candle on top. "Happy Birthday Adda!" he said after dropping the cake on her desk.

"Aww, thank you pest," she smiled, opening her arms for a hug. He smelled like 'Navy Black', and she was grateful he had abandoned his terrible 'oud' perfume. "The cake is courtesy of Baaba, Mami, Hamma, Hamma Mubarak, and I."

"You guys are so sweet."

"Can we cut it now?" he asked. "It looks like it's going to make sense."

"Glutton. Go and get a knife and plate then," she replied.

Khalifa happily skipped away, and Fatimè used her index finger to taste the cake's icing. It was her favorite. The sweetness lingered on her tongue, a perfect start to her birthday.

After Fatimè and Khalifa had finished watching a movie, the living room retained the setting of relaxation. A box of pizza lay half-empty on the coffee table, alongside a plate of small chops. The blinds were drawn open, allowing the sunlight to stream in, while the air conditioner hummed softly, maintaining a cool temperature in the room.

The doorbell rang, and Fatimè wondered who it could be, considering she was not expecting anyone. She silently prayed that whoever it was wouldn't disrupt her plans for an afternoon nap. Peering through the peephole, she saw it was Madina and quickly opened the door.

"Well, hello, birthday girl!" Madina exclaimed, enveloping Fatimè in a warm hug. Intisar stood beside her, radiating the fresh glow of a new bride. Fatimè returned the hug, feeling grateful for their presence, and ushered them inside.

"I didn't know you guys were coming..." Fatimè admitted, a hint of surprise in her voice.

"You didn't invite us to the party, so we took it upon ourselves to come over," Intisar said, plopping down on the couch. The state of the sitting room, led them to believe that Fatimè was celebrating.

"There's no party," Fatimè clarified. "Khalifa and I were just watching a movie."

Madina inquired about their parents, Mami and Baaba. Fatimè explained that they had left for Kaduna that morning for some function. She then turned to Intisar, curious about her recent trip.

"When did you return? How was your trip?" Fatimè asked, genuinely interested.

"Best trip ever! I had the time of my life. The food, the shopping, overall just being with Al-Qasim," Intisar exclaimed, sighing dreamily. "I wish it didn't have to end. I miss it already... take me back."

She playfully waved her arms, and Fatimè and Madina shook their heads at her theatrics.

"You can follow him, ai. It's not too late, you know," Madina suggested, a mischievous glint in her eyes.

Intisar rolled her eyes. "A wala hakkilo na? Do I look like someone who can fight?"

Fatimè couldn't help but laugh at their banter. She imagined Intisar, of all people, in the army and knew she wouldn't last more than a minute.

"You better go back to your cake business so you'll be less occupied with missing him so much," Fatimè teased.

Intisar's husband, Al-Qasim, was a flying officer in the Nigerian Air Force and spent most of his time away from home.

"Hmm. You're right. I miss baking anyway," Intisar admitted, a hint of longing in her voice.

The doorbell interrupted their conversation, and Fatimè rose to answer it. Gideon, their security guard, stood at the door, informing her of a delivery truck outside.

Confused, Fatimè followed him out to see for herself, with Madina and Intisar trailing behind. Their eyes widened as they saw the truck parked outside the gate.

"Miss Fatimè Ardo?" one of the delivery guys asked, looking up from his clipboard.

"Yes?" Fatimè replied, her curiosity piqued.

Madina and Intisar exchanged intrigued glances, wondering what could be in the truck.

"We have something for you. Can we start offloading?" the delivery guy asked, assuming her approval.

The three of them stared in surprise, all saying "offloading?" in unison.

Fatimè managed to ask, "Do you mind if I ask who they're from?"

"Mr. Kamal Maitambari," the other delivery guy replied.

"Crap!" Fatimè exclaimed inwardly, realizing she had forgotten to call him back after seeing his missed call earlier. Her frown deepened as she pondered Kamal's intentions. Why would he send her so many gifts?

As the delivery men began offloading the boxes from the truck, the shock on Fatimè's face intensified. There were 25 boxes in total.

"Ahn ahn! Airport guy is doing the most," Madina exclaimed in surprise. Fatimè, however, wore a frown, finding the gesture excessive.

Gideon was about to start moving the boxes inside with Intisar and Madina helping out and squealing in the process. They had no idea that Fatimè was boiling inside. She ignored them and picked up her phone to send him a lengthy message. It was just too much, and she did not like it at all.

"Well?" Intisar looked at her. "Aren't you going to open them?"

"No," Fatimè said, "I did not ask for them."

"And that is why they are called gifts; you don't ask for them. They are given to you. Besides, isn't it your birthday?" Madina hissed.

"Leave her alone jare. She doesn't know what she's saying," Intisar said, dragging one of the boxes toward her.

"Guys! I'm serious. Don't open anything. I am not comfortable with all of this, okay?"

She sat down on the floor, cross-legged with her face in her hands, while they looked at her like she had just grown two heads.

"They're just gifts, fa," Madina said.

"You mean you don't see anything wrong? With these?" Fatimè waved her hands in front of all the boxes splayed on the floor. "This is just..." Her voice started breaking, and the both of them rushed to her. "Tims, useni wallina hakkilo mada. What is it?"

"I'm just overwhelmed; this is a lot. I mean, who buys you all these stuff when there's nothing between you guys? It's just crazy."

"You can't blame him for going all out. He's just a man in love, and he thinks this is the best way to show it," Intisar said empathetically.

"He's a little extra, but who doesn't like a little drama in their lives, huh? He makes you smile, and I've seen your face light up when you talk to him," Madina added, trying to make Fatimè see reason.

Fatimè shook her head. "He's a responsible guy, and there's nothing wrong with him. I just feel like I'm betraying Khalid by trying to love another."

"Tims, I'm going to be upfront and honest with you," Madina said, turning to face her. "Khalid is gone, and he's never coming back." Madina looked at her cousin, feeling sympathetic for her. However, she knew she had to say what was on her mind. "You need to stop blaming yourself for what happened. It was an accident and it's not your fault," she said with a gentle tone.

Intisar chimed in, "I'm sure Khalid would have wanted you to be happy."

Fatimè felt conflicted, but the support from her cousins began to chip away at her reservations. She realized that holding onto the past wouldn't bring Khalid back, and perhaps it was time to consider moving on.

"And fine boys make you happy. That's a fact," Intisar added, playfully nudging Fatimè.

Fatimè couldn't help but laugh, appreciating the lightness that Madina and Intisar brought to the situation.

"Still doesn't mean I'm accepting all these gifts. I'm calling him right away," Fatimè declared, determination evident in her voice as she grabbed her phone and left the sitting room.

Madina called out after her, "Tims, wait!" but it was too late. Fatimè had already disappeared from sight, intent on confronting Kamal.

Madina and Intisar exchanged a knowing look. They understood Fatimè's stubbornness and knew there was no use in trying to persuade her further. They could only hope that she would come to her senses and give Kamal a fair chance.

Abuja, Nigeria

13th March 2017

"Salman has traveled, so where are you going to be staying?" she asked, taking a spoonful of her rice.

Zahra sat across from Fahad in the restaurant. Her appearance reflected her classy taste in a sage green dress with a subtle v-neckline and sleeves adorned with fine embroidery, complemented by a stylish turban that covered her hair. The restaurant buzzed with activity—the clinking of cutlery, the murmur of conversations, and the enticing aroma of spices.

"Anty Hauwa's." Fahad responded.

"Do you have to go there?" She asked, her tone laced with a hint of displeasure. She took another glance at her plate, her spoon lingering mid-air.

Confusion filled Fahad's expression as he looked up from his own plate. "And what do you mean by that? I should not stay over at my aunt's?"

Zahra couldn't fathom how Fahad remained oblivious to the threat Fatimè posed to their relationship. She responded with a sigh, her voice tinged with frustration. "That's not it... I don't like you around that girl; you are too close for my liking."

Fahad chuckled softly, finding her accusations slightly absurd. "That girl you're referring to is my cousin. She's family," he explained.

Zahra scoffed, her gaze intensifying as she leaned forward. "Is she your only cousin, eh Fahad? What about the other ones? Ehen, Madina fa? What about her? Why can't you go to their house? You have over a thousand relatives in Abuja, why does it have to be her? Why is it always her?" She fired off her questions, her jealousy shining through.

Fahad maintained his calm composure, trying to reason with Zahra. "At the last reunion for the Ardos here, we were a little over two hundred, so I think you're exaggerating the numbers," he replied, hoping to inject a touch of humor into the conversation.

However, her glare intensified, and Fahad quickly realized his attempt at humor had failed. "Babe... Look at me," he pleaded, seeking her attention.

Reluctantly, she turned her gaze towards Fahad, "What?" she replied, her voice laced with skepticism.

"There's nothing between her and me. You're my girlfriend, and she's my cousin. That's all," he reassured her.

Zahra remained silent, her attention momentarily drawn to a white Venza parked across the street. An unsettling feeling washed over her, but she couldn't quite grasp its significance.

Her voice softened as she continued, "You're trying to dismiss my concerns when, for all I know, you could get married to her."

Fahad let out a sigh. "Did I lie? Aren't you guys known for marrying your cousins? Prime example? Your parents, your sister... should I go on?"

He just wanted to put his hands on his head, "Fatimè and I are not getting married because I don't love her. The only person I love is you," Fahad said.

Zahra's mind whirled with conflicting emotions, and she found solace in the plate of food before her, diverting her attention momentarily.

Seeing Zahra's guarded response, Fahad made a sincere effort to bridge the gap between them. "Now you don't want to hear what I have to tell you?" he asked, his voice tinged with disappointment.

"Mhmm," Zahra replied nonchalantly, her eyes fixed on her plate, but a glimmer of curiosity remained.

Fahad seized the opportunity to share some positive news, hoping to uplift Zahra's spirits. "I spoke to Baba about us, and my uncles are coming to see your dad next week," he revealed.

Zahra's eyes widened, and a smile spread across her face, erasing the remnants of her earlier insecurities. "Are you serious?"

"Yes, In sha Allah. It's time for us to settle down, don't you think?"

"Yes, yes, baby. I love you!" Zahra exclaimed, her voice filled with enthusiasm and affection.

Fahad chuckled, embracing Zahra's unpredictable nature. "Oh, now you say it back?"

"Whatever. Now tell me about that project you're working on..." Zahra said, diverting the topic to something more lighthearted.

The woman in the white Venza watched their interaction with a mixture of envy and rage. She adjusted her veil and picked up her phone to dial a number. He picked up on the third ring, his voice raspy.

"What is it?" he said.

"He's seeing someone else," she replied.

"And how is that any of my concern?" he said. "I feel it's an added advantage for me."

"Oh really? That's what you're going to say, eh? You've gotten what you wanted, right?" she retorted.

"Woman, will you calm down?" he said, shutting her up. She knew better than to upset him, so she kept quiet. "My problem with you is you're impatient and you never listen. Stick to the plan, and everything will work out fine."

"But—" she started to say.

"But nothing. I have something to do," he said, cutting the call.

"Bastard." she cursed, banging her fists on the steering wheel. She did not need his help anyway. She could handle it on her own. Just then, Zahra and Fahad emerged, full of smiles, and she felt nothing but rage.

She could handle it right now. Starting the car, she planned to run them over and end this once and for all, but she decided against it and just drove past them. There was always another day.

Zahra could not take her eyes off the car, causing Fahad to ask, "What are you looking at?"

She shook her head and muttered, "Nothing." She did not know what it was, but one thing she was sure about was that it wasn't anything.

As the young woman drove away, she was seething with anger. She had been so close to getting what she wanted, but the sight of Zahra and Fahad had ruined everything.

Abuja, Nigeria.

13th March, 2017.

Fatimè glanced at her phone, its vibrant screen illuminating the neatly arranged vanity table before her. The table held a collection of her personal items; bottles of exquisite perfumes lined up in precise order, alongside an array of skincare products and carefully organized accessories. Soft ambient light from her bedside lamp bathed the room in a warm glow, creating a serene atmosphere.

As she delicately applied her night serum, the phone's persistent ringing interrupted her peaceful routine. Fatimè hesitated for a moment, contemplating whether to answer or not. Finally, she decided to pick up the call.

"You sent them back," Kamal's voice resonated through the phone as soon as she answered.

"I had to. I can't accept them. I'm sorry," Fatimè responded, her eyes fixed on her reflection in the mirror.

Kamal fell silent for a moment, absorbing her words. The hurt in his voice was evident as he gathered his thoughts. "If I may ask, can you tell me why you can't accept them?" he inquired.

"It kinda felt like you were trying to buy my affection or something," Fatimè replied, her voice laced with sincerity. She noticed a fleeting reflection of uncertainty in her own eyes.

A sharp intake of breath on the other end of the line revealed Kamal's surprise and hurt. Fatimè realized the impact of her words, but it was too late to retract them.

"What?" Kamal's voice wavered with a mixture of disbelief and pain. "Is that how low you think of me? That I'll try to buy your affection?"

Fatimè's heart sank, the weight of her words crashing down upon her. She wanted to explain, to apologize, but Kamal cut her off before she could find the right words.

"You don't have to explain. I get it. Goodnight," he said, his voice heavy with disappointment, before abruptly ending the call.

Fatimè stared at herphone, contemplating whether to call him back, but she sensed the anger andhurt in his voice. Giving him some space to cool off seemed like the betteroption. With a heavy sigh, she closed the serum bottle, plugged in her phone,and settled into bed. The room felt quieter now, and the shadows danced on thewalls as she reflected on the unforeseen turn of events.

Lagos, Nigeria.

Hafsah paused at the door of Kamal's study and peered inside, taking in the familiar sight of a well-lived-in space. The study had an air of comfort and functionality, with bookshelves lining the walls, filled with a diverse collection of literature. A large wooden desk occupied the center, strewn with papers and a laptop. The gentle hum of a distant air conditioner provided a subtle background noise.

Her concern was evident when she walked into the room without waiting for an invitation. She found her brother's face etched with annoyance, his brows furrowed and lips slightly downturned. Kamal was a reflection of his sister, although she was a light-skinned version of him, a complexion inherited from their mother, but Hafsah, being the younger of the two, had a youthful charm to her appearance. With chubby cheeks and captivating eyes, she was dressed in a simple gown, her hair styled in neat braids. With their age difference of more than a decade, Hafsah held immense respect for her older brother.

The fourth-year urban and regional planning student had decided to spend a few days of her vacation at her brother's house.

"Ya Kamal?" she asked, her voice tinged with concern. "Are you okay? Is something wrong?"

"I am fine. Do you need anything?" Kamal replied, his tone curt.

"No, I was going to ask what those boxes were for and-"

"Just put them in the guestroom or something," he interrupted, his irritation noticeable.

Hafsah sensed that there was something deeper troubling him and decided to patiently wait for him to open up.

Kamal rubbed his temples before finally letting out a sigh. "I met a girl," he confessed.

Hafsah's eyes widened in shock. Her brother, who had always been focused on his work and seldom showed interest in romantic relationships, had suddenly found himself smitten. "What?" she blurted out, unable to contain her surprise.

Kamal quickly tried to dismiss her curiosity. "Nothing," he replied, sensing his sister's desire to delve deeper into the conversation. He knew Hafsah's inquisitive nature too well.

But Hafsah was never one to shy away from a heartfelt conversation, especially when it came to her brother. She settled herself comfortably, patiently waiting for Kamal to continue.

"A few months back, I met this girl, and I would say it was love at first sight," Kamal admitted, a hint of a smile tugging at the corners of his lips. "I've been trying to court her, but she's a very difficult person. I understand it's due to certain things, but I've been patient because she's everything I want in a woman: determined, smart, and funny. We don't have many like her in the world, you see. And not to mention, beautiful."

Hafsah was taken aback by her brother's vulnerability. It was rare for Kamal to speak so openly about his feelings. "Wow," she said, her mind trying to process the unexpected news. She felt a surge of excitement, eager to meet the woman who had captured her brother's heart.

"Things were going well, but I'm afraid I might have messed things up by a little gesture I thought she was going to like, and now it's ended up upsetting her," Kamal confessed, his tone tinged with regret.

"By little gesture, I'm guessing those boxes are gifts you sent to her, and she returned them?" Hafsah asked.

Kamal exhaled loudly, "Yes."

Hafsah couldn't help but chuckle. "Ya Kamal, these are too much. Anyone would feel overwhelmed, especially since you said you're still trying to court her. She's not even your girlfriend yet."

Kamal rubbed his chin, realizing his oversight. "I didn't think about it like that. Honestly, I couldn't settle on one thing to get her, so I just thought, get her everything I knew she would want or like."

Hafsah facepalmed, amused by her brother's tendency to go overboard. She recalled a similar incident when she had casually mentioned needing art supplies, and Kamal had surprised her with an abundance of materials fit for an entire store. "Ya Kamal, you need to understand that this is not how things work. At this stage of your relationship, you need to take things slowly. I don't know the 'certain things' that are holding her back because we all know you're a great guy..." Hafsah paused, making a playful retching sound, before continuing, "Forget I ever said that."

"I am not playing here, missy," Kamal retorted, his tone serious, although a glimmer of amusement danced in his eyes.

"Ah, sorry," she apologized, her laughter still evident. "As I was saying, just take it slow. Don't apply too much pressure. And didn't you say things were going well?"

Kamal nodded, his gaze thoughtful.

"Toh. Then let things be. Everything will fall into place," Hafsah advised, emphasizing her trust in the process.

"Hmm," Kamal acknowledged, grateful for his sister's perspective. "Thanks."

"Maybe I should start charging for all this advice I dish out," Hafsah jokingly remarked.

"You want to start scamming people, dai? Kai, is there any money-making venture you do not know?" Kamal teased, a smile gracing his lips.

Hafsah shook her head playfully. "Me again? I have to make it in this life, o."

"Thanks for the advice, madam. You can go," he said, dismissing her teasingly.

Hafsah had already reached for the door when she turned to ask one last question, a mischievous glint in her eyes. "Since she doesn't want them, can I at least-"

He shot her a warning glare before she could finish her sentence. "If you touch any of those boxes, I'll cut off your head."

"Ikon Allah," Hafsah laughed, "No vex o. I shall stay away from the sacred boxes of your woman."

"Good. And I better not hear any of this from Maa," Kamal called after her.

Abuja, Nigeria.

15th March, 2017

Fatimè let out a groan when she spotted her aunt's SUV parked in front of their gate. If there was anything worse than her already terrible day, it had to be this. She and her aunt, Najma, always clashed because she was always meddling in Fatimè's affairs. Steeling herself for the inevitable drama, she went inside.

As Fatimè entered the living room, the air was filled with the pleasant aroma of turaren wuta. Small buckets of turaren wuta were placed on the coffee table, showcasing her Aunt Najma's bubbling business. The sound of the television set to 'Arewa 24' provided background noise, while a stack of vibrant fabrics by the side indicated that her Aunt had come to collect them to serve as anko for one of the numerous events she was fond of organizing.

Aunt Najma, a stoic and no-nonsense woman dressed in a simple cotton bubu with a matching veil, looked up and acknowledged Fatimè's presence. Her commanding presence demanded respect in the family as the eldest, and she often took on the role of a mother figure to all.

"Mami, Dada, Yan nyalli jam," Fatimè greeted them, perplexed at the huge grins on their faces.

Aunt Najma applauded when she saw Fatimè, almost making her take off her glasses to check for a smudge. "Fatimè am," her aunt exclaimed, "Your mother just told me the good news. I'm so happy for you. Congratulations, my dear!"

"What good news, Dada?" Fatimè asked, confused.

"Come on, don't be silly. Isn't getting married good news?" her aunt responded.

"Hmm," Fatimè said, feigning ignorance. "Who is getting married this time around?"

Aunt Najma's expression hardened as she looked from Fatimè to her mother, who was now pretending to watch television. "Who if not you?" her aunt retorted.

"Hmm," Fatimè replied, smiling.

"Jidda?" her aunt turned to her mother. "Didn't you say she was seeing someone? What's his name? Kamal ko?"

Fatimè shook her head in disbelief, unsurprised by her mother's behavior. She was always eager to share Fatimè's personal life with the family, and she enjoyed it. "Don't mind her," her mother said. "She's just being ridiculous."

"No, Dada. Kamal and I are not getting married. We're not even on speaking terms," Fatimè clarified.

"What happened?" her mother asked with concern.

"Nothing."

"What do you mean by nothing?" her mother began.

"Mami, Dada, I'm sorry, but I have to go. miwodi nawal hore," Fatimè excused herself.

"Are you sure this girl doesn't have jinns?" Aunt Najma muttered.

"Whatever it is, we'll take care of it. We will," Hajiya Hauwa assured her sister.

"Hmm. Let me get going. Salman is here. I'll call you later."

"Okay, Adda. Shafa?" Hajiya Hauwa called on their help to assist Najma with the fabrics to the car.

As Fatimè entered her room, she exhaled deeply, feeling the weight of the day on her shoulders. She slowly removed her atampa that was sewn into a simple yet elegant design of traditional Borno-style attire. With meticulous care, she untied her 'ture ka ga tsiya' head tie. The fatigue in her eyes was undeniable, and she longed for a moment of respite.

When her sister left, Hajiya Hauwa marched straight to Fatimè's room. "What do you mean by you and Kamal are no longer talking?" she demanded.

Fatimè rolled her eyes. "Nothing happened, Mami. We disagreed, and we're not on speaking terms anymore."

Her mother frowned. "You need to sort things out with him. He's a good man."

"I will, Mami. When the time is right," Fatimè replied, hoping to end the conversation.

"Good. I don't want you to miss out on a good man because of some silly disagreement," her mother said before leaving the room.

Fatimè let out a sigh of relief and flopped onto her bed. She needed a nap.

Fatimè stood in the kitchen, adorned in a comfortable gown and a neatly wrapped turban. The soft hum of the fridge provided a soothing background melody. On the cooker, a pot of aromatic miyan kuka for tonight's dinner bubbled gently, infusing the air with the fragrance of daddawa. She wasn't a fan of the soup, so she opted for some noodles.

Fahad, dressed in a simple t-shirt and trousers, sat across from her on the kitchen island, attentively listening to her words.

"What I am saying is I do not get why he's upset," Fatimè said, her voice filled with confusion.

Fahad cocked his head to the side, showing his concern. "It's valid, please. What you did was not nice at all. And also, you cannot tell people what to be mad about."

"So, you are on his side now ko dume?" Fatimè said, though deep down, she knew he was right.

"I feel the both of you need to talk about this. He needs to understand what you are okay with, and also, for you to understand that not all of his gestures have malicious intentions," Fahad suggested, offering a thoughtful perspective.

Fatimè chopped off the onions skillfully, adding them to the pot of noodles as she pondered Fahad's words. "Hm. I did not see it that way."

Her respect for Fahad grew, appreciating his ability to analyze situations from different angles. However, she couldn't help but feel frustrated that others, especially her mother, saw her as at fault. Their last conversation had ended in an argument, leaving Fatimè with a lot of unresolved thoughts.

"What was that big news you wanted to tell me again?" Fatimè asked, her attention momentarily shifting from her cooking. As the noodles neared completion, she added the seasoning.

"Zahra and I are getting married," Fahad revealed, a glimmer of joy in his eyes.

Fatimè clapped excitedly, her face beaming. "Whoa! Congratulations, my gee! I'm so happy for you. So, when is the wedding?"

Just then, Mubarak barged into the kitchen through the back door, still chewing on a pin-pop. His casual attire of jeans and a t-shirt, coupled with a camera hanging around his neck, indicated he had just returned from a photo shoot.

"So, who's getting married?" Mubarak asked, walking over to the pot on the fire. "Ouu, indomie!" he exclaimed, turning to Fatimè with pleading eyes. "Zanci, please. I'm famished."

Fatimè turned off the cooker, pouring the entire pot's contents onto a single plate. "Cook yours," she said to her brother, who had already grabbed a fork.

"Fahad's the one getting married," she answered his question, her voice filled with enthusiasm.

Mubarak playfully turned to Fahad. "Looks like I'm the only one left on the single train."

"Only because you chose to. Abuja's most wanted," Fahad teased, a playful grin on his face.

Fatimè made a gagging sound, pretending to be disgusted. "They must be really blind gaskiya."

"You of all people should not be talking, you know... four eyes and all..." Mubarak retaliated, provoking laughter from Fahad.

Fahad knew their bickering never ended, so he took that as a cue to leave. "I'm sleepy. Goodnight."

"I call dibs on official photographer sha," Mubarak called out as Fahad left the kitchen.

As the kitchen emptied, Fatimè hurriedly made her way to her room, giggling mischievously as she locked the door behind her. She knew Mubarak would come knocking in a few seconds, and she would gladly welcome him in. The taste of indomie was even better with him.

Katsina, Nigeria.

16th March 2017.

Hajiya Sadiya, in her late fifties, adjusted her shawl tightly around her shoulders. Through her glasses, the lines on her face spoke of the profound grief she carried. A deep sigh escaped her lips as she wrestled with the emptiness that clung to every corner of their home.

In the modest compound, pots of plants adorned the surroundings, their vibrant colors contrasting with the somber mood. The tall-looking fence provided a sense of privacy and security, while pairs of shoes neatly placed by the door hinted at the presence of a family within. Suddenly, a knock on the gate startled her.

"Imran! Imran!" she called out for her son, but she doubted if he could hear her over the video game he was playing in the sitting room.

A tall teenager, appeared in a 'Star Wars' t-shirt and shorts, bearing a striking resemblance to his late brother, Khalid.

"Na'am Mama?"

"Can you check who's at the gate? I heard someone knock just now," she said.

"There's no one at the gate," Imran confirmed after he returned.

Hajiya Sadiya reached for another date from the bowl on the stool next to her, trying to distract herself from the lingering sense of emptiness. "Hm. It must have been my ears," she mumbled, her eyes fixated on the gate

Imran occupied the empty seat next to her and picked up a date. "It's so chilly, Mama. You should come inside," he suggested.

She did not answer and focused on eating her date, her eyes still on the gate. There was a lingering silence with her thoughts on the last time her husband and son walked through that gate. She wondered when the feeling in her heart would change; when she would go back to moving with the world because now, it felt like the world was spinning without her in it. The grief had turned her into a ghost, a shadow of her former self, a specter frozen in time. She was moving through it like an open wound, and it felt like everyone around her was oblivious to the pain she was carrying.

Imran, sensing his mother's pain, moved his chair closer and rested his head on her shoulder. "It's okay, Mama. I'm here," he whispered softly. He understood the depth of their shared pain—the loss of a brother and father for him, and the loss of a son and husband for his mother.

Outside the gate, stood the stranger who had knocked. The man took another cautious glance at the house before retreating behind the transformer across the street, seeking refuge in its shadow. Questions raced through his mind. What had come over him? What if someone had seen him? How would he explain his presence? The weight of his actions burdened him as he wrestled with the unimaginable—his involvement in Khalid's death.

Chapter 7

♥

Lagos, Nigeria.

17th March 2017.

Good morning, everyone." Kamal greeted, striding into the spacious conference room. He handed a file to his assistant, Favor, who swiftly distributed copies to the team members seated around the long, polished table.

The room fell into silence as Kamal meticulously reviewed the report. His fingers drummed anxiously on the table, his eyes darting to the report but failing to focus. The weight of responsibility etched lines on his forehead, causing a silent turmoil in the set of his jaw.

After a few minutes, Kamal cleared his throat, breaking the silence, and addressed the team with a mix of seriousness and acknowledgment. "This is impressive," he said, his tone carrying a blend of approval and determination. "We are making considerable progress, although we still need to do more. But overall, good work, guys."

The team members exchanged glances, pleased with his acknowledgment.

Dressed in a dark suit and a neatly arranged tie, Kamal's appearance mirrored his serious mood. He occasionally glanced at his phone, his fingers instinctively reaching for it, only to be stopped by the need to maintain professionalism.

"What's the status of the 'Go-Stride' project?" Kamal asked, directing the question to Kunle.

The Go-Stride was a cab-hailing app they had been working on for the past few months.

"We are still on the beta version," Kunle replied.

Kamal frowned, his expression hardening. "You said a month. It is getting to two months now. You know how I get with deadlines and promises. Or should I take over? I believe I pay you for that, so why the delay?"

"I am sorry, sir," Kunle apologized. "We ran into some unforeseen issues."

"I do not want to hear your excuses," Kamal cut him off. "I want to see something by Monday. Meeting over. You can all leave."

As the team members filed out of the conference room, Kamal beckoned to Favor. "Please book a flight for tomorrow to Abuja for my sister and send the details."

"Yes, sir," Favor replied, nodding her head before leaving the room.

Across the table, Sa'ad, clad in a well-tailored kaftan with intricate designs, carried himself with confidence despite his large build, his presence a stark contrast to Kamal's somber demeanor.

"What's up?" Sa'ad asked.

Kamal shrugged, trying to appear nonchalant. "Nothing. Don't you have projects to oversee?"

"Perks of being a Vice President? I can chill," Sa'ad joked. "Now tell me, what trouble is going on in paradise?"

Kamal rolled his eyes. "What makes you think there's trouble?"

"For starters, you are missing that look you've had on for months." Sa'ad pointed out, leaning forward.

"What look?"

Sa'ad, who had been Kamal's friend since childhood, eyed Kamal with curiosity. They were inseparable growing up, sharing secrets and adventures—a bond that transcended the ordinary.

He scoffed. "Come off it, guy. Ever since you met that babe, you have been moving like you won the lottery or something."

Kamal hissed. "I am not in the mood for your nonsense, Sa'ad."

"Ahaps that confirms it. There is trouble in paradise. What did you do this time around?"

"Yes, everything has to be my fault. Of course."

"M.K, M.K. Relax." Sa'ad placed a hand on Kamal's shoulder.

Before Sa'ad could finish his sentence, Kamal's phone vibrated, providing a much-needed escape from the conversation. "I need to take this," Kamal said.

Sa'ad shook his head, understanding that Kamal was actively avoiding the conversation. The last time he checked, Kamal had never needed to take Rukayya's call.

Abuja, Nigeria.

2nd April, 2017

In her room, Fatimè sat cross-legged on her bed, engrossed in her work. Jumbo twists framed her face, a practical choice that required minimal maintenance.

A half-eaten pack of Fox's cookies rested on the bedside table—a guilty pleasure she indulged in while tackling her tasks. Despite fighting cramps earlier in the morning, she succumbed to her cravings, opting for sugar over an unsettled stomach.

The diffuser on her dresser emitted a calming fragrance as Shafa entered the room, bearing Fatimè's clean clothes. "Thank you," Fatimè said wearily, collecting the neatly folded clothes and placing them on the bed. Her mind, still occupied by her work, paid little attention to the state of her room.

"Mami said I should call you," Shafa mentioned, making her way to the door.

"Okay. I'll be right downstairs," Fatimè replied, saving her work and heading down to answer her mother's call.

In the kitchen, a bag of assorted fruits from her father's farm caught Fatimè's eye. Her mother, engrossed in her task, assembled a food basket with two coolers, a bowl of salad, and a variety of fruits. The kitchen buzzed with activity as Shafa returned dishes to their rightful place, and the aroma of stew teased Fatimè's taste buds.

Noticing Fatimè's presence, her mother turned around, her casual attire reflecting the day's relaxed atmosphere. "We are going to the hospital to visit your Aunt Rabi'atu."

"Which aunt? Who's sick?" Fatimè asked.

"Your Aunt Rabi'atu? Baba Gidado's daughter?" Her mother scolded. "How can you not remember your aunt? You children nowadays do not even bother to know your relatives. That is how you'll run into her somewhere and fail to recognize her." Placing her palm on her forehead, Fatimè listened to her mother's explanation, trying to keep up with the intricate web of family connections. She wondered if her mother understood that the Ardo family was too vast for her to know everyone intimately. Even among the relatives she did know, it was challenging to keep up, as the family seemed to grow every month with new births and marriages.

"Yauwa toh. Her son was admitted yesterday," her mother continued.

"Okay. Let me get ready," Fatimè said, heading to her room.

As Fatimè approached the carport, her mother stood there, clad in a simple abaya, a scowl etched across her face. Meanwhile, Fatimè herself wore a simple A-line gown completed by a stylish head-tie wrapped around her hair and a veil.

"What's wrong?" Fatimè asked, looking around.

Her mother let out a sigh of annoyance. "Is it not Sule? I specifically told him this morning that he'd be taking us to the hospital. And now he's saying he's stuck in traffic. Can you imagine?"

Just then, Fahad emerged from one of the rooms in the boy's quarters, dressed up and looking like he had somewhere to go.

"Mami? Are you going out?" he inquired.

"Yes. I want to take this to Rabi'atu at the hospital," her mother replied.

Fahad looked at Fatimè with a puzzled expression, silently pleading for help in understanding who Rabi'atu was. Fatimè stifled a chuckle, quickly covering her mouth to ensure her mother didn't notice.

"Let me drop you," Fahad offered, trying to avoid his aunt finding out he had zero idea who Rabi'atu was.

"Yauwa. Miyatti," his aunt said, calling out to Gideon, who was sitting at the guard post. "Gideon, please get the keys to my car. It's in that drawer in the center table in the sitting room."

Throughout the drive, Fatimè's mother continued to express her frustration, venting about the need for a new driver. Fatimè understood her mother's exasperation with Sule's incompetence and couldn't help but agree silently. Sometimes, opting for an Uber seemed like a more reliable option. If only she could touch the steering of a car again with the intention of driving. If only.

As they arrived at the hospital, the sterile scent of antiseptic filled the typical hospital ward. Rabi'atu, Fatimè's stocky and talkative aunt, bombarded them with pleasantries. "You have grown so big," she exclaimed to Fatimè. "The last time I saw you, I was changing your diaper." Fatimè and Fahad maintained smiles on their faces, but their expressions turned blank when she asked, "So when is the wedding?"

Her question was met with silence. Luckily, Fahad's phone rang, and he quickly excused himself, with Fatimè mouthing "traitor" after he left.

"Jidda. Don't they look good together?" Aunt Rabi'atu said, smiling.

The doctor opened the door, and Fatimè almost hugged him out of gratitude. She slipped away and found Fahad in one of the corridors. "Bloody traitor!" she said, lightly punching him on the arm.

"What?" he laughed. "It was a real phone call."

"Indeed. I'm glad the doctor came. It was like she was out to get me."

"I know, right?" Fahad agreed. "What is with all this shipping?"

"Help me ask. Every time marriage, marriage, marriage. Can you even imagine us getting married?" The both of them burst into laughter after playing out the scenario in their heads. Fatimè's laughter was short-lived when her eyes met his.

What was he doing here?

Fahad noticed her change in demeanor and turned his head to see the cause. He was coming out of the pharmacy that was facing the corridor, looking so casual in his coffee-brown jalabiya.

They didn't have to wait long, as Kamal walked up to them. "Assalamu Alaikum," he said, stretching out his hand to Fahad.

Fahad took it and answered, "Alaikumul Salam."

Fatimè had a straight face when he turned to her. "Hello. We meet again."

"Hi," she said, her mouth turning into a hard line.

Fahad looked puzzled, wondering who the guy was when Fatimè introduced him: "Fahad, this is Kamal, Kamal, Fahad."

"Ooh!" Fahad smiled. "This is the legendary airport guy. Nice to meet you."

"Same here," Kamal said.

Fahad's phone rang again, and Fatimè wondered if he was timing it to get out of the situation. "I have to take this," Fahad said. "Butterfly, call me when you're done. Once again, nice to meet you."

Kamal nodded as Fahad left them alone. "I see you are still appearing and disappearing," she said with a small smile.

"Situation demands it," Kamal replied. "And look how favorable it has been to me; I am always running into you."

Fatimè remained silent, examining the leather pouch he held in his hands. It contained drugs. Was Kamal sick? He looked exhausted and disheveled, which was unusual for a man who prided himself on his appearance. Something was up.

"Are you alright? Is something wrong? Are you ill?" Fatimè asked.

Kamal shook his head. "Not me. Adil."

"Subhanallah! What happened? How is he doing?" Fatimè asked, concerned.

"Alhamdulillah. Better than the past few weeks," Kamal replied, his voice heavy with emotion.

Two weeks? Adil must have been seriously ill.

"Yes," Kamal nodded. "He got into an accident."

Fatimè felt guilty for not returning Kamal's call. "That is terrible. I am sorry. Is he still here? Can I see him?"

Kamal scratched his neck, unsure of how to answer. He knew that Rukayya, Adil's mother, was there and didn't want to create an awkward situation. "Erh..."

The whiff of Rukayya's perfume announced her presence. She was drop-dead gorgeous. Fatimè couldn't help but notice the striking resemblance between Rukayya and Adil.

"The doctor wants to see us," Rukayya announced, casting a glance at Fatimè.

Fahad returned just then, and Fatimè took it as a cue to leave. "Butterfly, Mami is done. Should we get going?" Fahad asked.

"Yeah. Okay," Fatimè said as she turned to Kamal. "Regards to Adil. I wish him the speediest recovery."

"Thank you," Kamal said as they walked away.

Rukayya had already stalked off, leaving Kamal with a deep scowl on his face as he made his way back to the ward.

Butterfly? What was that?

"I am guessing that was his ex-wife," Fahad asked, breaking the silence as they made their way back to the ward to retrieve Fatimè's mother.

Fatimè sighed, feeling a bit uncomfortable. "Was it that obvious?" she asked.

Fahad chuckled. "Of course. Did you not see the look she was giving you?"

"Hm. I barely noticed," Fatimè admitted, although she had indeed noticed the ex-wife's glare.

"Well, I see where the airport guy gets all his confidence from," Fahad said, grinning. "He's one good-looking lad, and he's got a good eye for beautiful ladies."

Fatimè rolled her eyes. "Fahad, abeg. You sound like Madina right now."

Back in Adil's hospital room, Kamal sat silently in the corner while Rukayya sat at the edge of the bed. The doctor had just left, and Adil was asleep.

This had been the situation for the past two weeks: silence. There wasn't much to talk about, and Kamal didn't mind the quiet. But as he thought about Adil's impending discharge tomorrow, he felt a sudden urge to speak up.

"I intend to marry her," Kamal blurted out.

Rukayya's expression remained blank, and Kamal immediately regretted saying it. He wasn't one to speak so boldly about his feelings.

Rukayya didn't see the need for the information. It wasn't news to her, and today's conversation confirmed it. She got up from the bed and made her way to the door.

Giving Kamal one last look, she said, "I hope she knows."

5th April, 2017.

"This looks good, but I have some concerns about the orientation of the building. The bedrooms are facing east, and I think they will get too much sun in the morning."

There was a blueprint of a 4-bedroom house spread on the table with Fatimè and Seun standing over it. It was the latest project she was working on, and Seun and she were in charge.

Seun nodded, "We can adjust the orientation by 15 degrees to the north, which would solve the sun exposure issue." Fatimè considered this, "That could work. What about the materials? I was thinking about using a lot of glass for the facade to maximize natural light, but I am not sure it is cost-effective."

Seun leaned in, "Actually, there are some energy-efficient glass options that we could use that wouldn't break the bank. And the extra natural light could also reduce the need for artificial lighting, which would save on energy costs in the long run."

Fatimè smiled, "Okay, that's a great idea. Let's look into those options."

Just then, Rahila burst into the room, her face beaming with excitement. "Omo Fatimè, you don hammer!" she exclaimed, clapping her hands.

Fatimè raised an eyebrow. "Please tell me this hammering translates to millions of naira? My Japan trip needs funding."

"Abeg," Rahila hissed. "I am talking about 'v-f-b' waiting at the lobby for you."

Seun and Fatimè looked at each other, puzzled. "V-what?" they both asked.

Rahila rolled her eyes and facepalmed. "You guys are so ugh. Very fine boy, please. Uncultured lot."

"Please Rahila. No one says that" Seun said.

"Whatever," Rahila replied, turning to Fatimè. "A hunk is waiting for you in the lobby."

"Me?" Fatimè questioned.

"Ahn Ahn. You are no longer Fatimè Ardo abi what?"

"A tall, fine hunk," Rahila added dreamily.

Fatimè knew immediately that it was Kamal; he had called her earlier, but she had been too busy to answer.

"Can we finish this later?" Fatimè asked Seun. "It's time for lunch anyway."

Seun nodded as Fatimè left. He packed up the table and turned to Bisola. "Is she dating him?" he asked.

"Looks like it," Bisola replied.

Seun looked solemn, and Bisola squeezed his shoulder. "Pele ehn," she said sympathetically. She felt bad for him since he had been crushing on Fatimè since day one, but the barriers between them were too much.

In the lobby, Kamal was sitting, one leg atop the other, on one of the couches provided for visitors. He saw Fatimè and got up, smoothing his trousers. "Hey," he said.

"Hi. What are you doing here?" Fatimè asked.

"Looking for a lunch companion," Kamal said.

Fatimè raised an eyebrow. "In an architectural firm?"

"Fine. I came to ask you out for lunch, if you'd like to go, that is..." Kamal trailed off.

They hadn't talked for weeks until the meeting at the hospital, and Fatimè figured this was the best way to reconcile. "I'll get my bag," she said with a smile.

The cozy restaurant had just the right lighting for Fatimè, who wanted to be able to see her food. She ordered lamb rice, Caesar salad, and pineapple juice, sticking to the safest choices for an unfamiliar restaurant. When the waiter arrived with their food, she asked him, "How are you?"

Kamal smiled, grateful to hear someone ask. "Honestly," he began, "I am okay, Alhamdulillah. He was in terrible shape, though.

I desperately wished to take his place. My little boy was in a lot of pain, and there was nothing I could do about it. That was the biggest scare for me--not being able to do anything."

Kamal had recounted the incident where Adil fell from a towering slide at the playground, leading to a compound fracture of his left arm. The severity of the injury was such that the bone pierced through his skin, necessitating surgical intervention.

Fatimè listened attentively, struck by his last sentence. It reminded her of her own experience of losing her sister. "That's terrible, oh my God," she said. "I'm so sorry you had to go through that. Being in a situation where you're helpless is one of the worst things. I'm really glad Adil is doing better now."

Kamal's eyes focused on her fully. "Going through that ordeal knowing you and I were not okay made everything worse. It was plain torture, and I just want to say I'm sorry."

"I'm sorry too," Fatimè said. "I overreacted, and I didn't mean the whole buying of affection thing."

Kamal's relief was evident. "I just want you to know that whatever I feel for you is genuine, and if we were to have something between us, I want it to be out of your own volition. It wouldn't sit well with me if I were to buy your feelings. With you, there's no price tag, and even if there were, I couldn't afford it."

Fatimè fiddled with the ring on her index finger, trying to process everything he said when a familiar voice interrupted them. "Ta dimples," She was not surprised to see Yusuf, one of Khalid's friends approaching their table. All of his friends referred to her as 'Ta dimples', it was about the 'dimples' nickname she had given Khalid. She smiled and greeted Yusuf, and Kamal watched as they exchanged pleasantries. Yusuf also introduced his wife, Salma.

As Yusuf and his wife left, Fatimè felt a pang in her heart when she saw his walking stick. Kamal noticed and asked, "Are you alright?"

She sniffed, tears threatening to spill. "Yeah, it's just seeing him like that made me...sad...I don't know. I felt..."

Yusuf was the one in the car with Khalid when he had the accident and he was lucky enough to scrape through with a broken leg.

"It's natural to feel sad for him," Kamal said. "The ones who are left behind deal with all the pain, and you tend to ask yourself why you were the one who survived."

His accusing expression disappeared quickly, replaced by a reassuring smile. "It'll be alright, In Sha Allah."

Fatimè nodded, too overwhelmed by her thoughts to ask the many questions swirling in her head.

Yusuf sat in the driver's seat of the car, his hands gripping the steering wheel tightly, but he didn't start the engine. Salma joined him, letting out a sigh as she reached out to touch his shoulder in a gesture of comfort.

For a few minutes, they sat there in silence until Yusuf finally spoke, his voice barely above a whisper, "Every day I live with this guilt that everything is my fault."

Salma's eyes widened with surprise, and she withdrew her hand, looking at him with concern. "Why would you say something like that? How is it your fault? It was an accident."

"One that could have been avoided if only I had checked the car properly. Maybe Khalid would still be here with us," Yusuf replied, his voice heavy with regret.

Salma's tone was soft and soothing as she tried to console him. "Whether you checked or not, it was meant to happen. Allah has decreed it."

"I tried so hard to avoid her eye because there's something else, something I should have told her," Yusuf said, his voice wavering with emotion.

Salma looked at him, puzzled. "What do you mean?"

"I received a call after the accident. Someone claimed he knew who was behind it. I tried to get through to him, but he bailed when we were supposed to meet up. I should have pushed through and got to the bottom of it," Yusuf explained, his expression full of regret.

"But it's not your fault he bailed though. Might have even been one of those prank calls," Salma reasoned.

Yusuf shook his head, his eyes closed tightly as if in pain. "Maybe. But I should have at least done something."

Salma placed a comforting hand on his shoulder, giving it a gentle squeeze. "Well, it's too late now."

Yusuf rubbed his temples wearily, his eyes focused on some distant point. "Yeah. It's too late."

"Nabila drummed her fingers impatiently on the steering wheel, irritation mounting with each passing moment. The Grills101 parking spot was her chosen rendezvous, and tonight was crucial – she was on call. About to dial his number for the umpteenth time, relief flickered as she saw him approaching.

With a press of a button, she unlocked the central lock, but her greeting was laced with frustration, 'Why are you like this?'

"Nabz dollars!" he hailed, making an X sign with his hands. "How far now?"

"Abeg. Spare me all this hailing. Do you know how long I've been waiting here?" she scolded.

Straight to the point, she cut through the banter, 'I need that thing. Do you have it?'

"Is there anything I don't have for you, Nabz? You know me, L.K, your guy for everything. The only thing is you might have to drop a huge bar because you know how dangerous your parole is."

"Money is not a problem," she assured him.

"Nabz dollars!" He hailed again, "Just like the last time?"

"Yes, just like the last time."

With a nod and a mock salute, he exited the car."

Chapter 8

♥

A buja, Nigeria.

14th April, 2017.

Kamal took off his shoes at the door, the rich scent of lily and jasmine oil from a diffuser welcoming him home. His stomach grumbled with hunger for his mother's catfish pepper soup. The day had been long, and he needed some relaxation. The soft glow of a chandelier illuminated the tastefully decorated living room, furnished with plush velvet sofas and elegant wooden coffee tables. The TV played softly in the background, adding to the calming ambiance of the space.

The sound of the TV alerted him to the fact that his parents were home. He walked towards them and greeted with a Salam. His sister Hafsah was in a corner scrolling through her mobile phone, the dim light highlighting her round face with chubby cheeks.

He seated himself next to Hafsah and playfully pulled her ear. "Didn't you see my missed call?"

"I was just about to call you back," Hafsah replied, her face engrossed in her phone.

Kamal's father, a man who embodied the essence of wisdom with a snowy white beard and a furrowed brow that commanded respect, turned towards him, his back straight and his posture impeccable. "Do you plan on moving your business back to Abuja or what?"

Kamal was confused and looked towards his mother for an explanation, who gave him a questioning look.

"My business is doing perfectly fine where it is," he replied.

"I noticed you are in and out of here lately," his father added, his voice firm.

Feeling hurt, Kamal stood up, the frustration evident in his movements. "Oh wow. So it's now a crime to want to visit my family? I guess I'd take my leave since I am not welcome here."

His father did not care much about what Kamal said as he turned his attention back to the TV, his demeanor unchanged.

"Kamal," his mother called. "Sit down. You know that's not what your father meant."

He sat back down, not because of anything, but because he did not want to upset his mother. Besides, he had important news to tell her.

"He's in and out because of some other business," Hafsah said, trying to reduce the tension in the room.

Kamal glared at her, but it was of no use. She had already carried out her blabber-mouth duties.

"What business?" His father asked, his attention now back on them, his gaze unwavering.

His mother was also waiting to hear, her gentle and nurturing presence calming the atmosphere in the room.

"He's seeing someone," Hafsah said.

Kamal now felt like giving his sister a hard knock for what she had just done. This was not how he had intended to break the news, but he went ahead to finish the job.

"Yes. I have been seeing someone, and I intend to marry her."

No one said anything for a while, not that he was surprised. He was expecting this reaction. His parents, especially his father, had been really upset when they learned about the divorce. His father refused to speak to him for weeks and did not forgive him for ruining the relationship he had with Rukayya's father. Rukayya's father and his father were longtime friends and colleagues in the Nigerian Army.

"I hope this time around, it will last long. We all know your habit of dropping out of things," his father remarked.

"Hussein?" This was one of those rare moments where his mother referred to their father by his first name, her concern for her son evident in her voice.

She gave him a warning look, but he ignored her. "What? I just want to confirm before he gets married again, and he'll decide to divorce her after a year. I cannot handle any more embarrassment from him."

"Daddy..." Hafsah tried to talk, but he shut her up immediately, his authoritative nature taking over.

"You keep quiet. This is none of your business."

She gave her brother an apologetic look and left the sitting room, her exit showing her respect for her brother's privacy.

At this point, Kamal had had enough. "You know Rukayya and I's marriage was more of a sham. You arranged it, and I agreed to it because I wanted to make you happy, but then I realized I needed to make my own decisions."

"You sure make some great decisions," his father laughed, his tone sarcastic. "Dropping out of medical school is a perfect example."

Kamal's face screwed up in annoyance, his father's words touching a sensitive nerve. It had been years, but his father still held on to this issue. He had tried everything to make him understand that being a doctor was not his calling, but he just would not budge. It seemed like every time they talked, his father found a way to chastise him.

"And it will forever be the best decision I've made in my life," Kamal retorted, his resolve unwavering. "I'm sorry, but you have to live with your son not turning out the way you want."

Without waiting for a reply, Kamal made his way out of the room, needing some air to calm his emotions.

Hajiya Hillu looked at her husband, her mouth set into a hard line. "Why are you always so hard on him? Give him a break for God's sake."

"He needs to learn to make better decisions, and that won't happen if you don't stop treating him like a kid."

Hajiya Hillu shook her head, exasperated. "And what is wrong with him getting married again?"

"I will not argue about this, Hillu. I have a headache," he said, getting up. "Goodnight."

As he left the room, Hajiya Hillu let out a sigh. She was tired of the constant tension between her husband and son. She wished they could just find a way to see eye to eye.

15th April, 2017.

On a sunny afternoon, the warm rays of the sun enveloped Fatimè and her cousins as they sat on a mat in the backyard. Their hands and feet were freshly adorned with intricate henna designs by the henna artist who had just left. Fatimè let out a sigh, knowing she would be stuck doing nothing for the next two hours before she could take the henna off. She loved henna, but she hated the wait for it to dry, and the fear of it getting smudged if she moved too much.

Madina, with her hair neatly braided, broke the silence, "Have you guys seen Sadiqqa's anko?"

Mufida, dressed in a simple gown with her hair wrapped in a turban, adjusted her pillow to lie down and grunted trying to find the best position.

"Hm," Intisar, said, "You mean items to open a fabric store abi?."

They all laughed at Intisar's scrunched-up face.

"Ah toh. Because I do not understand all those atampas and laces she sent. Is she getting married or she wants to start a fabric business?" Intisar complained, looking comfortable in her new position.

"Me, I just said Allah hokku sa'a, how many events does she plan on holding that she needs all that anko?" Mufida waved off a fly that had come to perch.

"Is it that bad?" Fatimè asked. She had not opened her 'WhatsApp' all day, so she had not seen the message yet.

"She sent three atampas and three laces! Is she alright? What does she need six ankos for?" Madina said.

"Have you seen the price? 150k," Intisar added.

"Kai!" Fatimè could not help but laugh, "Who is going to buy anko of 150k? Cannot be me. I have better things to do."

"You have not seen the lineup of events. You would think she is hosting a carnival." Mufida said.

"I am sitting this one out. I am not even a fan of weddings. Allah hokkabe jode jam," Fatimè said with a nonchalant tone.

"Amin. Are we not going to that new restaurant again?" Intisar changed the topic. "We've been planning this thing for weeks."

"How about next weekend?" Mufida suggested.

"Ah. I can't make it." Everyone turned to look at Fatimè, their brows raised,

"Why?" Madina asked, "Are you going somewhere?"

Fatimè, dressed in a casual gown with her hair neatly packed in a bun, shifted a bit, feeling her back beginning to hurt, "Erh yeah, Kamal and I...."

Before Fatimè could complete her sentence, they all erupted in cheers. "Ahn Ahn! E don set kenan?" Intisar said with a huge grin on her face, her playful and high-spirited nature on full display.

Fatimè felt like disappearing; they were not going to let her rest.

"So are you guys now... you know, a couple?" Mufida asked, her curiosity getting the better of her.

"Of course. Can't you see they are even going on dates?" Madina answered the question before Fatimè had a chance.

"So do you like him?" Intisar asked, her eyes sparkling with anticipation.

"I do not know," Fatimè said honestly, her voice soft and uncertain. Since their reconciliation at the restaurant, Kamal has been flying to Abuja almost every weekend. Emails and phone calls were now frequent, and she was even reading books he had recommended. Fatimè hated reading, okay, maybe hate was a strong word, but she disliked reading. She preferred to watch a movie. All of this, but she still had no idea what she felt, her conflicted emotions hidden beneath her calm exterior.

Her cousins were oblivious to whatever it was she was thinking about and had now graduated to planning a wedding that had not even been set.

Gombe, Nigeria.

22nd April, 2017

Under the scorching sun, Fatimè wiped the sweat off her forehead with a tissue, feeling the heat taking its toll on her. She wondered why her sister-in-law, Fa'iza, was taking so long to come out. They had planned to go out to the farm to get some fresh air. Finally, Fa'iza emerged from the house, wearing a pale pink abaya with a veil donned in a talha, and sunglasses shielding her from the bright sun.

As soon as Fa'iza came out, one of Fatimè's older cousins, Zayyad, tall and a bit lanky, appeared from the house opposite where her brother and his wife lived. He waved and jogged up to her, asking all in one breath, "Tims! When did you get here?"

"Yan nyalli jam." She greeted. "A few days ago fa."

"And you did not come over?" Zayyad's face turned into a frown, showing his disappointment.

"I did, Hamma Zayyad. Dada said you had gone on a short trip," Fatimè replied, imagining the scenes if she had not visited any of her aunts and uncles. She would not hear the end of it.

"Oh yes, I just got back from Bauchi. I had to take care of some work," Zayyad said.

Fa'iza greeted Zayyad, and he replied with a smile, "Where are you guys off to?"

"The farm. Want to join us?" Fa'iza asked.

"Nah, I can't. I have an errand to run. I'll see you guys later though." Zayyad said and waved them goodbye.

When they arrived at the farm, B Yusuf, who was in charge, gave them a hearty welcome. Fatimè hadn't been to the farm in years, since her sister's death. A lot had changed; the ranch had grown bigger, and there were many new structures.

"It's been a while," B Yusuf said to Fatimè

She looked around and smiled, "The place looks nice and well taken care of."

"What can I say? This place is my whole life. I give it my all," B Yusuf replied with genuine dedication.

Fatimè knew he meant it with everything in him. He had been on the farm since he was a little boy. He taught her how to ride a horse and everything about the farm. There was always a passion in his eyes, and she was not surprised when her father left him in charge after they moved.

As B Yusuf led Fatimè around the sprawling farm, she couldn't help but be struck by the sheer scale of the operation. The farm, more like a ranch, was indeed successful and well taken care of. Everywhere she looked, there were signs of productivity and success. The land was covered in lush green crops, including groundnut, pepper, sugarcane, maize, millet, rice, cassava, okra, and onion, along with various vegetables. The fields were carefully tended, and the crops looked healthy and robust.

As they walked past the chicken coops, Fatimè couldn't help but admire the vibrant colors of the chickens' feathers, and the way they pecked and scratched around the yard. The cows in the nearby fields were grazing contentedly, their deep, resonant moos adding to the peaceful atmosphere. And the horses, with their rippling muscles and glossy coats, were a sight to behold.

The farm was a testament to hard work and dedication, with every corner of the land being put to good use. As they continued to walk, Ali pointed out the different crops they were growing.

"Let's go for a ride," Fa'iza suggested, her adventurous spirit taking over.

"Adddddddaaaa," Fatimè said, looking down at her feet, feeling a bit hesitant. "I'm not dressed for that, and I haven't been on a horse in years."

Her sunflower-patterned gown was indeed inappropriate for horse riding, but Fa'iza was not having any of it. "I have something in the car," she said with a cheeky smile, turning to B Yusuf. "Can you please get the horses ready while we change?"

B Yusuf nodded with a smile and walked away, leaving Fatimè and Fa'iza to prepare for their horseback ride.

Fatimè felt a mix of emotions as she rode the horse, the wind in her hair bringing a sense of freedom she hadn't felt in a long time. The exhilaration of horseback riding made her feel like she was soaring, and with every gallop, she felt her worries dissipate, carried away by the horse and left behind in the dust.

After their ride, they sat on a mat provided by B Yusuf, catching their breath and sipping water to quench their thirst. "That felt amazing," Fa'iza said, taking another drink.

"I have to admit, I feel so much better. I missed this," Fatimè said.

"See? I told you that's what you needed," Fa'iza replied with a smile.

There was a moment of silence before Fatimè finally spoke up, her thoughts about Kamal weighing heavily on her mind. "At what moment did you realize Hamma was the one you wanted to marry?"

Her question was genuine, tinged with a touch of fear and uncertainty.

Fa'iza chuckled. "Where is this question coming from?"

But when she saw the serious expression on Fatimè's face, she shifted her position and said, "When I tasted his grilled meat at one of Anty Najma's Eid barbecues."

"What?" Fatimè asked, confused by the unexpected response.

"I'm serious! You know I don't play with my naman sallah. I tasted it, and it was the best naman sallah I had ever eaten. At that moment, I knew I had to spend the rest of my life with that guy," Fa'iza explained with a playful grin.

Fatimè couldn't help but laugh. Her brother did know his grills, and Fa'iza's quirky way of expressing her feelings lightened the heavy mood.

"But on a more serious note," Fa'iza continued, her tone becoming more sincere, "These things happen differently for everyone. It could be a slow process, instantaneous, or somewhere in between. For your brother and me, it was somewhere in between. It went from saying hello as cousins to me looking forward to seeing him at family events. We finally had time for a lengthy conversation, and I didn't want it to end. He has always been intentional from day one. He makes me happier than I could be on my own and makes me feel like I'm the best catch."

"Ahn ahn. Una dey love o!" Fatimè teased, clapping her hands playfully.

"Shift joor. So tell me, have you met someone you like?" Fa'iza asked, now genuinely curious about her sister-in-law's feelings.

Fa'iza's mother-in-law had made sure almost everyone knew she was seeing someone, but she still wanted to hear it from Fatimè herself.

"Kamal proposed to me a week ago," Fatimè confessed, her heart fluttering as she recalled the romantic night they spent at a drive-in cinema.

As they lay in the back of a blue Tundra filled with blankets and pillows, Kamal pointed to a star in the sky and said, "It's so beautiful, just like your eyes when you're happy. I want to make you happy."

When he asked her to marry him for the third time, Fatimè had told him she needed to think about it.

"I don't know, Adda Fa'iza. I'm so confused," she said, exhaling deeply, showing her conflicted feelings and fear of giving him a chance.

"Don't beat yourself up," Fa'iza said, putting an arm around Fatimè in a comforting gesture. "I can't tell you if he's the one, but one thing I can assure you is that you'll know if you want to spend the rest of your life with him. And the only reason you should marry someone is that you want to marry them."

They lost track of time, talking about anything and everything until Fatimè's brother called, telling them to come home.

As Fatimè put on her seatbelt, she burst into laughter. "I just can't believe he bought your love with naman sallah."

Abuja, Nigeria.

23rd April, 2017.

Rukayya and Sumayya sat in Rukayya's bedroom, surrounded by the familiar elements of her personal space. The TV played in the background, providing a soft noise as they admired the design pictures of the restaurant Rukayya was planning to open soon.

On the dresser, an assortment of perfumes and humra jars were arranged neatly, giving the room a pleasant fragrance. In one corner, an unfolded praying mat and neatly folded hijabs awaited their next use.

"Wow. This is beautiful Rukks! The architect did a fantastic job, Ma sha Allah. I love the design," Sumayya said with genuine admiration.

"I'll soon be the owner of a restaurant, In sha Allah," Rukayya said with a smile, her excitement palpable.

"I'm so happy for you. May Allah put barakah in it," Sumayya replied, her mood shifting to a more serious one.

"Amin Amin," Rukayya said, closing the laptop with a satisfied expression.

However, Sumayya's intentions were far from congratulatory. She cleared her throat loudly, catching Rukayya's attention. Rukayya knew her friend well; whenever Sumayya had something to say, it was written all over her face. Finally, Sumayya spoke up.

"What are you doing about this news?" She asked, unable to contain her curiosity.

"News? What news?" Rukayya pretended not to know what She was talking about, but the worry lines on her face betrayed her.

"Don't give me that," Sumayya said, leaning forward. "You know I'm talking about your husband getting married again."

Rukayya corrected her, "Ex-husband. And I'm not going to do anything."

"What do you mean you're not going to do anything?" Sumayya frowned deeply. "Some babe swung out of nowhere and is about to take your man. I wouldn't be surprised if she's the reason behind your separation. And you're here telling me you don't care? Haba Rukks! We're talking about the father of your child here."

Rukayya remained unfazed, avoiding eye contact and instead focusing on her phone as if it held the most captivating content in the world.

"What happened between you and Kamal?" Sumayya prodded further. "There has to be something that's making you act unbothered."

Rukayya's nonchalant attitude was apparent with the way she remained tight-lipped, refusing to divulge her true feelings and the hurt she had been holding onto for so long.

"You say I'm not worried?" Rukayya suddenly stood up, her emotions finally breaking through her calm exterior. "Well, let me tell you one thing, the person who should be worried here is that babe. She has zero idea what she's getting herself into."

Lagos, Nigeria.

23rd April, 2017.

Sa'ad stood at the doorstep in a button-up shirt and khaki pants as he rang the doorbell. The door opened, and he greeted Mrs. Simon with a cheerful smile.

"Mr. Sa'ad. How nice to see you." She welcomed him, "Please come in."

The living room was comfortably cool, thanks to the air conditioner softly humming in the background with soft, well-placed lighting casting a gentle glow throughout the space radiating a warm ambiance. Sa'ad took a seat on the sectional couch, feeling at ease in the familiar atmosphere.

"You have not visited us in a while; would you like some tea or coffee?" Mrs. Simon offered.

"Part of the reason why I am here. I have missed your special tea," Sa'ad admitted, remembering the delightful taste of her homemade brew.

Mrs. Simon blushed, "I'll get you some then."

Sa'ad was almost done with his tea when Kamal appeared from a room downstairs, looking slightly disheveled and covered in sweat from an intense workout.

"What are you doing here?" Kamal asked, surprised to see his friend.

"Having a cup of tea. You?" Sa'ad replied casually.

"I can see that. You didn't tell me you were coming over," Kamal said.

"And you didn't tell me you were getting married," Sa'ad said, looking Kamal in the eyes, waiting for an explanation.

Kamal sighed, feeling the weight of the unspoken truths between them. "I was going to tell you. We haven't finalized anything yet, that's why."

"So, is it that girl?" Sa'ad inquired.

"The name is Fatimè," Kamal corrected. "And yes, I'm sure about this."

"Just trying to make sure Rukayya doesn't happen again," Sa'ad remarked with concern.

"What makes you think this is the same thing?" Kamal asked, his defensiveness growing.

"Come on, M.K. Piya...?" Sa'ad's voice trailed off.

Kamal closed his eyes briefly, trying to avoid the topic he knew his friend would bring up. "I don't want to talk about that."

"You didn't tell her, did you?" Sa'ad probed.

"Because I don't need to. It has nothing to do with her," Kamal snapped, trying to push away the guilt and fear.

Sensing the tension in the air, Sa'ad decided it was best to leave the conversation for another time. He stood up and smoothed out his trousers. "We'll talk about this some other time. Thank Mrs. Simon for the tea."

As Sa'ad reached the door, he paused and called out to Kamal. "M.K?"

"Yeah?"

"She needs to know," Sa'ad said earnestly before leaving, leaving Kamal alone with his conflicted emotions.

Chapter 9

♥

Abuja, Nigeria.

26th April, 2017.

Zahra and Khajja stood outside, awaiting Zahra's ride. The sun dipped low, casting a warm glow on the quiet neighborhood. Khajja turned to Zahra, a light breeze tousling their veils, and asked, "So has the date been set?"

Zahra shook her head, her eyes shining with excitement, "No, not yet. They are coming next week for the formal introduction."

Khajja's face lit up with joy, "Ma sha Allah! I am so happy for you."

Zahra beamed, her anticipation palpable, "I know right? I am so excited."

Meanwhile, in a sleek white Venza parked a few houses away, a woman with an air of mystery about her was on the phone with someone. The wind whispered through the trees as she inquired, "Is it done?"

"Yes," the person on the other end replied, their voice tinged with secrecy.

"Exactly like I asked?"

"Yes. The message has already been delivered."

"Good. You'll hear from me soon," the woman said before ending the call. With a confident smile, she started the car and drove past Zahra and Khajja, the engine's hum fading into the evening. Little did Zahra know, she was about to face something she never saw coming.

Abuja, Nigeria.

28th April, 2017.

"Ah, gaskiya dun wattako, This would put our family's reputation at stake..." Fatimè heard her aunt say as she stepped into the house. The TV was off, and a tray with a bowl of half-eaten danwake sat on the coffee table. Her aunt only nodded to her greetings, and she shrugged off her aunt's dismissive response, making her way upstairs to Madina's room.

The atmosphere in the house was heavy, the air thick with tension as Fatimè entered. The room, though slightly messy, offered a glimpse into Madina's life—a pile of books on the reading desk, an open notebook, and a textbook on business law hinted at diligent studying.

Madina was seated in front of the dresser, engrossed in the task of loosening her braids. Fatimè tapped her shoulder to get her attention, and Madina took off her air pods, which were blasting music in her ears.

"Keh!" Fatimè said, and Madina turned to face her with a smile. "Tims!? When did you get here?" Madina asked, curious about her cousin's sudden appearance.

"Just now, ko fe'i? I met Umma in the sitting room, and she was looking very upset. She did not even answer my greetings," Fatimè explained.

"Hm, is it not your cousin?" Madina replied nonchalantly.

"Do not give me yeye gist, please. Be more specific," Fatimè urged.

"Fahad..." Madina started, and Fatimè's eyes widened. Fahad was known for being responsible and level-headed, so this news was surprising.

"Fahad kuma? Hah, what did he do?" Fatimè asked in disbelief.

As Madina loosened her braids, Fatimè took the other mitsilla from the dresser and began helping her out. "It is not him per se. It is Zahra," Madina explained.

"Ahn, his girlfriend? What happened?" Fatimè asked, intrigued.

"Turns out she was involved in a scandal. Nudes scandal," Madina revealed.

Fatimè's mouth opened in surprise, not at the scandal itself, but at the fact that Zahra was involved. Nudes scandals were unfortunately common, with girls sending explicit pictures to men they trusted, only to have their trust betrayed.

"Zahra?" Fatimè exclaimed, "I thought she was a calm babe? Kai! Wait, so how did Anty Zainabu find out? Does Fahad know?"

"Someone sent it directly to Anty Zainabu's phone, and now she's saying the only way Fahad is marrying her is over her dead body," Madina explained.

"Ah! Directly to her phone? But how and why would someone do that? That is wicked Walahi," Fatimè commented, her heart going out to Fahad.

"Yes. Via 'WhatsApp'," Madina said, continuing to comb her hair.

"This is a very terrible thing, and I feel for Fahad," Fatimè said, shaking her head in dismay.

"Well, with the way things are going, Anty Zainabu is not going to change her mind," Madina said.

"With Umma on her side?" Fatimè clicked her tongue. "I doubt it."

"Exactly. With the way Umma sings the Ardo legacy and principles," Madina added.

"I feel her, though," Fatimè admitted. "I mean—"

"You think Fahad should not marry her too? Ahn, ahn. Finding a way to keep your love alive, I see," Madina teased playfully.

Fatimè gave Madina a light smack on her back, chuckling.

"Ouch! I was joking now," Madina laughed.

"As I was saying, I understand where Anty Zainabu is coming from. To us, we are woke, but we also have to be realistic. These things have consequences, and one thing is, the internet never forgets," Fatimè explained, trying to see the situation from both sides.

"You are right, but then again, it has already happened, and it cannot be erased. Besides, Fahad knows, and he still wants to go ahead with the marriage," Madina replied, understanding Fahad's perspective.

"There are so many things involved here, Madina. You need to understand that marriage is not just about the two of you alone. It is a union of two families, and with this kind of scandal, issues are bound to happen. I feel bad for Fahad, though. Convincing Aunt Zainabu is going to be hard," Fatimè said with concern.

"Walahi kam. I just hope everything works out fine," Madina said, agreeing with Fatimè.

"In sha Allah. Me that just came here to drop a package for Umma, you have gotten me to loosen half of your braids. You are just a fraud, Madina," Fatimè playfully teased.

"Please tell me the package is not one of Hajja's numerous experiments?" Madina asked, hoping it wasn't.

Fatimè laughed, while Madina shook her head. Hajja was known for her unconventional mixtures of herbs and chemicals, swearing they were a solution to every illness. However, her concoctions often ended up causing more harm than good.

"She needs to be stopped," Madina complained. "Before she blows up the whole of Gombe with her yeye inventions."

Fatimè was trying not to die of laughter as she remembered the past incidents. "Relax, madam. It is not from her. This one is from Dada."

"Au ho," Madina let out a sigh of relief. "She should be glad I did not sue her for damages."

"Honestly!" Fatimè agreed with a grin.

6th May, 2017.

Kamal sat nervously in the living room of Alhaji Faruk's house, wiping beads of sweat off his forehead despite the air conditioner humming quietly in the background. The TV was set to BBC News, and a tray containing a jug of zobo and a bowl of dambun nama was placed on the coffee table. He couldn't help but feel anxious about this meeting.

As Alhaji Faruk walked down the stairs, he carried himself with a commanding presence, his tall and lean figure attired in a well-ironed kaftan. Though streaks of silver had appeared in his once dark hair, he exuded an air of wisdom and authority. Kamal stood up, rubbing his palms together in anticipation. "Please sit," Alhaji Faruk said after exchanging greetings. Kamal took a seat on a single-seater opposite Alhaji Faruk and cleared his throat.

"I am sure you are wondering why I called you here," Alhaji Faruk began. "Well, I am not one for many words, so I'll go straight to the point. Do you remember our first encounter and what you said to me?"

Kamal nodded, even though he knew the reason for the meeting. "I asked for your daughter's hand in marriage," he said, trying to hide his nervousness.

"Good," Alhaji Faruk said, scratching his chin. "And her reply at that time was a no. Now, I do not know what happened these past few months, but it seems to me that the both of you have become close and are rather fond of each other. So I am going to ask you now, what do you want with my daughter?"

Alhaji Faruk's piercing gaze made Kamal feel the weight of the question. "Nothing has changed," Kamal replied, trying to sound confident. "I still want to marry her."

"And did you discuss this with her?" Alhaji Faruk asked, looking for reassurance.

"Yes. She has agreed to my proposal," Kamal said, trying to steady his voice.

"And your parents? Your family? Where are you from?" Alhaji Faruk inquired, wanting to know more about Kamal's background.

"My parents are both from Sokoto, but they live here in Abuja. I have just one sibling, Hafsah. We are a really small family," Kamal explained.

Alhaji Faruk nodded, taking in all the information. "She told me you have a son," he said, and Kamal confirmed it.

"Yes, with my ex-wife. It was an amicable split," Kamal replied, hoping that his past wouldn't be an obstacle.

"And why do you want to marry my daughter?" Alhaji Faruk asked, wanting to understand Kamal's intentions.

"Perhaps we should take a walk? Stretch our legs? The weather looks perfect for one," he suggested.

Kamal agreed, and they both got up, with him walking behind his soon-to-be father-in-law. One thing he loved about Fatimè's house was the presence of trees and flowers. The environment was so serene and meticulously taken care of. So many times when he sat in the garden with her, he could not help but pass comments about the beautiful atmosphere.

As they walked, Kamal decided to answer the question. "My reasons for wanting to marry Fatimè are because I love her. This happened from the first day I set my eyes on her, and as I got to know her better, I realized she is the one I want to spend the rest of my life with. I also have no doubts that she will be an amazing partner for me, seeing as she has all the qualities I want in one: her knowledge, compassion, kindness, and listening skills, amongst others. And I dare not forget to mention how beautiful she is, both inside and out."

Alhaji Faruk hummed as he listened attentively, observing Kamal's sincerity. "And do you agree on core values? Goals? Dreams?" he asked, wanting to ensure their compatibility.

"It is hard to agree on everything," Kamal replied honestly. "We do have our differences, but at the end of the day, we can come to a compromise. We have a lot of similarities too," he added.

"That is a good thing," Alhaji Faruk said, acknowledging Kamal's perspective. "How do you plan on supporting her? You know what she has been through, right? Are you ready to be there for her hundred percent?"

"Absolutely," Kamal said with determination. "We have talked about her problems, and I am ready to be there for her so she can get better. I am capable of taking care of her. I run my own company, and Alhamdulillah, it is doing well. I can afford all the necessities and a few luxuries for her, in sha Allah."

"Excellent," Alhaji Faruk said, pleased with Kamal's responses. "From the little I have gathered and from this conversation, you are a responsible man. It was nice meeting you again, Kamal." He extended his hand for a handshake, and Kamal gladly took it, his face filled with joy.

"Thank you so much. I appreciate it," Kamal said, relieved and grateful for the approval.

"I'll send her to you now," Alhaji Faruk said and turned back to walk towards the house, leaving Kamal standing in the garden.

Kamal sat down on one of the chairs in the beautiful garden, relieved that the meeting with Fatimè's father had gone well. He decided to reply to a few emails on his phone while waiting for her.

As he was working, he heard the soft rustling of footsteps and looked up to see Fatimè's radiant smile approaching him. It was one of his favorite things to see, even more so than watching 'Ronaldo' play football. She looked stunning in an A-line gown with flair hands, adorned with little purple hexagon patterns that seemed to reflect against her glowing skin. Her signature head tie and a large veil gave her an elegant and regal appearance, making her even more captivating.

She cleared her throat, getting his attention. "Lower your gaze," she reminded him with a playful smile.

"I am sorry," he apologized, momentarily distracted by her beauty. "It is difficult not to admire how beautiful you look, ma sha Allah."

"Thank you," she smiled, blushing slightly. "So, how did it go?"

Suddenly, Kamal's face changed, and Fatimè's heart almost skipped a beat. What did her father tell him?

Kamal let out a defeated sigh, "I'm sorry, but Baaba said he did not want to see my face anymore and only allowed me to say my final goodbyes to you."

"What?" Her voice began to shake until Kamal laughed.

"Relax," he said, his eyes twinkling mischievously, "I was just kidding."

She rolled her eyes, "Not funny."

"You were already imagining life without me, huh? Don't worry, I am not going anywhere," he reassured her.

"Of course not. I was just..."

"Wanted to admit you like me?" Kamal teased.

"Of course, I like you. You're my friend."

"Yeah, right," he said, his voice laced with sarcasm.

"What did you talk about?" she asked, curious to know the outcome of their conversation.

He cocked his head to the side, a playful glint in his eyes, "That is for me to know and for you to find out."

"Oh, is that how you want to play? Cool then."

As they continued their banter, Kamal's rose and woody scent wafted towards her, adding to the pleasant atmosphere around them. However, his phone rang, interrupting their conversation, and he excused himself to answer the call.

Fatimè tapped her feet impatiently as she waited for him to finish the call. She couldn't help but wonder about the outcome of his discussion with her father. Kamal soon returned with an apology written all over his face, "Something came up, and I need to go."

"Nothing serious, I hope?" she asked, concerned.

"No, no, but it is urgent. I'll come to see you tomorrow, and we'll talk. I promise."

"Okay," she nodded. "See you then."

When Fatimè returned to the house, she could not help but feel a sense of relief when he told her he was joking about her father's request. What was this feeling?

18th May, 2017.

"Are you sure I should go?" Madina asked as she parked the car in front of the bustling supermarket. Fatimè came down from the car and stood by the passenger's window, "Yes, don't worry, Hamma Mubarak would pick me up. You need to beat that Gwarinpa traffic anyways."

"Okay then, I'll call you when I get home," Madina said and zoomed off.

As Fatimè entered the supermarket, a mix of relief and excitement washed over her. There was just something therapeutic about walking from aisle to aisle, surrounded by the colorful array of products and the familiar sounds of grocery shopping.

At the counter, Fatimè patiently waited for the cashier as she worked on the PoS machine. The cashier looked apologetically at Fatimè after trying about three of the machines. "Madam, I'm sorry. It seems your bank has network issues. Perhaps you'll pay in cash?"

Fatimè retrieved her wallet from her handbag but noticed it was empty except for some loose change and her other ATM card, which had expired. She had planned on getting another one and also withdrawing some money, but today was such a busy day. This was not a good day to be an adult.

"Um, I don't have any cash on me right now. How about a bank transfer?" The cashier nodded and proceeded to give her an account number.

Fatimè spent an ample amount of time trying to transfer, but it just would not work. It was now looking like a race between her bank and service provider on who would end up killing her first. "Is there an ATM nearby?" she asked.

"Yes. Just across the street, take your left, it's by the corner," the cashier replied.

Hurrying to withdraw, Fatimè was about to leave when she came face to face with a pretty-looking lady. The woman had an aura of elegance and sophistication that caught Fatimè's attention. She couldn't help but return the woman's warm smile. "All of them are out of service, except the one I used," she informed.

The pretty lady spoke, her voice carrying an air of confidence. "Oh, I'm not here for that. I'm here for you," she said calmly.

"Me?" Fatimè was puzzled.

"Yes, so I'll just cut to the chase. That guy that you are seeing? Kamal, yeah? Stay away from him, or you are going to regret it." The lady's words sent a shiver down Fatimè's spine, and before she could respond, the woman had walked away, leaving Fatimè feeling both confused and fearful.

Fatimè's heart was now pounding, and she couldn't shake off the feeling of unease. Who was that woman, and how did she know about her relationship with Kamal? The encounter left her with more questions than answers, and a sense of foreboding settled over her.

Chapter 10

♥

Abuja, Nigeria.

20th May, 2017

Fatimè found solace in the smallest of things amidst the chaos of the world, such as the breathtaking beauty of sunrises during her morning runs. It was what she needed after the unsettling encounter she had two days ago, and by the time she got home, drenched in sweat, she felt relatively better. As she gulped a cup of water from the dispenser in the dining room, she overheard a conversation between her brothers, Mubarak and Khalifa.

The aroma of coffee and the sizzling sound of frying chips hit her when she stepped into the kitchen. That was when she realized how hungry she was. Khalifa was toasting some bread while Mubarak was making a cup of coffee.

"Hamma Mubarak, useni, Just this once," Khalifa begged.

"Shafa, I want a plate of that, please," Fatimè said to their help who was standing over the cooker, turning the chips.

"With eggs?" Shafa asked.

Fatimè shook her head and said, "I'll eat with yaji."

"Hamma Mubarak, answer me now," Khalifa begged again.

"No," Mubarak replied firmly, "I am not shooting your girlfriend for free. I can consider giving you a discount, but free? Nope. I have told you several times to avoid dating broke babes..."

"Who's dating a broke babe?" Fatimè asked, interrupting their conversation.

"Whoa!" Both of her brothers screamed at the same time.

"What?" Fatimè asked with annoyance written all over her face.

Khalifa was the first to reply, "You. You are in your workout gear..."

"And so?" Fatimè asked, not understanding their sudden interest in her morning routine.

"You haven't gone for your morning run in ages... since..." Mubarak said, trailing off.

"Well, I felt like it today. Now can you two stop staring at me like you've seen some aliens?" Fatimè said it with a hint of irritation in her voice.

"Hmm," Mubarak said.

Fatimè ignored him as she collected the plate of chips from Shafa and grabbed a jar of yaji from the cupboard.

Mubarak and Khalifa exchanged looks when Fatimè left the kitchen. "Something is up," Khalifa said.

Mubarak had known something was wrong since he picked her up the day before yesterday, but his sister had become so adept at masking her emotions with the "I am fine" facade that he decided to let her be.

Fatimè descended the stairs after a refreshing shower, her emerald-green dress complementing her radiant complexion. The fitted waist flared out into a flowing skirt, and her head was wrapped in a stylish turban. As she entered the sitting room, there was a lingering scent of bakhoor mixing with his subtle woody fragrance. His visit did not come as a surprise to her; after all, he was in the habit of appearing and disappearing. She didn't say a word to him and simply focused on sipping the tea she had asked Khalifa to make for her.

Kamal cleared his throat, "Sunshine." He called, "Did something happen? You haven't been answering my calls or text messages. Are you okay? Is everything fine?"

Fatimè's response was blunt, "Why don't you ask that girlfriend of yours? I'm sure she has an answer."

Kamal was taken aback. "What are you talking about?"

Fatimè stood up, her frustration evident as she dropped the cup, and replied, "You're seriously asking me that?"

Kamal was now more puzzled than ever, trying to make sense of Fatimè's anger and accusation.

"I don't know what girl you're talking about, Fatimè," Kamal tried to explain.

"Kamal, please. I've had zero drama in my life before you came into it and intend to keep it that way," Fatimè declared firmly before leaving the living room, her steps indicating she was still upset.

He put his head in his hands and sighed. He couldn't understand what she was talking about.

What was this about a girlfriend? So many thoughts ran through his head, but he knew exactly who he needed to talk to as he made his way to his car. She was going to get it from him.

The living room, adorned with traditional furnishings, emanated a warm and inviting atmosphere. Ammatullah, a gracious woman in her late forties, entered with a tray of refreshments. She wore a simple A-line gown, her hair covered in a large veil, and her warm smile greeted her cousin, Faruk, who was seated on the carpet next to her husband, Abubakar.

"Some kunun tsamiya for you and dates to accompany," Ammatullah offered with genuine hospitality. "How has work been?"

Faruk, a smile playing on his face, accepted the refreshments. "Ammatullah, you're a lifesaver. You always know how to make the best kunun tsamiya. Miyatti. The farm's flourishing and we've just harvested the most exquisite fruits. I'll send you a basket."

Teasingly, Ammatullah responded, "I'll be waiting eagerly for that. Anything for a taste of your fresh fruits." With that, she left them alone to delve into more personal discussions.

Faruk took a sip of the kunun tsamiya, relaxing in the conversation.

"Are there any new developments on the farm?" Abubakar asked.

Faruk leaned back, a thoughtful expression on his face. "The farm is thriving, Hammadi is doing a good job with the management, Alhamdulillah. We've expanded the crops, and the livestock is doing well. Can't complain.

"Alhamdullilah. Hammadi has always excelled with work, he is a good lad. Alhmadullilah for our children, Allah ya cigaba da masu albarka." Abubakar responded, "How about the company?"

Faruk chuckled, "Well, you know how it is – the hustle and bustle of city life. But speaking of that, I've been seriously considering handing over the reins of the company to Muhammad. Perhaps retire to Gombe and just rest."

"You that loves work?" Abubakar laughed, "Anyways, it is a good idea, You've worked hard all these years. Maybe it's time to enjoy the fruits of your labor. But don't disappear completely. Stay involved, and maybe keep some shares. You never know when your expertise might be needed."

Faruk chuckled, "You sound like Jiddu, always telling me not to retire completely. I suppose you both are right."

"Well you know our women," Abubakar said, and they both laughed.

Faruk shifted the conversation to a more serious note.

"Now about this boy I asked you to look into, dume fe'ata?

Alhaji Abubakar's demeanor shifted slightly, sensing the gravity of the topic "Faruk, I've checked into his background thoroughly, and from what I have seen, the man dropped out of medical school, ventured into a haulage and logistics business, and has been successful. No history of drugs or any other vices. From what I've gathered, he's a responsible man who minds his own business."

He continued, "He also hails from a respected family in Sokoto. His father is a retired general from the Nigerian Army, and his mother is a businesswoman. There are no scandals, and everyone who knows them speaks highly of their integrity."

Faruk, reassured by the information, nodded appreciatively. "Thank you, Habu. I just want the best for Fatime. I trust your judgment."

Alhaji Abubakar grinned, lightening the mood. "Well, I'm known for having a good eye. And don't worry, if he ever steps out of line, we'll handle it."

Both men shared a hearty laugh, the tension of the investigation momentarily forgotten.

Kaduna, Nigeria.

20th May, 2017.

Hajiya Zainabu was serene as she stood in her bedroom, arranging her clothes in the wardrobe. Her radiant glow illuminated the room, and her braided hair displayed a mix of natural curls and hints of grey, a testament to her wisdom and grace. The bedroom walls were painted in soft neutral tones, creating a calming atmosphere. A queen-size bed took center stage, adorned with crisp, patterned bedding that added a touch of elegance.

As she hummed a song, trying to distract herself from the conversation with her son, Fahad, he persisted in following her to where the wardrobe was situated. She gently placed a stack of neatly folded atampas inside, displaying a meticulous mannerism that showcased her attention to detail.

"Ammi, please listen to me," Fahad implored.

She turned to face him, her expression determined. "There's nothing to hear, Fahad. So, please do not bother trying to convince me. You are not going to marry that girl, sam."

"Just give me a chance to explain. This thing happened when she was young and naive, but now, I promise you, Zahra is nothing like that. She has learned from her mistake," Fahad pleaded.

"A mistake that is going to haunt the both of you for the rest of your lives? Come on." Hajiya Zainabu shook her head in disapproval.

He attempted to speak again, but she cut him off. "This thing is huge, no matter how you choose to look at it. It is not something that will go away. They'll always look at your wife with it. This is someone who would give birth to your children one day. How do you think they would feel seeing their mother's naked pictures all over the internet? Fisabillahi!"

Fahad knew it was not going to be easy to get his mother on his side, but it did not hurt to try. "Ammi, you have always talked about second chances."

"Yes, for people who deserve them, but in this situation? Gaskiya wadtake sam." Her voice held firm, unwavering in her decision.

"Ammi, Walahi, I love her," Fahad declared, his voice trembling with emotion.

The shock of Fahad's statement was mirrored in his mother's expression. It took him months before he could open up to her about seeing someone, and here he was, confessing his love for a woman.

Hajiya Zainabu was taken aback, but she still did not falter, even after hearing Fahad's heartfelt plea. "And you can love another. She is not the only woman in the world. You are a successful young man. You can have your pick. You have so many cousins you could choose from. They are all decent girls. Madina is an example."

"Ammi, I have told you I am not interested in this auren zumunci thing."

"You say it like it is a bad thing. Look at your sister. Is it not the auren zumunci? She's living peacefully, isn't she?"

"And that is because she loves him, Ammi. Why can't you see that I love her too?"

His mother was now done with arranging her clothes, and she felt it was time to put an end to the conversation. "I did not oppose this relationship when you came to me, but this scandal has changed everything, and I am sorry to say, but I cannot agree to this union. My decision is final."

Fahad let out a defeated sigh as his mother left the room. The stern look on her face was enough to tell him that she was never going to change her mind. He remained standing in the bedroom, the faint scent of bakhoor lingering in the air.

Abuja, Nigeria.

20th May, 2017.

Nabila looked tired as she stepped out of the hospital after her 24-hour shift. Her lab coat covered a dove-gray two-piece ensemble, and the exhaustion was evident on her face. She wasn't surprised to see Kamal waiting for her in the hospital's parking lot. He had no time for pleasantries and went straight to the point.

"What did you do that for?" Kamal's voice was sharp with frustration.

Nabila feigned innocence, "What are you..?"

"Cut the crap, Nabila. You know damn well what I am talking about." Kamal's anger was evident.

Realizing that denying her actions would only make things worse, Nabila let out a sigh and came clean, "I was only trying to help."

"Help? Come on, Nabila." Kamal kicked one of the tires of his car, and the sudden motion made her step back a bit, startled. "You just ruined a relationship I've been working hard on based on your speculations."

"M.K., you know this relationship is doomed from the start."

"And who are you to decide that, huh?" Kamal's voice was raised.

"I'm your best friend, and I know why you want this so bad. I'm telling you it is a bad idea, and that girl is bad news. Piya would..." Nabila tried to reason.

"Don't," Kamal warned, his tone cutting her off. "Don't you ever mention her name again, and stay out of this, or I'll forget whatever friendship it is that we've had."

The sound of Kamal's car zooming off was enough evidence of how upset he was, but Nabila was not going to relent. She loved him too much to let him do this to himself.

22nd May, 2017.

Madina drove towards Lokogoma and let out a sigh of relief when she saw the exit. Missing an exit in Abuja could lead to a long detour, which could mean ending up in Suleja or even Kaduna, and she couldn't afford that. When she arrived at Fatimè's house, she walked straight to her cousin's room without knocking. As she opened the door, the room was dimly lit by a desk lamp, which was unusual. Fatimè usually kept the room well-lit.

Madina switched on the overhead light to reveal the state of the room. Fatimè's work bag was sitting on the ottoman, the clothes she had removed earlier draped on a chair by the corner, and a half bottle of Sprite sat on the bedside. She found Fatimè sitting at her desk, hunched over a coloring book. She was dressed in a sleeveless floral knee-length gown, her hair packed in a lazy bun.

Fatimè looked up at Madina, who was wearing a black Palazzo pantsuit with a high-neck long-sleeved top, subtly pleated along the neckline. She completed her look with a matching black turban, evidence that she had come to Fatimè's house straight from work.

"A jamo?" Madina asked, but Fatimè didn't answer. Dropping the things she was holding on the bed, Madina walked over to the desk to get a closer look at what Fatimè was doing.

She saw that Fatimè was coloring an anime character. Fatimè only colored when something was bothering her, so Madina asked again, "A jamo?"

Fatimè shrugged, "Nothing. Just tired."

Madina responded, "Hmm. Kamila sent the stuff; come, let's check them out."

Fatimè replied, "Not now. I am not in the mood."

Madina was surprised by Fatimè's behavior and asked, "Did you fight with your airport guy? Ehn amaryan Kamal?"

Fatimè hissed and said, "Drop the amarya talk. There's no wedding taking place."

"Dume fe'ata?" Madina asked with an incredulous look on her face.

Fatimè groaned, "Nothing. I am no longer interested."

Madina was shocked and said, "No longer what? Fatimè Faruk Ardo, what is wrong with you? A few days ago, you told me you said yes, so what changed?"

"I don't know," Fatimè said. "Some girl accosted me yesterday at the ATM after you guys left and said if I knew what was good for me, I'd stay away from Kamal; if not, I'll regret it."

Madina asked, "Did you tell Kamal this?"

"Erh, not exactly," Fatimè replied.

Madina said, "So how are you sure he even knows this woman? I think you are rushing into making a decision. Why not give him a chance to explain?"

Fatimè groaned, "Explain what, Madina? Don't you get it? I do not care who she is. I am not interested in any drama, especially dealing with any of his women. He already has an ex-wife to begin with."

Madina laughed and teased, "Ah, do I smell jealousy here? You have fallen for the airport guy."

Fatimè replied, "Abeg! That is not the bone of contention here..."

Madina continued, "Look, Tims, he deserves to be heard. For all we know, the woman is just trying to scare you so she can have him all for herself. I mean, Kamal is the total package, and it makes sense if women are after him. What matters is that he is only after you."

Fatimè remained quiet, mulling over what Madina said. She knew her cousin was right, and she should have given Kamal a chance to explain himself. But she was scared. What if the woman was right? She let out a frustrated sigh and went into the bathroom to wash her face.

As she emerged from her room, Fatimè found Khalifa and Madina engrossed in a conversation. Khalifa was dressed in a jersey and shorts, holding his football boots.

"Adda Madina, please don't forget," Khalifa implored.

"You're my only hope. My favorite. The best sister in the whole world," he continued, trying to persuade Madina.

Fatimè rolled her eyes at her brother's antics. "If you fall for his tricks, Madina, you'll be disappointed. Just last week, he said I was his favorite."

"Don't listen to her; she's just jealous," Khalifa retorted, trying to defend himself.

"You wish," Fatimè said with a smirk. "Please take him with you, Madina. He's always bothering me."

"No, thank you." Madina laughed. "My three brothers are enough for me."

"You're such a spoilsport," Khalifa said, shaking his head. "Anyway, Hamma Kamal is here. He asked me to come get you."

"See?" Madina clapped. "Go on and listen to what he has to say."

Fatimè grabbed one of the hijabs, folded neatly on the ottoman, and put it on. "Fine, but don't eat any of my Pringles. I counted them."

"Kai! Just go," Madina said, shooing her away playfully

The woody and luxurious fragrance of Kamal's perfume seemed to be competing with the sandalwood scent emanating from the bakhoor that was slowly burning in one of the kaskos in the sitting room. Fatimè sat on the couch close to him, and he cleared his throat to get her attention. "Are you ready to listen to me now?"

"If I wasn't going to, I wouldn't have come downstairs," Fatimè replied.

"I spoke to Nabila," Kamal said.

"Nabila?" Fatimè's brows were now raised. "Who's she?"

"It wasn't that hard to figure out. She's a longtime friend."

"And do all your 'friends' go around harassing women you want to marry?"

"Nabila was just being dramatic," Kamal said.

Fatimè couldn't help but laugh. "She threatened me, and you are calling it being dramatic?"

"I know, I know," Kamal said, "Nabila, my ex, and I used to go to the same school."

"Rukayya?"

"No, not Rukayya."

"Oh lord. How many exes do you have?" Fatimè was now getting frustrated; she did not want to deal with any 'ex' drama.

"I promise you, it's just this one, then Rukayya. When my ex and I broke up, Nabila took it personally, and she's still salty about it. Kamal explained.

"And that is what I am avoiding. Drama, issues, and exes from years ago. I don't have the energy for all of that baggage. Fatimè stated.

She knew she sounded hypocritical when she said baggage because if there was anyone who had the most baggage, it was her.

Dealing with Khalid's death alone was enough, and in a way, that was why she did not want any additional stuff.

"You won't hear or have to deal with any of this again," Kamal assured her.

"Fatimè?" He called when he noticed she still looked unconvinced and said, "I want you to know, I want this, I want us, and I do not want to lose you. I worry that I may fail you or that I won't be enough, but I have also come to understand that worry is also part of loving someone. Believe it or not, I feel as though I am learning to love for the very first time."

Fatimè let go of whatever reservations she had because, if consistency and assurance were a person, it'd be Kamal, and that was all she needed.

15th July, 2017.

"Do you like them?" Kamal's mother asked, gesturing towards the abayas spread out on her bed. Kamal nodded, confident in his mother and aunt's choices and knowing that Fatimè would love them too.

"I'll ask your Aunt Rahina to get more since you said that's what she likes to wear. We'll make it thirty. The atampas and laces will arrive tomorrow in sha Allah, and the other items by next week. Everything should be ready by the end of the month," his mother said, her voice filled with excitement.

"Thank you so much, Maa." Kamal hugged his mother in gratitude. She had taken care of all his wedding preparations, making things easier for him.

"Best in mother and son!" Hafsah announced her presence, interrupting their moment.

Kamal released his mother and walked over to his sister, who picked up an abaya and sized it up. "Wow, Maa. This is so beautiful. I just remembered I'm due for new abayas," Hafsah said, admiring the garment.

"That's for your brother's bride," their mother corrected her, collecting the abaya.

"All of these? Enjoyment!" Hafsah exclaimed, giving Kamal a light punch on the arm. "You still haven't introduced me to her."

"Is that necessary?" Kamal asked.

"Yes!" Both Hafsah and their mother said in unison.

Hafsah moved to her mother's side, "I need to meet this woman that has gotten you in a chokehold."

"Are you crazy? Who's in a chokehold?"

"Ahaps. Keep lying to yourself."

Ignoring their banter, their mother began to gather the dresses on her bed. After some playful back-and-forth, Kamal finally agreed to take Hafsah to meet Fatimè, and his sister ran off happily, muttering about a gift for her new sister-in-law.

Kamal was about to say goodbye to his mother when she stopped him. "Have you talked to your father?" she asked.

Kamal shut his eyes briefly and mumbled a no.

"Kamal..." His mother's tone was reproachful.

"Maa, please, what do you want me to say to him? He has already shown me he does not want to be a part of this."

Kamal understood his father's message when he refused to be part of the entourage that had traveled to Gombe the previous week to formally seek Fatimè's hand. Instead, he cited business and delegated Kamal's uncles to attend on his behalf. Kamal knew that his father's excuse was just to show that he was not supportive.

"He's not against it, you know," his mother said. "He's just still upset about the fallout with Rukayya's father."

"And it's not my fault their friendship is based on their children. It has been four years. He should get over it."

"Just try..." his mother's voice trailed off.

Kamal did not like the look on his mother's face at the moment. He knew that he would have to try to make amends with his father just for her. "I'll talk to him," he said, earning a smile from his mother. "Allah ya maka albarka.

16th July, 2017.

Kamal should have known better than to assume that with women, a few minutes meant a few minutes. Just as he was about to call his sister, the back door opened, and Fatimè stepped out.

"I hope she did not give you much trouble," Kamal asked, addressing Fatimè.

Hafsah, who had just arrived, scowled at her brother. "I did not know you had that little faith in me, Ya Kamal."

Kamal raised an eyebrow. "We all know your ability to run someone's ears off with your chatter," he retorted.

Fatimè interjected with a smile, "I had a great time."

Hafsah grinned smugly. "See? At least someone recognizes the great company."

Kamal turned to Fatimè. "I'm glad you had a good time."

Suddenly, Hafsah let out a scream. "I knew it!" she exclaimed, grabbing the attention of Kamal and Fatimè.

"Knew what?" Kamal asked, clearly annoyed.

"Ya Fatimè. I knew she looked familiar, and I have been trying to recall where I'd seen her, then I remembered the fun fair..." Hafsah continued. "That one you picked me up from, at City Park? She was at the stall."

Fatimè was impressed with Hafsah's memory. "Oh, that one?"

Kamal looked confused, trying to remember the incident.

The fun fair had happened years ago when Madina suggested they get a stall to have some fun, but Kamal couldn't seem to remember meeting Fatimè there.

"I have somewhere to be, and I am running late. I'll call you later." Kamal said, eager to end the conversation and get going.

Fatimè nodded in agreement. "It was nice seeing you, Hafsah."

Hafsah moved in for a hug, exclaiming, "Me too. New sister, oh my God!"

Kamal shook his head at his sister's excitement; she was a handful. Nonetheless, he was happy that they had hit it off.

As they got into the car, Hafsah brought up the topic again. "You do not remember her from the fair? You were even staring at her, and I had to tap you. I even thought that was where you guys met...."

"Hafsah," Kamal warned, "I told you I don't recall seeing her."

Hafsah knew better than to push the issue. Her brother's tone made it clear that the conversation was over. Deep down, she knew her memory wasn't the one failing.

Chapter 11

♥

Abuja, Nigeria.

17th August, 2017

Kamal skillfully cleared all the pins, relishing the satisfaction that accompanied a well-executed bowl. Contemplating another round, he opted against it, choosing instead to head to the restaurant adjacent to the bowling area. Settling into a seat, he signaled a waiter, requesting a refreshing glass of orange juice. Having enjoyed a hearty meal at his mother's earlier, hunger wasn't a pressing concern.

Savoring the juice delivered promptly, Kamal shifted his focus to the daunting task of addressing the numerous emails that awaited him. Sa'ad had overseen matters in Lagos during Kamal's absence due to his upcoming wedding, but a few loose ends demanded his attention. Despite vowing to disconnect completely from work during his honeymoon, the demands of entrepreneurship offered little respite.

As Kamal immersed himself in his phone, he sensed someone pulling out the seat across from him. Glancing up, his expression immediately transformed into a frown. "Stalking doesn't suit you," he remarked sarcastically. "You should stick to being a doctor."

Nabila, sincerity evident in her eyes, responded, "I'm sorry." Observing her genuine remorse, Kamal nodded and replied, "Apology accepted."

A brief pause ensued before Nabila ventured to ask, "Are you still going ahead with it?" Kamal, known for his stubbornness and lack of receptiveness, failed to recognize the underlying message. Oblivious to the fact that Fatimè might not be the right person for him, he remained impervious to Nabila's unspoken concerns. She felt compelled to find a way to make him see the truth—how deeply she truly cared for him.

Suppressing her feelings, Nabila forced a smile and inquired, "So, when is the wedding?"

19th August, 2017.

Fatimè hesitated for a moment at the top of the stairs, her heart sinking at the sight of the sitting room below. If she had known she would be descending only to encounter one of her haughty aunts, she would have preferred to stay in the comfort of her room. The atmosphere in the sitting room was quiet, with a tray of cold zobo and a plate of samosas and spring rolls set before her father's cousin, Anty Beeba. A movie on 'Africa Magic Epic' played softly in the background.

Anty Beeba, with her dusky skin bearing a few faint age spots and deep-set brown eyes, looked up as Fatimè descended the stairs. Her aunt took great pleasure in meddling in Fatimè's affairs and embodied the quintessential "Nigerian aunty."

Matters had worsened when Fatimè declined her son's marriage proposal, prompting her to avoid Anty Beeba at all costs. Steeling herself, Fatimè mustered a smile and greeted her aunt, "Anty Beeba, yan nyalli jam."

Anty Beeba responded with a standoffish tone, "Jam."

Expecting such a response, Fatimè merely nodded, ready to retreat, but her aunt called her back, halting her departure. "Your mother says you are getting married," Anty Beeba remarked.

Fatimè affirmed, "Yes."

Anty Beeba probed further, "O pullo na?"

"No," Fatimè replied.

"Hm. Shame," Anty Beeba commented.

Fatimè opted to remain silent. When dealing with Anty Beeba, it was often wisest to keep one's thoughts unspoken.

"When is he bringing the lefe?" she asked.

"After the wedding in sha Allah."

Anty Beeba wore an incredulous expression, causing Fatimè to wonder if her aunt's eyes might pop out of their sockets. "And when have you ever witnessed a wedding taking place without lefe? Inalillahi wa inna ilaihi rajiun."

Fatimè averted her gaze, fixating on her feet as her aunt continued to lecture her about the illogical nature of her decisions and how she was being utterly ridiculous. Anty Beeba concluded her tirade with a parting shot, "Maybe they are right; you definitely have aljaanu.

"She said that?" Intisar asked, her disbelief evident after Fatimè recounted the incident from earlier in the afternoon.

They were gathered in Madina's room, where she had taken charge of planning the upcoming wedding. The room was strewn with various fabrics of different colors and patterns, and a vision board adorned one of the walls, displaying pictures of wedding themes and decor ideas. If there was anyone who embodied the term "extra," it was Madina.

"Why are you acting like you don't know Anty Beeba?" Madina chimed in as she emerged from the bathroom. "She said that and more, I'm certain."

Intisar shook her head and turned to Fatimè. "Are you serious about the lefe stuff, though?"

Fatimè replied, "Yes, of course. It's like creating an avenue for gossip. What did he bring and what did he not bring? It's such an eyesore."

Both Intisar and Madina nodded in agreement, and for the next hour, they busied themselves with selecting outfits, with Madina taking the lead.

While Fatimè insisted on a simple wedding Fatiha, Madina, and Intisar wouldn't hear of it, emphasizing the necessity of having a traditional kamu ceremony. The only option seemed to be giving in to one event, or they wouldn't give her a moment's peace. She decided to allow them to have their way, but with one condition—it had to be an all-female event, and she adamantly opposed any social media presence.

Madina grumbled, playfully calling her a party pooper. "This is the year of hashtags, and you're depriving us of it. Do you have any idea how much #CatchingFlights&Feelings would have blown up?"

Intisar noticed that Fatimè seemed distant, so she gently tapped her arm. "Are you okay?"

Fatimè took a moment to gather her thoughts before responding, "This time four years ago, I was planning my wedding with Khalid, and it's just weird that I'm now marrying someone else... I don't know. I've accepted it and I'm moving on, but it still feels surreal.

Grief is truly a strange thing because most of the time, you're fine and at peace, but then, out of nowhere, a wave of sadness hits you and drags your heart on the floor."

2nd September, 2017

Ever since he was a child, the gigantic shelf in his father's study had always fascinated Kamal. The study was a room of sophistication and elegance, with rich dark wood paneling adorning the walls. A grand ornate desk sat regally in the center of the room, complemented by plush velvet armchairs. Soft, muted lighting from a crystal chandelier cast a warm glow over the space. Kamal often found solace in this room, surrounded by the accomplishments and victories of his family, both his and his sister's.

Gracefully, Kamal walked along the shelf, examining each item with interest. Pausing at a picture frame, he picked it up and gently ran his hand over it. The frame held a picture of his family from a trip they took eight years ago.

Lost in the smiles captured in the photograph, Kamal's reverie was interrupted when the door swung open, revealing his father. Kamal greeted him, but his father responded with a grunt before taking a seat on one of the plush velvet armchairs.

Kamal's father was a man of striking appearance, with piercing eyes framed by a few well-earned wrinkles. His square jawline was sprinkled with gray stubble, and his tall and sturdy frame carried an aura of resilience.

There were a few minutes of uncomfortable silence as Kamal held onto the frame. Finally, his father broke the silence, his tone abrupt and direct. "I'm sure you didn't come here just to look at my face. So, out with it. What do you need?"

Kamal disliked this aspect of his father—his straightforwardness. Sometimes, he felt his father couldn't distinguish between being a soldier and being a father.

His father glanced at the frame in Kamal's hands, and suddenly his expression changed. It reminded Kamal of the hurt that flashed through his father's eyes when he had announced his decision to no longer pursue medicine.

They had been sitting in the 'Peat Inn' restaurant when Kamal had mustered the courage to reveal his true feelings. The ensuing silence at the table was deafening.

"What?" his father had asked, trying to process Kamal's words.

"I don't want to be a doctor anymore," Kamal had repeated.

He had attempted to explain himself to his parents, but his words fell on deaf ears as his father stormed off in anger. The following two days felt torturous as if Kamal's world had turned upside down. His father refused to speak to him, his mother tried to mediate, and even his sister was upset with him for ruining their vacation.

Three months had passed, and yet his father's anger remained unchanged. The worst part was that Kamal still didn't know what he truly wanted to do. However, one thing he was certain of was that medicine was not his path.

His mother had suggested a trip to Sokoto, where he could spend a few weeks with his cousins. Kamal eagerly seized the opportunity, knowing that any chance to travel and clear his head would be beneficial, especially since his father had cut off his allowance.

On the eve of his trip, Kamal met up with a friend who asked him to deliver a parcel to his aunt in Kebbi, as it was on his way. In a joking manner, Kamal had requested a delivery fee, and his friend obliged. Little did he know that dropping off that package would lead to picking up another one to be delivered in Sokoto, for which he received a small payment.

Thus began Kamal's months of driving around the country, delivering messages and packages. He dismissed it as a way to combine his love for traveling with making some money, given that his father had stopped supporting him financially. Sa'ad, fresh out of university, joined him, and with his mother's support, they expanded their business from local deliveries to a full-blown haulage and logistics company.

Despite the tremendous growth in their business, Kamal still missed his father's presence. It was partly why he had accepted the proposed marriage to his friend's daughter, hoping to reconcile their strained relationship. Little did he know that it would only serve to further estrange them.

"I want you to understand that I wasn't cut out to be a doctor. Pursuing that path would have made me miserable. And as for Rukayya..." Kamal paused, taking a deep breath before continuing, "I tried my best, truly, but it just didn't work out between us. It was better for both of us to let go before causing any more hurt."

His father's expression remained stern as he spoke, his disappointment profound. "I once told you that your word is your bond. Keeping your word demonstrates your credibility and the trust people can place in you. I asked you repeatedly if becoming a doctor was truly your desire, and you assured me it was. Four years later, you come home and go back on your word. Do you believe that actions have no consequences?"

Kamal's head dropped in shame. All this time, he had thought his father was being unreasonable, but he had no idea how deeply his actions had hurt him. He would have preferred his father's anger or even a physical confrontation over this look of profound disappointment.

"I'm sorry," Kamal muttered, his voice barely audible.

His father's tone softened slightly as he replied, "Mere apologies won't solve anything. I hope your apology comes with a genuine effort to make amends. You're intelligent enough to know that your actions carry more weight than your words. And with Fatimè, I hope you will keep your promises because there is no greater fraud than a man who does not keep his word."

With those words, his father patted Kamal's shoulder and left the room, leaving Kamal to contemplate the weight of his actions. "There is no greater fraud than a man who does not keep his word," echoed Kamal's mind as he sank deeper into the sofa, realizing the immense consequences that stemmed from something he had once sworn to take to the grave.

5th September, 2017.

"What is the meaning of this rubbish?" Fatimè heard her mother exclaim as she swung open the door to her room. The room was a haven of comfort, with the walls adorned with textured wallpaper in a subtle cream tone. Soft lighting from a bedside lamp cast a warm glow, and a kasko of turaren wuta sat on the nightstand.

Her mother stood before her, wearing a pastel floral cotton nightdress, her hair covered in a plain silk headscarf, looking visibly upset. Fatimè abandoned her concerns for the moment; clearly, this was not a good time to discuss anything.

"Ko fe'i?" Fatimè inquired, trying to keep her voice calm.

"Can you imagine? Why is it that people never follow instructions? I specifically asked Hamma to send pictures of the house renovation progress, and do you know they painted the sitting room 'off white' instead of 'pure white' as I told them..." Her mother's frustration poured out in a torrent of complaints.

Fatimè had initially advised her mother that the house didn't require any major renovations, but her mother had proceeded anyway. Now she regretted even bringing up the topic.

"And as if that wasn't enough, the clothes I gave to the tailors two months ago were supposed to arrive today, but they're saying they're not ready. Will they be ready on the wedding day?" her mother continued, her voice filled with exasperation.

"Mamiiiii..." Fatimè interjected, attempting to soothe her. "Take a deep breath and relax."

Fatimè moved closer to her mother, placing her hands on her shoulders and giving them a gentle squeeze. She began massaging them, applying just enough pressure to help her mother unwind.

"It doesn't matter if the sitting room is painted off-white, and your clothes will be ready before the wedding, in sha Allah. We still have a few weeks left," Fatimè reassured her, trying to ease her worries.

"But..." her mother started to protest.

"But nothing. I want you to stop stressing yourself out. The house will be fine, Hamma will take care of it, and your clothes will be ready. Everything else will fall into place."

"I just want everything to be perfect," her mother sighed, her voice filled with longing.

"Nothing in this world is perfect, Mami. We just do our best and leave the rest to Allah," Fatimè gently reminded her.

Her mother nodded, silently acknowledging her daughter's words of wisdom. Fatimè wrapped her arms around her mother, resting her head on her shoulder.

"I want you to know that I love you, and I'm going to miss you so much. I appreciate everything you've done for me, and I never take it for granted. Miyatti Mami am," Fatimè expressed her gratitude, her voice filled with warmth.

A tear escaped her mother's eye as she replied, "Allah wadanma barka be bangal mada, Fatimè am."

When Fatimè emerged from the room, she found her father in the sitting room, enjoying a cup of tea.

"Baaba am," she called out, walking over to join him.

"Na'am," he responded, looking up from his tea.

Fatimè poured herself a cup of tea and settled beside him. "I managed to get Mami to rest. She looked so exhausted."

"I'm glad you convinced her to take a break. I've been trying for days. The way she's been bustling around, one would think it's her wedding," her father remarked, a hint of amusement in his voice.

"Isn't it?" Fatimè teased, struggling to contain her laughter.

"Fair point," he conceded, sharing in the laughter. They both understood the dynamics of a typical Nigerian home, where the wedding often felt like it belonged to the mothers rather than the bride and groom.

Her father put down his cup of tea and cleared his throat. "How are you? No bandu mada?"

"Okay, I suppose," Fatimè replied, her voice tinged with uncertainty. "But there's this strange feeling... Not necessarily good or bad. It's just... there. Like I'm floating, you know?"

Communicating her emotions to her father always came naturally. She never felt the need to hold back or pretend. He understood her in ways that others couldn't.

"I want to know if you're doing this for yourself," her father said, his tone serious. "Not for your mother, not for me, not for him, or anyone else. For you. Because it's what you truly want."

Fatimè nodded, a determined look in her eyes. "I'm sure, Baaba. This is my choice and my decision. But if ever I feel like it's not what I want anymore, I know you'll call it off in an instant. - fa idha 'azamta fatawakkal 'alal laah; innalaha yuhibbul mutawakileen - and once you have taken a decision, place your trust in Allah, surely Allah loves those who place their trust in him."

The recitation earned her a gentle smile from her father, and he nodded, "Indeed Ati am, indeed.

Gombe, Nigeria.

4th October, 2017.

Man, with the way you've been pacing this room, you're gonna burn a hole in the carpet. Calm down, please," Sa'ad remarked, trying to lighten the mood.

The room in the guest house the bride's family had provided for the groom and his friends had a simple yet comfortable ambiance. The curtains were drawn, casting gentle shadows on the patterned carpeted floor, muffling any outside noise.

Kamal ignored Sa'ad's comment and remained standing by the window, deep in thought, the soft glow from the lamp accentuating the contemplative expression on his face.

Sa'ad couldn't help but chuckle at his friend's restlessness. "Why are you acting like it's your first time getting married?"

"Shut up," Kamal hissed. "It feels different this time, you idiot because it's real. I truly love her."

"Romeo!" Sa'ad burst into laughter. "Man, the last time I saw you like this was with Piya."

Kamal shot him an annoyed look, but Sa'ad continued to tease. "Does Fatimè know, though?"

"I've told you, Piya has nothing to do with this. This is my life now, with Fatimè..." Kamal replied, his voice filled with determination.

Their conversation was interrupted by a knock on the door, making Kamal pause. He glanced at Sa'ad and asked, "Are you expecting someone?"

Sa'ad shook his head. "Maybe it's one of the guys. Go ahead and check."

The rest of Kamal's friends occupied the other rooms available at the guest house.

Kamal approached the door, expecting to see one of his friends on the other side. However, he was taken aback when he opened it and found himself face-to-face with someone he hadn't seen in four years.

"How the hell did he find me?" Kamal wondered aloud, his surprise evident.

Chapter 12

❤

Gombe, Nigeria.

5th October, 2017.

Amidst the lively chatter from her cousins and the whirlwind of events, Fatimè couldn't pinpoint the exact cause of her pounding headache. The exhaustion from the week-long journey to Gombe and the relentless wedding preparations seemed to have taken a toll on her. They had arrived in Gombe just a week ago for her wedding—her wedding, she reminded herself. Even the joyful chants of "Amarya" couldn't fully register in her mind.

Every ritual felt like a physical formality, a series of steps her body mechanically went through while her mind floated elsewhere. Her aunts paid no heed to her preferences, insisting on bathing her with nono despite her aversion to the qarni that came with it. Safiyya, her skilled cousin, had transformed her unruly hair into neat shuku braids, and the dambordu ritual was a delight, where she was cleaned, perfumed, and patterned with henna, all the while her aunts and cousins showered her with blessings. Despite her request for no bridal shower, Intisar and Madina had organized a surprise one, and the haggling at the kamu event between Kamal's aunts and her cousins showed the significant amount settled, judging by Madina's wide smile.

Fatimè had feared not being accepted by Kamal's family, but her worries were laid to rest when his aunts embraced her warmly, smiles of "amaryar mu" on their faces. Anty Khadija had thoughtfully allocated a separate house for Fatimè and her bridesmaids. Currently, they were gathered in the sitting room, enjoying a meal and chatting animatedly. However, Fatimè had only managed to nibble on a piece of suya, as her nerves prevented her from having a proper meal. A hot shower had provided some relief, and she was grateful to have shed the intricate komolè ensemble she had worn for today's event. The word "beautiful" didn't quite capture the essence of the outfit, especially when adorned by her. She gave credit to Madina for meticulously taking care of all her outfits, leaving Fatimè with the simple task of attending fittings.

Returning to her nervousness and anxiety, Fatimè absentmindedly played with the heart-shaped locket hanging from her neck, wondering if Kamal felt the same way. Madina's gentle tap snapped her back to the room's lively conversation. "Are you okay? Your phone is ringing," Madina informed her, handing over the device. Meanwhile, her cousins began singing "ango misses amarya." Fatimè shook her head, excusing herself from the room to answer the call in solitude. Glancing at the caller's name, her heart skipped a beat—it was Khalid's mother.

6th October, 2017

Fatimè leaned against the balcony railings on the second floor of her aunt's house, taking in the refreshing air and admiring the houses and birds scattered around. The sky was clear and beautiful, and she adjusted her veil to shield herself from the chilly weather.

Without hesitation, she lifted the veil to her nose, inhaling the familiar scent of 'Lancôme en rose'. Sniffing her clothes had been a habit of hers, and Khalid would often playfully pull her hands away, teasing her for acting like a baby. Smiling at the memory, Fatimè wiped away a solitary tear that had escaped onto her cheek. She missed him dearly.

Last night's phone call from Khalid's mother contributed to her current state, even though all his mother did was wish her a happy married life. It was difficult for Fatimè to maintain contact with Khalid's mother because she couldn't help but tear up every time they talked. The love they both shared for him was incredibly strong.

Her aunt's house was a few meters from the mosque, where most of the Ardo family's wedding ceremonies took place. So when she heard the loudspeaker announcing, "An daura auren Fatimè Ardo da Kamal Maitambari..." she wasn't surprised. Fatimè had silently said her prayers before her cousins rushed into the balcony, showering her with hugs, exclamations of "Ma sha Allah," and congratulations.

Fatimè had pleaded with Madina to create a distraction so she could find a quiet place to pray before the groom and his friends arrived. Her aunt's room provided much-needed privacy, and as she recited her adkhar, her phone beeped with a message from Kamal: "Alhamdulillah, I cannot wait to see you and whisper 'my wife' in your ears." The words echoed in her mind, filling her with joy.

As she heard the door open, Fatimè silently hoped Madina wasn't coming to fetch her. She needed a few more minutes. Turning her head towards the door, she saw him. "Madina, let me in," he said, his voice trailing off. "I just needed to see you, you know, before it all..." The comfortable silence that followed was exactly what Fatimè needed at that moment.

She imagined the forthcoming chatter as soon as the groom arrived—her mother's expression as her dreams came true, witnessing her daughter getting married.

"I thought your wedding day was supposed to be your happiest day." He broke the silence.

"And who said I was not happy?" Fatimè retorted, mentally rolling her eyes. He had asked her this question a billion times since she accepted Kamal's proposal.

"Are you sure?" he asked, turning to look at her.

She sighed, "Are you here to congratulate me or...?"

"I'm sorry. I'm just looking out for you. But I truly pray that you're happy with this decision."

"Yes, I am," Fatimè affirmed.

He gazed at her for a few moments before standing up. His hand went into his pocket to retrieve something, but he quickly changed his mind. "Congratulations, butterfly. I wish you a delighted married life."

Fatimè smiled warmly. "Thank you, Fahad. I appreciate it."

Just then, Madina appeared and informed him that he needed to leave. Fatimè noticed how Madina didn't spare him a glance. "What's up with you guys?" she inquired.

Madina shrugged and tugged at her arm. "We need to get you ready. Your husband will be here soon.

In thirty minutes, Fatimè had transformed into a light ivory fit-to-flare lace gown with intricate embellishments along the bodice and a long train that cascaded down to the floor in soft ruffles. The bridal veil framed her face and fell gracefully over her shoulders. She wore minimal makeup and listened as her cousins bombarded her with advice on what to do when she saw Kamal. Their suggestions were utterly ridiculous, and there was no way she would follow them.

Madina announced that Kamal had arrived, and Fatimè made her way downstairs. She paused momentarily, catching a glimpse of him in a sky-blue 'babbar riga.' He looked incredibly handsome, and she couldn't help but smile, knowing he was now hers. As they stood face to face, she noticed the huge grin on his face, reminiscent of 'Luffy's' expression when he met with 'Zoro' in 'Wano'. Okay, only a true otaku thinks of anime on her wedding day.'

Fatimè was relieved when he simply took her hands instead of going in for a hug, as she couldn't bear the "awws" that typically accompanied whatever people referred to as a 'halal hug.' Madina stood beside her, whispering, "Mr. and Mrs. Airport Guy, inspired by Madina Hamidu." Fatimè couldn't help but chuckle as they took their seats.

The grin remained on Kamal's face as Fatimè toyed with her bracelet. Amidst the chorus of "Ma sha Allah" and congratulations, she heard his voice clearly as he said, "You look so beautiful, sunshine. So beautiful. This color suits you." Fatimè blushed at the compliment, feeling his hands gently squeeze hers.

The photo session left Fatimè with sore cheeks from all the smiling she had to do. She had taken off her glasses, and the flashes from the camera were giving her a headache. Kamal, on the other hand, continued to smile, unable to describe the joy he felt in his heart. He was still coming to terms with the fact that he had won Fatimè's heart.

"Are you okay?" he whispered in her ear, noticing her discomfort.

"What do you think?" she replied, just as the photographer captured another shot. Kamal understood what was going through her mind and chuckled, recalling a conversation they had a few weeks ago when she confessed her fear of falling asleep on her wedding day.

"Let's get out of here," he suggested.

Fatimè's eyes widened, "What? We can't just leave..."

"I'll tell them you need to take a shit."

"What?!"

Fatimè tried to hold him back, but he had already approached Madina, who stood next to the photographers. Seeing Madina struggling to contain her laughter, Fatimè knew he had shared the same plan with her. Ya Ilahi! She covered her face with her palms until he returned.

"Situation handled. Let's go," he declared.

Without waiting for anyone's reaction, they left the sitting room together. She kept her head down until they reached the room upstairs. Kamal opened the door, and the scent of bakhoor wafted into her nostrils. Fatimè stepped into the neat room and noticed her blanket and pillow arranged on the bed. The fact that he had prepared a room for her to take a power nap almost brought tears to her eyes.

She plopped onto the bed, taking a deep breath, which made him smile. Sleep truly made her happy, and he found it cute. He turned to leave, but before he could, Fatimè got up and hugged him. Kamal held on to her, even though he could not believe she initiated the hug. As if she could hear his thoughts, Fatimè broke free from the hug. He laughed, "It's allowed, you know? We are married."

Fatimè smiled and walked over to the bed. She took off the veil first and proceeded to remove every piece of jewelry on her, dropping them on the bedside drawer. When she came out of the bathroom after changing into a cotton gown she had picked from her aunt's wardrobe, He was no longer in the room, leaving behind the saffron and lavender scent of his 'Initio' perfume.

Several times, Madina had warned Fatimè about the potential danger of getting kidnapped while she slept. One might think it was just an exaggeration, but everyone knew that Fatimè slept like the dead. A live band could be playing in the room, and she still wouldn't wake up, but if you switched off the fan or the AC, her eyes would snap open.

Madina decided to put this to the test, and the next few minutes had Fatimè rubbing her eyes, trying to untangle herself from the duvet. "Toh amarya, you have succeeded in making us miss our flight..." Fatimè panicked and jumped off the bed. "What?! Why didn't you wake me up? Subhanallah..."

"Relax," Madina laughed. "I was kidding."

Fatimè shot her a glare, and Madina moved away slightly, lest Fatimè threw a pillow at her. "Your husband said we should let you sleep; that's why. Isn't that sweet?" Madina held her hands to her chest and let out a sigh. "I love love."

Fatimè shook her head and stifled a yawn. "What time is it?"

"12:08 PM. Intisar just texted me that all the aunts are on their way, and our flight is at 5:00 PM, so we need to get ready."

Fatimè nodded and headed into the bathroom to freshen up. Intisar and Mufida joined them by the time she came out, with Madina laying out her outfit on the bed. They helped her get ready, exchanging light-hearted chatter, and when they were done, they looked at her with pure love and admiration. "Ma sha Allah, Tims. You look stunning," Madina said.

Fatimè's eyes welled up with tears as she enveloped them in a bone-crushing hug. "Thanks, guys..."

They all sat through an hour of counsel from Fatimè's aunts in the sitting room downstairs.

"Marriage is work, actual work." Aunt Najmah, her oldest aunt, said, "You will adjust your communication, your tone, your money management, your addiction, everything. You will work to accommodate, tolerate, and compromise. It is not a walk in the park or a bed of roses. It is work. Throw away the idea that everything is ice cream and pizza, even though sometimes it is. Sometimes it is a water bed, a bouncing castle, and a window near the ocean, and other times it is a thorn, a storm, or thunder. But one thing is certain, and that is the fact that you will work."

Each aunt shared her wisdom, and Madina pinched Fatimè when one of the aunts repeated the famous saying, "In yace bari ki ba ri..." They struggled to contain their laughter, fearful of their aunts catching them and delivering a scolding.

Fatimè's mother found it difficult to speak and instead shed tears as if there was no tomorrow. At one point, Fatimè wondered if her mother was the same person who had been pushing for the marriage.

Their hug was tight, and her mother whispered into her ears, "Do not let anyone maltreat you; you are an Ardo, granddaughter of a king, a gem, but also, treat him with respect and kindness, Allah ya hada kanku..." At that point, Fatimè succumbed to her tears too.

Kamal sensed the weight of respect attached to his father-in-law's presence as he cleared his throat, prompting immediate silence.

Placing Fatimè's hands in Kamal's, he spoke with a mix of authority and warmth, "I am giving you her hand, and I am pleased to have married her to you. I trust that you will both take care of each other with love and fill your home with happiness and laughter. Baarakhallahu laka, we baarak alayka, wa jama'a baynakuma fee khair."

Fatimè heard the crack in her father's voice and knew he was trying to hold back his emotions. Tears welled up in her eyes when he walked her to the car, and she moved to embrace him, realizing that she was truly leaving. "I'll miss you so much, Baaba am," she said amidst tears.

"Me too, Ati am, me too. Now go, your husband is waiting."

The drive to the airport was filled with Madina and Sa'ad's lively conversation, while Fatimè counted the minutes until her next nap. She couldn't contain her laughter when they arrived and saw her brothers in the parking lot, looking all serious.

"Ahn Ahn, su queen's guard! I hail," Madina exclaimed.

"Just making sure he knows what he's up against in case he tries to act funny," Mubarak said with a smile.

"She's too special for me to act funny, and with this defense, I dare not," Kamal replied, surrendering his hands. Hamma gave him a curt nod, expressing his approval.

Fatimè's goodbyes to her brothers were heartfelt, and she laughed at Khalifa's attempt to give her marital advice. "What do you even know?" she teased.

"I know that you managed to bag someone who supports a good club, so don't ruin it," Khalifa retorted.

Hamma shook his head and pulled Fatimè aside, leaving the rest of the group chatting as they awaited their flight. "I don't have much to say," he began. "Baaba has said it all, but I want you to know one thing: I am always here for you. Please never forget that, baby petel."

She nodded and rested her head on his shoulder, knowing she could always count on her brother.

Sokoto, Nigeria.

Just a few of Fatimè's relatives and friends accompanied her to Sokoto for the budan kai. She was relieved that it was a small and intimate event since she was exhausted. Kamal's mother wore a wide smile as she lifted Fatimè's veil and commented, "Ma sha Allah. She's a beautiful one."

The following hour felt like a blur as Fatimè struggled to stay awake. Once they arrived at their apartment, everyone went straight to bed. What a day, and what a wedding!

Fatimè's entourage left early the next morning, and Kamal arrived soon after for their trip to Lagos. His mother and aunts playfully teased him about being so eager with his wife, causing Fatimè to feel embarrassed. They met with his father and uncles, who accompanied them with prayers before their departure.

"Until I come visiting," Hafsah said, bidding them farewell at the airport.

"Don't come and disturb my wife, please," Kamal jokingly warned.

"Of course not. I'm the better company, and she knows that," Hafsah retorted.

Fatimè observed their banter until their flight was called. Three flights in one week and two hours of Lagos traffic had drained most of Fatimè's energy, but she felt revived when Kamal opened the door to their house and the scent of bakhoor greeted her nose. It was her favorite combination: sandal and kajiji.

A hot shower, some tea, and a good sleep would be the best things for her right now. After freshening up, she joined Kamal in the sitting room, where he had set up two prayer mats. They proceeded to pray together, with Kamal placing his hands on her forehead as they recited the du'a, "Allahuma inni as'aluka min khayraha wa khayra ma jubilat 'alaihi, wa a'udhu bika min sharriha wa shari ma jubilat 'alaih."

Both of them were too tired to eat, so they settled for tea. Kamal lovingly tucked Fatimè into bed, saying, "Sleep well, wifey," before planting a gentle kiss on her forehead. She immediately dozed off, and Kamal watched her for a few minutes before quietly leaving the room.

In less than an hour, Fatimè was tossing and turning, finding it hard to sleep. She always had trouble being comfortable anywhere but in her room, making her avoid traveling.

The room was an oasis of quiet, and when she got up from the bed, her movement echoed. Switching on the lights, she took her time to look around. The room was adorned with smooth-textured wallpaper in muted shades of gray and beige. Large windows welcomed the soft glow of natural light, offering a serene ambiance.

The best part was its clutter-free nature. Only a few pieces of furniture adorned the room, and everything was neatly tucked away in drawers or on shelves.

Unable to go back to sleep, she decided to check her phone for a few minutes. Replying to messages, a chore for Fatimè, became especially tedious on occasions. Now, as a married woman, she anticipated the flood of congratulatory notifications the moment she switched on her data—a stream from different apps: Twitter, WhatsApp, Instagram, and more. She missed her brother Khalifa, her ally in such situations, who would read aloud the messages as she dictated replies.

After more than half an hour, she gave up, having answered only half of the messages. She'd tackle the rest later. Craving a hot bath, she tiptoed through the extra-quiet room, every step resonating like an echo. The silence was stifling, prompting a fleeting thought of calling Kamal to wait for her while she bathed. She dismissed the idea, opting instead to leave the TV on to dispel the unnerving silence.

The bath worked its magic; she felt a thousand times better. She approached the closet and switched on the light. The custom-built closet had mirrored doors, a masterpiece of organization that only Madina could achieve, knowing precisely how Fatimè preferred her clothes arranged.

As she rummaged for a pair of pajamas and a scarf to cover her hair, her eyes caught a pile of boxes in a corner. Curiosity got the best of her. Walking toward them, she was awestruck when she realized what they were—the gifts Kamal had sent on her birthday. The same gifts she had mailed back to him.

She wondered at the sentimental soul she married. He had kept them for her.

Amid the anticipation, she decided to open the gifts. The first box contained the new Goalrilla CV basketball system. She had to keep herself from screaming; it was still nighttime. She had watched a review of the system on YouTube and thought it was amazing. It came attached to a Spalding basketball customized with her name. The next box revealed a Rocket reusable smart sketchbook, a must-have for any architect. And that was not all—a pair of floral-embroidered lace pumps caught her eye. She looked at the box and covered her mouth with her hands. It was one of the most beautiful shoes she had ever seen. Another box was scanty except for a piece of paper sitting pretty in it, and when she read the contents, it was a one-year subscription to her favorite anime streaming site, 'Crunchyroll.'

She couldn't believe she had let months of it waste away, and now she felt a twinge of regret.

She was just on the fourth box but couldn't go any further, so she lay back on the carpet and looked at the ceiling. This man was just too much.

Abuja, Nigeria.

7th October, 2017.

Rukayya was relieved to find the supermarket parking lot nearly empty, as she had no desire to navigate through a crowd. However, her relief was short-lived when she spotted a man leaning on her car with his arms crossed. His intense gaze made her stumble over her words as she managed to say, "Excuse me?"

"Mrs. Maitambari," he said, smirking.

"We are no longer married..." Rukayya responded, her voice wavering.

"Hm. I see. Anyway," he continued, "I have a message for you."

Confusion etched across her face as she wondered what message he could have for her. "It's for your ex-husband," he clarified. "Tell him I am coming."

As he began to walk away, he turned back and added, "My regards to Adil."

Rukayya's heart skipped a beat.

Chapter 13

♥

"**W**ow. I love this." Kamal had the most boyish grin on his face as he held the GPS golf smartwatch. "This is one of the best things ever, and it will certainly make golf much more enjoyable."

Fatimè felt fulfilled; it was worth it. She had felt the urge to get her husband a wedding gift, just because. These two weeks had been unforgettable for her, as she had savored every moment—the bliss, companionship, sleep, Kamal cooking, the absence of work stress, and, oh yes, the sleep. All they did was revel in each other's company; it was truly a honeymoon.

"Thank you so much," Kamal said, reaching out to hug her.

"There is more," she whispered in his ear.

He released her and watched as she led him to his closet. Fatimè opened a cupboard, and there it was, sitting pretty—the 'Boadicea the Victorious Ardent' perfume. Kamal almost gasped—how did she know?

He couldn't contain his joy as he lifted her and spun her around. "You are the best wife ever!"

Fatimè giggled and silently thanked her sister-in-law, who had helped her choose the gift. "Wristwatches and perfumes," Hafsah had said. "He never has enough."

Fatimè thought Hafsah was exaggerating until she ventured into Kamal's room while he was out on an errand and saw the array of perfumes he had lined up in a drawer. No wonder he smelled like a billion bucks. She knew he was into wristwatches because he had mentioned it before—his wrist was rarely devoid of a stylish timepiece.

"Is this why Hafsah was asking me for perfume recommendations, claiming it was for someone?" Kamal inquired.

Fatimè made a 'zipping my mouth' sign with her hands.

"Is she seeing someone?" Kamal's protective brother mode kicked in.

Fatimè laughed, having witnessed this behavior from her brothers. "No, she is not," Fatimè reassured him. "Come..." She held his hand and led him to the sitting room.

Kamal wondered what surprise she had in store this time. She had already given him two of the best things ever and fulfilled his top wish list items. Any more would make his heart burst.

Upon seeing the setup in the sitting room, his mouth formed an 'O' of surprise. The Nintendo Switch console was placed next to the DSTV decoder.

"This woman will be the death of me," he exclaimed. "What am I going to do with you?" he asked playfully.

"You like it?" Fatimè asked sheepishly.

"Like? I love it!"

"Well, they say a console is the glue in every marriage."

Kamal laughed. "And by 'they,' you mean Fatimè Ardo, right?"

Fatimè nodded. "Just speaking facts."

An hour into the game, Kamal's hands found hers. She had grown accustomed to his touch by now—the gentle forehead kisses, hugs, and holding hands. She didn't mind them at all.

"Are you trying to distract me so I won't win?" she asked playfully when he poked her.

She turned to look at him, and he wore the most mischievous smile on his face—the 'I am going to tickle you' smile.

Oh no.

Oh no.

She hated tickles. If someone tried to tickle her, they might end up with a kick in the face.

Before she could utter a word, he had already launched his attack. The laughter that erupted was loud and pure. Kamal loved it; it was one of the most beautiful sounds he had ever heard. He would give anything to hear it echo throughout the house every day.

She tried to protest, but it was futile. He knew all the right spots, and he was stronger than her. Amidst the laughter and her desperate attempts to free herself, she unintentionally blurted out, "Khalid, please stop."

Immediately, the atmosphere changed. She knew what she had done, and there was no taking it back. Kamal cleared his throat and stood up, the hurt evident in his eyes.

She was left speechless, and even if she had words, he didn't stick around to hear them. He grabbed his keys and left.

Abuja, Nigeria.

18th October, 2017.

Zahra sat in the passenger's seat, her arms crossed tightly against her chest. The silence was becoming unbearable, so she finally broke it. "So, where are we?"

Fahad closed his eyes for a moment, collecting his thoughts, before responding, "Ammi still wouldn't budge. I don't know what else to do. I was hoping Baba would be able to convince her."

"It's okay," Zahra interjected softly, unable to bear his words any longer. Deep down, she knew it was already over.

Tears welled up in her eyes, but Fahad tried his best not to look. He despised seeing people cry, especially when he knew he was the cause of their pain.

"I'm sure she's happy now," Zahra muttered.

"What?" Fahad questioned, confusion evident in his voice.

"Your cousin. She can have you all to herself."

Fahad let out a sigh of 'Please do not start again.' "She's married," he said. "There's Madina. How am I sure they did not plan all of this?"

Zahra's remark caught Fahad off guard, and frustration seeped into his voice. "Are you being serious right now? You want to blame them for something you are responsible for?"

Zahra was taken aback by his outburst. "Wow. Wow. Wow, Fahad? Are you judging me now?"

"You know that's not it," Fahad replied, his tone tinged with exasperation. "I have never, for one second, judged you for this. But we can't absolve you of any blame. I want you to try, for once, to be accountable for your actions and stop trying to shift the blame onto others."

"Fahad..." Zahra tried to interject.

"Let me finish," Fahad cut her off, his voice filled with urgency. "This whole situation is incredibly frustrating, and it's driving me nuts. Can we please focus on finding a way out of this? Instead of investing energy in blaming my cousins, channel it into praying so my mother might change her mind."

"I'm sorry," Zahra whispered, her voice filled with remorse.

Fahad started the car, ready to leave. "I have to go. I have a meeting."

Zahra nodded silently and moved to exit the car.

"Fatima Zahra," Fahad called out, his voice softer now. "I love you, and I don't want to lose you. Never forget that."

Lagos, Nigeria.

Kamal struggled to find the right words to describe the turmoil he felt. He wished he could turn back time and not hear what his wife had said. A deep ache settled in his chest. How could his day go from pure bliss to utter despair so quickly?

He gulped down another glass of orange juice, the acidic liquid doing little to quell the bitter taste of disappointment. A guttural groan escaped him as he grappled with his emotions, the weight of frustration and hurt bearing down on him. Why him? Why did life always seem to go haywire the moment he found happiness? On the 11th day of his honeymoon, he was consumed by anger and hurt because his wife was still fixated on her ex. If only the man were alive, Kamal thought, maybe he could find some solace in punching him.

He covered his face with his hands, seeking refuge from the harsh reality, and let out a heavy sigh. He was at a loss for what to do. Despite his efforts, nothing seemed to resolve the situation. The frustration was overwhelming. Just as he was lost in his thoughts, his phone rang, and he glanced at the caller ID.

"Oh God, not now," he groaned inwardly, knowing he had to answer. Rukayya only called if it was an emergency.

"Rukayya," Kamal answered, his voice tinged with apprehension.

"I swear, if anything happens to my son, I will never forgive you." Rukayya's voice trembled with hysteria, sending shivers down Kamal's spine. Before Kamal could respond, the call abruptly ended.

Could his day possibly get any worse?

Back at home, Fatimè sat on the couch, gently rubbing her temples. She couldn't help but wonder what was going through Kamal's mind. She knew that what had slipped out of her mouth wasn't intentional at all. She reached for her phone on the side table and dialed Madina's number.

"Mrs. Airport Guy! Do you now remember that you have a cousin? Aure dadi," Madina's voice came through the phone, laced with a hint of playfulness. "ajamo?"

"Madina, I messed up."

Madina's tone became calm as she asked, "What did you do?"

Fatimè narrated the entire incident to Madina, and she waited for her cousin's usual reprimand. As Madina spoke rapidly and loudly, Fatimè's mind began to drift. There was no point in talking; she needed guidance.

"I deserve all of that, thank you. Now tell me what to do."

Two hours had passed, and Kamal still hadn't returned. Fatimè felt apprehensive, despite her attempts to reach him through calls and messages. She understood his anger and knew she had hurt him deeply. Regret consumed her ever since she uttered Khalid's name. She needed to accept that she was now married to Kamal and let go of her lingering attachment to her ex. It was a struggle she had been wrestling with ever since she and Kamal transitioned from friendship to something more. Erasing Khalid from her life and memories was difficult, but she knew she had to try harder. She needed to fix things.

Determined to find Kamal wherever he was in Lagos, Fatimè picked up the car keys from the drawer. However, she suddenly remembered that she hadn't driven a car since the accident seven years ago. Panic set in as she realized her limited options. Taking an Uber late at night felt unsafe, and she didn't even know where to begin searching for Kamal.

Luck was on her side as she heard the gate opening. Peering through the blinds, she saw Kamal's car driving in. Letting out a silent prayer of relief, she hurried to open the door.

As soon as Kamal stepped inside, he was enveloped in Fatimè's embrace. "I'm sorry," she cried, her voice filled with genuine remorse. "I didn't mean to upset you. Please forgive me. It won't happen again. I'm sorry..."

Kamal called her name softly, breaking free from the hug. He looked into her tear-filled eyes. He couldn't stand seeing her cry, but he also didn't want her to use it as a means to bypass the issue at hand. He knew she was truly sorry, and he could sense it in her gaze.

"I told you it's fine, and I understand," he reassured her.

Fatimè released herself from the hug and locked eyes with him. Her tears continued to flow as she spoke, "No, I swear, it just slipped out. It wasn't my intention."

Uncomfortable with the crying, Kamal replied, "I understand, Fatimè. It's fine."

He caught a glimpse of the dining table and noticed that she had prepared something. "Did you cook?" he asked, surprised.

Fatimè nodded. "I thought you might be hungry."

Kamal knew that Fatimè wasn't particularly fond of cooking. They had discussed it from the beginning of their relationship, and he didn't mind taking charge of the meals himself or relying on Mrs. Simon's cooking.

"Yes, I'm very hungry. Let's eat."

Both of them were grateful for the silence as they ate. No one wanted to relive what had happened a few hours ago. Kamal had accepted her apology, and Fatimè, on the other hand, had vowed to do better.

"We should go on a trip; what do you think?" Kamal suggested, breaking the quietude with a hopeful tone.

Abuja, Nigeria.

August 2010.

There was nothing more therapeutic for her than sitting alone with her thoughts. She relished the feeling of introspection, reflecting on past moments and analyzing them. After completing a session, she felt much better than when she had arrived, until someone took a seat beside her on the bench.

Not in the mood for interaction, she ignored the person and focused on observing the people bustling in and out of the hospital. However, she couldn't help but notice the pleasant scent of his cologne. Leaning back in his chair and clasping his hands behind his head, he spoke up.

"Do you know what drives us to ridiculous extremes?" he asked, his voice capturing her attention.

Pausing briefly, he answered his question, "Hope. Hope that one day we will get what we want."

His words resonated deeply with her, perfectly describing her feelings. There was nothing more agonizing than yearning for something desperately, knowing it may never come to fruition, yet still clinging onto that tiny glimmer of hope.

"I'm Kamal Maitambari, and my story is that I fell in love," he introduced himself. "What is your story?"

The interruption grated against her solitude like a discordant note. However, she found Kamal's words strangely compelling, striking a chord within her own experiences. The vulnerability in his voice hinted at a shared human struggle.

Should she share her story? Opening up to a stranger felt daunting, yet the connection forged through shared sentiments made her reconsider. Taking a deep breath, she decided to let go of her guarded demeanor, at least for a moment.

Chapter 14

♥

Tokyo, Japan

30th October 2017.

When Kamal mentioned a trip, Fatimè had no idea he was referring to her dream country. She couldn't believe her ears when he told her they were going to Japan. Every otaku dreams of visiting Japan at least once in their life. It turned out he had been planning the trip ever since she said yes to him. Oh, what was she going to do with this man?

Today was their eighth day in Japan, and every second of it had been thoroughly enjoyed by Fatimè. The majestic shrines, refined culture, therapeutic hot springs, adventure, and picture-perfect sights made it all worthwhile. The happiest place on earth—'Disneyland'—was where their journey started. The pure bliss she felt was unmatched as Kamal unleashed the inner child in him.

Two days were spent in Hakone, where she finally learned how to ride a bike after numerous failed attempts. The 'Kinkakuji' temple had them holding hands, enjoying the serene ambiance. And what would a trip to Japan be without tea? Kamal made sure it was on their itinerary, knowing how much Fatimè loved tea. Meeting a real-life 'geisha' made the experience even more special.

Plans for a post-wedding shoot were made by Fatimè, and the Japanese wedding photo shoot was perfect for that. Pictures that made her feel a bit embarrassed had her cousins gushing over them. Kamal, on the other hand, got lost in museums and attractions, and his inner photographer ignited with Fatimè playfully teasing him about quitting hisjob so he could focus more on taking pictures.

Kamal's love for books was on full display as they spent hours at 'Bunkitsu', with her having to drag him out, but not before acquiring over twenty books. The highlight of his trip was when Fatimè surprised him with tickets to his favorite author's book signing. He smothered her with kisses upon finding out that he would meet the famous 'Haruki Murakami'.

Overall, the trip was amazing for both of them. Given the chance, they would have stayed longer, but their jobs were waiting for them. On a group video call with Madina, Intisar, and Mufida, stories about the trip were enthusiastically shared by Fatimè.

You guys wouldn't understand." Fatimè exclaimed, "I don't want to go backkkk."

"Toh, tell him you're not returning," Intisar said with a mocking tone.

"Yes," Madina added. "You both can quit your jobs and just stay there forever."

Fatimè couldn't help but laugh. "As much as that sounds tempting, na love, we go chop?"

"Oho!" Mufida chimed in, "You better pack your bags and come back home. This baby can't wait any longer."

Mufida was due in a few weeks, and as the official godmother, Fatimè couldn't miss it.

"Yes, ma!" Fatimè replied. "I have to go now; my husband is back."

"Ahn Ahn!" Intisar clapped. "My husband, FC. It's not easy o."

"Abeg, get out," Fatimè said, ending the call.

She felt Kamal's hands on her waist as he kissed her neck. "Hi, baby."

Gently taking his hands off, she turned to him and placed her index finger on his chest. "Hi, baby. Shower, please."

Kamal had just returned from the hotel's gym and was looking a bit sweaty. Sweat, even her own, was something Fatimè had an unhealthy aversion to.

He shook his head and said, "Okay, ma'am," before disappearing into the bathroom.

While Kamal showered, the rest of their packing was finished up by Fatimè. Their flight was scheduled for tomorrow at 10 a.m. The hustle of the morning rush was detested by her, so the night before a trip was when she always packed.

Twenty minutes later, freshened up, Kamal emerged, and a hug was moved in for. "Clean enough?" he asked.

"Mhmm." Fatimè nodded, giving him a peck on the cheek. "We're going to be late for lunch."

They got ready together, with Fatimè wearing a peach A-line abaya with crystal details and Kamal sporting a linen shirt and suede espadrilles. At the entrance of the restaurant, a lady approached them with a smile. "Irasshaimase!" she greeted.

"Arigatoo," they both responded with a smile.

The lady led them into a private room with a 'zaishiki'-style sitting arrangement—a short table with two cushions facing each other. As they sat down, they were served tea, and in a concentrated Japanese accent, the lady said, "Someone will be here shortly to take your order."

Fatimè turned around, taking in the beauty of the interior. "That's a lot of plants," Kamal remarked.

"And that's one thing I've always loved about Japanese culture," Fatimè replied. "The way they respect nature and maintain a strong connection with the natural world. Their design style is often inter-twined with nature."

"Madam architect," Kamal teased, a grin on his face. "School me some more. What other facts do you have?"

"If you look closely, all the doors here are sliding wooden doors. Do you know why?" Fatimè asked.

Kamal shook his head. "Why?"

"Well, they're important elements of Japanese interior design. Due to the high cost of houses and lack of space, Japanese homes tend to be small by Western standards. That's why the 'shoji', as it's called, is a traditional Japanese screen that plays a significant role in the interior of country houses. Unlike doors, the screen slides back and forth rather than swinging, saving much-needed space," Fatimè explained.

Kamal listened to her with rapt attention, his eyes filled with admiration. He loved listening to her talk. Just in time, a waiter appeared to take their order. "Moshi Moshi," he cheerfully greeted them. "What would you like to have?"

Kamal chuckled lightly. "Please forgive us; we didn't even check the menu. I was too busy with my human Japanese encyclopedia here."

"Don't worry. Take your time. I'll wait," the waiter assured them.

They had a difficult time deciding what to order, as the menu was extensive.

"The only time we're fated to lose is in fictional stories. This is our drama, and we decide what the plot will be." The waiter quoted, making Fatimè raise her head as she heard the statement.

He smiled and pointed at Fatimè's phone case. It featured a picture of 'Kagami Taiga' from her favorite anime, 'Kuroko no Basketball.' The quote was from the anime.

Fatimè couldn't help but grin. "I didn't know Africa had 'otakus'," the waiter remarked.

"Excuse you? Africa has thousands of otakus, and Nigeria has the highest number," Fatimè proudly informed him.

"Sō desu ne! Sadly, we stan different MCs in 'Kuroko'," the waiter said as he unbuttoned his work uniform, revealing a picture of 'Aomine Daiki'.

'Aomine' was 'Kagami's' rival, and Fatimè knew this was going to turn into a face-off.

The perfect quote came to her mind: "If we understood how people felt, then nobody would start a war," Fatimè quoted, smiling at the waiter.

He grinned back and responded, "Well, sadly, the only one who can beat me is me."

"And the only one who can beat you here is her husband if you don't get to bringing our meal," Kamal interjected.

Fatimè turned to see Kamal giving the waiter a deathly glare. She was beyond shocked and couldn't process what had just happened. "What was that?" she asked, visibly upset.

"I didn't like the way he was smiling and looking at you like he was flirting..." Kamal's voice trailed off.

"Are you serious right now?" Fatimè couldn't believe what she was hearing. Kamal's jealousy was unwarranted.

Ignoring her, Kamal got up, put his hands in his pockets, and pulled out his wallet. He dropped some notes on the table and said, "I've lost my appetite. I am leaving."

The anger in his voice was profound as Fatimè watched him leave without even a backward glance. She was dumbfounded, first at his behavior towards the waiter, second at his disregard for the waiter's apology, and third at leaving her by herself.

She had no intention of going after him. Kamal had displayed a certain level of immaturity, and she wasn't going to be a party to that nonsense.

The waiter arrived with their food and had an apologetic look on his face. "I'm so sorry," Fatimè said. "What he did was not right, and I apologize on his behalf."

The waiter smiled, placing the food on the table. Fatimè decided she wouldn't let Kamal's actions ruin her appetite. She ate her fill before asking for a takeaway package for Kamal. She wasn't about to deny him this amazing meal

Her plan was to take a solo walk before returning to their hotel since he had obviously left her alone. However, her hopes were dashed when she saw Kamal waiting for her outside. She chose to ignore him and started walking away.

Kamal knew he had messed up when he saw the look on her face. "I'm sorry. Please wait, let's talk," he pleaded.

Fatimè didn't spare him a glance and hailed the first cab that stopped for her. She got in, leaving Kamal standing there, regret written all over his face.

Back at the hotel, Kamal impatiently waited for Fatimè to return. This was not how he had envisioned the end of their trip. The door opened, and Fatimè walked in, holding some shopping bags. He watched her drop them and disappear into the bathroom. Yes, she was still mad.

She emerged from the bathroom and spent the entire time ignoring him as she concluded her packing. Kamal couldn't hold it in any longer, so he spoke up. "Fatimè, I'm sorry."

"It's not me you should be apologizing to, you know," she replied, her voice cold.

"I know. I did apologize to him before I left, but I also feel like I owe you an apology for embarrassing you," Kamal admitted, feeling remorseful.

Fatimè mumbled a barely audible "hmm" as she zipped the last box.

"I overreacted, and I'm sorry. I was just jealous," Kamal explained, his voice filled with sincerity.

"Jealous? Jealous of what, Kamal? A harmless conversation with someone who I was probably never going to meet again?" Fatimè questioned, her tone still laced with frustration.

"You don't understand. It was just the way you were with him, in your element. We don't have that," Kamal expressed, his voice tinged with sadness.

"We don't because you're not interested in anime, and that's totally fine. We're not expected to be into the same things. But you keep forgetting that we have a lot of other things we share in common, and I value them," Fatimè responded, her words tinged with a mix of understanding and disappointment.

She stood in front of him now, looking him in the eyes. "I understand that I shouldn't have gotten too comfortable, and I'm sorry it made you upset. But it is no excuse for your behavior back there. Next time, maybe talk to me rather than lashing out at innocent strangers."

Kamal let out a sigh, realizing the truth in her words. "Again, I'm sorry," he said, his voice filled with remorse.

"I cannot stay mad at this handsome face anyway, sooooo..." Fatimè started to say, trying to protest.

"Oh, I'm handsome?" Kamal interrupted with a mischievous smile.

"Uh-oh..." Fatimè began to protest, but her words faded as he planted a kiss on her lips.

Abuja, Nigeria.

31st October, 2017.

"No! No! No! No! This cannot be happening!" Madina screamed so hard that her entire body began to shake.

She grabbed the bedside lamp and flung it at the wall in a fit of rage. But it wasn't enough to quell her anger and frustration. With tears in her eyes, she swept the contents of her dresser onto the floor. Bottles crashed and shattered, some of the shards cutting her skin and causing her to bleed. Tears streamed down her face as hysteria began to set in.

The crashing sounds caught her mother's attention, and she burst into the room. "Madina?! Dume fe'ata? What's wrong?" She asked, her words rushed.

Her eyes scanned the room and landed on the chaotic scene. "Subhanallah! What happened here?"

Madina remained bent over the dresser, unable to answer her mother. Instead, she continued to cry.

Umma walked slowly towards her daughter and held her. "It's okay. I'm here now. It's over."

Madina clung to her mother, crying as if her life depended on it. "Umma, Mi somi, mi somi walahi," she sobbed.

Her mother didn't ask any more questions. She simply held her and let her cry.

"This has happened before?" Mujahid asked Umma, his voice filled with concern.

"No," she replied, her voice heavy with worry. "I have never seen her like this."

"This is not normal," Mahir said, his eyes fixed on his sleeping sister. "It cannot happen again. What if she hurts herself?"

"No! No! No!" Madina cried out in her sleep, causing everyone to rush to her side.

"Madee? Madee?" Mujahid called, trying to wake her up.

She opened her eyes to find her mother and two of her brothers standing over her.

"What happened?" she managed to say, her voice groggy.

The last thing she remembered was reading a message on her phone.

"I should be asking you that," Umma said, concern etched on her face. "I found you in a hysterical state, and I have no idea what caused it."

"No bandu mada?" Mahir asked, worry evident in his voice. "Do you feel any pain?"

Apart from the pounding in her head and the band-aids covering the cuts, Madina felt okay.

"I'm fine," she replied, pushing herself up into a sitting position.

Mujahid looked at her intently. "You need to tell us what happened. What triggered this frenzy? Have you been missing your appointments?"

"Hamma," Mahir interjected, his voice filled with compassion. "I don't think she's in the right frame of mind to answer all these questions."

"Mahir is right. You should rest," Umma said soothingly. "Whenever you're ready to talk, we'll be here for you."

"You should eat something," Umma suggested, concern evident in her voice. "I'll make you some pepper soup."

Madina nodded, realizing that she was indeed hungry. She adjusted the duvet, seeking comfort and warmth.

The door opened, and her other brother, Muhammad, walked in. "Umma, I got your text. Ko fe'i? Is she okay?"

He took one long look at Madina and said, his voice laced with anger, "It's because of him, right?

Lagos, Nigeria.

6th November, 2017.

"Do we have to go?" Kamal whined, pulling the duvet over his head.

Fatimè rolled her eyes. "Yes, get up." She tugged the duvet away from him.

They were supposed to return to work today after their holiday. The room was still dark, so Fatimè went to draw up the blinds and switched off the air conditioner. She switched on the lights, and Kamal groaned as they hit his eyes. He didn't feel like going to work.

Rubbing his eyes, Kamal noticed that Fatimè had already showered and was in a bathrobe. "I'm going to get dressed. Please, don't go back to sleep."

Kamal nodded and disappeared into the bathroom. As he hummed in the shower, he realized he was in a good mood today. He was normally cranky in the morning, he never understood how people had so much energy in the morning. It took him an hour or two to fully interact with the world, as his sister Hafsah would say. It was as if he needed time to marinate for the day.

After dressing up, he joined Fatimè in the dining area for breakfast. Fatimè was clad in a green abaya with crystallized sleeves, and her veil was rolled into a talha style.

"Whew, at last," she said when she saw him. "I was about to go get you."

"You should have. I needed help with a few things," Kamal replied.

Fatimè shook her head. "It's too early for your shenanigans."

He kissed her forehead. "Good morning."

Just then, Mrs. Simon entered the room, catching them in a tender moment. Fatimè quickly murmured, "Good morning."

Kamal had made it his life mission to always embarrass Fatimè with his PDA in front of their housekeeper. Mrs. Simon responded to their greetings and then turned to Kamal. "What you asked for is ready. Should I package it?"

"I'll do it myself. Thank you," Kamal replied.

They finished eating, and Kamal asked Fatimè to give him five minutes to gather something.

"How do you manage to always be on time?" she asked when he returned in exactly five minutes.

"Discipline," he replied, starting the car. "When I was younger, my father had a timetable for me. Everything had a fixed time, and you dared not be late for anything. It became ingrained in me. Something about being a soldier's son and whatnot. I'm very conscious of time. I don't like my time wasted, and I don't like to waste anyone's time either."

The drive was silent, with their hands intertwined. Her eyes would glance, and several times when he was controlling the steering with one hand, she would feel a little tingle and her body screaming, "I want him to drive me the way he's driving this car; turn me the way you are turning that steering." It was embarrassing how watching him drive did things to her.

When they arrived at Fatimè's workplace, Kamal offered to go in with her. "This is not my first day at school," she laughed.

"See you later," he said, kissing her cheek.

Fatimè took a deep breath and walked toward the entrance. This branch of the company was no different from the one in Abuja, except that it was a bit bigger. At the lobby, she met the receptionist, who escorted her to the HR department.

Within an hour, she settled into her new office, which she shared with another female architect named Adaeze. Adaeze was bubbly and energetic, reminding Fatimè of her friend Bisola. Adaeze showed her around and introduced her to everyone as her "new friend."

Fatimè was laughing at a joke Adaeze had just told when they heard a knock on the door. "Come in," Adaeze said.

The door opened, revealing a man in a well-tailored kaftan. The scent of his 'Aventus Creed' cologne wafted into the room as he walked in.

"Afternoon, ladies," he said with a cocky smile.

Adaeze waved at him. "Hey, Sadiq."

Fatimè's phone beeped, and she excused herself, leaving the two of them alone.

Sadiq casually sat on the edge of Adaeze's desk and asked, "Who's that?"

"The new transfer from Abuja," Adaeze replied.

"I know," Sadiq rolled his eyes. "You know what I mean, Ada. Details."

Adaeze shook her head. "Uh-uh, Sadiq. This one is not for you. Quit it."

He scoffed at Adaeze's warning. "We'll see about that, honey."

Meanwhile, Fatimè returned to the office, taken aback when she found Sadiq standing in front of her with a crooked smile.

"I believe I have not properly introduced myself. I am Sadiq, but you can call me anything you like. What's your name?" He asked, still wearing that ridiculous smile.

Fatimè was instantly irritated. He was standing way too close to her, invading her personal space. One more inch, and his lips would be on hers. She shifted back, a look of irritation plastered on her face. "Fatimè. Mrs. Fatimè," she emphasized on the "Mrs." part, hoping he would get the hint.

"Beautiful name for a beautiful woman. I was hoping we'd be friends. Maybe I can show you around?" Sadiq persisted.

Adaeze shook her head, knowing how persistent Sadiq could be. Did he not see that Fatimè was married?

"Thanks for the offer, but Adaeze has already shown me around. Excuse me," Fatimè said curtly, returning to her seat.

Sadiq, undeterred, turned toward her desk but was interrupted by a knock at the door.

"Delivery for Mrs. Fatima," the delivery person announced.

"Fatimè," she corrected, collecting the package. "Thank you."

If Fatimè had a dollar for every time she had to correct people about her name, she would be on 'Forbe's' list.

"I'll see you later," Sadiq said with a smirk before leaving the room.

"Ignore him," Adaeze advised, sensing Fatimè's discomfort.

Fatimè shrugged and opened the package, immediately noticing the black bow attached to it. She knew it was from Kamal. There was always a handwritten note accompanying everything he sent her, so she eagerly looked for it.

"Hey, sunshine,

I hope your day is going well? Here is something to make it better, though.

Kisses."

She chuckled, capturing Adaeze's attention. "Ouu, someone is smitten," Adaeze teased.

Fatimè smiled, appreciating the thoughtful gesture from Kamal. It was always the little things that made her day.

"Rukayya, I told you. I'll sort it out. Nothing's going to happen, for God's sake," Kamal insisted, exasperated by his ex-wife's unfounded concerns about their son's safety due to a stranger she met in a parking lot. Her paranoia was starting to affect him too.

"Aziz is already on top of things. Just calm down," he reassured her.

"Whatever," Rukayya replied curtly before abruptly ending the call.

Kamal sighed and shook his head, frustrated by the situation. He then called for the person knocking on his office door to come in.

"Ango! Ango!" Sa'ad hailed as he entered. "How far? What's with the face?"

"Nothing," Kamal replied dismissively. He wasn't in the mood to discuss his family problems with Sa'ad.

"Do you have any plans to keep me away from my wife?" Kamal asked, gesturing toward the pile of papers on his desk.

"Eh, ehn! In your words, you said, 'Drop everything on my desk until I get back. I don't want to be disturbed.' And since when did you not like work? Na wa o. Newlyweds be doing the most," Sa'ad teased.

"It's not my fault you cannot relate," Kamal retorted.

"Wow. Wow!" Sa'ad playfully held his chest, feigning hurt.

"Can you stop being dramatic so we can finish this up in good time?"

Kamal rolled his eyes at Sa'ad's complaints, but deep down, his mind was preoccupied with the issue Aziz had reported. He needed to resolve it as soon as possible.

Meanwhile, Fatimè finished praying Asr and eagerly looked forward to going home. Her day had been great, but exhausting at the same time. Kamal had texted her that he was on his way, so she made her way to the parking lot, only to come across Sadiq.

"We meet again," Sadiq said when he saw her.

Fatimè rolled her eyes. She assumed Kamal was stuck in traffic, which was why he was running late. Now she had to deal with Sadiq.

Sadiq hadn't noticed any strange cars in the parking lot, which made it the perfect opportunity for him to offer her a ride.

"Beautiful girls should not be kept waiting, you know," Sadiq remarked confidently, attempting to charm her.

Fatimè scoffed, ignoring him. She couldn't believe the audacity of some men.

Seemingly immune to her disinterest, Sadiq continued, "How about a ride home? My car and I wouldn't mind some company."

He flashed his car keys, hoping to impress Fatimè with his BMW.

She resisted the urge to hiss at his persistent behavior. "Where the hell was Kamal?" she groaned inwardly.

Just as she spotted Kamal's car approaching, she felt a wave of relief. Kamal stepped out of the car and walked towards them, giving Sadiq a stern look. He then put his arm around Fatimè's shoulder.

"Sorry, I'm late. Traffic," Kamal apologized. "Are you waiting for something?"

"This is Kamal, MY husband," Fatimè introduced Sadiq to Kamal, emphasizing the "my" possessively.

Immediately, Sadiq's demeanor changed. Nevertheless, he extended his hand for a handshake. "I'm Sadiq. We work together."

"Nice to meet you," Kamal responded with a straight face. He then turned to Fatimè.

"You must be tired, shall we?" Kamal suggested, indicating that they should leave.

Fatimè nodded gratefully, relieved to have Kamal by her side. They walked away hand in hand, leaving Sadiq with a deep sense of disappointment in his chest.

"Damn it!" Sadiq cursed under his breath. He couldn't believe it. She was married? He had thought it was just an excuse women used to ward off unwanted attention.

"Oh well," Sadiq smirked, brushing off his disappointment. "The guy looked like stiff competition, and one thing with him was that he loved competition."

Meanwhile, as they approached the car, Kamal opened the passenger door for Fatimè, a small gesture of chivalry that never failed to make her smile. She thanked him as she got in and buckled her seatbelt.

Kamal walked around the car and slid into the driver's seat, starting the engine. They sat in comfortable silence for a moment, the weight of the day slowly dissipating.

When they got home, Kamal insisted on covering her eyes because he had a surprise for her.

"Wow," Fatimè said as he saw the brand-new car that was parked in front of her.

"Do you like it?"

Fatimè smiled and said, "Yes, I love it. Thank you very much. It's beautiful."

The car was indeed perfect. Her favorite brand; 'Kia' with all its features.

"Want to take it out for a test drive?" He said handing her the keys.

Fatimè's eyes were already filled with tears when she said, "I can't drive."

Chapter 15

♥

Abuja, Nigeria.

July 2011.

"Adda! Adda!" Fatimè called as she sprinted up the staircase.

"Tims," Fatimè's sister scolded, giving her a stern look. Fatimè adjusted herself and greeted her with a Salam, but her excitement was still evident on her face.

"Now, what has gotten you so giddy that you are calling my name like that, eh?" Furaira asked curiously.

"Guess what, Adda? I just collected my driver's license!" Fatimè exclaimed, her face beaming with a huge grin.

"Yay! Welcome to the big girls' club," Furaira said, hugging her. "Now I can rest from driving you around."

"I know, right!" Fatimè replied, relieved that her sister would no longer have to chauffeur her around. Furaira loved driving as if she had an extra life hidden somewhere.

"I'm going to the salon. Want to come?" Furaira offered.

"Yes, please. I am due for a blow-dry. Will you make jumbo twists for me later?" Fatimè requested.

"Chab! That your hair that takes hours?" Furaira remarked, wondering how her sister coped with the amount of hair she had. It was just crazy.

"Haba mana Adda, useni," Fatimè pleaded, hoping her sister would agree.

Furaira waved her away dismissively. "I'll think about it. Go and get ready."

Downstairs, Fatimè attempted to negotiate a car with her father, who was trying hard not to laugh. "Okay, how about that Kia we saw on Top Gear?"

"Maybe Baaba should buy you a plane. Na a walwai gonga," Mubarak chimed in from the dining room, having overheard their conversation.

"Hamma Mubarak, you are ruining my pitch," Fatimè cried out.

"Madam, you're trying to scam our father. I have to step in," Mubarak teased.

Their father listened to their banter for a few minutes before intervening. "Mubarak, leave your sister alone."

Fatimè stuck her tongue out at her brother while her father added, "No car for you until you are 22."

Mubarak burst into laughter, teasing her further, "Sorry for you."

When Furaira appeared, she shook her head at her siblings' drama. They were at it again over God knows what. Ignoring them, she turned to her father, "Baaba, Tims and I are going to the salon."

He nodded. "Make sure you come back before Magrib."

"Okay," Furaira responded, giving him a side hug.

"Drive carefully," their mother advised when they encountered her in the kitchen. "Furaira, please watch your sister; you know how she can be."

"Yes, Mami. I will," Furaira assured her.

Fatimè crossed her arms in protest. "Mami, I am not a child."

"Yet you behave like one. Please, go and get that crazy hair of yours in order," her mother scolded.

"As if I did not inherit it from you," Fatimè muttered under her breath, but her mother overheard and quickly moved to smack her with a plastic spoon.

Fatimè was swift as she dodged the spoon and ran out laughing.

Furaira had already bid farewell to their mother, but she felt the need to return and hug her. "See you later, Mami," she said again before finally leaving.

"Toye yahata?" Hammadi asked his sisters.

He had just returned from a polo match with his friends and looked exhausted.

"The salon," Furaira replied, handing the keys to Fatimè. "Oya, bring the car out."

Khalifa, standing by the gate with his football boots in his hands, shouted, "You're going to let Adda Tims drive? Aren't you scared for your life, Adda?"

"Shut up," Fatimè retorted. "You're just jealous because you can't drive."

"I'm in no mood for your bickering," Furaira interjected. "Meet me in the car."

"Hamma, the chocolate money," Fatimè asked, approaching her brother.

"Kai, ke dai kina da naci. Come and collect," Hammadi responded, handing her two 1000 naira notes. Fatimè thanked him with a huge grin.

"Adda Tims, buy for me too, please," Khalifa pleaded.

"After you rubbished my driving?"

"Hamma please tell her to buy for me too."

"That one is between you guys," Hammadi said, walking away.

"Fatimè Faruk Ardo!" Furaira yelled from the carport. "Yan dillu!"

Fatimè quickly ran off before her sister could scold her any further.

It was a few minutes before 5 pm when they finished at the salon, and Furaira tossed the keys at Fatimè. "You're driving us back."

Fatimè's mouth turned into a pout, but she caught the keys. "But Adda..."

"But what? Weren't you jumping up and down a few hours ago because you can drive? Ikon Allah."

"Yes, but I'm tired now..." Fatimè protested.

"So, it's me who's not tired?" Furaira questioned.

"Adda now..."

"Adda Tims nowwwww," Furaira mimicked. "Please, drive the car, let's go. It's getting late."

Furaira hit play on the dashboard screen, and the song 'Price Tag by Jessie J' started playing.

"Oh my God, just kill me already," Fatimè groaned. "You're obsessed with this song."

Furaira pretended not to hear and continued singing along. She playfully extended her hand toward Fatimè, as if offering an imaginary microphone.

Fatimè gave her a playful glare but had no choice but to join in singing along, their horrible voices blending together as they sang word for word.

"See? I'm tired. Enough of this CAR-aoke," Fatimè declared.

Furaira continued changing songs using a button on the steering wheel. 'Adele's Rolling in The Deep' started playing, but Furaira quickly pressed next.

"No way! Put it back. That's my song!" Fatimè protested.

Suddenly, Furaira snatched Fatimè's phone from the phone holder, causing Fatimè to reach out and try to grab it back. In the process, the phone accidentally flew to the back seat.

"See your life? If you break your phone, you're on your own," Furaira warned.

"If it breaks, you'll replace it," Fatimè retorted.

Furaira unbuckled her seatbelt to reach for the phone at the back. "I can't reach it," she said.

Fatimè turned slightly to glance at the rear seat. "You have to move to the back to get it, ai?"

As Fatimè turned her attention back to the road, a delivery bike suddenly made an illegal overtaking maneuver, swerving right in front of her and catching her off guard. She tried to dodge the bike, knowing that slamming on the brakes would likely result in a collision. She instinctively veered to the left, hitting the pavement with a screech and then a loud bang as the car somersaulted twice before finally landing back on all four wheels.

Voices seemed distant to Fatimè as she slowly regained consciousness. She groaned in pain and forced her eyes open, her broken glasses making it difficult to see the crowd that had gathered around her.

Realization hit her like a ton of bricks as she pieced together what had just happened. "Innalilahi wa inna ilaihi rajiun," she whispered under her breath, seeking solace in prayer.

As she tried to assess her own condition, she felt sharp pains all over her body and the wetness on her face. Thoughts of Furaira flooded her mind, and she frantically searched the scene, desperately seeking her sister.

"Adda! Adda! Where is my sister?" she cried out, her voice filled with anguish.

Tears welled up in Fatimè's eyes as she scanned the surroundings, hoping for a glimpse of her beloved sister. The shattered remnants of her glasses prevented her from seeing clearly.

An elderly man from the crowd shouted, "Madam, you're not supposed to move!"

Ignoring his warning, Fatimè disregarded her own pain and continued to search for Furaira. Her heart pounded in her chest, and tears streamed down her face.

And then, she saw her. Furaira lay motionless on the bare ground, covered in blood. Fatimè rushed towards her sister, her cries blending with the sounds of sirens and commotion around her.

"Adda, please wake up! Pleaaaaaseeeeeeee. Useni Adda Don Allah. Wake up," Fatimè pleaded, her voice filled with desperation.

Deep down, she knew it was futile. The first thing Furaira had taught her as a medical student was how to check for a pulse, and Fatimè had done just that. There was none.

Her sister was gone.

Time seemed to stand still as Fatimè clung to Furaira, her cries echoing through the air. The world around her became a blur as grief enveloped her, shattering her heart into a million pieces.

"That was the last time I drove a car," Fatimè uttered, her voice filled with a mixture of sorrow and fear. The accident had given birth to a deep-seated post-traumatic stress disorder (PTSD) within her.

The mere thought of driving again sent shivers down her spine, and her anxiety escalated when she attempted to drive months later, resulting in a debilitating panic attack.

Emotional trauma consumed her as she constantly blamed herself for not being able to save her sister. The pang in her chest intensified each time she pondered the tragic events, accompanied by the haunting feeling that it should have been her instead.

Her parents had sought the help of a therapist, which proved beneficial to some extent. It provided a support system and offered coping mechanisms, but it couldn't completely erase the pain she carried within.

Kamal felt grateful that Fatimè had opened up to him. During their conversation, she had briefly mentioned losing her sister in an accident before closing off, tears welling up in her eyes. Sensing her fragility, he decided to give her space and wait until she was ready to share more.

He had always assumed that Fatimè's choice to not drive was simply a preference, perhaps a love for being a 'passenger princess.' The revelation of her emotional trauma shed light on the depth of her pain.

"I am so sorry," Kamal said softly, wrapping his arms around her for comfort. "I can only imagine how terrible it must have been for you. I should not have..."

"It's fine," Fatimè interrupted, her voice trembling but resolute. "I'll have to find a way to move forward at some point."

"And I'll be right there beside you, every step of the way," Kamal assured her, giving her shoulders a gentle squeeze.

"I don't want you to gooooo," Kamal whined, holding Fatimè by the waist.

She gently took his hands off and turned to face him. "Mufida would have my head if I don't show up, and besides, I'm the godmother."

Kamal held her hands and pulled her close, pressing her back against his chest. He placed his hands on her stomach and whispered in her ear, "This stomach is too flat. Maybe I should do something about it..."

Fatimè let out a soft giggle. "You're not serious. Allow me to pack, please."

"I would have accompanied you, but Sa'ad keeps filling my desk with work. Looks like he wants payback for the long vacation I took."

"As should be," Fatimè laughed, putting another abaya into the box. "Don't leave all the work for him."

"I see he has recruited you to his side."

"I'm always on your side, baby, you know," she replied, a playful smile on her face.

Kamal smiled back. "Hm. If you smile like that again, you are definitely going to miss your flight."

Abuja, Nigeria.

"Adda!" Khalifa yelled when he saw Fatimè at the door.

"I missed you too," she said, giving him a bone-crushing hug.

"Pest!" Mubarak called from the sitting room. "What are you doing in our house?"

She rolled her eyes and let go of Khalifa. Stepping into the house, she retorted with a smile, "Last time I checked, this is still my father's house."

"Always and forever," her father's voice chimed in as he came downstairs.

"Baaba am." She ran to hug him.

"Ati am. Mi yaunima" he replied, embracing her warmly.

She held onto her father while her brothers made retching sounds at their public display of affection.

"How are you? Noy lawol? Your husband?" her father asked, overflowing with curiosity.

"All good, Baaba. Alhamdulillah. Where's Mami?"

"Upstairs. She has been waiting for you," he informed her. He then turned to the boys. "Yalla, shall we? An kira sallah."

"Adda, don't open your box until I return, please. I want my gifts intact," Khalifa instructed.

"Yes, boss."

Mubarak decided to give her a pinch as his welcome-back gift. "Small marriage and you've added kg. Tsk."

Fatimè opened her mouth to respond, but Mubarak was already out the door. She would respond when he returned.

Before heading to her mother's room, she stopped by the full-length mirror at the staircase to see if she had gained weight or if it was just Mubarak messing with her. Whatever the case, she made a mental note to get back to working out full-time. She had joined Kamal a couple of times at their mini gym at home, but she knew she needed to do better.

When Fatimè reached her mother's room, she found her mother saying her prayers and joined in. By the time they both finished, her mother had concluded her Adkhar, and Fatimè engulfed her in a hug.

"Mami! Your favorite child is back," Fatimè exclaimed.

"Favorite child that got married and left me?" her mother teased.

Fatimè couldn't hold back her laughter at her mother's response. "Were you not the one who was pushing for it?"

"You look well," her mother remarked. "I am happy he is treating you well."

"Yes, Mami. Alhamdullilah." They chatted for a bit before they left as Madina was already bombarding her phone with texts.

They were supposed to meet the new mother at Aunt Ammatullah's house since Mufida was back home for the customary wankan jego. The party of aunts she encountered at the house made her cheeks hurt from forcing smiles as they kept asking if she was expecting. Fatimè couldn't wait to disappear to Mufida's place. What was it with people and asking such personal questions? It was nobody's business whether she was pregnant or not.

"Hey, hey, hey," Fatimè exclaimed when she opened the door to Mufida's old room. It remained the same, with only the addition of the baby's items. Mufida's sister, Nadia, was in the room with the baby, and they exchanged pleasantries before Nadia left to get some refreshments.

The bathroom door opened, and Mufida appeared, beaming at the sight of Fatimè. "Tims! You're here. Finally. I was about to revoke your godmother status."

"You cannot try it, ai," Fatimè replied, walking over to give her a warm hug. "Congratulations, habibty. No bandu mada?"

Mufida couldn't hide the smile on her face. Finally, someone asked how she was doing. "Alhamdulillah," Mufida said. "I am well, just trying to get used to the new status and all."

Mufida picked up the baby and handed her to Fatimè, who was now gushing, "Masha Allah! So precious and Handsome.

They talked while Mufida fed the baby, and their conversation was only interrupted when Mahmud appeared. Fatimè wondered how he had managed to escape the scrutiny of their aunts downstairs, but from the look on his face, he missed his wife and didn't care about anything else.

"Our one and only godmother is here," Mahmud announced.

Fatimè smiled. "Hamma Mahmud, en yalli jam?"

"Jam, Alhamdulillah."

"Congratulations. Allah maunin barkindi."

Just then, her phone rang, and Fatimè took it as a cue to excuse herself and give them some privacy. She answered the call outside the house, not wanting to endure another round of her aunts bombarding her with questions. It was Kamal calling.

"Sunshine, how was your trip? Did you arrive safely? How's everyone at home?" he asked in rapid succession.

"Alhamdulillah, everyone is fine. I'm at Mufida's."

"How are the new parents? And the baby?"

"All well, Alhamdulillah. And you? How are you?"

"Missing you terribly. Can't wait for you to come home."

Fatimè blushed. "I miss you too. I'll talk to you later when I get home."

"Okay, laters, baby," he said before ending the call.

The next thing Fatimè felt was someone grabbing her from behind. "Tims! Mi yaunima!" Madina half-yelled.

"Too tight," Fatimè croaked, trying to break free.

"Oh, sorry," Madina laughed and released her grip. "When did you get here?"

Umma appeared behind them and lightly slapped Madina on the back. "When will you grow up, ehn? Look at you, running around like a little girl."

Madina moved away a bit and scratched her back, feeling a bit embarrassed. Her mother had no idea how much she had missed Fatimè.

Fatimè chuckled and moved to greet her aunt.

"Fatimè am," her aunt greeted back, "How are you?"

"Jam, Alhamdullilah" Fatimè replied.

"Aha, you look well, my dear. And your husband?" her aunt asked.

"He's fine, Alhamdulillah," Fatimè replied.

Umma nodded and left them outside. Fatimè turned to Madina, asking, "You're not going in?"

Madina shook her head. "So that they'll attack me with the 'and you, when are you bringing a husband?' No, please."

"They just finished me too with the 'Are you pregnant?' question," Fatimè sighed.

"What are Fulbe aunts if they're not constantly in your business?" Madina said, laughing.

"I know, right? It's only been a few months. Let me catch a break, please."

"You should be glad you crossed over to Lagos. Imagine if you were living close to any of them,"

Fatimè shuddered at the thought.

"So, what have you been up to?" Fatimè asked.

"Nothing," Madina shrugged. "The usual work, work, work. Pretty boring since you left."

"Oh, come on, Madee. Intee and Mufida are here now."

"Yeah, yeah, but you know things are different. They're married and all, with responsibilities," Madina said, a hint of loneliness in her voice.

Fatimè knew how Madina felt, and she put her arms around her. Madina was her best friend, her confidante, her sister. "I know, boo. I know. It gets lonely over there too."

"Come off it. At least you have Airport Guy, and you still haven't given me the Japan deets, you know," Madina winked. "Did you...?"

"Ah, you naughty child. What about that guy you were telling me about?" Fatimè tried to change the topic.

"Talking stage," Madina replied.

"Kai, Madina! What kind of talking stage lasts this long, eh? And wait, I don't even know anything about this guy, apart from the name Mr. X," Fatimè said, curious.

"Chill. All in due time," Madina teased. "It's going to be the biggest surprise ever!"

Fatimè couldn't wait to find out who this mystery guy was because getting Madina Hamidu to fall for someone was no easy task.

Back home, Fatimè and her brothers were in her room, unpacking the gifts she had brought for everyone. On one side of the bed, she had kept all the gifts she got for them. Mubarak was still expressing his gratitude over the camera and lens cleaning kit she had gotten him. "Thanks, baby petel. I needed this, Wallahi," he said with a grin.

"You're welcome," Fatimè replied with a smile. She opened another box and handed a rectangular carton to Khalifa. He was ecstatic. "Adda! Oh my God!" he squealed. "You're the best sister ever!" It was the 'Corsair HS50' gaming headset, with its sleek design and immersive sound quality.

"Damn," Mubarak remarked. "You really went all out. So you can be sweet?"

"Someone has to be the good one around here," Fatimè jokingly replied. They spent some time chatting and Fatimè tagged all the gifts. She was almost done when she noticed a pack she had almost forgotten.

"Oh," she said, picking it up. "I don't know what this is, but Kamal got it for you." She handed it to Khalifa, who eagerly accepted it. "Wow. He remembered our conversation? We were talking about the latest spy gadgets," Khalifa said, a big grin on his face.

"Geeks," Fatimè muttered playfully.

Khalifa focused on setting up the hidden camera detector his brother-in-law had gotten for him. "Whoop," he exclaimed when he finished. "Let me sweep your room first, Adda. Let's see if anyone finds your life interesting."

"You're crazy," Fatimè laughed.

Mubarak decided to indulge his little brother, and together they decided to test the device. They asked Fatimè to keep quiet, and she shook her head at their ridiculousness, but deep down, she was also intrigued by the spyware.

At first, there was no sign of anything suspicious until Khalifa suggested they switch off the lights and unplug all the devices. Then, the detector started beeping, growing louder. Mubarak used the flashlight on his phone to investigate. "I saw something. Come closer," he said to Khalifa.

Fatimè listened to them, wondering if they were playing a game or being serious. Mubarak picked up the desk plant that was sitting on the shelf in the corner of her room. He asked Khalifa to switch on the lights so he could examine it properly. There was a crack on the vase, and that's where Mubarak pulled out a small camera.

"What?" Khalifa exclaimed. "How?"

Fatimè looked at them in disbelief. "What? What is that?"

"Guess someone found your life interesting after all," Mubarak said, trying to make sense of the situation.

"If this is a joke, you guys better stop it," Fatimè said, her voice filled with concern.

"Come and see now," Mubarak said, handing the small camera to her. "Someone has been spying on you."

"I don't understand. Spying? Why? How? What?" Fatimè's mind was racing, and she started to freak out.

"Relax, Adda. We need to find out if there are more," Khalifa said calmly, trying to reassure her.

Fatimè sat back down and watched as her brothers turned her room upside down, searching for hidden cameras. In the end, they counted ten of them: two in the electrical outlets, one in her table clock, one in a picture frame, the one from the desk plant, one in her bedside lamp, another attached to her curtain rod. And that wasn't all.

They discovered four more hidden cameras in her closet and bathroom. The revelation left Fatimè beyond shocked. It felt as if she were trapped in a movie or some twisted nightmare. Why would someone be spying on her? The invasion of her privacy made her stomach churn with disgust.

She had never felt so violated and confused in her life. How long had those cameras been there? Had someone been watching her every move, even during private moments like taking showers? The thought sent shivers down her spine.

"What else is there?" Fatimè whispered, her voice trembling. "Is my phone bugged too? Is this person following me everywhere I go?"

Her mind raced with a barrage of questions, each one more disturbing than the last. The realization that her life had been under surveillance by some unknown individual was terrifying.

Overwhelmed by the weight of it all, Fatimè instinctively covered her mouth to stifle a scream. The questions swirling in her mind became unbearable, causing her head to spin and her vision to blur. Before she could comprehend what was happening, her legs gave out, and she collapsed onto the floor.

Mubarak reacted quickly, catching her just in time to prevent a harsh impact. "Tims! Tims!" he called out in alarm, gripping her and turning to Khalifa. "Get some water. Quickly!"

June, 2013.

Khalifa knocked on his sister's door before entering. He found her standing by the bed, folding her clothes.

"Hamma Khalid is here," he informed her before quickly leaving the room. A smile spread across Fatimè's face as she had been eagerly awaiting Khalid's arrival all morning. Their relationship had progressed from friendship to a serious commitment, and they were set to be married in a few months. She couldn't express how grateful she was to have Khalid in her life. He was everything she needed and more.

Khalid had been there for her during her darkest moments, helping her find meaning when she felt lost after the loss of her sister. Although she still carried guilt within her, he constantly reassured her that she was not to blame. Putting on a large veil over her gown, she made her way downstairs. Khalid was sitting in front of the TV, watching a football match, but his distracted expression didn't go unnoticed by Fatimè.

"Baby am," she clapped her hands to get his attention.

"Mhm. Yes, yes," he responded with a smile. "How are you?"

"Good. Why do you look like that?" Fatimè inquired, concerned by his obvious worry. Khalid was usually a carefree and cheerful person, making his troubled state apparent.

"Nothing," he replied dismissively. "Sit down, mana. Is that how you welcome the love of your life? Your husband-to-be? The father of your unborn children?"

Khalid playfully shifted the conversation, trying to lighten the mood. Fatimè raised her finger to her lips, teasingly hushing him. "Shh. Before Mami or Baaba overhear you, Subhanallah."

Khalid chuckled, enjoying their banter. "Shy shy bunny. I'll be quiet then. But don't do all these 'kunya' things for me when we get married."

"Have you ever seen a Fulani girl without 'kunya'?" Fatimè retorted playfully.

"Fair point," Khalid conceded. "Have you finished with your supervisor?"

"After dribbling me, ba, finally," she replied, smiling.

Their conversation continued as they finalized the remaining plans for their wedding. However, Fatimè couldn't shake the feeling that something was bothering Khalid. She couldn't ignore it any longer and brought it up again.

"Baby am, tell me what is going on. I know something is up," she insisted.

Knowing Fatimè's persistence, Khalid finally relented. "I think someone is stalking me."

"What?" Fatimè's voice rose in alarm. She pushed her glasses up her nose, trying to comprehend his words.

"Yeah, I don't know if it's just paranoia or something else, but for the past few weeks, I've had this unsettling feeling whenever I go out. It's as if someone is watching me," Khalid explained.

"Inalilahi! Did you tell anyone about it? Mama? What about Yusuf? I should tell Baaba. He can talk to Uncle Abubakar. You know he works with the D.S.S. He can..."

Khalid tried to contain his laughter at Fatimè's dramatic response. "Bunny, bunny. DanAllah, relax. I told you, it's just a feeling."

"How can you tell me to relax? You just said someone is stalking you! What if something happens to you? God forbid! We need to take precautions. Please..." Fatimè's voice trembled with concern.

"I said 'think.' I'm not sure. I have to gather all the facts first, and then we can decide what to do. Besides, why would someone be stalking me? I have nothing to offer. I'm just a normal guy who works at a construction company. How much is in my bank account, sef?" Khalid chuckled, attempting to lighten the mood.

But Fatimè didn't find it amusing. "You think this is a joke? Do you know how wicked people can be? How they love to attack innocent individuals? Wallahi, Khalid, I'm not taking this lightly."

"Haba, Babyn Khalid," he said, trying to calm her down. "Fine, I'll talk to Yusuf, and we'll handle it. I don't want you to stress yourself. I need you to relax as much as possible. I'll be fine, insha'Allah."

"Hm. You promise to talk to Yusuf and get back to me?" Fatimè's eyes searched his face for reassurance.

"Yes. I cross my heart. The heart that belongs to Fatimè, my one and only, Babyn Khalid, my cutest bunny, my 'yar fillo," Khalid pledged, hoping to alleviate her worries.

Her face softened, and she covered it with her hands. Khalid realized that she had become so anxious just from hearing a fragment of the truth. If he were to tell her about the attempted hit on his life, he couldn't fathom how she would react.

Fatimè slowly opened her eyes and found herself lying on her bed. Her brothers and father were gathered around her, concern etched on their faces.

"Are you okay?" her father was the first to ask, his voice filled with worry.

She coughed weakly and winced, placing her palm on her forehead, feeling the onset of a throbbing headache. "My head hurts," Fatimè replied, her voice strained.

Her father turned to Khalifa, issuing a command. "Khalifa Please, Get her some Advil and a cup of tea." Khalifa hurriedly left to fulfill his father's request.

"I don't want you to dwell on this too much, okay?" her father reassured her, placing a gentle hand on her shoulder. The worry lines on his face softened as he tried to comfort her. "Just try to relax. I'll get to the bottom of this."

Fatimè trusted her father's words, finding comfort in his presence. The concern in his eyes mirrored her worries. "Okay, Baaba," she replied, grateful for his assurance.

"And not a word of this to your mother," he added firmly. Both Mubarak and Fatimè nodded, understanding their father's instructions.

The next morning, Fatimè awoke with a splitting headache. She stretched for a few minutes before reaching for her glasses on the bedside drawer. Once she put them on, she could see Kamal sitting in the hammock chair in the corner, facing her bed.

Closing the novel he had been engrossed in, Kamal approached her with a warm smile. "Good morning, sunshine."

Fatimè blinked, pleasantly surprised. "When did you get here?"

"Just this morning," Kamal replied. "I tried calling you multiple times last night, but you weren't picking up. So, I called Mubarak, and he informed me you weren't feeling well. What happened?"

Kamal gently placed his hand on her forehead, his brows furrowing. "Looks like you're running a temperature."

"I'm fine," Fatimè insisted, attempting to downplay her discomfort. "It's just a headache."

As she sat up, Fatimè began recounting the unsettling events of the previous day to Kamal.

"Wow," Kamal murmured, his eyes reflecting a mix of concern and curiosity. "This is crazy. I'm still trying to piece everything together. Who would do something like this, and why? What could be the motive behind it?"

Frustration laced Fatimè's voice as she shared her confusion. "I've been asking myself the same questions. I've considered everyone who has access to my room, but nothing adds up. Nada. I can't make any sense of it."

Suddenly, a surge of bile rose in Fatimè's throat, and she hurried to the bathroom. Kamal followed closely behind, his voice filled with genuine concern. "Are you okay?"

She vomited, the unpleasant sensation leaving her weakened. It was the third time she had thrown up since the previous night.

Fatimè emerged from the bathroom, feeling weak. Kamal guided her back to bed, his expression turning more serious. "Okay, that's it. We're going to the hospital."

"Kamal..." Fatimè began to protest, but he gave her a stern look, effectively silencing her.

"My sister is here!" Hafsah squealed in delight and leaped onto Fatimè, engulfing her in a hug.

"Keh, keh. What is this? Do you want to break her bones?" Kamal shot Hafsah a glare, and she retreated with a pout. "Ahn, masu wife," she muttered.

Fatimè chuckled softly, understanding Kamal's behavior. The news from the hospital had made him overly protective. He had even mentioned that, if it were up to him, she wouldn't lift a spoon again. She found it ridiculous. She was pregnant, not incapacitated. Nonetheless, they were both ecstatic about the baby, even if Kamal was being a bit extra.

"Hello, sweetheart," Fatimè greeted her sister-in-law, giving her a warm hug.

They all went inside, with Hafsah filling the room with her constant chatter. Fatimè's mother-in-law smiled upon seeing her. "Fatimè, dear. It's so nice to see you. How was your trip?"

"Alhamdulillah, Maa. How is everything?"

"Alhamdulillah, my dear," her mother-in-law replied. She then turned to Kamal. "Your father will be downstairs shortly."

They enjoyed a hearty lunch, made even livelier when Kamal announced the good news. Fatimè wished the ground would open up and swallow her, as Kamal clearly didn't understand the concept of 'kunya.' How was she supposed to face her in-laws again?

But to her surprise, nobody seemed to mind. Everyone was simply excited about the baby that was on the way.

Fatimè later found herself praying in Hafsah's room. Afterward, she spent some time admiring the portraits displayed on the canvases. Hafsah was indeed a talented artist.

An open photo album on the desk caught Fatimè's attention, and she picked it up, flipping through the pictures. Most of them were family pictures, and she couldn't help but admit that Kamal was an adorable child.

However, her gaze froze when she reached a certain picture towards the end. She thought her eyes were failing her. Removing her glasses, she cleaned them and put them back on, but the face remained the same. It was Furaira's picture.

Confusion and a rush of emotions washed over Fatimè as she tried to comprehend why Furaira's picture was in the album.

Chapter 16

♥

Fatimè decided against bringing up the picture on their way to her parent's house. The discussion required a calm and sane atmosphere, so she decided to wait until they got home, especially since they were leaving for Lagos that day. The trip had drained all her energy, from the camera incident to the pregnancy news, and now this picture has left her head feeling fuzzy. She had so many questions she couldn't wait to ask.

"Please don't dwell too much on what happened," her father assured her. "I'm handling it."

Fatimè and Kamal said their goodbyes to everyone, but her mother called her aside at the last minute. "Ajamo?" she asked, lifting Fatimè's chin with her index finger.

Fatimè swallowed nervously and replied, "Yes, Mami, Mijamo."

"Hmm..." Her mother scrutinized her, her gaze filled with knowing. "Take care of yourself and eat properly since you're now eating for two," she added.

Fatimè felt beyond embarrassed. Her mother knew, which meant her father would know, and by tomorrow morning, the news would spread throughout Abuja and Gombe.

There goes her plan to hide for nine months.

Lagos, Nigeria,

"Are you alright?" Kamal asked for the hundredth time after they arrived home. He had noticed that she had been acting strange ever since they left his parents' house. Could this be the beginning of hormonal changes?

Fatimè sat on the couch in the living room, staring off into space, pondering the best way to approach the topic. This is a delicate situation, and I need to handle it carefully.

"I found something at your house..."

"Okay?" Kamal waited for her to continue, curiosity etched on his face.

Fatimè produced the picture she had taken without Hafsah's knowledge and handed it to him.

Confusion filled Kamal's face. "Why are you giving me a picture of my cousin and her friends?"

Now it was Fatimè's turn to be confused. "Take a closer look at the picture."

Kamal examined the picture again. "Isn't this your sister?" he asked after a second look. "Did she happen to go to Istanbul University?"

He doesn't recognize Furaira in the picture. How is that possible?

"Yes," Fatimè replied.

Kamal pointed to the girl on Furaira's left. "This one. She's my cousin, Safaraah. She also attended the same university."

Oh, so that's the connection.

"Oh, no wonder," Fatimè said. "I was wondering why my sister's picture was in your family's photo album."

"I've never noticed it before. Safaraah used to spend holidays at our house, so she must have forgotten the picture during one of her visits," Kamal explained.

It's a simple explanation, but why did it bother me so much?

Fatimè nodded. Her sister had a reputation for making many friends, so it wasn't surprising that Furaira had even connected with Kamal's family.

"What a small world," Kamal remarked. "Unrelated, but you and your sister really look alike, Kaman twins."

Fatimè asked, referring to Furaira's picture, "Can I keep this?"

"Of course. Why not?" Kamal replied.

Fatimè looked at the picture again. They did bear a striking resemblance.

6th January, 2018.

I thought we bought a bag of these two weeks ago?" Kamal asked as Fatimè tried to hide a bag of cheeseballs behind her, but he caught her in the act.

"Ya qarei? Wow, you're embracing this 'eating for two' concept," Kamal teased, leaning on the trolley.

Fatimè playfully slapped his shoulder and threw the bag into the trolley. It was true; she had developed a craving for cheeseballs lately and could easily down 5–6 packs in one sitting.

Kamal chuckled and pushed the trolley toward the coffee aisle. As he reached for two bottles of 'Mount Hagen' from the last shelf, he turned and came face to face with a smug smile.

"Hello, Kamal Maitambari," the stranger greeted.

Kamal furrowed his brow. "What are you doing here?"

"Am I not allowed to shop?" the man retorted.

Fatimè joined them, holding two packs of Twinings, observing the exchange between her husband and the stranger.

"This must be your wife," the man said with a smile. "She is gorgeous, I must say."

"Yes, she is," Kamal replied, the frown still evident on his face.

"Well, I'll leave you two," the man said, touching Kamal's shoulder and giving it a friendly tap. "Nice to see you again, Kamal."

"The feeling is not mutual," Kamal muttered as the man walked away.

The tension in the air was palpable, and Fatimè couldn't help but ask, "Who was that?"

"An ex-business partner who nearly cost me millions of naira," Kamal explained.

"Hm, I see why you looked like you wanted to strangle him," Fatimè remarked.

"Come," Kamal said, breaking the tension. "I still need to get some toiletries."

The night hung heavy with silence as Kamal paced back and forth in his study. The soft glow of the desk lamp cast long shadows on the walls, accentuating the tension in the room. His phone vibrated, the sudden sound echoing through the quiet space. He hesitated for a moment before reluctantly picking up the call.

"Kamal Maitambari," a voice on the other end of the line, spoke, its tone measured but filled with an undercurrent of unease.

Kamal leaned against the desk, a faint smirk playing on his lips.

"Did you think you could escape it forever, Kamal?" The voice quivered. "Living with guilt is a heavy burden, isn't it?"

Kamal chuckled, a nonchalant expression on his face. "I don't know what you're talking about."

"You know exactly what I'm talking about," the voice stammered.

"What do you want?" Kamal asked, his voice dripping with indifference.

"Oh, you know what I want," the voice replied, a trace of desperation in its tone. "

A cold confidence enveloped Kamal as he listened to the voice unravel. He glanced around the room, his eyes settling on the framed degrees on the wall.

The voice confessed, "I can't take it anymore."

Kamal crossed his arms, a steely resolve in his gaze. "That sounds like a personal problem."

The voice hesitated, as if searching for words. "Maybe we can make a deal. A new arrangement. One that eases the guilt for both of us."

Kamal's smirk never wavered. "I'm not interested. Handle your guilt on your own."

As the call ended, Kamal's attention shifted to the phone on his desk. He dialed a familiar number, and after a couple of rings, Aziz answered.

"Sir?"

"Dispose of the issue. Swiftly and discreetly," Kamal commanded, his tone unwavering.

"Yes, sir," Aziz replied before ending the call.

Kamal leaned back in his chair, the corners of his lips curling into a satisfied smile. The game was still in his hands, and he intended to play it well.

12th January, 2018.

"Thanks, Henry. That will be all for today. I don't think I'll be going out again," Fatimè said, utterly exhausted. She just wanted to sleep for hours. Work had become more hectic for both her and Kamal at a bad time. While she was grateful for not experiencing much morning sickness, the fatigue and the desire to doze off by midday were overwhelming.

She pressed the doorbell, but there was no answer. As she turned the handle, the door opened. Mrs. Simon must have heard the car pull in and left the door open for her. Fatimè dropped onto the couch, removing her veil.

Mrs. Simon emerged from the kitchen and greeted her, "Ma, you have a visitor."

"A visitor? Who?" Fatimè wasn't expecting anyone today.

Before Mrs. Simon could respond, a voice startled her, causing her to almost jump off the couch.

"Wow, this smoothie is really good."

"Madina!" Fatimè exclaimed. "When did you get here? What are you doing here?"

"Today," Madina casually replied, sipping her smoothie. "I'm here to see my favorite cousin, of course, and also to introduce myself to my godson or daughter. I don't want any mistakes."

Fatimè chuckled at her cousin's eccentricity. "You're ridiculous. We still have months to go."

"It's never too early," Madina said, narrowing her eyes playfully. "Aren't you going to hug me? Na wa o. I guess I'm the only one doing the missing."

"Of course not," Fatimè replied, moving to hug her. "I was just surprised, that's all. You didn't tell me you were coming."

"Because I wanted to surprise you, duh."

"I'll set the table for dinner," Mrs. Simon interjected, leaving the two.

Madina pointed to the cup in her hand and asked in a hushed tone, "Did she make this too?"

Fatimè nodded.

"Okay, now I'm looking forward to dinner!"

Fatimè understood Madina's enthusiasm because Mrs. Simon's culinary skills were exceptional. Ever since she had a taste of the watermelon juice Mrs. Simon made for lunch two weeks ago, Fatimè had asked for a cup every day.

"So, this is what you've been enjoying? Ahn ahn! No wonder you're glowing and shining and all that," Madina teased.

"Madee, please," Fatimè laughed. "Come, let's go up to my room. I need to change out of these clothes."

Madina spent the entire time in Fatimè's room, filling her in on the latest gossip.

"Madee, please tell me you didn't say that to her." Fatimè covered her mouth with her hand, shocked by Madina's response to one of their cousins who had asked about her marriage plans.

"Do you want me to repeat it?" Madina smirked. "I told her to let people in happy marriages ask me that question."

"Subhanallah, Madina. What did she say afterward?"

"I didn't even give her a chance to respond. And, honestly, did I lie? Next time, she won't be asking me stupid questions."

Fatimè wasn't surprised; she knew her cousin's ability to hold her ground against anyone who crossed her.

"Nikam, come and see the 'what I ordered vs. what I got' mishap with Anisa." Madina handed her phone to Fatimè, who burst into fits of laughter as she viewed the image.

"Kai, kai! What is this atrocity? Who is this tailor?" Fatimè exclaimed, amused by the fashion disaster.

"Some girl on Instagram. I told her the vendor was bad news, but she didn't listen," Madina explained, shaking her head.

Leaving Fatimè engrossed in the pictures and videos from Mujahid's wedding, Madina began browsing through the clothing in Fatimè's closet. Holding up a teal abaya, she exclaimed, "Seeing this makes me want to go shopping, walahi. It would look so good on me."

"You always want to go shopping," Fatimè chuckled. "Now tell me, what's this about a therapist? What's going on?"

Chapter 17

♥

Lagos, Nigeria.

"Wow. I cannot believe you kept all this from me..." Fatimè's face showed clear hurt after her cousin's revelation.

"Tims, I told you, it's nothing," Madina insisted.

"Nothing? Are you for real, Madina? Come on. Do you know how I feel right now? Like utter shit. What's the point of being sisters if I can't be there for you?"

"You had so much on your plate—Adda Furaira's loss, then Khalid's. I just didn't think it was fair to add to it, you know? I could handle it, and I am," Madina explained, trying to justify her decision.

"How long?" Fatimè asked, her voice filled with sadness. "How long have you been in love with him?"

"It's been a couple of years, but I'm over it, honestly. I've made peace with the fact that it wouldn't work," Madina revealed, hoping to reassure her cousin.

"And are you okay?" Fatimè pressed, concern evident in her voice.

"Jeez, Tims! What's gotten into you? Abeg," Madina chuckled, trying to lighten the mood. "Of course, I'm okay. You worry too much. You'll end up stressing this baby... Wait, have you started shopping for baby stuff? I can't see any lying around. I saw this page that has some nice items, and..."

Fatimè let out an exasperated sigh, unable to comprehend how the conversation had suddenly shifted to baby talk.

Abuja, Nigeria.

15th January, 2018.

"So what do you think about the soil and foundation?" Rukayya asked as they inspected the building site for her restaurant.

"Based on our initial assessment, it looks stable, but we are in the process of conducting another test just to make sure it is suitable for construction. It won't take long, just a few more days," the engineer in charge of the project responded.

"What about the materials for the exterior? What do you suggest we use?"

"Considering durability, maintenance, and cost, we have included different options..." He handed Rukayya a file. "You can go through this to see which one works for you. We have provided all the information and also included our recommendation for this project. What kind of equipment will you need in the kitchen?"

"I plan on having a large kitchen," Rukayya explained. "With commercial-grade equipment, I would need space for refrigeration, cooking appliances, and a prep station. What about the outdoor seating we discussed earlier?"

"It is feasible. I have included all the plans in the file too, including parking and everything else."

Rukayya nodded and began perusing through the file. It seemed like the project was in good hands, and she couldn't wait to see it through.

"This looks good," she finally said. "I'll still go through it later, and if I have any additions, I'll let you know."

"That's fine by me. We'll commence work next week, in sha Allah," the engineer confirmed, heading towards his car.

Rukayya watched him walk away, contemplating whether or not to approach him. She had intended to keep things strictly professional, but the nagging feeling in her heart couldn't be ignored any longer. It had been there for a very long time, and she knew she needed to do something about it.

"Wait," she called out, stopping Fahad in his tracks.

He turned, waiting to hear what she had to say.

"I need to talk to you. It's about your cousin."

Lagos, Nigeria.

18th January, 2017.

You know those days when everything just feels bleh and meh and weh? That was how Fatimè felt at the moment. She had called in sick at work and just wanted to spend the whole day in bed, being a potato.

The house was quiet, and she had to admit she missed Madina. The one day she spent with her was a breath of fresh air for Fatimè. Stuffed and tired of sleeping, she decided to work on a drawing. She reached out for her glasses on the bedside drawer, but they were not there.

"Huh? That's weird," she muttered to herself. She could swear she had left them there last night before going to bed. Letting out her 65th groan for the day, she proceeded to search for them.

It didn't come as a surprise when her search yielded no fruit; she couldn't see anyway. The 66th groan escaped her lips as she re-membered that she didn't have a spare pair. The spare had replaced the main when it got lost, and she had forgotten to request another spare.

"Welp. There goes the drawing," she sighed in frustration. Today was really today-ing; first, she woke up with a banging headache, then there was the slow Wi-Fi, or was it the chaos in the sky?

I am going to be a father," he announced.

Dr. Tiwa did not miss the huge smile on his face; this meant the session was bound to be interesting. She had observed that Kamal had a knack for yapping when he was very happy or upset.

"Well then, congratulations are in order. And how does that make you feel?" Dr. Tiwa inquired.

"Excited. Being a father is one of the best things that has happened to me, and getting to do it again with someone I truly love, well, is great. Amazing, if I may add. Another thing that makes me feel good is that this will bring us closer."

"Closer?" Dr. Tiwa probed.

"Yes, with my wife. I feel the baby would be a great help in our bonding. I feel there is a lot of work to be done like we are not there yet. I want us to be solid."

"And why do you think your marriage is not 'solid'?"

"I am really happy. Fatimè is an amazing woman, and I am grateful to have her in my life. But sometimes I feel overwhelmed and scared that I would mess up."

"Have you talked to her about your fears and concerns? You know how important it is to be open and honest with your partner, right?"

Kamal nodded. "I suppose so. I am gradually easing into it."

"She might have her fears and concerns as well, and talking about them can help you both feel more supported and connected. More solid. What do you think your biggest fear is?"

"You know how my previous marriage was. I feel guilty, like I failed as a husband and father. I did not make any effort, and being that she had no issues or problems whatsoever made the divorce even more complicated. I love my son, and I want to be a better father to him, but I feel like I let him down by not being able to make the marriage work, by not trying to save it at all."

Dr. Tiwa refilled her glass of water and offered to do the same for Kamal, who declined. "It is understandable to feel guilty and regretful about a failed marriage, especially when it affects your relationship with your child. But it is important to recognize that you are doing your best to make amends and be a good father to him. How are both of you doing now?" she asked.

"Well, I try to spend as much time as I can with him and let him know I love him. But sometimes I feel like I am not doing enough, and even though he is still a kid, I cannot help but feel he resents me for the divorce."

"That must be difficult for you," Dr. Tiwa acknowledged. "He might still be a kid, but kids begin to realize the changes around them when they start being constant. Have you considered talking to your son about your feelings and seeing how he feels about the situation?"

"Well, I should do that. I don't want us to be estranged. You know, like my dad and I..."

"And how are things with you two? Any progress since our last talk?"

"A little, but it is still complicated. He is coming around, though."

"It can be difficult to have a desired result, especially if you have a strained relationship with a parent. Have you ever considered tagging along in a family counseling session?"

Kamal couldn't help but chuckle. "Good luck getting that old soldier to sit in a room and talk about his problems. I think I should handle this on my own."

Dr. Tiwa nodded, understanding the challenges of dealing with traditional Nigerian parents. There were a few minutes of silence before Kamal broke it.

"I have this unsettling feeling of my past mistakes catching up to me. There are some things from my past that I am not proud of. I have made some mistakes, and I am afraid they'll come back to haunt me and my family," Kamal admitted.

Dr. Tiwa's gaze was fully on him as she responded, "It is natural to have concerns about your past, but you can work to make amends and move forward."

Kamal shook his head slowly, knowing that there was nothing like 'making amends' with this situation. "It is important to remember that you cannot change the past," Dr. Tiwa added. "Just work on yourself and make positive changes. Focusing on the present and building a happy and healthy future is the most important thing."

The session ended with Kamal feeling relatively better. He just wanted to go home and cuddle with his wife. But then it hit him—his wife. He had been buried in work all morning and then this session with his doctor. He had forgotten to check up on her.

Earlier that morning, she had complained about feeling unwell, and when they spoke a few hours ago, she told him she was still in bed. Kamal pulled out his phone from his pocket, and the sight of the missed calls almost gave him a heart attack.

There were about eight missed calls from Mrs. Simon, three from Henry, Fatimè's driver, and two from Aziz. Something was wrong.

He dialed Mrs. Simon's number first, and she picked up on the first ring. "Mr. Kamal..." she answered, sounding tense, "I have been trying to reach you. Something happened to Mrs. Fatimè. We had to rush her to the hospital..."

"What? What happened? What hospital?" Kamal asked anxiously.

"Reddington Hospital."

"I am on my way!" Kamal said urgently and rushed out. This was not a situation he expected, and fear gripped his heart as he raced to the hospital.

Chapter 18

♥

January, 2005.

"Hello, is this seat taken?" She asked, standing at one of the tables at the outdoor café.

Kamal didn't bother to look up from his book and simply shook his head in response.

Pulling the seat opposite him, she let out a sigh before proceeding to devour her sandwich as she was famished. Today's classes had started at 7 a.m., and she was rushing through her one-hour break.

She finished eating and cleared her throat, which caught Kamal's attention. He raised his face to see who his companion was. The rose gold timepiece on her wrist caught his eye, and he couldn't help himself. "Wow. Nice watch!" he exclaimed. "Is that the..."

"The slide rule bezel Breitling Navitimer with a fantastic chronograph?" She finished the sentence for him, and they both smiled.

"It looks like someone knows her wristwatches. Impressive."

"A watch is more than a timekeeper. It is a work of art that tells a story."

Kamal nodded in agreement and looked at her in awe. She was beautiful, with her talha done perfectly, a great dentition, and the heavenly sandalwood bakhoor scent emanating from her.

The first time he saw her, she stood out in the crowd of students, her presence like a magnetic force pulling him in. It wasn't just her physical appearance; it was the way she carried herself, the subtle confidence in her walk, and the genuine interest she showed in the world around her. Kamal couldn't help but be captivated by the way she spoke, her mannerisms, and the expressions that danced across her face as she engaged in conversation. It was more than attraction; it was an unexplainable connection that left him intrigued.

This wasn't normal. No woman had such a profound effect on him.

Her phone rang, breaking him out of his trance. "Hello?" she answered. "Okay. Mido wara."

Fulfulde had never sounded any better.

She grabbed her bag from the table and stood up. "I have to go, or I'll be late for my class."

Kamal watched her walk away, and he was about to leave too when he noticed she had left her jotter on the table. Picking it up, he glanced at the first page, and there it was, written in cursive, "Piya..."

26th January, 2017.

Kamal woke up with a throbbing headache, the remnants of a haunting dream lingering in his mind. Images flashed before him, and he rubbed his temples to dispel the lingering tension. This was not the time for disturbing dreams.

He glanced over to his side, finding Fatimè fast asleep. He felt a twinge of gratitude for the temporary respite sleep offered them both. The past week had been a harrowing ordeal, especially for Fatimè. Sleep had become elusive for both of them.

After all, she was the one who went through the D&C. The words "Your wife has suffered a miscarriage" kept replaying in Kamal's head, a relentless echo of despair. The heartbreaking look on Fatimè's face when he stepped into the ward was etched in his memory.

He held her for a long time as she cried, feeling utterly useless at that moment. Even with her family's presence, she remained withdrawn. The vibrant smile and glow on her face were replaced by a shroud of grief. It was only natural that she was mourning.

He was mourning too. The anticipation of welcoming a baby had been replaced by the heavy burden of loss. Kamal blamed himself, grappling with thoughts of what he could have done differently, replaying the moments leading to the hospital visit.

In the words of his mother, who was trying to console him, "haka Allah yaso..." and he held onto that, seeking solace in the faith that time would eventually heal their wounds.

The clock read 7:58 a.m., and Kamal decided to go to work today. He needed something to occupy his mind, a temporary distraction from the weight of their shared sorrow.

Fatimè stood in the closet as Kamal adjusted his tie. He noticed her reflection in the mirror and turned to give her a tender kiss on the cheek.

"How are you feeling, my love? Did you manage to get some sleep?" he inquired, his concern evident in his voice.

"Yeah," Fatimè replied softly.

"I have a few things to check at work. I'll be back early, though. Is there anything you need?" Kamal asked.

Fatimè shook her head, her gaze fixed on the cufflinks she was fastening on his shirt.

"I've asked Mrs. Simon to prepare something for you. Are you sure you don't need anything else?" He persisted.

"I'm fine," she replied, summoning a weak smile to reassure him.

He reached out for a hug, and she held onto him, finding solace in his embrace. "Are you sure, my love? Maybe I should stay back. I can ask Sa'ad to..." Kamal's voice trailed off.

"No, I'll be okay," Fatimè interrupted.

"I'll be back early, I promise," he reassured her, gently brushing away a stray strand of hair from her face.

"Sure." She nodded, releasing herself from his comforting hold. "See you later."

Abuja, Nigeria.

26th January, 2017.

"They've set a date for our convocation. Finally. Someone can rest now. Although I haven't picked a dress yet, I was thinking..." Zahra paused when she noticed her boyfriend's attention was elsewhere. He seemed lost in thought.

"Fahad!" she clapped her hands in front of his face. "Are you even listening to me?"

"Mhm," he mumbled. "Yeah, yeah, sorry. What were you saying?"

"I was telling you that they've fixed a date for my graduation. What's on your mind, ne wai?"

"I'm sorry. I received some bad news a few days ago. Ammi was telling me that Fatimè..."

"Ah! This Fatimè again? Even after getting married, she still won't let us be? I'm still suspecting..." Zahra interjected, her frustration evident.

"Zahra! What's wrong with you?" Fahad's voice grew stern.

She scoffed and turned away, feeling the weight of her frustration. He had no idea how their situation was affecting her. His mother's disapproval of their marriage, the stress from school, and then, there was always Fatimè. Always.

"I told you to drop this agenda, ko? You didn't even hear the news. She lost her baby," Fahad explained, his tone softer now.

Zahra felt a pang of embarrassment. Yes, she wasn't a fan of Fatimè, but she didn't wish bad things upon her either. "I'm sorry," she said sincerely. "I hope she's okay."

"Yeah, I haven't spoken to her though."

"Are you still traveling to Bauchi today?" Zahra asked, attempting to change the topic.

Fahad checked his watch. "Yes. My flight is in four hours. I wanted to say goodbye to my love first."

"You can be sweet, sha," Zahra smiled.

"Now, what were you saying about a dress?"

Zahra drifted off into talking about dresses, while Fahad's mind wandered back to his conversation with Rukayya. With the latest news, he wondered if this was the right time to tell Fatimè about it. What if Rukayya was lying?

Lagos, Nigeria.

Kamal sighed as he stared at his watch. His plans of quickly popping in and out of the office were thwarted as soon as he arrived. His secretary, Favor, had informed him of an important meeting, and he had no choice but to stay back.

"The machine learning algorithm on the platform designed would be used to analyze traffic data, weather patterns, and other variables to help make better routing and scheduling decisions," Shamsudeen explained.

Kamal raised an eyebrow. "Can I see how it works?"

Shamsudeen, the team lead for the project, pulled out a tablet and tapped on it. A map appeared on the screen, showing a network of delivery routes and real-time traffic data.

"With this, we can input our fleet data, and it will analyze various scenarios to find the most efficient routes and schedules based on current conditions," Shamsudeen explained. "It can also help identify potential bottlenecks or delays and suggest alternate routes to avoid them."

Kamal leaned back in his chair, listening attentively as Shamsudeen launched into a list of potential benefits of the platform. "We are talking about improved on-time delivery rates, reduced fuel costs, lower maintenance expenses, better customer satisfaction, and so on."

"Sounds promising, but how do we know this is better than what we already have?" Kamal inquired.

"The free trial period would be used to test it out," Shamsudeen replied.

Kamal nodded. "Okay then. We'll run it for a month and see how it goes. Is that all?"

"Yes," Shamsudeen confirmed. "I'll keep you updated."

With the meeting concluded, Kamal stood up, signaling the end. They all left the conference room, and on his way out, Kamal bumped into Sa'ad at the door.

"Guy, where are you rushing to, haka? How was the meeting?" Sa'ad asked.

"Home," Kamal replied. "Fatimè is still not feeling well."

"Oh, Allah sarki. My regards to her, please. How are you holding up?"

"Alhamdulillah. Can you check on those advertising guys for me? They are coming in an hour."

"Sure, no wahala."

When Kamal arrived home, he called out for Fatimè, but there was no answer. The house was quiet, and it seemed like Mrs. Simon, their housekeeper, was out running an errand. As he entered their room, he noticed it was empty, and the unmade bed caught his attention.

Fatimè never left the bed unmade, even if she was running late. He had always teased her about it, but this was not the time for reminiscing. Something was wrong somewhere.

Ten minutes passed, and his gut feeling was proven right. He couldn't find her anywhere. He had checked every nook and cranny, but there was no sign of her. A defeated sigh escaped his lips as he dialed Fatimè's number.

Switched off.

"Hmm, where did she go to?" Panic began to set in. Just then, he heard the front door open. It was Mrs. Simon, holding a bunch of shopping bags.

"Mr. Kamal, you're back already. I went to get something for dinner," she paused when she noticed the expression on his face. "Is something wrong?"

"Where's Fatimè?" he asked, his voice laced with worry.

"She's not in her room? She told me she was going to take a nap before I left."

"No, she's not even in the house."

"Maybe she went out for a walk?"

Kamal dialed Fatimè's number again, hoping for a different outcome. But once again, it went straight to voicemail.

"Get Henry for me, please," Kamal requested, his voice filled with urgency.

Mrs. Simon nodded, concern etched on her face, and hurried away to find Henry, their driver and trusted employee.

As Kamal made his way back upstairs, he went straight to Fatimè's closet. There, he noticed that one mini trolley was missing. His heart sank, and he let out a defeated sigh. She was gone.

Abuja, Nigeria.

Hajiya Hauwa paced around the living room in full panic mode. She had always talked about how Fatimè would be the one to give her a heart attack, and it looked like it was about to happen.

"Jiddu," her husband called, "Panicking is not going to make us find her any faster. Useni wallina hakillo mada."

Still standing, she turned to face him. "How do you expect me to be seated while my daughter is God knows where a week after losing a baby?"

"I know, but like I said, it won't solve anything. We need to approach this carefully."

"Of course you'd say that." She waved her hands. "Were you not the one indulging in her shenanigans? Whatever was going on in her life, she'd just up and leave all in the name of 'needing a break,' now look at it."

He shook his head and excused her behavior, sensing the tense atmosphere. "Has Kamal gotten back to you?"

"No, and Zainabu said she's not at her house either."

Her sister-in-law's house was her first guess, as that was mostly Fatimè's hideaway. They had also called everyone, but no one seemed to know where Fatimè was.

Mubarak announced his presence with a salaam, his face looking all shades of distressed.

"Any luck?" his father asked after returning the greeting.

"No, and her phone is still switched off."

"Your sister wants to kill me," Hajiya Hauwa cried.

"Mami." Mubarak put his hands around her shoulder. "We'll find her, in sha Allah. We are doing all we can."

That calmed her a bit as she sat down and prayed fervently for her daughter to come home safe and sound.

Meanwhile, Kamal's face showed signs of frustration and anguish. It had been two days of not knowing where his wife was. He felt like he was going crazy, like his whole life was falling apart.

All the leads they had followed had amounted to nothing but dead ends. Couldn't she have at least sent a text? Just something to hint that she was okay. It was the uncertainty that was killing him, not knowing what had happened.

He had grown accustomed to the numerous calls that came in, but when his phone rang, he didn't think twice before swiping to answer.

It was Aziz.

"Anything?" Kamal asked, hoping for some good news.

"Yes. I'll forward the details."

Kamal waited for Aziz's message, and when he saw it, he let out a sigh and said, "Oh, Fatimè Ardo, the things you do to me.

Chapter 19

♥

Abuja, Nigeria.

30th January, 2017.

"It's been three days, fa. This can no longer be seen as her usual stint. What if something has happened to her?" Intisar still couldn't wrap her head around her cousin's disappearance. The whole thing was worrying, and she just wished Fatimè had reached out or something.

Mufida was the one who replied to Intisar, "In sha Allah. She's fine. I'm still suspecting she just wanted to get away. Things like that happen, I mean the loss hit her hard."

"I told you guys, we should have gone to see her. At least it would have helped. When things like this happen, you need people around you..."

"Why are you talking as if we just refused to go?" Mufida said, picking up baby Abdallah.

The 2-month-old had woken up from his nap and had started crying for his mother's attention. Mufida settled to feed Abdallah before she turned to Intisar. "You know we all had concrete reasons for not going. Or is it with this bulging stomach that you want to travel all the way to Lagos?"

At the far end of the bed, Madina was lying face up with the back of her palm on her forehead, oblivious to the conversation taking place around her. Why was her life like this? Always ten steps forward and twenty backward. This was why she hated hope; it was such a liar. Every time there was a glimmer of it, and it looked like things would finally work out, it would just dash away. Can't life just give her something good for once?

"Ehn toh, I know," Intisar said. "I'm still insisting one of us should have been there. What about Madina? It's not like she has anything going on."

Madina caught the last part and got up. "What do you mean by 'it's not like I have anything going on'?" When Intisar didn't answer, Madina repeated her question. "I'm asking you, what do you mean? Ohh, yes... Madina has nothing going on. Why would she sef? It's not like she has a husband to take care of or a baby... zero responsibilities..."

"Madee..." Intisar called, trying to placate her. "That's not what I meant walahi... I was just..."

"Just what? You are talking about one of us being there as if it was not a week or two ago that I visited her? Tell me, when was the last time you showed up for anything? You are one to talk when you are always whining about every minor inconvenience in your life as if others don't have problems. I set up meetings and you guys present excuses, 'oh I can't make it, you know Alqa is around,' 'I'm sorry Madina, Mahmud and I are going somewhere.' If I don't come to your houses, shikenan, I won't see you guys. You sit down here talking about us being there for each other and how I have nothing going on when I AM ALWAYS THE ONE MAKING AN EFFORT."

Madina grabbed her bag and walked out, slamming the door. The room was now silent, Abdallah had fallen asleep again, and Mufida put him back in his cot.

"We need to do better," she said.

Bauchi, Nigeria.

30th January, 2018.

The TV in the living room was tuned in to the E! channel, showing 'Keeping Up with the Kardashians'. She pictured her brother's response every time he saw her watching the show. He'd always go, "Why are you watching this rubbish?" To him, he didn't see why someone would sit and watch strangers act out their lives and call it a reality show. There was nothing realistic about these guys, he'd say. But she did not care. It was like a comfort show for her, an escape from her reality.

"I made awara. Do you want some?" Na'ima offered.

She shook her head. "I'm still full from that rice."

"Okay. I'll keep it for you, in case you still want it."

Fatimè smiled at her friend and was grateful for her hospitality. When she was desperate to get away for a day or two, she knew this place was her best bet. Fatimè and Na'ima had stayed in camp together during NYSC, and they had remained in touch ever since. When she reached out to her, Na'ima was more than happy to oblige. Her husband was a businessman who traveled around often, so they had the house to themselves. She understood more than anyone why her friend needed this, as she was no stranger to losing babies. She had lost the third one last year.

Someone knocked at the door, and Na'ima made a move to check. She then turned to Fatimè. "It's your cousin."

Fatimè nodded and grabbed her hijab. "I'll just talk to him outside."

"This can't continue," he said quietly. "I understand your needs and feelings, but you also need to consider your family and friends. Everyone is worried sick about you. Do you know how many times Mami has called to ask if I knew where you were?"

She didn't say anything, but deep down, she felt really bad. He was right, and she also did not want to involve him in her problems, but what choice did she have after she ran into him at the airport? She had begged him to not tell anyone where she was. Leaving her house was not intentional; she just needed to get away from it all and have some fresh air. The whole "almost everyone loses their first baby" or "another baby would come" was suffocating.

"I am sorry," he said. "I cannot keep lying. I feel like an accomplice to murder or something. We need to inform them of your whereabouts. At least let everyone know you're safe."

A car pulled up in front of the house where they stood, and Fatimè turned to look at him. He gave her an 'I-do-not-know-too' look, and they waited to see who it was. Fatimè's expression when she saw her husband was of surprise mixed with guilt because she had no idea how he found her or how to start explaining why she disappeared, or the main question which she was sure was running through Kamal's head right now, as to what Fahad was doing here.

Kamal looked at her and then Fahad, waiting for one of them to start talking. This was what Fahad was avoiding; the last thing he wanted was to have any issues with Kamal. He cleared his throat. "It's not what you think..."

Kamal was looking at him squarely when Fatimè interrupted.

"Can you excuse us, please?" she asked, turning to Fahad.

He nodded and walked to a corner. It was not Fahad's place to explain anything, and with the way Kamal's face looked, she'd rather do it herself.

"Why?" was the first question he threw at her. "Why would you do this to me?

"This has nothing to do with you," she said.

"Of course, it has everything to do with me!" he said, almost yelling. "From the moment you said yes to being my wife, everything about your life involves me. I cannot begin to describe the barrage of emotions I have felt from the day before yesterday when you disappeared till today. Do you know how fucking scared I was? Not knowing where you were or if something had happened to you? The mere thought of you not being okay was enough to give me a heart attack, but you're standing there looking into my eyes telling me it has nothing to do with me. Come on, Fatimè!"

"I'm sorry... it wasn't my plan to..." The tears had already started to form in her eyes.

"Oh no, no. Sorry, won't cut it this time around. And to think you were here with him?" He gestured toward Fahad. "What is he doing here anyway?"

"It was all a coincidence."

"A coincidence?" He gave a sarcastic laugh. "A coincidence that you ran away to Bauchi, and your cousin who happens to be in love with you is also here?"

What? Fatimè let out a sigh. What was it with everyone thinking Fahad was in love with her? In all the years they had spent together, Fahad had never told her he was in love with her. Their relationship was purely platonic, so she always wondered where the whole 'love thing' was coming from.

"Do not act like you do not know what I am saying. I have seen the way he looks at you..."

She decided to ignore his comment.

"It is not what you think. I just needed some fresh air, and I decided to fly over here, and..."

"Yes, and fresh air translates to Fahad, right?"

He couldn't believe his wife right now.

"Kamal," she begged. "I promise you are misunderstanding everything... If you could just let me explain..."

"Of course, you would explain to me why my wife needs to catch a break with another man." He crossed his arms and leaned on the wall. "And oh, it had better be a good one."

"I was not catching a break with Fahad, okay? Like I told you, it was pure coincidence. We met at the airport, and it turns out he was there for some office work. I'm staying with a friend. You can come in and see, walahi. Fahad just showed up now and was even advising me on calling you before you came in..."

She paused and looked at him. He was still standing with his arms crossed against his chest, and she hoped he believed her because it was nothing but the truth.

"I just wanted to be alone, okay? That house was killing me. It reminded me of my loss, and if I had spent one more day there, I would have gone crazy."

"And you think going away without informing anyone was the best decision? What happened to communicating? I wasn't going to hold you from getting some space. Wai, what do you think I am?"

He had a sad look on his face, and Fatimè felt bad.

"I am not going to lie to you, but what you did is just not it at all. I understand this is a difficult time for you, but did you stop to think about me? How I was faring too? In case you have forgotten, the baby was also mine."

"Kamal..." she choked. She knew she had hurt him so badly; it was evident on his face.

He didn't even answer and walked towards the door to leave.

"I'm so..." she began, her voice trembling.

"Don't," he turned, cutting her off. "There's no need. I am just really glad that you are okay. That's all that matters. I'll let you be." He said and got into the car.

Fatimè stood there, her face in her hands, as tears streamed down her cheeks. Fahad watched her, but he didn't say a word because, omo, she had really fucked up.

1st February 2018.

Fatimè listened quietly as her mother berated her on the phone. "A wala hakkilo na?" she shouted. "Kai! You should be grateful to God it's your husband who found you because the whole of Bauchi would not have contained you and me. I would have beaten the madness out of you..."

She did not say a word because she deserved it.

"Wadu munyal," she mumbled.

"Sorry for yourself!" Her mother said and hung up.

Tired was an understatement for how she was feeling at the moment, and to top it all off, she had a flight to catch. Yes, she needed to go back home and fix whatever mess she had made.Spending two more days alone had done her a lot of good. She was able to process her thoughts, and now she was ready to go back.

Kamal still wasn't picking up her calls, but he had sent an email checking up on her. She had returned the gazillion calls and messages she had missed, and now her main focus was to reconcile with her husband.

"How are you feeling now?" Na'ima asked.

"Better. Thank you so much, Na'ima. I really appreciate it. Thank you."

"Shh. You don't need to. I'm glad I was able to help. Just focus on getting better, okay? And about your husband, things will work out fine, in sha Allah."

She nodded.

"Now let's go before you miss your flight to Romance."

She scoffed. "Give up on making jokes. You suck."

Na'ima laughed. "I know."

Fatimè was unsettled throughout her flight. She thought about how to sort out her issues with Kamal. As usual, there was no reply, even when she sent him a message telling him she'd be returning today.

The air in Lagos was h for hot when their plane landed. She did not miss the weather. She pulled out her phone to order an Uber but paused when she saw him standing in the parking lot with his hands in his pocket.

The sun was shining on his crisp blue kaftan, and she just wanted to run into his arms and get lost in the scent of his Maison Martin. Kamal loved to match every outfit with a fragrance, and he reserved this particular one for his kaftans.He took off his sunglasses as she dragged her trolley towards him.

"Hi," she said.

He only nodded and collected the trolley. The drive home was quiet, with only the radio in the background. Fatimè was glad today's traffic was not so bad; the silence was already choking. She should have just taken her Uber jeje, or he would have sent Henry to get her instead.

Even when they got home, Kamal still did not utter a single word and went straight to his room. Mrs. Simon had asked to leave early, so she ate dinner alone. She tried calling a few people, but either they were busy or they did not want to talk to her. Even Madina was not picking up her calls, which was strange.

After three episodes of 'Bleach', she decided to call it a night. She was exhausted, and she had work tomorrow. She opened the door to his bedroom and found him sleeping. It was just a few minutes past 8 p.m. Damn, he really did not want to talk to her. Fatimè sighed and got into bed. The night light shone on something on the bedside drawer — a post-it note. "Here are your meds, don't forget to take them." She smiled as she took the meds. What did she do to deserve this man?

Bauchi, Nigeria.

"Ammi, come on," Fahad begged, his voice filled with remorse. "I said I was sorry."

His mother's voice rose as she berated him, "Do you know the magnitude of trouble you caused? How could you hide her whereabouts when you know everyone was worried about her? Even if she asked you not to, it was a very foolish thing to do. You should know better!"

Fahad mumbled another apology, his voice filled with guilt.

"I understand the relationship you have with your cousin, but you need to understand that she is married now. There should be boundaries..." His mother cautioned, her tone firm.

"Yes, Ammi. I understand. Wadu munyal," Fahad responded, his voice laced with sincerity.

"I hope it never happens again," his mother said sternly. Then she asked, "Did you go to that place?"

Fahad scratched the back of his head, searching for excuses. "Erh... I have been so occupied..."

His mother rolled her eyes, aware that he was just making up excuses. She decided to play along, knowing that he would eventually come around. She was determined to make sure of that.

"Make sure you go to that house before you leave Bauchi. Goodnight," she said, ending the call.

Fahad let out a groan, realizing he had no way to escape the situation now.

Lagos, Nigeria.

2nd February, 2018.

"Yep, that is all you need to catch up on," Adaeze said, handing Fatimè the laptop.

Fatimè rubbed her eyes, feeling exhausted even though it was barely 10 am. It seemed like she had just slept for two minutes before her alarm went off. Coupled with her husband giving her the silent treatment, she was beyond stressed.

"I'll get to it," Fatimè replied, her voice reflecting her weariness.

Adaeze embraced her in a hug, offering support without words. Fatimè felt grateful for her friend's presence. They worked for a while until Adaeze suggested they get lunch from the cafeteria, mentioning the new caterers and the delicious food they offered.

Finding a table in the cafeteria, Fatimè waited for Adaeze to return with their food. She was engrossed in her phone when she heard the sound of the chair opposite her shifting. Raising her head, she saw Mr. Annoying sitting there, wearing the same crooked smile that irritated her.

"Hello," he said, attempting to engage her.

Fatimè ignored him, determined not to let him get on her nerves that day. She wondered what kind of dunderhead he was for not understanding her repeated words of "stay away from me," especially after she had told him she was married.

"I see the cat's got your tongue today, but I don't mind doing all the talking," he persisted.

Fatimè glanced towards the counter, growing impatient as she wondered why Adaeze was taking so long.

"I haven't seen you in a while," he continued, undeterred by her lack of response. "Where have you been? I missed seeing your pretty face."

Fatimè paid him zero attention. Instead, she focused on her game of Candy Crush, determined to ignore him completely.

Just then, Adaeze appeared and scrunched her face upon seeing him. She was well aware of Sadiq's persistence and disliked his intrusion.

"Sadiq, what are you doing here?" she asked sharply.

"What does it look like?" he shot back, his tone defensive. "I am keeping your dear friend company."

Adaeze dropped the tray she was holding, her frustration evident. She turned to Sadiq, her tone laced with irritation. "Look, Sadiq, I have told you countless times that Fatimè is not available, especially for your nonsense shenanigans. So please, leave her alone."

Sadiq rolled his eyes at Adaeze, feeling unfazed by her words. He couldn't understand why she was so persistent in keeping him away. After all, he believed himself to be the whole package, and who wouldn't want him? This was precisely why he couldn't leave Fatimè alone. No one had ever said no to him, married or not.

"Why don't you let her speak for herself?" Sadiq retorted, making a move to hold Fatimè's hand.

In an instant, the cafeteria fell into silence as a loud slap echoed through the air. Sadiq held his palm to his cheek, his expression one of shock and disbelief.

Adaeze's face registered a mix of surprise and satisfaction, while Fatimè's eyes were burning with rage. She took a deep breath, adjusting her veil, and spoke with an intensity that demanded attention. "Don't you ever, in your pathetic life, try to touch me again, or I swear my fist will connect with your face."

The entire cafeteria was now watching the scene unfold, their curiosity piqued. Fatimè continued, her voice steady and determined, "And if you don't leave me alone, I will make sure you regret it. You do not want to mess with me."

With a dismissive huff, Fatimè turned and walked away, leaving Sadiq standing there, rubbing his cheek in disbelief. Adaeze quickly followed after her, concern etched on her face.

The cafeteria buzzed with whispers and murmurs, and Sadiq felt a mix of embarrassment and anger. He never expected such a reaction from Fatimè. He watched as she disappeared, realizing that he had underestimated her strength and resolve.

As the commotion died down, Sadiq slumped back in his seat, nursing his wounded ego. He vowed that he would find a way to get back at Fatimè for her audacity. However, deep down, a small part of him couldn't help but admire her spirit and the fire within her.

Kamal turned in his chair, his fingers locked, feeling the throbbing pain in his head intensified. Just when he thought his day couldn't get any worse, he glanced at his phone and saw an incoming call.

"Could this day get any worse?" he muttered to himself, rubbing his temples before reluctantly picking up the call.

"Oh, you finally decided to pick..." the voice on the other end began.

"Well, hello to you too," Kamal interjected, his tone laced with weariness.

"I did not call for pleasantries, Kamal," the voice continued, clearly annoyed.

He let out a sigh, realizing he had been neglecting his responsibilities. "I'm sorry. I have been really busy, but I promise not to miss the next meeting."

"Good. I'll be expecting you next week," she replied curtly, abruptly ending the call.

Kamal pressed the intercom button, summoning his assistant, Favor, who promptly appeared. "Sir?"

"Please cancel all my meetings," Kamal instructed.

Favor raised an eyebrow in surprise. "Even the one with the Huawei representatives?"

Shit! Kamal cursed internally. How could he have completely forgotten about such an important meeting? He couldn't afford to miss it.

"I thought it was next week?" he attempted to reason.

"Originally," Favor corrected him, "But their representative called and asked for it to be moved to today. I informed you."

Kamal's memory jogged, realizing he must have missed the email notification. Something was off. He rarely missed important details like this.

"Oh," Kamal recollected, "What time is the meeting?"

"In an hour," Favor replied, her surprise still evident.

"Okay, just cancel my other meetings," Kamal instructed.

Favor nodded, about to leave the room when Kamal called her back. "Wait, set up a meeting with Tiwa, please. Let's schedule it for next week Thursday."

Favor acknowledged his request with a nod, making a note on her tablet.

August 2009.

"Come on, babe, you can do it!" Khalid yelled enthusiastically from the stands, the only spectator at the basketball court. Fatimè was attempting to shoot the ball into the net from a reasonable distance, and he was there, cheering her on with all his might.

Fatimè took a deep breath, focused on her target, and threw the ball. The triumphant cheers from Khalid confirmed that she had successfully made the shot.

In his excitement, Khalid rushed toward her with an enormous smile on his face, as if she had just won a championship ring. "My little LeBron James!" he exclaimed, extending his fist for a celebratory fist bump.

Fatimè playfully crossed her arms across her chest, challenging his choice of words. "I am not little."

Amidst their banter, Khalid couldn't resist teasing her further. "Well, I'm taller than you, so you're little to me."

"Whatever," Fatimè replied, rolling her eyes.

Khalid grinned mischievously and mimicked her response, playfully mirroring her. Fatimè couldn't help but burst into laughter, enjoying their lighthearted exchange. These were the moments that made her appreciate Khalid's presence and the love they shared.

Fatimè channeled her thoughts and frustrations into the solitary game of basketball she was playing behind the house. Anything to distract herself from the anger she felt at that moment. It had been three hours since the incident, yet she was still seething. The audacity of that man to try and touch her, even after she explicitly told him she was married.

Scratch that, even if she wasn't married, it was a complete violation of her consent. She had no regrets about slapping him; he deserved it, and she wouldn't hesitate to do it again.

Adaeze's calming presence had helped to some extent, but Fatimè couldn't focus on anything else at work, so she decided to leave early. When she arrived home, Kamal wasn't there, and Mrs. Simon was occupied with her tasks. Fatimè was relieved that Kamal wasn't home yet, as she couldn't handle his silent treatment on top of everything else she was going through. Losing a baby, an upset husband, and someone provoking her—it was enough to drive her crazy.

Basketball was her sanctuary, her escape. It was something she knew would make her feel better, so she found herself playing her favorite game behind the house, desperately trying to forget. But suddenly, a sense of uneasiness washed over her. She took a deep breath, attempting to push the familiar feeling aside. Picking up the ball, she began dribbling, trying to find her rhythm. However, the more she played, the more anxious she became.

The atmosphere felt distorted, and the ball slipped from her trembling hands. Her vision blurred, and she struggled to see anything. Her heart raced, her hands shook, and she felt as if the entire world was closing in on her. Breathing became a struggle, and sweat started to form on her forehead. Clutching her chest, she felt a sharp pain, followed by dizziness. Losing her balance, she began to stumble backward, but before she hit the ground, strong hands caught her.

Chapter 20

♥

Lagos, Nigeria.

2nd February, 2018.

Kamal had arrived just in time, steadying her in his arms. "Fatimè," he called softly, concern evident in his voice. She wanted to respond, but her mouth wouldn't cooperate. He comforted her by holding her hand and gently rubbing her back. "It's going to be fine," he whispered, attempting to soothe her.

Once he was certain she had stabilized, Kamal carried her back into the house. Mrs. Simon inquired about the commotion when she saw them. "Uh, panic attack. Could you please get her a glass of water?" Kamal requested urgently.

"Sure," Mrs. Simon replied, rushing off to fetch the water.

When she returned, Fatimè had regained some stability and was sitting up, though her head throbbed relentlessly. Kamal handed her the glass of water, which she gratefully finished before resting her head back on the couch. The pounding in her head persisted.

"How do you feel now?" Kamal asked, his voice filled with genuine concern.

"Groggy," she replied weakly.

"That's expected. You should get some rest. Let's get you to bed," he suggested, worriedly.

Fatimè did not attempt to get up. Understanding her fatigue, Kamal gently scooped her up in his arms, carrying her as if she were a bride. He carefully laid her down on the bed. "Comfortable?" he asked, seeking her assurance.

She nodded in response.

"Okay, I'll be working downstairs, but I'll check up on you in a bit. If you need anything, just call me," he said before leaving the room.

Yep, he was still mad.

3rd February, 2018.

Fatimè stirred in her sleep, groaning as the sound of her phone woke her up. She tried to locate it, but by the time she did, the ringing had stopped. Glancing at her phone's screen, she saw that it was 2:33 a.m. She had been out for that long?

Curiosity piqued, she checked her phone to see who had called, and it turned out to be Madina. Seriously? Fatimè had informed her cousin about the panic attack before going to sleep, and it was now Madina chose to respond.

"Sorry, I missed your call. Are you okay? Maybe you should see someone. Call me when you get this. Xx."

Fatimè shook her head after reading Madina's message, dismissing it as an overreaction. It was just one panic attack in how many months? Besides, it was bound to happen. This month had been dreadful. Yawning, she decided to get out of bed and make herself a cup of tea. Kamal wasn't in bed, which was unusual. He typically had an early bedtime of 10 p.m. Was he still avoiding her? Whatever the reason, she wanted it to end today.

Fatimè found him in the downstairs living room, engrossed in his laptop. He didn't notice her arrival until she spoke up. "What are you still doing awake?" she asked.

"Working," he replied, raising his head to meet her gaze. "You're supposed to be sleeping."

"I've had enough. I'm going to make a cuppa. Want one?"

"I don't mind."

Fatimè returned with two mugs and handed one to Kamal. She settled on the couch, sipping her tea while watching him work. Her headache had subsided, and she felt relatively better.

"I'm sorry," she blurted out, tired of the silence. "I'm sorry I left. I know you're still mad at me for that, and I'm sorry."

"You think I'm mad because you left?" Kamal questioned, his eyes fixed on her.

"Then what? I don't understand."

"You still don't get it, do you?" He replied, his disappointment evident. "I'm not even mad. I'm just disappointed and hurt that my wife doesn't feel comfortable enough to discuss her feelings with me. I mean, even if you needed to get away, what happened to just telling me? It's evident you still don't trust me, and..."

"No," she interjected, struggling to find an explanation for her behavior. "It's not that... I..."

Her words faltered as Kamal mentioned Fahad once again, re-opening that wound. Fatimè rubbed her temples, feeling another headache coming on.

"I told you meeting Fahad there was purely coincidental, and we didn't even discuss anything," she protested. "I only asked him to keep quiet about my whereabouts."

"Yeah, right. I'm finding that hard to believe."

"Are you accusing me of something else?"

He remained silent, refusing to answer.

"Seriously?" Fatimè's temper flared.

"Don't blame me. You've given me enough reasons."

"You're being ridiculous," she said, frustration evident in her voice. "Do you seriously think something is going on between my cousin and me? My God! You better erase those thoughts from your mind, because there's absolutely nothing. I swear, and I'm really sorry about leaving. I shouldn't have done that."

Kamal approached her, holding her hands gently. "I'm sorry too. My emotions were all over the place when I came home and didn't see you. I got scared, and I didn't know what to do. I thought you had left me forever and wouldn't come back. I just don't want to lose you. I don't think I could survive it."

"I understand," Fatimè said, her voice filled with empathy. "This is the only place I want to be right now. This is home, and you are home."

Tears stained Kamal's T-shirt as Fatimè hugged him tightly. "I'm so sad, Kamal. I'm so sad," she whispered.

"Me too, baby. Me too," he replied, his voice filled with compassion. "But I'm always here for you. Don't forget that."

He let her cry for a little while longer before gently releasing her from the embrace. "There, there, no more crying. We don't want you to end up with another headache. Just hold on a moment, let me finish up, and then we can go to bed, okay?"

Fatimè nodded, wiping away her tears, and went to clean her face.

9th February, 2018.

Leaning against the wall with her arms crossed and a frown on her face, Fatimè looked at her sister-in-law. "I can't believe you needed a tragedy to happen before you could pay me a visit, hmph."

"Ahn Ahn. Haba mana, Tims. Don't say it like that. It's Hamma, Walahi. You know how your brother is now? Anytime I bring up visiting you, he keeps postponing the trip."

"Ehen? So it's like that? It's me and him."

"You and I cannot fight; you know that, as per your favorite siste r-in-law..."

"And the only one too." Fatimè laughed. "You'll always be number one."

"So, tell me, how are you?" Fa'iza asked. "And don't give me the usual."

She knew Fatimè's habit of hiding and bottling up her emotions.

"I'm fine," Fatimè responded. "I'm just finding it hard to adjust, you know? How emotions just hit you randomly as time passes. You think you're good, and then you see that stroller you bought or that baby and mama email you forgot to unsubscribe from. It's so hard. Sometimes, I think I'll never heal."

"Of course not. You'll heal, in sha Allah. It'll take time, but you will. Just know we are all here for you."

Fatimè nodded and proceeded to fold the hijabs they had prayed with.

"Have you talked to Fahad?"

"Since Bauchi? No, why?"

"I need you to talk to him. You're the only one that can convince him."

"About what?"

"This Zahra thing. Tell him to let go."

It was almost as if Fa'iza was begging, and Fatimè let out a sigh. She had no idea it was this bad.

"I thought this issue had died down?"

"Which died down? It's just getting worse day by day. He wouldn't budge, and Ammi wouldn't either. Me, I'm just tired because I'm in the middle of it all. They both keep reporting to me... ahn."

"But why won't Ammi let them be? I mean, this thing happened in the past, and the girl seems..."

Fa'iza chuckled. "We're talking about Ammi here, fa."

"Okay, what about Adda Farida?"

"She's with Ammi on this. As always. Just try to make him see reason?" Fa'iza's phone pinged, and she looked up. "Toh, your brother has started..."

"Ahn already? You've only been here for three hours, fa. He won't even let you sleep over?" Fatimè pouted.

"Hamma din?"

"Gaskiya ne! Adda na Hamma... ina yinku walahi."

"Let's go before he starts blasting my phone with calls," Fa'iza said, laughing and pulling Fatimè out of the room.

They met Hammadi and Kamal in the sitting room, laughing over something.

"Ahn, Hamma, I thought you'd be spending the whole day here? Or even leave Adda for me?"

"For what? See this girl, fa. Please leave my wife alone..."

"Ah, lallai." Fatimè feigned hurt. "I know where I stand."

"Yes, with your husband, and me with my wife. Kin gane?" He turned to Kamal and stretched his hand out for a handshake. "Thank you so much for the hospitality and for taking care of this big head."

"Anytime," Kamal said, smiling.

"Shall we?" Hammadi beckoned to Fa'iza. "I hope we can make it to Aunt Najma's because of the traffic in this town, sai a hankali..."

They all stepped out, with Hammadi pulling Fatimè to the side and whispering, "Next time you run off like that, I'll cut off your ears, walahi."

"Better than Mami, who wanted to cut off my neck."

"I don't blame her. You gave us quite the scare." Hammadi paused and placed his hands on her shoulders. "Please take care of yourself and call me, okay?"

"Thank you so much, Hamma, for coming. I really appreciate it."

Kamal and Fatimè returned to the house after waving their guests goodbye. "Your siblings should visit more often; see how you're smiling."

"I've missed them. It's nice to have people around." She picked up the tray of snacks and drinks left on the center table. "When is Adil coming again?"

"Next week. He's coming together with Hafsah since their holidays are clashing."

"For real? Whew! Finally, some noise. This house is too quiet."

"Are you calling me boring? Wow, Fatimè, wow."

"You're not boring." Fatimè laughed. "You're just reserved and quiet. It's comforting."

She moved to embrace him and added, "Very comforting."

The fruity scent was doing things to him as he held on to her. "My God, I love this woman so much."

The decision to get frozen yogurt was made after they planned to watch a movie and insisted on getting some to enjoy while watching.

Fatimè was now standing in front of Yogurberry, waiting for Kamal to bring the car around, when someone yelled out her name.

"Adda Nafisa!" she exclaimed, walking towards her to hug her.

Nafisa was a close friend of her sister, Furaira. "Long time!" Nafisa said. "How have you been?"

"Alhamdulillah. You? Kin guje mu."

"No, fa. I haven't been to Abuja in a long while. What are you doing in Lagos?" Nafisa asked.

"I live here, with my husband."

"Wow! Ma sha Allah." Nafisa beamed. "My junior sister is already married. Tabarkallah. Furaira would be so proud."

Fatimè smiled. "Please give me your number so I can stop by one of these days."

"Sure, sure... we should catch up. I've missed you. How's Mami and everyone? My regards to them, please."

"In sha Allah."

They were exchanging numbers when Kamal appeared, and Fatimè introduced them. "This is my husband, Kamal, and this is Adda Furaira's friend..."

"Oh, nice to meet you," Kamal said.

There was a long pause before Nafisa responded, "Yeah, same..."

She looked at him long enough that Kamal started to feel a bit uncomfortable, so he cleared his throat. "Uh, shall we?" he said to Fatimè.

"Sure." She turned to Nafisa and gave her a side hug. "I'll give you a call."

As they walked away, Nafisa was more than convinced that she had seen Kamal before, but she wasn't sure where.

Abuja, Nigeria.

10th February, 2018.

Zahra mindlessly scrolled through Instagram, saving anything that caught her fancy until a call interrupted her. She quickly answered, expecting his call.

"Are you home?" he asked.

"Yes, what's up?"

"Come out..."

"Now?"

He hissed, "No, yesterday. Please come out. My problem with you is that you're not serious."

"Sorry, sorry." Zahra laughed. "I'm coming."

As soon as Zahra stepped into the car parked in front of the house, the AC hit her face. "What's going on?" she asked.

"We've tracked down the culprit."

"Is it the person I told you about?" Zahra's joy knew no bounds, and she couldn't wait to tell Fahad, 'I told you so.'

She had shared the intimate pictures with her ex-boyfriend, and after confronting him, he claimed that someone had stolen his phone a week before the incident, so he had no idea how the pictures got out. Zahra berated herself for initially believing that he had deleted the images a long time ago.

After much persuasion, Fahad managed to obtain the number that sent the message to his mother, hoping that her cousin in the DSS would be able to track it. Two months later, Fahad told her to give it up.

The damage had already been done.

But relenting wasn't in Zahra's dictionary, and, well, it paid off. She listened as Kabir explained how they managed to track down the culprit.

"The phone theft was premeditated," he said. "Someone was paid to steal the phone from your ex, obviously to gain access to the pictures."

Zahra was bewildered. Why would someone go to such lengths to ruin her? For what? Seriously.

"Then why didn't they post it on some platform or something? If they aimed to tarnish my reputation, why did they send it directly to Fahad's mother? How did they even get her number?"

"Hey, calm down. Am I not here to tell you everything? The bad news is that we cannot pursue the culprit because, even after tracking the number, it didn't match the ID. It was some random SIM card that they probably threw away, and we have no evidence that they paid for the images."

Kabir handed her a file, and when she opened it, she exclaimed, "What?!"

Zahra's eyes widened in shock as she flipped through the file Kabir had given her.

Lagos, Nigeria.

13th February, 2018.

"Why are you so nervous?" Adaeze asked, laughing. "It's just a presentation."

"Arc. Akinyemi will be there; you know how that man loves to grill."

"Yes, but chill. I'm sure they will love it, and besides, from what I've seen, that presentation is too good."

"You think?" Fatimè opened the door to their office and found Sadiq leaning over her desk.

"What are you doing here?" Adaeze asked.

Sadiq stood up, his expression serious, much to Fatimè's relief. His crooked smile had always annoyed her. "I am the project architect for RCD, in case you've forgotten, so I need the designs for the new residential complex. If you had bothered to check your emails, I wouldn't be here."

Adaeze grabbed the designs from under her desk and handed them to him. Sadiq took them without sparing them a glance and left the room.

"I Am tHe PrOjEcT aRcHiTeCt..." Adaeze mocked him after he closed the door, and they both laughed.

"You're not serious, I swear," Fatimè said, picking up her laptop. "Let's go. I'm going to be late."

Fatimè's initial sketches were displayed in the conference room as she spoke. "As you can see, I focused on creating a building that is both functional and visually striking..." The slide on the projector showcased a 3D model of the building. "The main entrance is designed to be welcoming and provide an excellent first impression. I have incorporated a lot of greenery and natural light to create a relaxing atmosphere," she added.

"This shows a lot of potential," Arc. Akinyemi said, and Fatimè smiled. She was glad she had impressed him.

"Do you have any ideas on how we can cut costs or expedite the construction process?" Arc. Jada asked.

"Yes," Fatimè responded. "I believe there are a few areas where we could make some changes without sacrificing the overall quality of the design."

She explained some of the adjustments she had made to the project to reduce costs without compromising the design.

"Can I see a video of that render again?" It was Arc. Akinyemi asked this time.

Fatimè nodded and accidentally clicked on another file in the folder. Before she could react, the video started playing.

The sound emanating from the video echoed through the room, silencing everyone. The stares Fatimè received from her superiors were laden with disbelief and curiosity. She rushed to turn it off, but her laptop chose that moment to freeze, pushing her to the brink of panic. The awkward silence persisted until Arc. Akinyemi unplugged the projector cable, and the screen went blank.

Fatimè held her head in her hands. "I'm sorry, I had no idea..."

Arc. Jada cleared his throat. "It's alright. Just step outside, compose yourself, and come back when you're ready."

Walking out of the room felt like a walk of shame. She was beyond embarrassed, but the big question was, how the hell did a video like that end up on her laptop?

Chapter 21

♥

Lagos, Nigeria.

17th February, 2018.

You know that thing where you get scolded for something you did not do? – That was what Fatimè's predicament was looking like. She remembered when she was much younger, her brother, Khalifa would misbehave and her mother would scold her too. It was always, 'Where were you?' 'Why did you not stop him? 'Did you not see him?' as if she was not struggling with her poor eyesight already.

Fatimè cursed whoever planted the embarrassing video that made her look bad in front of her bosses—recalling her talk with HR Manager Arc. Yemi, she apologized, genuinely shocked about the video.

"I didn't expect this from you, Mrs. Fatimè."

"I know, sir, and I am deeply sorry. I swear I have no clue how that video got into my system. I'm as shocked as you are."

Arc. Yemi, who'd known Fatimè since childhood as the daughter of one of their partners, vouched for her character. He acknowledged her hard work and decency even before she joined their company.

she never for once, used the title of her father being the owner of the company as a ground to misbehave.

"I understand," he said, "But the problem is the video was inappropriate for a professional presentation. Unfortunately, there have to be consequences. You'll be off the project temporarily while we investigate."

Fatimè felt really disappointed. She loved that project. She nodded and left his office, relieved she wasn't suspended or fired.

The ringing of her phone interrupted Fatimè's thoughts. It was Fahad. She felt relieved as she recalled promising Adda Fa'iza to talk to him.

"Butter... Fatimè. How are you?"

He was still trying to get used to not calling her by the nickname he had given her years ago.

"Alhamdulillah. How are you?"

"Great," he replied, sensing something off. "You sure you're okay? You don't sound good. Still thinking about the baby?"

"No, not that. Something happened at work..."

"That's messed up!" Fahad exclaimed after Fatimè spilled the details. "Any idea who did it?"

"No. No one has access to my work laptop. But why would someone do this to me?"

"People do things, you know? Maybe someone at work has a grudge."

Fatimè paused, recalling the incident with Sadiq. "Nah, can't be him. He wouldn't stoop that low."

"What happened?" Fahad asked.

Fatimè explained about Sadiq and the cafeteria incident. "Think he's behind this?"

"We can't say for sure. We need proof. Check if he touched your laptop, maybe office cameras can help."

She decided to discuss it with Adaeze on Monday.

"Enough about me," Fatimè said. "I've been wanting to talk to you. About Zahra..."

Fahad groaned. "Not you too. Adda Fa'i put you up to this?"

"No, but we're just looking out for you..."

"This is draining. Everyone thinks they know what's best for me. No shit, I just want to be with this girl. I wish Ammi understood, but I'm hopeful. Been praying, and I know it'll happen."

"In sha Allah," Fatimè said.

"Gotta take this call. We'll talk." Fahad hung up, another failed attempt to discuss his talk with Rukayya.

A knock echoed through her door, and upon opening it, Fatimè found Hafsah with a stack of books. "What's up?" Fatimè inquired. "Have you guys had lunch?"

"Yes. Yes." Hafsah replied. "Full to the brim that it knocked Adil out. Whew."

Fatimè chuckled, understanding Hafsah's relief. For the past few days, managing Adil's boundless energy had been a challenge, his preference being running around and playing with slime.

"I'm trying to complete this mid-semester homework and need a flash drive to print something. Do you happen to have one?"

"Erhm, I don't think so, but Kamal might have one. Let me check for you," Fatimè offered, retrieving a flash drive from Kamal's study.

"Thank you! Let me hurry and finish before nephew Gremlin wakes up," Hafsah said as she walked out.

Upon returning, Hafsah caught Fatimè putting away her laundry. "Ahn, you've finished already?" Fatimè asked, observing Hafsah suppress a giggle.

"No. no," Hafsah laughed. "Ya Kamal is really into you, it's cute."

Fatimè hung the abaya she was holding and tilted her head. "You have started ko?"

Hafsah, in her typical 'awing' and 'cooing' manner, showed Fatimè her laptop screen. "This flash drive is filled with your pictures. Like hundreds of them..."

"What? Let me see..."

As Fatimè scrolled through the pictures, she discovered over a hundred images, some unfamiliar. Bewildered, she clicked on one, recognizing an outfit from ten years ago, a gift from Baaba.

What?? She wondered, perplexed by Kamal's extensive collection. The pressing question remained – where did he get all these pictures?

"Thank you," Kamal murmured as she unbuttoned the last shirt button, planting a soft kiss on her neck before disappearing into the bathroom for a shower. Re-emerging in a plain t-shirt and sleep pants, he yawned and rubbed his neck.

"Walahi, I cannot wait for this project to be over. I am so exhausted. I hate keeping late nights," he expressed, sinking into the bed.

"When are you finishing?" Fatimè asked.

"Hopefully by the end of this week," he replied, letting out another yawn.

Fatimè dropped her phone on the nightstand and shifted toward the center of the bed.

"I miss you," Kamal admitted, resting his head on her chest. "I don't like being away from you."

As she ran her fingers through his damp hair, the scent of his Aveda body wash enveloped her. His breathing slowed, and he visibly relaxed. Being in his wife's arms was all he needed to shake off exhaustion.

After a while, Fatimè cleared her throat. "So, Hafsah needed a flash drive today for her assignment, and I got one from your study."

"Oh," Kamal mumbled, still enjoying the head rub.

"Yes, but I saw something else."

"What?" Kamal asked nonchalantly.

"It was filled with my pictures, and I was just wondering where you got them from. The pictures aren't recent, some I don't even know about them."

He released himself from her hold, "oh, oh, oh. Oh jeez. You were not supposed to see that. Damn."

"What do you mean?" Fatimè asked, now confused.

"The surprise has been ruined. I was planning a little something for your birthday, a picture collage from a gift page on Instagram. Madina helped me collect pictures of you over the years."

Everything now made sense, and Fatimè understood the unexpected pictures.

"I was just shocked, you know..." she admitted.

"That a man has a flash drive with pictures of his wife? Come on," Kamal laughed.

"I'm sorry I ruined your surprise."

"It's fine. I am still getting it though, it's too good," Kamal assured her, returning to his previous position. Moments later, he was snoring away in her arms.

Fatimè shook her head; he really was exhausted.

Abuja, Nigeria.

19th February, 2018.

"No, listen to me. If I'd known you'd mess this up, I wouldn't have asked you to handle it," Madina seethed, frustration crackling through the phone's touchscreen before she abruptly ended the call.

At that moment, Madina's mother gently pushed the door to her room ajar, arms laden with a colorful assortment of fabrics that she dropped onto the bed. "Who are you fighting with now?" she asked, curiosity and concern evident in her voice.

Madina, still visibly annoyed, replied, "Just some guy from work. He's been botching up a critical case we're handling."

"Oh," her mother remarked, taking a seat on the bed amidst the sprawl of fabrics. "I picked these up from Jidda. Choose the ones you like so we can get them to the tailor in time."

Madina sifted through the richly adorned wrappers, selecting three and handing them to her mother. "I'm not sure about the style yet, but it has to be something simple. We don't want a repeat of last year."

Her mind flashed back to the fashion fiasco of the previous Eid, prompting her to give away the disastrous clothes and opt for an abaya.

"Alright. These should look lovely on you," her mother commented. "I'll have Usman come by tomorrow to collect them. Does he still need to take your measurements?"

Madina nodded and cleared her throat. "Um, umma, I wanted to talk to you about Fahad."

"Ehn ko fe'i?" her mother responded, furrowing her brow with intrigue.

"Umma, come on," Madina implored. "You know what I mean, and you're the only one Aunt Zainabu would listen to. Please, talk to her. Useni. Honestly, Fahad is miserable. You should've seen him the last time he visited."

"So, you support him marrying a girl like that?"

"Umma, I'm pretty sure Fahad knows what he's doing, and he's okay with it. People make mistakes, and everyone deserves a second chance if they're sincere about making amends. Just imagine if it were me..."

"God forbid!" her mother exclaimed, almost startling Madina. "Allah hoinu."

The conversation took a sudden turn into a sermon, and Madina rubbed her temples as she let her mother continue.

"Umma, please, relax," she implored, her voice calmer now. "In sha Allah, I won't do something like that, trust me. But this isn't about me; it's about Fahad and how he's being denied the chance to be with someone he loves. In today's world, finding someone you love who loves you back is rare..."

Madina felt a lump forming in her throat, making it difficult to speak. She quickly composed herself. "Please, just let him be if that's what he truly wants."

Her mother shrugged and gathered the fabrics from the bed. "I'll call Zainabu tomorrow," she said before leaving the room.

Lagos, Nigeria.

24th February, 2018.

"Adil, hold still," Kamal warned as he attempted to tie the boy's shoelaces. However, Adil seemed determined to break free and run around the airport.

"Let me do it," Fatimè offered, squatting beside Kamal. Her nimble fingers swiftly completed the task just as their flight was announced. The holiday had sadly come to an end, and Adil and Hafsah were set to return to Abuja today.

"Are you absolutely certain you haven't forgotten anything?" Kamal inquired, his tone tinged with a touch of exasperation. "I don't want to receive any 'can you send over' requests from you later."

"Yes, Ya Kamal, I've packed everything," Hafsah reassured before leaning in to whisper to her sister-in-law. "But just in case, you'll be the one I'll call."

Fatimè chuckled and gave Hafsah a side hug. "Of course, I've got your back. Thank you for coming; I'm going to miss you."

"Will you miss me too?" Adil chimed in.

"Of course, sweetheart, I'll miss you more. I can't wait for you to come back during the next holiday."

"Daddy, don't forget the game, okay? The one you promised me," Adil reminded Kamal.

"As long as you pass your exams, I'll get it for you, In sha Allah," Kamal assured him. He turned to Hafsah. "And you, Hafsah, don't worry, I haven't forgotten about the 'iPad' you mentioned. Now, let's get going before you miss your flight."

Fatimè and Kamal exchanged hugs with their departing guests before sending them off to board the plane.

"Don't forget to call me when you arrive," Kamal reminded Hafsah as they walked away.

Hafsah gave him a thumbs-up, and he turned to Fatimè. "Where did you say her address was again?"

Fatimè had mentioned that she wanted to visit her sister's friend, whom she had met recently.

"Let me check," she said, scrolling through her messages. "It's in Maryland."

"Okay, that's at least an hour's drive, maybe more with traffic," Kamal observed, glancing at his watch. "It's already past 10; we should arrive before Zuhr."

Fatimè nodded and texted Nafisa that she was on her way.

"What about your work stuff?" Kamal inquired, ten minutes into the drive. "Have they still not investigated who's behind the video?"

"No," Fatimè replied, her mind weighing the decision to disclose her recent conversation with Fahad. She knew Kamal would be infuriated when he learned about the cafeteria incident involving Sadiq, but she had no choice. It was better he heard it from her.

"I might have an idea," she began, and Kamal listened to her with full attention.

Fatimè recounted the whole story, holding nothing back. Kamal clenched the steering wheel, and his jaw tightened in anger.

"That swine! I knew there was something off about him. How dare he???" Kamal seethed, his voice edged with fury.

"Please, calm down," Fatimè urged, reaching out to place her hands on his shoulders, trying to pacify his mounting rage.

Kamal's eyes remained fixed on the road, but the tension in his body was palpable. "Why didn't you tell me?"

"Because It's just a speculation, and I didn't think he could stoop so low. It's not..."

"It's not what, huh?" Kamal interrupted sharply. "Men like that infuriate me, men who lack respect for women. Regardless of the fact that you are married to me, he should not be treating any woman like that, period. He needs to get a grip, for God's sake. No should mean no."

Fatimè acknowledged that Kamal had every right to be angry, so she chose to remain silent.

"You're filing a complaint first thing on Monday, and if they don't take action, I will," Kamal declared with a stern determination that left no room for doubt. There was no sympathy for Sadiq in Kamal's tone.

As Fatimè stepped into Nafisa's welcoming home, the walls adorned with scribbles and the remote missing its back cover hinted at the presence of lively children. With Nafisa's family out for the moment, the house offered them a tranquil space to connect. Engrossed in hours of conversation, Fatimè felt a renewed sense of vitality, realizing how much she needed friends in this new town.

"Ah, Adda Nafi, this tea is amazing. I haven't had tea this good in a long while," Fatimè expressed with genuine appreciation.

"This is one of Furaira's special recipes. She practically bombarded us with it back in school; I have been holding on to it for years," Nafisa replied, pouring herself another cup.

"No wonder, Adda made the best teas. No exaggeration," Fatimè added. She loved tea, but when it came to brewing it, her sister Furaira was in a league of her own. Besides her medical career, Furaira had taken brewing teas seriously, even compiling a book of her recipes. Fatimè and their father had been her designated taste-testers.

Nafisa sighed as she sipped her tea. "I miss her. A lot. We had so many plans, and we were on our way to becoming the best neurosurgeons this country had ever seen. This whole doctor thing just doesn't feel right without her."

"Me too. I don't even know how I'm managing without her. Adda was someone I could always rely on, no matter what. She was just always there," Fatimè shared.

"Furaira was that way with everyone," Nafisa added, her voice wistful. "Once she took you under her wing, shikenan. She'd always have your back."

"Sometimes, I wonder how life would have been if she were still here."

Both of them took another sip of tea in silence, each offering a silent prayer for Furaira. Just as the moment grew heavy with nostalgia, Fatimè's phone beeped.

"Okay, I'll see you soon," Fatimè said after answering.

Nafisa looked surprised. "Are you leaving already? I was hoping to drop you off."

"That's too much trouble, Adda Nafi. Please don't bother. Kamal is already on his way," Fatimè declined with a warm smile.

"This husband of yours is quite dedicated, coming all this way to pick you up despite the distance and traffic."

Fatimè grinned. "He had some work to do around this area."

Nafisa raised an intrigued eyebrow. "So, where did you two meet?"

Fatimè chuckled. "You won't believe it. At the airport."

"Wow, people are finding love in the most unexpected places. Allah ya barku tare."

"So, did you have a good time? You look happy," Kamal observed, glancing at Fatimè with a warm smile.

"Yes, I did," Fatimè replied, a genuine smile lighting up her face. "This is a sign that I should make more friends in this town."

Kamal chuckled. "I've been saying that, but you'd always say, 'Nah, I'm good.'"

"Well," Fatimè conceded, her smile faltering slightly, "getting friends isn't the issue; it's finding the quality ones. There's just no one like my friends and cousins back home. But you're right, I'll try to be more open to it."

"That's the spirit. I'm glad to see you happy; that's all I ever want for you."

As they spoke, a message appeared on Fatimè's phone, and she instinctively opened it to check. Her body visibly tensed, a reaction Kamal immediately noticed.

"What?" he inquired with concern. "What happened?"

"Nothing," Fatimè replied a bit too quickly, her gaze fixed on the phone screen, her voice slightly trembling. "Just one of those graphic broadcasts that aunts share now and then."

"Hmm, okay," Kamal acknowledged, though a flicker of concern passed over his face. "I'm going to stop by Spar to pick up a few things."

Fatimè nodded absently, her mind consumed by the ominous message she had received: 'If you want to know what happened to Khalid, meet me at Mushin by 4 pm tomorrow. Come alone.

26th February, 2018.

Mr. Abdullahi..." Mr. Etim called, "I believe you know why we are here." "No," he responded.

Sadiq eagerly awaited the end of the meeting, yearning for the cup of coffee awaiting him on his desk.

"An incident occurred two weeks ago during a presentation by one of our senior designers, where an inappropriate video was played..."

"Okay?"

"Well, from the report we received, you were in her office a few minutes before the presentation?"

"Yes, I remember. I went there to get some drawings."

Mr. Etim narrowed his eyes. "Are you sure you were only there for the drawings?"

"Yes, and I left immediately."

"This is a report from the IT department." Mr. Etim said, handing a file to Sadiq. "It shows that there was a log-in to Archvault at 9:45 am and from this CCTV footage..." he turned the laptop to face Sadiq, a clip playing, "You were in her office at 9:40 am and proceeded to her desk, where her laptop was..."

"What?" Sadiq watched the clip in front of him and face-palmed himself. He had forgotten about the cameras. "

All evidence points to you, I'm afraid. Mrs. Fatimè also informed us that you harassed her at the cafeteria before the incident..."

"This is all a misunderstanding..." Sadiq said. He had no idea how to explain what he was doing on her laptop, and that was when he remembered what a friend had told him a few years back, 'beautiful women would be the end of you, my guy.' Looked like it had come to pass, and all Sadiq did was let out a sigh.

"I'll have you know your actions were not only inappropriate but completely unprofessional. You have put her reputation and the company's at risk and also shown total disregard for your fellow architect's work. You will be suspended without pay for the next two months. In addition, you will be required to complete a sensitivity training course and also write a formal apology to the senior designer whose work you sabotaged."

Sadiq nodded, knowing he'd rather die than explain himself.

"I can't believe Sadiq went that far," Adaeze said when they got back to the office. "I mean, how could he?"

"Honestly, I'm just glad all of this has been cleared up, even though I cannot get over the look on all the principals' faces. I wanted the ground to open up and swallow me."

"Aww, my friend. I understand. Do you think they fired him, though?"

Fatimè shrugged, "I could not care less. Whatever it is, and I need him to stay away from me."

"Of course, after this, he would not dare try anything stupid." Adaeze noticed Fatimè's expression and asked,

"Why do you still look solemn, though? I thought it was what you wanted."

Fatimè contemplated telling her about the message she received last night. She still had not told anyone, even Kamal. She feared it was unwise. Since the incident during their honeymoon, Fatimè avoided anything that had to do with Khalid; she had relegated all thoughts and memories to the back of her head. Adaeze knew the story, so when Fatimè showed her the message, she understood.

"First things first, how sure are we this is not some trap? Have you tried calling or texting back? It could be someone messing with you, but on the other hand, this might be legit and it'll provide you the closure you need. The only way we can find out is to reach out to the person. What do you think?"

Fatimè nodded, agreeing with Adaeze. It was worth the shot. If Khalid's death was not an accident, she'd want to know what happened. Yes, it would not bring him back, but it was enough for her to let go.

Adaeze suggested calling the number, but there was no answer.

A message came in a few minutes later, an address with the caption, "Come alone."

"Uh, uh. Hell no. I am not letting you meet up with a stranger alone."

"But what..."

"Ah! This is Lagos o, Fatimè, and we are still not sure who this person is. Look, this is how we are going to do it...."

Chapter 22

♥

Gombe, Nigeria.

5th March, 2013

The enthusiastic shout of "GOOOOOAL!" reverberated through the hotel lobby, blending harmoniously with the chorus of cheers from other patrons.

"Oh, what a moment!" exclaimed the commentator on the television. "Ronaldo, the prodigal son, back at Old Trafford, has conjured something truly extraordinary. He has just turned the tie on its head, Real Madrid now ahead, 3-2 on aggregate."

Yusuf, Abdurrazaq, and Ayman's expressions tightened with hope as they yearned for Manchester United to stage a comeback. However, their aspirations crumbled when the final whistle blew, leaving the score unchanged.

"That Ronaldo goal was poetry in motion," Khalid grinned, savoring the triumph.

"Absolutely." Abba nodded. "No defender or keeper could have stopped that. We're talking about a classic Ronaldo move."

"Please, please. It was just a lucky break," Yusuf retorted, rolling his eyes. "We'll get you guys next time."

Khalid shot him a mocking smile. "It'll take a legendary comeback for you guys to do that."

Just then, Khalid's phone rang, prompting him to excuse himself for the call. Ayman seized the opportunity to interject, "So, congratulations! You've won a ticket to the quarterfinals. Not like you'll go much further."

Abba responded confidently, "Oh, we're going far. The Champions League is calling, my friends."

The banter continued for the next half-hour until they realized the lobby was nearly empty.

"How far? Where Khalid go?" Abba inquired.

"He's still on the phone; check outside," Yusuf suggested.

As Ayman rose to investigate, Khalid reappeared. "You're still having marathon calls with someone you're marrying tomorrow?" Abdurrazaq teased.

"As in, babe he'll be seeing you for the rest of his life o," Ayman added.

"Abeg," Khalid hissed. "You guys will not understand."

"Tirr!" They burst into laughter as they headed to their room, only to discover that Khalid had forgotten their keycard on the table downstairs.

"Too much love, you don dey forget things. Na wa."

After retrieving the keycard, they entered the room, with Khalid heading straight for the shower. As he approached the bathroom, he blurted, "I can't believe this is my last shower as a bachelor."

Laughter erupted from the group as Yusuf responded, "Shey you no go bathe tomorrow morning?"

6th March, 2013.

The hotel lobby buzzed with anticipation as Khalid's friends gathered, preparing to depart for the Wedding Fatiha. Khalid, confidently attired in his white babbar riga adorned with intricate aska tara traditional embroidery, completed his look with a kɜndai cap that accentuated his facial features flawlessly.

"How far? Is the car ready?" Khalid turned to Yusuf. "You know angos like us are not supposed to be stressing themselves, anyway. You can't relate."

Yusuf shook his head, offering a congenial smile. "It's your day, so you get a pass with whatever. That is my wedding gift to you."

"Nice try," Khalid responded with a playful smirk. "Better get my gift ready."

Yusuf strolled towards the parking lot, and just as he was about to get into the car, he noticed a man in a red face cap struggling with his car's battery beside theirs. The distressed man looked up as Yusuf pressed the unlock button on the car key.

"Salam Alaikum," the man greeted.

"Walaikumul assalam," Yusuf responded.

"Please, brother, I need a favor from you," the man said. "My car won't start; I think the battery must have gone cold overnight. Can you please help me out with yours so I can start mine?"

"Sure," Yusuf replied, retrieving a jump cable from the boot. After connecting the batteries, the man's car roared to life.

"Sorry, it's like I heard someone calling you from the lobby," the man apologized.

"Oh, that must be Khalid," Yusuf explained. "I'll be right back."

In the lobby, the group was capturing moments with photographs. "Ahn! Group pictures without me? What gives?" Yusuf exclaimed, quickly joining in for a few shots.

"Where's the car?" Khalid inquired after the impromptu photo shoot.

"I thought you needed something when you were gesturing towards me at the car park."

"When? I was waiting for you, dai," Khalid clarified.

"The guy I was helping out told me you were..."

"We are almost late fa," Ayman interjected. "Let's be going abeg..."

Yusuf returned to the parking lot a bit confused. He looked around, but the man seemed to have disappeared. Bringing the car to the front of the lobby, Khalid got in, and they joined the convoy of cars waiting to escort them to the mosque for the Wedding Fatiha.

"Who told you I was calling you?" Khalid asked, recalling Yusuf's earlier statement.

"The guy I was helping out said he saw someone calling out to me, and I thought it was you," Yusuf replied.

"Oh." Khalid nodded. Then he glanced to his side. "Wait, why are we the lead car in this convoy?"

"Well, we were running late, so there was no time to arrange who leads," Yusuf explained, focusing on the road. "And we are still running late, guy."

Khalid chuckled. "Speed up, abeg."

Yusuf accelerated, and suddenly, there was a deafening sound as the passenger's wheel broke off, the car veering violently off the road. It narrowly missed a bystander before hitting the pavement.

"Innalilahi wa inna ilaihi rajiun," Khalid and Yusuf uttered as the car swerved violently to the right, coming to a stop after colliding with a streetlight. The airbags deployed just in time, and Yusuf turned around to check on Khalid after collecting his thoughts.

The streetlight had lodged into Khalid's door, halfway through the passenger's seat.

Exiting the car, Yusuf rushed towards Khalid, just as other cars began parking to assess the situation.

"He has lost a lot of blood," Yusuf exclaimed as they managed to get Khalid out of the passenger's seat. "We need to get him to the hospital!"

The frantic scene that followed, with everyone battling to extricate Khalid, portrayed the abrupt shift from celebration to crisis.

A few meters away, the man in the red facecap sat in the car and dialed a number. The recipient picked up on the second ring. "Is it done?" he asked.

"Yes..."

"And?" The person on the other end demanded, eager for more details.

"He is bleeding and looks unconscious, almost like he's dead."

"Good. I hope he is. Keep me updated," he said, cutting the call.

Lagos, Nigeria.

26th February, 2018.

Fatimè fervently prayed that she wasn't about to walk into danger, realizing that this was one of the riskiest things she had ever done. She could only hope that it would turn out in her favor. The only comfort she had was knowing that Adaeze was a few meters away in a pharmacy. The plan had been for Fatimè to proceed alone and find a nearby place to stay, while Adaeze accompanied her with a police officer friend as a precaution.

She wiped her sweaty palms, her phone beeping with a message from the informant. It instructed her to watch out for a man in a red facecap. As she nervously adjusted her glasses, her eyes darted around anxiously. The gravity of what she was about to uncover weighed heavily on her. It was more than just an accident. Should she pursue the killer? What was the right course of action?

Suddenly, her gaze caught a man attempting to cross the street, his head down. Fatimè's heart raced, and she braced herself for the encounter. But before she could react, a piercing scream escaped her lips as an oncoming car collided with him.

Frozen in place, Fatimè's heart pounded in her chest as she watched people rush to his aid. Adaeze urgently pulled at her arm, guiding her toward the car.

"We need to leave this place," Adaeze insisted, her voice urgent, a mixture of concern and fear.

Abuja, Nigeria.

26th February, 2018.

Mufida and Intisar sat together on the edge of the bed, engrossed in scrolling through the pictures sent to the family group chat. The sound of baby Abdallah's cheerful voice echoed from the living room, where he played under the watchful eye of his nanny. Meanwhile, Intisar's newborn son, Muhammad, peacefully slept in his crib.

"This Zahra babe is too stunning. No wonder Fahad was ready to go to war over her. She's something," Mufida commented, nodding in agreement.

"I'm relieved that Ammi finally agreed to the wedding," Intisar chimed in, showing her approval. "Maaa-deee!" she called out. "Come and see these pictures. Isn't she incredibly beautiful?"

Madina rose from her chair and took the phone, inspecting the photos. She calmly remarked, "Well, she looks alright."

"Ah! Madina, how can you look at this girl and just say 'alright'? She's way more than that," Intisar countered.

"What? Why are you two making it seem like she's the first beautiful girl to join this family? You know the Ardo men always get the cream of the crop," Madina responded casually.

"Or perhaps you're just feeling a bit jealous?" Mufida suggested with a sly smile.

Madina let out a sarcastic laugh. "Jealous of what? Please, don't make me laugh. I'm completely content, and you both know it."

Not in the mood for their usual banter, Mufida swiftly changed the subject. "Are we still planning to attend Adda Farida's shop opening?"

"Absolutely," Intisar confirmed. "Although, I'm still struggling to find something to wear." She walked over to the full-length mirror and scrutinized her reflection. "None of my clothes fit me anymore."

She spent the next few minutes complaining about her post-pregnancy weight.

"Madina," Mufida called out, finally noticing her cousin's silence. "You haven't said anything. Are you coming with us?"

Madina glanced at the clock and rose from her seat. "I won't be able to make it. I have some things to attend to. See you both later," she said, quickly packing her belongings.

"What's gotten into her?" Mufida wondered aloud after Madina left.

"Do you want to hear my theory?" Intisar asked, her eyes narrowing with suspicion. "I think she's in love with Fahad."

Mufida let out an exaggerated sigh. "And how did you come up with such nonsense?"

"I just have this feeling. Can't you see how she's acting because we called Fahad's girlfriend pretty?"

"You and your 'feelings,' Intisar! I don't think that's enough to conclude that she has feelings for him. Besides, I've never noticed anything between them. It looks like a typical cousin relationship to me."

"You also didn't see it when I told you that Mahmud and you would end up together."

"Intee, please," Mufida laughed. "Let me head back home. I'm sure Mahmud is on his way back. What comforts me is that I prepared dinner before leaving..."

"We'll see if I'm right or wrong," Intisar said, following her cousin out of the room.

Lagos, Nigeria.

"Here," Adaeze said gently, handing Fatimè a steaming mug of chamomile tea. "It'll help calm your nerves."

Fatimè nodded gratefully and accepted the warm cup, her mind still reeling from the shock of witnessing a man's death. A whirlwind of thoughts raced through her head, but one question loomed largest: was the hit-and-run a mere coincidence, or was someone deliberately trying to hide the truth from her? Could the man she had seen die be connected to the accident? She had so many unanswered questions.

Adaeze settled on the couch beside her, letting out a sigh. "What a day," she muttered before turning to reassure Fatimè. "Try not to dwell on it too much. Everything will be okay."

Fatimè glanced at the wall clock and gasped, realizing how late it had become. "Oh, God! Where's my phone?"

Frantically, she rummaged through her handbag and finally located her phone, only to discover that it had run out of battery. This was the worst possible time for her phone to die on her.

She had informed Kamal that she would be working late and had asked Henry to pick her up at 6. Originally, she had thought she could make it back to the office, but after the traumatic incident and how shaken she felt, Adaeze brought her to her house to help her collect herself.

Now, it was just minutes before 8 p.m., and Fatimè needed to get home ASAP. Adaeze, sensing her urgency, offered, "I'll drive you home," as she grabbed her keys.

Kamal greeted Fatimè with a calm demeanor when she walked into the living room. He sat on the couch, engrossed in a copy of 'Paul Beatty's The Sellout'.

During the drive back home, Fatimè pondered what explanation to give Kamal. She didn't want to lie, but telling him the truth was also not an option.

"I was with Adaeze," she finally said.

Kamal raised his head from the book, his gaze piercing. "And you didn't think to inform me of your whereabouts? Do you know how worried I was when Henry called and said he couldn't find you at the office? To top it off, your phone was unreachable."

"I just lost track of time," Fatimè replied, her voice trembling slightly.

Kamal rose from the couch and walked toward her, his voice growing colder. "I was here, worried sick about you, and all you have to say is that you lost track of time?"

His grip on her arms tightened, and she could feel her whole body vibrating with fear. If he didn't let go soon, she feared she'd have a dislocated arm.

"Kamal, please let go. You're hurting me," she pleaded.

"I'm sorry. I'm sorry," he said, immediately releasing her and reaching out to comfort her.

In an instant, her trembling body and his soothing words brought her back to reality, and she recognized the Kamal she knew. Who was that person just seconds ago?

"I didn't mean to," Kamal apologized sincerely. "Did I hurt you? Let me see that."

He tried to reach for her hand, but she didn't spare him a second glance as she rushed to the bedroom and locked the door.

Chapter 23

♥

Lagos, Nigeria.

3rd March, 2018.

Mubarak let out a frustrated sigh, the umpteenth one since they'd been stuck in Lagos traffic for nearly two hours. Fatimè chuckled, understanding his irritation all too well.

"Why are you acting like this is your first time in Lagos?" she teased.

He shot her an exasperated look. "I thought things had gotten better here. If I had known, I wouldn't have accepted this gig."

Mubarak had come to Lagos for the weekend to cover an event, while Khalifa had a gaming tournament. However, the traffic had taken a toll on Mubarak's mood.

Khalifa, sitting in the backseat, chimed in, "Hamma Mubarak, you know complaining won't make the cars go any faster, right?"

"Toh, king of reason. Thanks for your input," Mubarak retorted. Fatimè decided to tune out their conversation and focus on her phone. She wasn't in the mood for small talk.

Finally, they arrived at the restaurant, and Khalifa spotted an old friend, leaving the table to say hello.

"Baby petel," Mubarak called out, bringing Fatimè's attention back. "What's wrong?"

"Nothing, Hamma Mubarak. I'm just tired, you know, from work..." Fatimè replied, not entirely truthful.

"Hmm. Is it today you started working? There's something else bothering you. You're the poster girl for 'I'm fine.' You haven't said more than five sentences since we got here like you were not jumping with excitement a few days ago when we told you we were coming."

Mubarak's voice carried a tone of concern, and Fatimè knew she was being unfair. She had been excited about her brothers visiting, but the recent incident had weighed heavily on her.

"Something happened a few days back," she admitted reluctantly.

"Are you crazy?" Mubarak half-yelled once Fatimè recounted the entire story. "A strange number texts you, and you decide to meet them? You didn't even tell anyone, not even your husband?"

"Hamma Mubarak, I was just curious. It's about Khalid..." she began.

"Still, what if something had happened to you? What if it was a trap? Wallahi, sometimes I'm in awe of your craziness. Do you think your life is an experiment?"

Fatimè knew her brother was right; it had been a reckless move. She waited for him to calm down before she continued, "Well, it happened, and I'm safe. But I'm still worried. I don't think that guy's death was a coincidence."

"Of course not," Mubarak agreed. "It doesn't look like one. But if he was telling the truth about Khalid's death not being an accident, the real question is, why would someone want to kill Khalid? Do you know if he had any enemies or something?"

Fatimè shook her head. "Khalid was friends with everyone. I've never seen him in a fight. But a few weeks before our wedding, he mentioned something about being stalked."

"Stalked?" Mubarak repeated.

"Yes," Fatimè confirmed with a nod. "I wanted to tell Baaba, but he insisted I forget about it. I don't know; everything is just messing with my head. So many unanswered questions, like the cameras in my room. Why would someone be stalking me? Why go after Khalid? What was it about us...?"

Fatimè's voice trailed off as she became overwhelmed with emotion. She was on the verge of tears.

"Hey, hey," Mubarak reached across the table to hold her hands. "Calm down. Stop thinking about all these things. There are no explanations yet, but you shouldn't let it consume you. Investigating Khalid's death won't bring him back. I suggest you leave things as they are—unfortunate accident. But if it'll bring you peace, I can talk to his friend Yusuf."

"Yes," Fatimè agreed. "I ran into him a few months back..."

"Good. I saw him at an event I covered once, and we exchanged contacts. I'll reach out to him, and we'll see what we can find to put your mind at ease."

"Thank you so much, Hamma Mubarak. You don't know how much this means to me."

"Anything for you. I don't like seeing you so worried." Mubarak paused and glanced around. "Where's the food, though? I'm starving, seriously. Why is everything so stressful here?"

Fatimè tilted her head back and laughed. "Welcome to Lagos life.

Kaduna, Nigeria.

5th March, 2018.

"I can't believe you, Fahad... The one time you were supposed to stand up for me..."

Fahad could hear the anger in Zahra's voice, and it was entirely expected.

"Zahra," he tried to pacify her. "Can you please listen to me?"

"There's no point. I'll take care of this on my own..."

"Babe, wait..."

Fahad's words were drowned out as Zahra abruptly ended the call.

"Shit," he cursed, punching one of his pillows. His life seemed to be getting more complicated by the day. This was what he got for being a man who sought peace.

"Fahad, you haven't checked that thing for me," Fa'iza interrupted, entering the room. "You know I'm leaving tomorrow."

Fahad's distressed state caught Fa'iza's attention. "What's going on with you?" she asked as she took a seat on the edge of his bed. "Is it the price of super-wax?"

Fahad couldn't help but laugh. "I wish..."

"Fahad funds," Fa'iza teased. "Seriously, though, Ko fe'i?"

Telling his sister the entire story was as good as doing what Zahra wanted, something he wanted to avoid. However, he needed to give Fa'iza some explanation, or she wouldn't leave him alone.

"It's Zahra," he said.

"Ah, pre-wedding quarrels," Fa'iza mused. "I'd recommend them. They give you an insight into what married life will be like. I bet it was over something silly."

"Yeah," Fahad played along. "We'll figure it out, insha'Allah."

"That's the spirit. So, what are you planning for the wedding events?"

"Getting married?" Fahad replied, feigning innocence.

Fa'iza rolled her eyes at her brother. "Of course, you're getting married. I don't even know why I asked. I should know better."

"Exactly. Whatever she wants, is fine with me. Ask Fadila; they must have talked about it."

Just then, their younger sister, Fadila, appeared, munching on Pringles. "Ask Fadila what?"

"Amebo," Fa'iza said. "What have you been discussing with Zahra?"

"Hamma Fahad's girlfriend?" Fadila teased.

"No, his sister," Fa'iza clarified.

"Oh, come on, Adda Fa'i," Fadila laughed. "Nothing much, really..."

Fahad tuned out their conversation because he had one thing on his mind: he needed to talk to Madina as soon as possible.

Istanbul, Turkey.

october, 2010.

Piya, Seesa, and Meenal found themselves seated on a blanket spread out under a sprawling oak tree. The fragrance of blooming flowers and the soft chatter of other students in the distance created a peaceful ambiance. The trio, all engaged in a lighthearted conversation, sipping tea from their favorite mugs.

"Guys, you won't believe what happened in our Advanced Neurology seminar today." Piya said, "Professor Sharma tried to delve into the intricacies of cortical mapping, and I swear, it felt like he was unraveling the mysteries of the universe!"

Seesa, her eyes twinkling, responded, "Oh, don't get me started. I thought I signed up for medicine, not a crash course in astrophysics. And Meenal, you were navigating those neural pathways like a pro!"

Meenal giggled, "Guilty as charged! But hey, we aced the last clinical rotation, didn't we?"Now, what about that cute guy in our advanced cardiology class?"

Piya playfully nudged Seesa, "Yeah, Seesa, spill the tea! You were blushing during the last heart dissection."

Seesa rolled her eyes. "Oh, please, it was just a slight fever. And, you know, lab coats can make anyone look good."

Meenal chuckled. "Seesa, I've seen you blush before. This is different. Something's cooking."

Seesa shook her head. "Alright, fine! Maybe he's got a nice collection of medical dramas on his laptop. A girl can dream, right?"

They burst into laughter as the conversation seamlessly transitioned to Grey's Anatomy, Taylor Lautner, and, of course, the happenings in their lives outside of academics.

As they chatted, Seesa, with her keen perception, noticed a guy observing them from a distance. A sly smile crept onto her face. "Ladies, it looks like we have an admirer." She gestured discreetly toward the curious onlooker.

Piya glanced over her shoulder and asked, "Where?"

Seesa pointed subtly, "By the hedge. The guy in the blue jacket."

Meenal quipped, "Well, well, aren't we becoming celebrities in our little garden show?"

Piya, the prankster of the group, winked. "Should we give him a wave?"

Seesa joined in the fun, raising her hand in a mock greeting. "Hello, secret admirer! We hope you're enjoying the show."

With a final burst of laughter, they gathered their belongings and rose from the blanket, leaving the garden with playful waves. As they strolled away, Seesa couldn't help but glance back and caught the guy quickly looking away, pretending to be engrossed in a book.

"Smooth," Seesa whispered to her friends, and they shared one last laugh before heading off.

Abuja, Nigeria.

July, 2011.

"I still can't believe Torres is going to Chelsea," Sa'ad remarked.

"Toh, they need a top-class striker, ai," Muhammad replied. "It's a huge gamble, but if anyone can make it work, it'll be Torres."

Saif emerged from the kitchen, holding a bottle of water. "I'm just thinking about Rooney's form. Gaskiya, we need fresh blood in our attack."

"A hat trick from Torres against Liverpool is all I need," Jalaal laughed.

Sa'ad eyed him. "You're just bitter you couldn't beat us this season."

As Sa'ad and Saif engaged in their banter, Jalaal noticed Kamal's silence and decided to tap him. "How far? What's on your mind?"

Sa'ad chimed in, "Love, man. He's busy thinking about a girl who won't give him the time of day."

"Ah, M.K. has a girl?" Jalaal interjected. "I must be slacking."

Kamal responded, "Don't mind this idiot. I don't know what he's talking about."

"You'll deny it, I know," Sa'ad said. "Since he doesn't have the balls to tell her how he feels."

"Haba now," Saif added. "I don't believe there's any girl that MK can't win over. He's smooth."

"Toh, this one looks different," Sa'ad said. "Check her out now..."

Sa'ad pulled out his phone and opened Facebook. "See her account..."

Kamal was taken aback. "How did you find her account?"

"Beautiful girls aren't hard to find," Sa'ad replied.

"Bastard," Kamal muttered as Sa'ad showed a picture to Jalaal and Muhammad.

"Kai!" Jalaal exclaimed. "She's gorgeous. Man, you need to make your move ASAP."

Kamal snatched the phone away from Jalaal. "It's okay, please."

"Relax," Jalaal laughed. "Nobody's making a move on your girl."

"Does she have a sister, though?" Saif asked from the corner.

"Shege!" They all burst out laughing.

Kamal's phone rang, and he stepped outside to take the call. It was Nabila, probably calling about school stuff.

"Nabila? How far?"

"Where are you?" she asked urgently.

"At Sa'ad's. What's up? Why do you sound like that?"

Nabila struggled to find the courage to break the news to him, but she had to do it.

"Something happened... Piya..."

"Piya..." Kamal called for the second time in his sleep. Fatimè looked up from her prayer mat, wondering if she should wake him up. He seemed to be trapped in a nightmare, his restless tossing and mumbling disturbing the peace of the room. After a brief internal debate, she decided to let him be and resumed her prayers.

Kamal turned to the other side and continued his fitful slumber. The night was fraught with haunting dreams, and Fatimè couldn't help but feel concerned for her husband.

In the morning, Kamal entered the dining area with a quiet "Good morning." He leaned down to plant a soft kiss on her forehead before taking a seat opposite her. Fatimè couldn't help but notice that he looked different today, more present and composed. It was a welcomed change from the tension that had enveloped their home recently.

Fatimè, accustomed to Kamal's recent habit of skipping breakfast, was surprised to see him at the table. The silence between them lingered as they sipped their morning beverages.

Finally, she broke the ice. "Did you sleep well last night?"

Kamal paused in pouring his coffee and looked at her, his expression somber. "Not really," he admitted. "I had a troubling dream."

Fatimè was immediately curious. "Who or what is Piya? You kept calling that name in your sleep. Should I be concerned?"

Kamal knew it was time to open up about a part of his past that he hadn't shared before. He took a deep breath. "Piya was someone I used to love."

Fatimè felt a pang of surprise at his confession. Her husband dreaming about another woman stirred mixed emotions within her. But then she remembered her slip-up, uttering her ex's name just days into their marriage.

"It was a long time ago, during our university days," Kamal continued, his voice tinged with sadness. "But she's no longer with us. She passed away."

Fatimè could see the pain in his eyes, recognizing it all too well from her grief over Khalid.

"I'm sorry," she offered sincerely.

Kamal nodded in acknowledgment. "Thank you," he replied. "I should have told you about this earlier. I'm also sorry for what happened that night."

Fatimè nodded in agreement, understanding that they both had their share of regrets. "I shouldn't have disappeared like that and made you worry."

Kamal got up from his seat and walked behind her, planting a tender kiss on her back as a sign of reconciliation.

"We should go on a trip," he suggested, his voice warmer now. "I believe we need some fresh air."

Fatimè smiled at the idea, relieved to sense a glimmer of normalcy returning to their relationship.

Abuja, Nigeria.

8th March, 2018.

Intisar and Mufida entered the sitting room, where the soft hum of conversation wafted from the adjacent kitchen.

"Ya gida? Ya aiki?" They said, exchanging warm greetings with the help they met in the dining room.

Fahad suddenly spotted them and abruptly halted his conversation with Madina. "I guess I'll take my leave now," he declared, nodding a greeting to Mufida and Intisar.

Intisar couldn't help but notice Fahad's tense demeanor and was immediately curious. "What's doing him?" she asked.

"Wedding jitters," Madina answered. "What are you guys doing here?" She was surprised, considering their recent disagreement during their last meeting.

"We cannot visit you again?" Intisar replied.

Mufida, not wanting a repeat of last time, quickly said, "We couldn't stay away. We wanted to apologize."

"No, I should be the one apologizing. I'm sorry about what I said. I know how stressful it is with a long-distance marriage, being pregnant, and you with the baby and everything. I just felt lonely with Fatime living on the other side of the country, and you guys are always busy," Madina said.

Intisar added sincerely, "I'm sorry about what I said too. I honestly didn't mean it like that."

Madina shrugged, her smile returning. "It's fine. It was just a heated moment."

Madina then left briefly and returned with a plate of samosas and spring rolls. Intisar and Mufida had huddled up, engrossed in something on their phones.

Mufida remarked, "Ah lallai Tims. She's really chilling."

Curious, Madina inquired, "What?"

Mufida nudged Intisar, and they both shared a knowing look. "Didn't you see the snaps Tims sent?"

Madina shook her head, then grabbed her phone. "Ah, iyye! Look at that dress!"

Intisar chimed in, "I know, right? She's making me crave another honeymoon."

Madina and Mufida exchanged amused glances before Mufida teased, "Honeymoon indeed. What about the girl's trip we've been planning to go on? You guys should be serious, Abeg."

Intisar shot back playfully, "Look at this woman. Weren't you the one who went ahead and got pregnant?"

Mufida rolled her eyes and retorted, "Ehen, didn't you get pregnant right after?"

Their laughter filled the room, and Madina couldn't help but join in. "How about next year?" she suggested. "We can go to Bauchi."

"Bauchi?!" Mufida and Intisar exclaimed in unison.

Their laughter continued as Intisar quipped, "This one is no longer a trip; it's ziyara."

Lagos, Nigeria.

28th May, 2018.

Kamal's attention remained fixed on the screen in the conference room as Kunle, the project manager, provided an overview of the 'Stride' app and user feedback.

"Overall, the app has been performing exceptionally well. We have seen a significant increase in user downloads and active users," he reported.

"That's great news," Kamal replied, trying to immerse himself in the project's progress. "Are there any specific areas where we need to focus or make improvements?"

Nadia, the marketing specialist, chimed in, "Our marketing campaigns have been successful in spreading awareness about the app, but we have noticed a slight drop in user retention after the first few weeks. We should look into strategies to enhance customer loyalty and engagement."

Kamal nodded thoughtfully. "Customer retention is crucial for the long-term success of the app. Let's brainstorm ideas on how we can create a more personalized experience for users and offer incentives to keep them coming back."

Nadia, one of the designers, spoke up. "I have been working on some UI enhancements that could improve the user experience. Simplifying the interface, adding clearer navigation, and incorporating user feedback into the design could make a significant difference."

Kamal appreciated Nadia's input. "Please present your design proposals in the next team meeting. We'll discuss them in detail and decide on the best course of action."

The meeting concluded, and Sa'ad and Kamal walked back to his office. "We're still going to Jalaal's later, abi? He called me this afternoon."

"Yeah," Kamal nodded. "The games are in my car already. I have unfinished business with Saif."

Kamal's phone interrupted their conversation, and he picked up. "Yes? This is him? ....What? Subhanallah. Okay. Okay. I am on my way. " He said and rushed out quickly, with Sa'ad trailing behind him.

Kamal's heart pounded as he rushed through the hospital doors, his mind clouded with fear and uncertainty. The news of Fatimè's bleeding had sent him into a panic. He approached the reception desk, desperately seeking answers.

"I need to see my wife, Fatimè. Mrs. Fatimè Ardo. She was brought in earlier," he said.

The receptionist quickly checked the records and directed him to the room where Fatimè was being attended to.

"I'll wait here," Sa'ad said, and Kamal nodded. His steps were hurried, and his mind was racing with worry as he approached the door.

Entering the room, Kamal found Fatimè lying on the hospital bed, her face pale and her eyes filled with a mix of pain and confusion. He rushed to her side, taking her hand in his.

"Baby, how are you? Are you okay? What happened?" Kamal's voice was filled with concern.

Tears welled up in Fatimè's eyes as she spoke weakly, "I don't know. One minute I was in the office with Adaeze, and the next thing was sudden pain, and then the bleeding started. I was so scared."

Kamal held her tightly, trying to offer whatever comfort he could. "It's going to be okay, baby. I'm here now."

Just then, the doctor entered the room, accompanied by Adaeze, who wore a sympathetic expression. She greeted Kamal and stood by the side.

"Mr. Kamal, I am Dr. Rahman. We have examined your wife, and I have some information to share with you."

They all turned their attention to the doctor, and Kamal's grip on Fatimè's hand tightened.

Dr. Rahman spoke gently but directly, "I am sorry to inform you that your wife has lost the baby. We managed to stabilize her condition, but the fetus could not be saved. I'm sorry."

Kamal and Fatimè's world shattered at that moment. They both struggled to process the news, as they both had looks of confusion, grief, and pain. He looked at Fatimè, her eyes filled with tears, mirroring his own.

She was devastated, as she had just found out two weeks ago and was looking for the best way to break the news.

"Can we speak privately, Mr. Kamal?" Dr. Rahman said.

Kamal nodded. "I'll be right back." He said to Fatimè and kissed her cheek.

"I understand this is a distressing situation." Dr. Rahman said when they got to his office, "But I have more information to share. When your wife was rushed to the hospital due to bleeding, we conducted a thorough examination.

"Yes? Go on, doctor." Kamal said.

"In addition to our earlier findings, we discovered some additional factors that are concerning. Your wife's medical history shows that this is not the first time she has experienced the loss of a pregnancy. That, coupled with the current situation, raises more questions."

"And what are those questions?" Kamal asked.

"Given her history and the fact that the pregnancy was only two weeks old, it becomes even more unlikely that this was a natural miscarriage. We found traces of medication in her system that is typically used for inducing abortions." Dr. Rahman informed.

"What?" Kamal said with shock written on his face, "I don't understand. Are you saying the pregnancy was deliberately terminated? Like, my wife had an abortion? What?"

"I am deeply sorry." Dr. Rahman apologized, "The evidence strongly suggests that this was not a miscarriage. We have a responsibility to share this information with you, and your wife needs to receive the emotional and psychological support she needs during this difficult time.

Chapter 24

♥

Abuja, Nigeria.

September, 2011.

The living room was tense as Alhaji Hussein sat in his armchair, with an unspoken tension hanging in the air. Hajia Hillu moved about the room, trying to dispel the discomfort by preparing tea. Alhaji's stern gaze followed her, and when tea was finally served, he spoke in a commanding tone, "Hillu, we need to address Kamal's lack of direction. He left medical school, and although he claims this business venture is successful, I still question his decisions."

Hajia Hillu nodded nervously, aware of the strained relationship between father and son. "Yes, I have also noticed he has been distant and troubled lately. But pushing him too hard might worsen the situation."

Just then, Kamal walked into the room. The weight of his father's disapproval hung in the air, making the atmosphere even more stifling for him as he greeted with a cautious "Assalamu Alaikum."

His father acknowledged him with a curt nod, his stern expression unyielding. "Wa Alaikumul Salaam. Sit down."

Kamal took a seat, his mother's worried eyes meeting his briefly before she lowered her gaze, pouring the tea.

"Kamal," his father began, his voice a blend of authority and disappointment, "I've made a decision regarding your future."

Kamal's eyes widened, a mix of surprise and apprehension flashing across his face. His father's expectations, like a looming thundercloud, seemed ready to burst.

"I've spoken to an old friend," his father continued, his gaze unwavering, "and I believe it's time for you to settle down. Rukayya, his daughter, is a suitable match."

The news hit Kamal like a sudden gust of wind, leaving him momentarily breathless. He struggled to maintain composure, his eyes darting between his father's stern face and the untouched tea in front of him.

"This alliance is not just for the family's benefit but for your stability," his father asserted.

Kamal's internal conflict was visible in the clenching of his jaw and the subtle furrow of his brows. He fought to keep his emotions in check, his hands unconsciously gripping the edge of the seat.

His mother, sensing his silent struggle, shot him a sympathetic glance. The room felt like a battlefield of unspoken words, with the weight of expectations pressing down on Kamal's shoulders.

Alhaji Hussein, seemingly satisfied with Kamal's silence, concluded, "Good. This decision is final. You will meet Rukayya and her family soon. It's time to put your responsibilities first."

Kamal was still silent, the turmoil within him mirrored in the conflict etched on his face. As the weighty conversation continued, he grappled with the clash between his desires and the expectations imposed upon him by his father.

Lagos, Nigeria.

June 2012

In the dimly lit study, Kamal sat hunched over his desk, his face shrouded in shadows, staring blankly at a series of documents scattered across the mahogany surface. The soft glow of a desk lamp highlighted the desperation etched into his features. A heavy silence hung in the air, disrupted only by the distant hum of the city beyond.

The door creaked open, and Rukayya hesitated on the threshold, watching her husband with concern etched across her face. She hadn't seen him like this before --- a tempest of emotions raging beneath his usually composed exterior. Stepping into the room cautiously, she could feel the palpable turmoil synchronizing with the pounding of her own heart.

"Kamal, what's wrong?" Rukayya's voice was gentle and filled with genuine worry as she approached him.

He didn't respond immediately, his eyes fixed on the table that seemed to carry the weight of the world. Slowly, he lifted his gaze, revealing a storm of conflicting emotions — grief, anger, and an unsettling emptiness.

The room seemed to close in on them, and she felt an overwhelming urge to reach out to him to offer comfort in the face of such unforeseen devastation.

As reality settled in, Kamal's stoic facade crumbled. He crumpled the document in his hands, his breaths ragged. Rukayya, forgetting the strained nature of their relationship, rushed to his side and gently placed a hand on his trembling shoulder.

"Kamal, I'm so sorry," she murmured, her own eyes glistening with empathy.

His vulnerability spilled over, and he leaned into her touch, seeking solace in the unlikeliest of places. Rukayya, for the first time, felt a connection beyond the surface of their arranged marriage. She wrapped her arms around him, offering the warmth of her embrace, and in that moment, the boundaries that had separated them began to blur.

Grief and solace intertwined, and as they clung to each other in the quiet study, the lines of their strained marriage softened. In that unexpected intimacy, a fragile connection formed — a shared understanding of loss and perhaps the tentative emergence of something deeper between two souls bound by unforeseen circumstances.

Abuja, Nigeria.

29th May, 2018.

"Rukayya Abbani, Wikki drive," Rukayya informed the security guard as they reached the gate. A quick call on the intercom, and the gate swung open, allowing her entry.

"Mummy, did you pack my swimming trunks?" Adil's voice piped up from the back seat, filled with anticipation of his upcoming trip.

"Yes, Adil, I did, along with everything else you asked for," Rukayya replied, her tone infused with motherly patience. Adil's excitement about his journey to Lagos, especially the promised beach visit, had been palpable.

"We're here," she announced upon reaching Kamal's parents' house. Having instructed the gatekeeper not to bother opening the gate, she had no intention of a prolonged stay. Her relationship with her ex-in-laws remained unchanged, but she preferred to keep her distance.

Hafsah, Kamal's sister, emerged as their driver pulled up, having just returned from school. "Ya Ruuks!" Hafsah greeted her cheerfully when she stepped out of the car. "Ina yini? Aren't you coming inside?"

"Lafiya lau, Hafsee," Rukayya replied with a warm smile. "I'm just here to drop off Adil; I have somewhere to be."

"Oh, okay. Well then, little gremlin, let's go," Hafsah said playfully as she helped Adil out of the car.

"Bye, Mummy," Adil waved to his mother.

"Goodbye, baby. Have a safe trip. I love you," Rukayya replied before turning to Hafsah. "And please give my regards to Maa."

Hafsah nodded and escorted Adil inside the house.

Hajiya Hillu's presence was announced when Hafsah caught a whiff of her humra. "What time is your flight?" she asked.

"I don't know yet," Hafsah responded, tossing a set of atampa into her box. "Ya Kamal hasn't sent me the details. I called him twice, but there was no answer."

"Perhaps he's busy with work. You know how he can get," her mother replied, a hint of concern in her voice.

"Yeah, I'll try calling him again later."

Hajiya Hillu handed Hafsah two buckets containing turaren wuta and said, "Take these to Fatimè, please. Also, make sure the humra doesn't spill."

"Sure thing. Is Adil awake?" Hafsah asked as she took the items.

"I'll check on him," her mother replied.

Adil was still asleep when Hajiya Hillu decided to call Kamal. After a few rings, he picked up.

"Maa. Ina yini? An sha ruwa lafiya?" Kamal greeted, his voice heavy with an unspoken burden.

"Lafiya kalau, Ya gida? How is Fatimè? Your sister has been trying to reach you, but you haven't been answering."

"Yeah... um..." Kamal hesitated, struggling to find the right words.

"What's wrong?" his mother asked, sensing the gravity of the situation.

"We just got back from the hospital," Kamal finally admitted.

"The hospital? Are you or Fatimè sick? Tell me what's going on," his mother pressed.

Kamal took a deep breath before revealing the painful truth. "Fatimè had a miscarriage."

"Inna lillahi wa inna ilaihi rajiun. Subhanallah," his mother murmured, her voice filled with sorrow. "Is she okay? How is she?"

"She's been discharged, and she's resting now," Kamal replied, his emotions raw. "But I'm just..."

"I know, I know. I'm so sorry. Allah yasa me ceto ne. I'm so sorry," his mother consoled him.

"Can you please tell Hafsah and Adil to hold on for a bit?" Kamal requested. "We just need some time."

"Of course, Kamal. Take all the time you need. I understand. Please give my regards to Fatimè and call me when she wakes up."

"Insha Allah," Kamal replied, ending the call.

He let out a sigh of defeat, feeling a complex mix of emotions. His mind was filled with confusion, regret, and grief. He couldn't believe that they had lost their second child, and the revelation about the miscarriage was shrouded in mystery.

However, Kamal couldn't forget the conversation he had overheard just a few weeks ago between Fatimè and Madina.

Fatimè had laughed and said, "No, Madina, you're crazy. Just because I mentioned craving Ya Hajja's danwake doesn't mean I'm pregnant. Come on, get out of here."

"No, I'm serious. The way you married people like to move, I would not be surprised..."

"But for real, Madina, if I were pregnant, I don't know how to feel about it," Fatimè continued.

"What do you mean?" Madina had inquired.

"We need more time to be husband and wife. Mummy and Daddy can come later. A baby is not what we need right now," Fatimè had said, unknowingly within earshot of Kamal.

As he recalled that conversation, Kamal couldn't help but wonder if Fatimè had been carrying their child and, if so, why she hadn't told him.

"Baby?" Kamal called out as he scanned the room, "Did you see my card? The Zenith one?"

"It's in my wallet," Fatimè replied from the bathroom, where she was brushing her teeth.

Kamal walked over to the bedside, where her handbag lay, to retrieve his card. As he searched for it, something unexpected caught his eye—a piece of paper had fallen from her wallet.

Nabila arrived at the quiet restaurant, and Kamal, who had been waiting for about twenty minutes, greeted her with a strained smile. The weight of the discovery pressed on him, and it was evident in his demeanor.

"You're late," Kamal remarked, trying to maintain a semblance of normalcy.

Nabila shrugged, unfazed. "Ah, come on, you know how crazy the traffic can be in this town."

Kamal ordered a glass of water when the waiter approached. Nabila, on the other hand, requested orange juice.

"Anyways, I'm here. What's up? That seminar drained me. I can't wait to return to sanity."

"As if there's anything sane about being a doctor? Location doesn't matter," Kamal quipped, attempting to divert the conversation.

"You know what? Fair point," Nabila conceded with a chuckle. "I'm not even going to call you out on checking out. Now, out with it. What's wrong?"

Kamal took a sip of his water, contemplating his words, before handing Nabila the piece of paper he had found in Fatimè's wallet the previous night.

Nabila examined the paper, her brow furrowing. "What is this?"

"I found it in Fatimè's wallet," Kamal replied.

"What?" Nabila exclaimed, looking back and forth between the paper and Kamal.

Kamal nodded and proceeded to explain the situation in detail, sharing his confusion and concern. "I don't want to believe my wife aborted our child, but unfortunately, everything seems to point in that direction."

Nabila couldn't hide her shock and concern. "Did you ask her about it?"

"I was hoping we'd discuss it when she's feeling better," Kamal admitted. "But then I found this... I don't know what to think anymore."

"You need to confront her," Nabila advised firmly. "This is a very serious issue. You mentioned overhearing her saying she didn't want a baby... Could that be related?"

Kamal fell silent, contemplating the possibilities. Only Fatimè could provide the answers he needed.

Kamal parked the car and remained seated for a while, his mind a whirlwind of thoughts. He needed to gather himself before facing Fatimè. Upon entering the house, he found Mrs. Simon in the living room, seemingly piecing things together.

"Mr. Kamal, welcome," she said with a warm smile.

He managed a weak smile in response. "Where's Fatimè?"

"In her room," Mrs. Simon replied.

Kamal nodded and made his way upstairs. Fatimè was lying in bed, watching a movie, when he entered. She looked up at him, her face brightening.

"Salam Alaikum," she greeted, getting up to hug him.

However, Kamal's response was unexpectedly cold. He stepped back, leaving Fatimè bewildered. "Is something wrong?" she asked, her concern growing.

"We need to talk," he said solemnly.

"Okay," Fatimè replied, her curiosity tinged with worry.

"At the hospital," Kamal began, choosing his words carefully, "when the doctor called me..."

Fatimè listened attentively, her heart pounding in her chest.

"He said they found some drugs in your system, and your 'miscarriage' was actually an abortion."

Fatimè's eyes widened in shock. "What? I don't understand."

"That's what I need you to explain because I was going to dismiss it until I found this." Kamal handed her the receipt he had discovered in her wallet.

As Fatimè read the receipt, her disbelief deepened. Her name was boldly written on it, 'Mrs. Fatimè Ardo...'

"Where did you get this?" she stammered.

"I should be asking you that. It has your name on it," Kamal replied firmly, his frustration mounting.

Fatimè was dumbfounded, unable to comprehend how he had found such a receipt and what it meant. Abortion pills? Her head spun with confusion.

"Kamal, I'm telling you I don't know anything about this. Why would I want to get rid of our baby?"

Kamal's voice wavered as he replied, "You did tell Madina you didn't want a baby, though."

Fatimè's eyes widened with shock at this revelation. "What? How?"

"I overheard the conversation," he confessed.

Tears welled up in Fatimè's eyes as she realized the gravity of the situation. "Yes, I admit I said a baby wasn't what we wanted..."

"You," Kamal corrected, his tone cold. "Because I don't remember us discussing it, and besides, I had to find out about the pregnancy at the hospital."

"I was waiting for the right time to tell you!" Fatimè protested desperately.

Kamal walked away from her and stood by the window, rubbing his temples as he struggled to make sense of it all. Fatimè was left on the verge of tears, feeling misunderstood and wrongly accused. All the evidence seemed to point against her, and she couldn't help but resent her husband for doubting her.

"I need some air," Kamal finally said, his voice strained, and he walked out of the room, leaving Fatimè to grapple with her overwhelming emotions.

Chapter 25

♥

G ombe, Nigeria.

16th June, 2018.

Between the daunting tasks of packing and unpacking, Fatimè found herself in a dilemma. The box before her seemed to hold the weight of her decisions, and a heavy sigh escaped her lips. Nearly a week in Gombe, and the unpacking remained untouched.

Her room, a sanctuary frozen in time, retained its familiar elements — the two single beds against the wall, a small drawer between them, the 'Jonas brothers' poster adorning her sister's bed, a stack of books on her desk, and the walls still adorned with the remnants of purple and pink paint, a testament to the bond she shared with her sister.

This room encapsulated her entire childhood, a repository of memories from sleepovers with cousins, animated discussions about boys, and the latest TV shows.

Her phone buzzed, interrupting her reflections. She didn't need to check the caller ID; she recognized his number.

"How are you?" he inquired when she answered.

"Alhamdulillah," Fatimè replied. "And you?"

"I'm okay. And everyone?"

"Alhamdulillah."

A moment of silence lingered before he asked, "Do you need anything?"

"No," Fatimè responded, her tone curt.

She wanted to inquire about his well-being, whether he had eaten, but the unspoken words hung between them.

"I have to go," she stated.

"Okay. Take care, and regards to everyone," he calmly replied.

Fatimè released a sigh when the call ended. Their conversations had devolved into mere exchanges of greetings and terse responses. They skirted around the issue, the unspoken tension palpable in the house.

That's why, when she requested to come home for Eid, he didn't object. Space seemed necessary. Fatimè hoped that by the time she returned, the ordeal would be behind them.

Mufida knocked and entered, holding a plate of samosas.

"You're still not dressed? I'm sure they've started grilling..." Mufida began.

Fatimè yawned, contemplating whether attending her aunt's Eid barbecue party was worth the effort. It promised stress, yet the distraction seemed needed.

"I still can't decide what to wear," she confessed as she pushed her suitcase toward Mufida, grabbing a samosa for herself.

Sifting through the clothes, Mufida settled on a simple six-piece skirt with a peplum blouse. As Fatimè picked it up, an envelope fell out, bearing the words, "Eid Mubarak sunshine," in his neat handwriting.

"Ah, your husband is sending you off with love letters? Soyaya!" Mufida teased.

Fatimè sighed and opened the envelope, revealing a bundle of 500 naira notes with a note, "Eid Mubarak, enjoy yourself."

She dropped the envelope on the bed, attempting to focus on getting ready.

"Aren't you going to read it?" Mufida asked.

Fatimè shrugged, moving so that Mufida could help her zip up.

"Something is wrong," Mufida observed. "You've not been yourself all week."

Fatimè sat on the bed and turned to Mufida. "I lost another baby a few weeks ago."

"Inna lillahi wa inna ilaihi raji'un," Mufida exclaimed. "Why didn't you tell us? Subhanallah, are you okay?"

"No," Fatimè admitted. "And that's not the only thing. The doctor said it was an abortion, as they found some drugs in my system..."

"Abortion?" Mufida's face twisted in bewilderment. "I don't understand."

"Exactly, Mufida. I am as confused as you are," Fatimè began explaining everything to her cousin.

"The doctors we can dismiss as a misdiagnosis, but the receipt—where did it come from?"

"I don't know," Fatimè replied, her voice shaky. She held her face in her hands, and Mufida moved closer to console her.

"I believe you," Mufida said.

"But he doesn't! He doesn't!" Fatimè cried. "My husband really thinks I killed our baby."

"You need to understand how he feels," Mufida said gently. "He's just as confused as you are. I'm sure about that. And with the receipt, the doctor's report, and what you told Madina, he's bound to be even more confused. Didn't you say he proposed for the matter to be buried?"

Fatimè nodded. "But it's like it's still hanging in the air."

"You need to give it time," Mufida advised. "Pray for things to be sorted out. I'm sure everything will fall into place."

"I need to know where that receipt came from."

"When you return, I'll suggest that you find the pharmacy. That's a good start."

"Yes," Fatimè agreed, nodding. She felt a glimmer of hope that they would uncover the truth, but the uncertainty still weighed heavily on her heart.

Lagos, Nigeria.

16th June, 2018.

"What would you like for lunch, sir?" Mrs. Simon inquired, emerging from the kitchen.

"I'm fine with tea," Kamal responded.

Mrs. Simon started to leave but hesitated. "You have not been eating, sir," she observed, concern evident in her voice.

Kamal managed a smile. "I'm fine, don't worry."

Their conversation was abruptly interrupted by the doorbell. Mrs. Simon went to answer it, and Sa'ad stood at the entrance.

Greeting her with a smile, he walked straight in. "I need to have a conversation with madam," he said. "Just because she's not around, you're forcing me to spend time with you."

"Aren't you happy? It's not like you have a wife and kid at home," Kamal quipped.

"Wow, M.K., I'll vex and marry this year."

"Trust me, you'd all be doing us a favor. There's no denying you need a woman in your life."

"Check that your wife's side now. Looks like she has a hell of a lot of fine cousins. At your wedding, I was just dropping 'Ma sha Allah.'"

Kamal shook his head. "Did you bring what I asked for?"

Sa'ad handed him a sheaf of papers. "Yes, and everything is in order. I have set it up, and Hafsah is the only one that has access to it."

Kamal nodded. "The meeting with the Almeri guys has been confirmed. Are you sure you want me to go in your place?"

"Of course. If there's anyone I can leave the affairs of my company to, it's you."

"You're still going ahead with the sale of the shares?"

"Yes, and only to you."

"But why? M.K., I don't understand. You wake up one day and decide you no longer want to be in charge? Who does that?"

"I just think it's time for me to pursue other interests."

"What do you mean?"

"I've always wanted to retire at 40 so I can travel and spend time with my family while doing things I enjoy. My watch here is done."

"Why are you talking as if you're about to die?"

"Leave drama for women, please. Look, everything is fine. I just have other businesses to attend to, and there's no better person I'll leave the company to."

"But..."

"Do you want something to eat? I'll ask Mrs. Simon to fix you something—rice? Pasta? Let me make a cup of tea for you. Start the game for us; it's been a while since I wiped someone in FIFA.

Gombe, Nigeria.

The atmosphere at Aunt Najmah's residence buzzed with chatter and soft music. The expansive backyard had undergone a vibrant transformation with colorful decorations, grills, platters of diverse meals, and the joyous sounds of children frolicking. The delightful scent of fried meat wafted through the air, teasing Fatimè's senses.

"Tims! Mufida!" one of their cousins called out upon spotting them. "Sai yanzu?"

"She was busy looking for an outfit," Mufida explained.

"Haba amarya, allow the younger ones to shine now," Ramlah said with a smile.

"As if you are not doing the same," Fatimè teased. Ramlah's outfit was a dazzling blend of colors that perfectly complemented the lively atmosphere.

"Is that little Abdallah?" Ramlah asked, reaching for the toddler in Mufida's arms. "Ma sha Allah. He's so handsome."

They strolled around, greeting family members, and Fatimè was taken aback by the compliments on her appearance.

Seated with a group of cousins, she relished the delicious food when an entourage, consisting of her little cousins, nieces, and nephews, approached them. They greeted in unison, "Addas! Yan nyalli jam. Barka da sallah."

"Ahn, all these gayu. You guys are not playing this Sallah," Salma, one of Fatimè's cousins, commented.

"You all deserve Barka da Sallah," Mufida replied. Fatimè reached into her bag and handed each of the young ones a 500-naira note.

"Thank you, Adda Fatimè!" the children chorused before happily skipping away to show off their newfound wealth.

Mubarak, her brother, joined them, holding a plate of well-fried meat. "Tims Funds!" he hailed his sister. "Should I send you my account number?"

"Haba Hamma Mubarak, as big as you are?" Fatimè teased. Mubarak laughed and exchanged pleasantries with his cousins. Then the teasing began.

"When are you bringing us a wife?" Safiyya asked, joining in.

"Aha, finally, I have been begging him to settle down," Fatimè chimed in.

"Gaskiya," Mufida added. "It's about time. Bring us a beauty. We trust your taste."

"Is this an ambush?" Mubarak laughed. "Y'all are slowly becoming Fulbe aunts."

"Oho dai," Safiyya said. "Do and find a wife."

Fatimè left the grilling of her brother to her cousins and went off to get some water.

"Tims!" Fa'iza called when she saw her. "I have been looking for you. Where's the danwake?"

"Kai Adda Fa'i!" Fatimè laughed. "I kept it for you in the kitchen."

"Did you hide it? You know Hamma with danwake, let him not eat it fa."

"Don't worry, it's safe," Fatimè assured her sister-in-law. As expected, Hamma was at the grill with most of her male cousins. He handed her a plate, and she took a bite, then whispered to her sister-in-law, "I understand. He does know his grills.

Fahad parked in front of his aunt's SUV, stifling a yawn. It had been an exhausting day, and all he wanted was to go home and sleep. However, he had an errand to run for his mother. Upon entering the house with Salam, he found his aunt and Fatimè engrossed in a conversation.

"Fahad, you're here," his aunt said, looking up.

"Yes, Yan nyalli jam," Fahad greeted.

"Jam. The items, ko? Let me get them for you," she said, rising.

Fahad turned to Fatimè. "Hi."

"I did not see you at the barbecue," she said, a hint of surprise in her voice.

"I left early. I had some work," Fahad explained.

"Work even on Eid?" she asked incredulously.

"Work never stops for an engineer," Fahad replied.

"How are preparations going?" she inquired.

"Alhamdullilah."

Aunt Sa'adatu soon returned with a bag and handed it to Fahad. "Tell Adda Zainabu that these are the ones I got. The rest are coming in next week."

"Okay," Fahad agreed, taking the bag. "I should get going."

"Me too," Fatimè said, getting up. "It's getting late."

"Yes, yes. Fahad should drop you off," Aunt Sa'adatu concurred. "Don't forget what I told you."

Fatimè smiled. "Okay, Aunt."

In the car, Fahad drove in silence until they reached Fatimè's parents' house. "Can we talk?" he finally said.

"Sure, what's up?" Fatimè responded.

Fahad cleared his throat. "It's about Madina."

"Madina?" Fatimè was taken aback by the mention of Madina. What did she have to do with anything now?

"Zahra found out Madina was responsible for those pictures," Fahad revealed.

"Wait, what? Madina?"

Fatimè was beyond shocked at Fahad's revelation.

"Yes," Fahad continued, "She admitted to it too, but I am still trying to understand the reasons behind her actions."

Fatimè was stunned. "It's because she's in love with you."

"What?" Fahad was equally surprised.

It was now Fahad's turn to be shocked by the revelation.

Lagos, Nigeria.21st May, 2018

The small pharmacy was dimly lit, shelves neatly stacked with an array of medicines. The scent of disinfectant lingered in the air as customers moved quietly, seeking remedies for various ailments. At the far end of the store, a woman approached the counter.

The cashier, a middle-aged woman with a friendly demeanor, looked up from her magazine as the woman placed a box of drugs on the counter.

"Good evening, dear. How can I help you?" The cashier inquired, scanning the item.

The woman flashed a polite smile. "I have a prescription," she said, handing her a paper.

The cashier nodded sympathetically. "I understand. Can I have a name for the receipt?"

With a rehearsed pause, the woman replied, "Mrs. Fatimè Ardo."

The cashier typed the name into the system, completed the transaction, and handed over the drugs. The woman accepted the purchase, the subtle nervousness beneath her facade carefully hidden.

Meanwhile, Fatimè browsed the aisles, selecting a few items for her purchase.

As the woman made her way toward the exit, she inadvertently collided with Fatimè near the pharmacy's entrance. Startled, Fatimè mumbled an apology.

"I'm so sorry," the woman said, recovering quickly. In the brief encounter, she managed to discreetly slip the receipt into Fatimè's bag.

Unaware of the exchange, Fatimè nodded and continued towards the cashier to pay for her items. The woman, satisfied with the successful mission, exited the pharmacy without raising suspicion.

GLOSSARY:

Soyaya - Love.

Sai yanzu? - Is it now?

Yan nyalli jam - Good afternoon.

Barka da Sallah - Happy eid.

Gayu - fashion.

Chapter 26

♥

Lagos, Nigeria.

17th June, 2018.

Kamal stood on the pristine golf course, his golf club cutting through the crisp morning air with calculated precision. The lush greenery surrounded him as he focused on the perfect swing. The ball soared gracefully through the clear sky, and, satisfied with his performance, he turned to retrieve another golf ball, only to find himself unexpectedly face to face with Nabila.

Momentarily startled, Kamal quickly composed himself. "What are you doing here?" he inquired, his tone guarded.

"Attending a wedding, and then I decided to come say hi to my bestie," Nabila replied with a warm smile.

"Hm. How are you?" Kamal deflected, attempting to shift the focus away from himself.

"I should be asking you; you look terrible," Nabila remarked, her concern evident.

"Thanks for the observation," Kamal retorted sarcastically.

"No, I'm serious. What's going on, MK? Sa'ad's call had me worried," Nabila pressed.

"What are you guys now? Lovers? CEOs of the 'Let's Pity Kamal Foundation'?" Kamal quipped, frustration bubbling to the surface.

"MK..."

"No, I need to understand why you guys are staging an intervention. Did I tell you I had a problem?" Kamal's irritation was palpable.

"It's obvious, isn't it? You're selling your shares, and there's the issue with your wife," Nabila gently pointed out.

"My wife and our issues are none of your concern. Why are you guys discussing my wife, anyway?" Kamal's voice grew louder, anger taking hold.

"We're just worried about you," Nabila replied, trying to defuse the tension.

"And I can take care of myself, goddammit! I'm not leaving my business. I'm just trying out something new, and as for my wife, we'll sort it out," Kamal retorted, his frustration reaching its peak.

"When was the last time you saw Tiwa?" Nabila asked, her concern deepening.

"I'm not crazy, okay?! I don't need anybody telling me what to do with my damn life." Kamal hissed and walked away, leaving Nabila standing there, shaking her head.

She immediately placed a call, urgency in her voice. "He's struggling again. We need to do something ASAP.

Abuja, Nigeria.

6th March 2013.

Madina stood outside and dialed him again; this was the third time she had called, but he did not answer. Fortunately, this time around, he picked.

"What are you going to do?" she asked in a half-whisper.

"I don't see why you care." He responded.

"Look, I don't want to be a part of this anymore..."

He laughed, a deep one, "Too late, sweetheart."

"Madina!" Intisar yelled from the balcony, and Madina hurriedly ended the call, "What are you doing? It's time for pictures. Hurry!"

Madina nodded and headed inside, but not without the terrible feeling in her chest.

17th June, 2018.

The same terrible feeling had roused Madina from her sleep that morning, and she let out a low hiss. Her head was pounding, and she groaned in discomfort. This was why she detested road trips; they always gave her a headache.

Mahir, her brother, opened her bedroom door after knocking politely. The room's curtains were drawn, casting a soft, filtered light across the space. He entered with a plate of chips and eggs, the scent of which immediately piqued Madina's interest. She sat up, rubbing her temples.

"You're still in bed?" Mahir asked, taking a seat in the small corner chair.

Madina yawned. "Ehen. Didn't you see how tired I was last night?"

"Everyone was tired," he replied matter-of-factly.

She ignored her brother's comment and headed for the bathroom, realizing she needed to use it. When she returned, she found Mahir's plate empty.

"Kai, Mahir! You finished it already?" Madina exclaimed.

"Yup." Mahir got up, making a move to leave.

"Get me a plate too, Useni. I'm hungry," Madina requested.

Mahir nodded and exited the room, leaving the door ajar. Madina hissed softly, wondering why brothers seemed to have a penchant for such behavior.

At the staircase, Mahir crossed paths with Fatimè and greeted her with a friendly smile.

"To dun Madina?" Fatimè inquired. "I called, but she didn't answer."

"She's in her room," Mahir replied. "She just woke up; I think that's why."

"Okay, Miyatti," Fatimè said, heading straight to Madina's room.

She opened the door to find Madina standing in front of the mirror, combing her hair. The room had an air of disarray, with clothes scattered around haphazardly. Empty suitcases lay open on the floor, remnants of an unpacking process still in progress.

Madina turned when she noticed Fatimè's presence and asked, "When did you come back?"

"I called, but you did not answer."

"I was sleeping," Madina said, grabbing her phone from the bedside.

"How was Kano?" Fatimè asked.

"Hot, but I had fun," Madina replied, continuing to braid her hair into twos. "Did anyone miss me at the barbecue?"

"Of course. You and Intisar," Fatimè replied.

"She mentioned she was coming today," Madina said.

Intisar had spent Eid with her in-laws in Kaduna. The conversation shifted, and Fatimè decided to address a matter that had been bothering her.

"Fahad and I talked," she began. "He told me what happened."

Madina remained silent, focusing on her hair.

"Why? Why would you do something like that?" Fatimè's voice held a mix of disappointment and frustration.

Madina scoffed, flailing her arms. "Because I was desperate, ay?"

"Are you serious right now? Desperate? That's why you tried to ruin their relationship?" Fatimè questioned.

"Please. All I did was share an image that she had sent out herself. It's not like I was the one who snapped her," Madina retorted, trying to justify her actions.

"I cannot believe you are trying to justify what you did. Because of you, Fahad spent months fighting with Ammi and Zahra? Didn't you think this was going to ruin her reputation, even if she married him?"

"Well, then maybe she wasn't meant to marry him? I mean, a girl like that..."

"You have no right to say that, you know. At least, even for Fahad..." Fatimè's voice trailed off as she struggled to find the right words.

"Of course! You are always on his side, Fahad! Fahad! Fahad! Madina is the problem..." Madina snapped.

"No one said that..."

"Oh please, I did what I did because I felt he deserved better..."

"And that's you?"

"Ah yes. Here comes the condescension," Madina retorted.

Fatimè let out a sarcastic laugh. "Are you for real? You are the one thinking you are better than someone else."

"Of course. I deserve to be with Fahad."

"Now you are being ridiculous. What you did is even worse. At least hers can be called a mistake!"

"Yes, and you are a saint, right? Oh yeah, Fatimè, the perfect one who does no wrong, the one that everybody loves. Must be nice."

Fatimè looked at her Madina with bewilderment, trying to understand how this had become about her. Madina's emotions seemed to be spiraling out of control.

The next minute, Madina started crying. "Why can't I ever win? Why does everything bad happen to me? Why?"

Fatimè allowed Madina to cry for a while before speaking up, her tone softer. "Fahad not reciprocating your feelings is not the end of the world. You are not losing in life. I think that is an unfair thing to say. You are a lawyer, working at a successful firm; you are beautiful, and I have never met anyone who fills up a room with just their presence like you do. So, why do you think Fahad loving you is the only thing you need to win?"

Madina scoffed, still wiping away her tears. "Easy for you to say. He has always loved you."

"What is wrong with you?" Fatimè asked, her concern evident.

"Let's be real here, Fatimè. He has always loved you, ever since we were kids, No matter what I did to get his attention, he always chose you..."

The hurt in Madina's tone was evident, and Fatimè felt a pang of guilt. She didn't know what to say.

"You just chose not to see it," Madina continued, her voice trembling. "And the funny thing is, you didn't feel the same way. Life, yeah? I am begging for crumbs while you are throwing the whole bread away."

This time, Fatimè moved to Madina's side. "I don't know what else to say other than I am sorry. I am sorry it didn't work out with Fahad..."

"Madina is in love with Fahad?" Intisar chose that moment to appear.

18th June, 2018.

Fatimè gazed at the variety of dishes elegantly displayed on the dining table and wondered how her mother-in-law expected her to consume such an array of food. Despite her apprehensions about the amount, everything looked irresistibly delicious.

Hajiya Hillu emerged from the kitchen, carrying a sizzling plate of samosas and spring rolls. She noticed Fatimè's hesitation and asked, "You haven't started eating? Don't you like it? Should I prepare something else for you? Do you prefer sinasir?"

"No, no, Maa," Fatimè quickly reassured her. "I was just about to serve myself."

Hajiya Hillu smiled warmly, though she was well aware of her daughter-in-law's shyness. She took over the task of serving and said, "Relax, my dear. Let me do it. Just tell me what you like."

Fatimè nodded with a smile, allowing her mother-in-law to take the lead. Hajiya Hillu proceeded to plate a portion of every dish and arranged them before Fatimè, insisting, "Eat... eat."

Just then, Hafsah entered with a cheerful Salam. Spotting Fatimè, she hurried over. "Ya Fatimè! I didn't know you were coming. When did you get here? How are you? How are you? I was even thinking about coming over next week..."

"Keh," her mother scolded playfully. "Do you want to overwhelm her with your chatter? Please, let her enjoy her meal in peace."

Hafsah stuck her tongue out at her mother's teasing. "I'm just happy to see her. Let me go and change," she said, rising from her seat. "I'll be back; I have some juicy gossip for you."

Hajiya Hillu shook her head and adjusted the temperature of the air conditioner, ensuring the dining room stayed comfortable. Fatimè savored the taste of her meal, especially the catfish pepper soup. Kamal hadn't exaggerated when he claimed his mother made the best catfish pepper soup.

"This is really delicious," Fatimè commented, earning a warm smile from Hajiya Hillu.

"I'm delighted you like it. I prepared it especially for you."

Fatimè inwardly expressed gratitude for having a mother-in-law as wonderful as Hajiya Hillu.

"How are you doing? I hope everything is fine?" Hajiya Hillu expressed genuine concern in her voice.

"Yes, Maa. Everything is okay," Fatimè replied.

Fatimè would sooner perish than reveal whatever issues lingered between her and Kamal to his family. She trusted that they would eventually resolve everything together.

"Alhamdulillah. I pray Allah preserves the love between you both. Please continue to be patient with each other," Hajiya Hillu offered her blessings.

"Amin. Amin," Fatimè responded, focusing on her meal.

By the time Hafsah returned, Fatimè had finished eating. Hafsah's energetic and chatty presence was exactly what Fatimè needed to lighten her mood.

"I'm telling you, this is why I don't trust most of these 'Instagram' vendors. That's how..." Hafsah began her tale but was abruptly interrupted by Rukayya's greeting as she entered, carrying a sleeping Adil in her arms.

"Ya Rukayya, ina yini..." Hafsah greeted. "Little gremlin is out, I see. Let me take him upstairs."

Rukayya handed the sleeping Adil to Hafsah. Throughout the exchange, Fatimè remained silent. After all, what was she supposed to say to her husband's ex-wife?

20th June, 2018.

The atmosphere inside the car was thick with tension; a sense of unease hung between Zahra and Fahad as they sat side by side.

"You still haven't told me where we are going," Zahra broke the silence, her voice tinged with uncertainty. "I don't even know why I agreed to go out with you."

Fahad's gaze remained fixed on the road ahead as he replied, "Oh, so going out with your fiancé is now a problem?"

"I don't need to tell you the reason why," Zahra continued, her words trailing off. "I mean, with the way things are going... I doubt if we..."

Before Zahra could finish her sentence, Fahad interrupted, "Doubt what? What are you trying to say?"

"If someone is willing to go all the way to not see us together, I have every right to be afraid of committing to you," Zahra retorted, her voice laden with frustration. "Who knows what else she has up her sleeve? Look, I am just not ready to be fighting battles with your family. I already know what your mom thinks of me..."

Fahad sighed and rubbed the side of his head, "I know what you want to say, but trust me, all of that does not matter now. She has accepted that what happened was a mistake that you deeply regret."

"I can never get the image out of their heads," Zahra insisted, her anxiety showing. "Don't blame me for looking out for myself."

Fahad pulled over at their destination and gestured for Zahra to exit the car. She mustered a weak smile and walked into the restaurant, but her expression quickly shifted to a frown when she saw who was seated there.

Inside the restaurant, Fatimè wasn't surprised by Zahra's reaction.

"What is she doing here?" Zahra asked, her voice laced with skepticism.

Fahad, in an effort to mediate, urged, "Just talk to her."

After a moment of hesitation, Zahra pulled out a chair and sat down. The restaurant had an inviting ambiance, with soft lighting and elegant decor that created an intimate atmosphere.

"Hi," Fatimè greeted, offering a polite smile. "I know I am one of the last people you want to see, but I felt the need to talk to you."

"About?" Zahra asked, her tone guarded.

"Fahad told me what happened..."

"Yeah, yeah. Your cousin tried to sabotage our relationship?" Zahra scoffed. "She cannot show her face, so she decided to send you instead? As what? Her spokesperson? This is ridiculous. Who even knows if you were in on it?"

Fatimè felt her temper rising but maintained her composure, reminding herself that she was here for Fahad's sake.

She took a deep breath before responding, "Okay, I get that you are upset, but it's not like I want to be here. I have a million and one things to do with my time..."

Fatimè's outburst was enough to silence her for a moment.

"But," Fatimè continued, "Seeing as my 'cousin' is worried about losing you..." Fatimè chose her words carefully, "I have to take one for the team. What Madina did was terrible, but that is her issue. I am not here for her, but for the sake of the love you and Fahad share. I am begging you to let things be..."

"It's how everyone is asking me to let go," Zahra replied, her voice weary. "You think I want to drag this?"

"I understand where you are coming from," Fatimè empathized, "It's just that telling everyone Madina is responsible for sending those pictures is not going to change anything..."

Zahra appeared utterly disbelieving of what she was hearing, but Fatimè pressed on, "I am just being honest. She would get an earful, no doubt, but it'll only reopen old wounds, and I'm sure that is not what we want..."

With a scoff, Zahra folded her arms defensively. The situation had taken its toll on her, and she was growing tired of the conflict.

"Look," Fatimè continued, her tone gentle, "The bone of contention here is that Fahad loves you very much and he wants to be with you. Stop giving him a hard time."

"So she is just going to go scot-free?" Zahra asked, her voice tinged with frustration. "No repercussions?"

"Your marriage to Fahad is enough of a repercussion. Trust me," Fatimè replied with conviction.

"Thank you very much." Fahad expressed his gratitude to Fatimè when they stepped outside the restaurant.

Fatimè offered him a warm smile. "I just hope it works out. You deserve to be happy."

Fahad nodded and was about to leave when he halted in his tracks. "I have been wanting to tell you something."

"Sure, what's up?" Fatimè asked, intrigued.

"So there's this project I have been working on, and the owner is your husband's ex-wife."

Fatimè couldn't help but laugh. "There's no need to tell me. Personal lives should not get in the mix of business."

"No, it's not that," Fahad explained. "I think you two need to talk."

Chapter 27

♥

Abuja, Nigeria.

22nd June, 2018.

Rukayya stood at the entrance of the restaurant, her demeanor uncertain. The restaurant was still in the midst of its construction phase, with the scent of fresh paint and the echoes of hammering and drilling lingering in the air.

"Let's go to that side..." she suggested, her voice lowered. "There's so much noise in here."

Fatimè agreed, and they walked toward a quieter corner of the restaurant, seeking refuge from the ongoing renovations. As they settled into their seats, an awkward tension hung in the air. Fatimè was eager to hear what Rukayya had to say, as the situation had piqued her curiosity.

Rukayya broke the silence, her words carrying a mixture of emotions. "When I heard Kamal was getting married again, honestly, I did not care. But when I saw you, I became worried."

Fatimè raised an eyebrow, surprised by Rukayya's candid admission. She wondered if Rukayya felt threatened by her presence.

"Kamal and I's marriage was arranged," Rukayya continued, "So I did not go in with any expectations. But I thought both of us would try to at least make it work, and that was when I found out it was three of us in this marriage."

Fatimè was genuinely puzzled. "Three of you?"

Rukayya nodded. "Me, him, and the love of his life."

She was silent as she knew of the Piya situation but she waited to hear Rukayya's side, "This is where things get interesting, this girl and you.. are so similar."

Fatimè's eyes widened in surprise. She hadn't anticipated the conversation taking such a turn. "So, you think he married me because I look like the same girl he once loved?"

Rukayya sighed, her gaze distant as she recalled her experiences. "He was obsessed with this girl, a very unhealthy obsession. He had keepsakes of her—pictures, mementos, and more..."

Fatimè struggled to grasp the implications of Rukayya's revelations. "And what did you do about all of these?"

"I was already pregnant," Rukayya explained, her voice tinged with resignation. "I thought, why not try to make it work? At least for the baby. And I have to admit, things were going well until I almost lost Adil. I woke up one day bleeding, and we rushed to the hospital. Although the baby was safe, the doctor reported it was an attempted abortion."

Fatimè was taken aback. "Wait, what?"

"Yes," Rukayya confirmed with a solemn nod. "I was very confused until I overheard a conversation.

7th July, 2018.

The wedding hall was a grand spectacle, adorned with elaborate decorations ranging from cascading fairy lights to opulent floral arrangements. The air buzzed with lively chatter of guests and the rhythmic beats of the music, creating an atmosphere of celebration and joy for Fahad and Zahra's wedding.

Kamal sat at the far end of the hall, immersed in the festivities, sipping a cool diet coke as he swayed gently to the infectious beats. Unbeknownst to Fatimè, she spotted him from across the hall as she contemplated stepping outside for a breath of fresh air. Her surprise was evident as she approached his table.

"What are you doing here?" she asked, genuinely taken aback.

Kamal, with his usual charm, pulled out a seat for her. "Attending an event I was invited to," he replied, casually taking another sip of his coke.

Fatimè realized she had entirely forgotten that she had sent him an invite. "You did not tell me you were coming," she remarked.

"It was a last-minute decision," Kamal explained before offering a compliment. "You look beautiful."

Fatimè's cousin, Halima, couldn't contain her enthusiasm. She approached the couple with an infectious grin. "Fatimè!" she exclaimed. "So this is your husband? No wonder you've been hiding him. He is so handsome."

Fatimè cleared her throat at her cousin's suggestive comment but proceeded to introduce them. "This is my cousin, Halima," she said to Kamal.

"Nice to meet you," Kamal replied with a warm smile.

Halima didn't hold back her admiration. "You are so handsome, Ma sha Allah," she added again, her tone filled with admiration.

Fatimè felt like wiping the grin off her cousin's face. She swiftly got up, pulling Kamal along. "We have to go," she declared.

"But the event is not over," Halima protested.

Kamal stood beside Fatimè, struggling to stifle his laughter, while Fatimè shot him an annoyed look. "I have a headache. Excuse us," she explained curtly as she led Kamal away.

Halima shook her head after their departure, muttering, "What a snob."

Once outside, Kamal gallantly opened the car door for Fatimè, who still wore a frown on her face. He couldn't help but laugh. "What's funny?" she demanded.

"Nothing," he replied, but his laughter eventually overcame him. "You look so cute when you're jealous."

"I'm not jealous. Jealous of what?" Fatimè retorted defensively.

"Someone called your husband handsome, and I could see the smoke coming out of your ears. Is that not why you asked us to leave?"

"Of course not," Fatimè insisted. "I was not even bothered, and my head really hurts."

"Sorry, baby," Kamal said, gently placing his palm on her forehead. Her physical response to his touch was evident in the way she relaxed, her features softening.

During their ride home, he reached out for her hand, and she willingly offered it. "Kamal is only for Fatimè," he reassured her with a loving smile.

9th July, 2018.

Madina sat at her desk, immersed in reviewing legal statutes when Sarah entered her office. She looked up, acknowledging her colleague with a nod.

"Good morning, Madina," Sarah greeted. "Have you had a chance to review the Johnson case files yet?"

Madina nodded again. "Yes, I have. It appears to be quite intricate."

Sarah leaned in, a focused look in her eyes. "I've compiled a timeline of events to help us structure the argument."

Madina considered the approach. "Okay, I'll focus on analyzing the relevant precedents and case law."

"Excellent," Sarah said with determination. "Can we aim for a meeting by the end of the day?"

Madina readily agreed, "Sure, sure."

Their discussion was abruptly interrupted by Madina's phone ringing. Sarah excused herself from the office.

Madina picked up the phone, her voice laced with a mix of frustration and exasperation. "You finally decided to call me back, huh?"

The voice on the other end replied with an air of indifference, "Why are you bombarding me with calls?"

Madina retorted, "Oh, now I am bombarding you with calls?"

A hint of annoyance crept into the man's voice. "Ten missed calls, Madina. Do I happen to have your kidney?"

Madina's patience waned. "Do you think this is the time to be funny? My life is falling apart, and you're making jokes?"

His response remained unapologetic, "What am I supposed to do about that, huh?"

Madina's anger flared. "Oho! That's what you're going to say? You know I can ruin your life in split seconds."

His tone grew defiant, "Oh really? Please do your worst. I'd like to see you try."

As Madina listened to his words, tears welled up in her eyes. She felt overwhelmed by the situation, realizing the depths of trouble she had fallen into.

"You know what's funny?" he continued, unyielding. "You're deep in this mess, and I'm not going down without you."

Madina slumped in her chair, her grip tightening on the phone. Regret washed over her, and she couldn't help but feel trapped in a dire situation.

Lagos, Nigeria.

20th July, 2018.

"Here," Kamal said, handing her a bag containing two packs of frozen yogurt. "The blueberry one was unavailable, so I got you this instead."

"Thank you. How was your day?" Fatimè asked, her fingers already itching to dig into her froyo.

Kamal let out a tired sigh. "Meh. Meetings upon meetings."

Fatimè raised an eyebrow, curiosity piqued. "Did you get to set one with the Al-Sheikh guy?"

Kamal's eyes lit up with excitement. "Yes! We're set to meet on Monday. I just need to put some finishing touches on the software, and that's it."

For a long while, Kamal had been diligently working on a supply chain software, pitching it to several companies. Fortune had finally smiled at him when the owner of one of Dubai's largest manufacturing companies responded positively. He was now on the cusp of making millions.

"Congratulations," Fatimè said, her enthusiasm genuine as she hugged him tightly. "I'm so happy for you."

Kamal corrected her with a gleam in his eye. "Us, baby."

Their gazes locked, and before she knew it, his lips met hers. The kiss was slow, gentle, and filled with longing. It was evident that they had both missed each other deeply.

Abuja, Nigeria.

22nd July, 2018.

Khalifa felt like his legs were about to detach from his body. The weariness etched into his bones was evidence of his day's journey around Wuse Market. Accompanying his mother, they visited numerous stalls, engaging in relentless bargaining that had taken a toll on him.

"Please, just keep them there," Hajiya Hauwa said, her voice tired and drained of energy, pointing to the corner by the couch. "Kai, I am tired."

Khalifa flopped down beside her, mirroring her fatigue. Both of them let out a collective sigh of exhaustion.

"Yauwa, before you go, check what is wrong with this phone. I have been trying to send a WhatsApp message since yesterday..."

Khalifa took the phone and proceeded to investigate the issue. He suspected it was either a problem with her data or the need for an app update.

Mubarak announced his presence with a courteous salam and dropped at their mother's feet, his weariness mirroring Khalifa's.

"Mami, Yan nyalli jam? Mi somi walahi."

"You've finished the shoot already?" Hajiya Hauwa inquired.

"Yes, Mami. I am also hungry. Is there any food?"

Hajiya Hauwa rolled her eyes and mimicked Mubarak's question, eliciting a chuckle from Khalifa.

"At this age, aren't you supposed to be going home to your wife's meal?" she teased.

"Mamiiiiii," Mubarak whined. "This wife thing again?"

"Yes, this wife thing again," Hajiya Hauwa repeated with a warm smile. "You need to settle down, Mubarak."

Khalifa couldn't help but enjoy watching his brother being grilled, but the tables turned when Mubarak reminded him of his duties, "You are here laughing; don't go and repair that parking. How do you want Babaa to park?"

"But Hamma Mubarak," Khalifa protested, the idea of descending those stairs again weighing on him.

Mubarak responded with mock indifference, "Okay, fine. Let the car stay as it is."

Khalifa knew the scolding he'd receive from his father if he left the car as it was, so he begrudgingly got up and handed his mother her phone.

"I have updated the app; it should work now."

"Thank you, dan auta na," she said gratefully.

Mubarak couldn't resist making a gagging sound at their display of affection and managed to steer the conversation toward something else.

Hajiya Hauwa returned to the sitting room after a refreshing shower, her fragrant lemon sugar body wash delicately scenting the air. She found her husband seated on the couch, his cap and shoes still on, indicating his recent arrival home.

"Sannu e wartuki," she greeted warmly. "How was your day?"

The room was infused with the soothing scent of burning bakhoor as she moved to sit beside him, savoring its aroma as she leaned in.

"It was fine, although tiring," he replied, wrapping his arm around her. "I enjoyed the game."

He had attended a polo match organized in honor of one of his friend's sons, who was getting married.

"Shall I bring your food now?" Hajiya Hauwa offered.

He declined with a shake of his head. "I'll just have tea. How was your day?"

As she prepared the tea tray, she recounted the incident in the market where a vendor had attempted to cheat her.

"Can you imagine? He thought it was my first time buying it, so he doubled the price."

Moving behind him, she massaged his tired shoulders as he closed his eyes. The knots in his muscles slowly unraveled under her skilled touch.

"Have you spoken to your daughter?" she asked casually.

"Yes, this morning. Why do you ask?"

Her movements were gentle as she massaged him, her fingers working their magic on his weary body. He could feel the fatigue slowly leaving him.

"I don't know," she said thoughtfully. "I just have this feeling that there's something she's not telling us. Her little holiday, it was as if something was wrong."

"Did you ask her about it?" he inquired.

"You're behaving as if you don't know your daughter," Hajiya Hauwa replied with a soft smile. "She's always fine. But I suspect something happened between her and her husband."

"They looked fine to me before they left," he remarked. "And every couple has their little issues. They're adults; they can sort it out themselves. Besides, if it were something serious, she would let us know."

Hajiya Hauwa nodded in agreement but couldn't shake off the nagging feeling in her chest.

Lagos, Nigeria.

25th July, 2018.

Fatimè sat in front of the dresser, her hands running through her damp hair. She had no energy left to attempt a blow-dry, so she settled for a silk scarf to tie around her head. Her mind wandered to the squishy feeling in her stomach.

The scent of his cologne wafted to her nose, announcing his presence. He walked up to her and planted a soft kiss on her cheek. "What are you thinking about?"

"Nothing," she replied softly, biting her lips.

"Hmm." He placed his thumb on her lips. "If you keep doing that, we might have to take another shower."

Fatimè covered her face with her hands, and he chuckled. "Shy, shy."

He opened one of the drawers in the closet and picked out a T-shirt and shorts. Fatimè watched him dress without a word, still in her robe.

After he finished dressing, he stood behind her, his tall frame towering over her. "Are you okay?" he asked, placing a gentle hand on her shoulder.

She nodded slowly.

"I'm sorry," he apologized sincerely. "I should not have doubted you in any way. The receipt, the doctor... please forget about it."

"I still need to know where the pills came from," she said firmly. "Pills just found their way into my bag? What if it was an abortion? I know I did not do it, but someone did, and I need to find out who."

Kamal sighed. "Well, there are three of us in this house: you, me, and Mrs. Simon. If you and I did not do it, then..."

"No," she interrupted, her voice adamant. "Mrs. Simon would never..."

"Of course, I trust her 100 percent," he assured her.

Fatimè let out a frustrated sigh, and Kamal walked around to face her, kneeling and holding her hands. "This is why we need to let it go," he implored.

"Let it go? A lot of mysterious things have happened in my life. Remember the cameras in my room? Someone is out to get me."

Kamal understood her paranoia and rubbed her back. "I'm not saying I have all the answers, but we'll figure it out," he promised.

"I spoke to Rukayya," Fatimè suddenly blurted out. It seemed like the right time to seek an explanation from him.

"What? My ex-wife?" Kamal raised an eyebrow. "Why?"

"Did you marry me because I look so much like the love of your life?" Fatimè's eyes searched his, seeking the truth.

Kamal let out a sarcastic laugh but stopped when he saw the sincerity in her expression. "You're actually serious?"

"You haven't answered my question," she pressed.

He shook his head, his tone sincere. "One, you are the only love of my life, and no, that's not why I married you. But it's true I was once in love with this girl named Piya."

"Obsessed is a strong word, Fatimè. I loved her. Keyword – 'loved.' I understand why Rukayya is saying all of this. I have to admit that part of the reason why our marriage did not work was my inability to accept that Piya was no longer a part of my life. I have apologized for that. I've worked on it."

Kamal paused and narrowed his eyes, his voice taking a more serious tone. "Are you really comparing our marriage to my marriage with Rukayya?"

"No," Fatimè quickly clarified. "I just wanted to hear it from you. That's all."

Kamal knew there was more to her curiosity, but he didn't push. Instead, he kissed her goodnight, and they both retired to bed.

October 2011

This time around, she was the one who met him on the bench. As usual, the enticing scent hit her nose, and she wondered what could go wrong with a well-dressed, good-looking man. Yet, there she was too, seemingly perfect on the outside but fighting internal battles.

The silence between them lasted for a few minutes before she broke it. "I cannot believe I am here because of a man."

"That makes two of us," he said.

She gave him a look, and he quickly added, "I am here because of a woman."

"Oh," she said.

"So this man, what did he do?"

"Nothing," she replied, "Absolutely nothing. Just that I am madly in love with him."

"Let me guess, he doesn't feel the same way?"

"Yeah. He's into someone else who doesn't see him that way."

"Ah yes, the brutal circle of life. Does he know?"

"No."

"So, all of these are based on assumptions. You are not sure if he 'loves' this other girl?"

"Well, his actions say otherwise. He puts her above me, all the time. When she's there, it's like I don't even exist."

She remembered the first time it hit her; they were 10 and on their first horse riding lesson. The instructor had suggested one horse for two persons, and just when she picked him to be her partner, he preferred to go with the other girl instead.

"I'm sorry about that," he said, "I know exactly how unrequited love feels. Does she know, though?"

"Who?"

"The other girl. It seems like you're close."

"She's my cousin."

"That's close..."

"Yeah, she has no idea, even now that she's in a very serious relationship. He's only ever had eyes for her."

"What's with the other girl? What made her so special? Can I see her?" he asked, all in one breath, "Sorry. I'm being intrusive."

She laughed a little and handed him her phone.

He looked at the picture and let out a small gasp, "Looks like my lucky day, miss..."

"Madina..." she completed, "Madina Hamidu...

Chapter 28

♥

Lagos, Nigeria.

30th July, 2018.

The only sound in the car was the soft hum from the radio, and Fatimè's hands remained firmly clasped in Kamal's for the past thirty minutes. Neither of them wanted to let go. Her head still rested on his shoulder as they pulled over at her office. She raised her head and adjusted her veil.

"I should be back in a week," he said, his voice tinged with reluctance. "Are you sure I shouldn't get Hafsah to come stay with you?"

"I'll be fine. Mrs. Simon is here," she assured him, handing him a sweater. "I forgot to pack this. With the rain and all, it'll be cold."

"Sure, thank you, baby," he replied, giving her a tender kiss on the forehead.

Fatimè stepped into the office, her footsteps slightly weary, the rich flowing fabric of her pink abaya sat gracefully around her frame. The intricate embroidery on the sleeves and hem added an elegant touch to the attire, showcasing her style even on days when exhaustion threatened to take over.

The room was filled with the scent of freshly brewed coffee mingling with the sound of a pen gliding across paper.

Adaeze looked up from her computer screen as Fatimè entered, her neatly styled weave cascading down her shoulders, framing her face with its sleekness.

Fatimè sighed, collapsing into the chair next to Adaeze's desk, "Ah Adaeze, you would not believe the day I have had..."

"You look stunning despite the tiredness," Adaeze remarked with a playful grin. "I swear you can make even a long day at a construction site look glamorous."

Fatimè chuckled, her exhaustion momentarily lifting as she appreciated Adaeze's compliment. "Trust me, there is nothing glamorous about negotiating with contractors or dealing with unexpected changes."

"What happened?" Adaeze asked.

"We have made some significant progress with the foundation. The structural engineer came through and was able to address those concerns we had last week..."

"That's good news," Adaeze said. "You are on track. What about the interior spaces? Did you manage to finalize the layout?"

Fatimè leaned back, a touch of frustration crossing her features, "Not quite yet. We had some unexpected changes from the client. They decided to incorporate additional rooms on the second floor, which meant we had to go back to the drawing board and reassess the entire floor plan. It has been a bit of a headache."

"I can only imagine," Adaeze empathized, "clients and their ever-changing demands."

"I know, right," Fatimè said, "I have been brainstorming some new ideas to accommodate the changes. It is going to require some adjustments, but I think we can create something even better than we already planned.

The conversation shifted gears, and they began discussing the upcoming design presentation they had scheduled with the client.

Abuja, Nigeria.

30th July, 2018.

The room was filled with the soft hum of the air conditioner, creating a comfortable and relaxed atmosphere. Zahra was wrapped around Fahad, her arms holding him tightly. They enjoyed the peaceful moment until the sudden ring of a phone disrupted their tranquility.

Fahad reluctantly untangled himself from Zahra's embrace and reached for his phone. The caller's name displayed as "Madina." "Can we talk?" Madina's message popped up on the screen.

Fahad hesitated for a moment, his brow furrowing. "Are you alright?" he typed back. "I thought we were done with this."

Madina's response appeared almost instantly. "It is very important. It is about Fatimè. I think she is in danger."

Fahad sighed, his concern growing. "Madina, I am in no mood for your antics."

"I am dead serious, Fahad. Please come outside. Let's talk."

Fahad detected the seriousness in her tone, prompting him to open the door and step out. He spotted Madina's Venza parked a few houses away and walked up to her.

Madina let out a sigh of relief when she saw him, and Fahad didn't waste any time. "What is wrong with Fatimè?"

Madina hesitated for a moment before responding, "Nothing..."

Fahad hissed in frustration, "Look Madina, if this is one of your antics, I'd suggest you put a stop to it. I don't have time for nonsense."

"Her husband, he is not who you think he is."

Fahad's curiosity was now piqued. "And where did you get this information from?"

"Because I know him, daresay more than his wife."

Fahad's confusion mixed with disbelief was evident in his expression. "We met at a hospital... Way before he knew Fatimè. We had the same therapist. We often sat in silence until we opened up to each other. I told him about you and how I thought Fatimè was standing in the way of us being together."

"What?" Fahad exclaimed, "Again with this nonsense? I never liked Fatimè that way; I saw you all the same, as my cousins. Besides, wasn't she with Khalid?"

Madina scoffed, "You know that is not true. You and her were always close. It was like you were in love with her, ever since we were kids."

Fahad refrained from admitting he used to have a crush on Fatimè.

"At that time, her and Khalid had some issues, and it looked like something was going to happen between you two. So, I asked Kamal to step in..."

"What do you mean, 'step in'?"

"The plan was for him to just make sure you two didn't end up together. But I guess he fell in love at first glance. Before he could make a move, Khalid came back into the picture. You see, with Khalid back, there was no need again, but he did not let go. I did not understand why. It was like he had something personal against her. He would stalk her, and it started to look like it was now an obsession."

"And you kept all this away from her? How did he even end up marrying her? Were you in on it?"

Madina kept quiet.

"Answer me, Madina!" Fahad's anger was evident, and Madina felt a pang of fear.

"I tried to get him out of it, but he was already crazy, talking about revenge and all. I was scared he would do something to me because something is telling me he had a hand in what happened to Khalid..."

"What? Khalid's death was an accident, right?"

"Right now, I am not so sure. The day I told him Fatimè was getting married to Khalid, he said he'd make sure it never happens."

"Inalilahi. Madina, are you serious right now? With all of this, you were still..."

"I did not have any proof, and again, it was another opportunity for you and her to be together, so I..." She stuttered, "I helped him get her. I set up the meeting at the airport, gave him all the information. He promised me he was going to take care of her; he told me he loved her..."

"Kai!" Fahad exclaimed, banging his fist on the dashboard. "You are the most selfish and despicable person I have ever met. All this for what?"

"I just wanted to be with you..."

Fahad let out a sarcastic laugh, "And tell me, how is that going for you, huh? You jeopardized someone else's life all for your stupid selfish gains. Fatimè is like your sister, for crying out loud. I don't even think there is anyone she trusts in the world more than you, and you went ahead to set her up with a freaking psychopath."

"He has been treating her well, hasn't he? Is she not happy? Was she not the one who consented to marrying him? All I did was help; I did not force her."

"Oh my God. I cannot believe you right now. You are still delusional. You still see nothing wrong with what you have done..."

"I am trying to fix it, goddammit! Is that now why I am here?"

"Why did you say she is in danger? Is he planning to hurt her or what?"

"I don't know. But I can feel something is up. We need to get her out of there ASAP."

Fahad couldn't believe he had to deal with all of this in the midst of his honeymoon, but he had no choice. He would never forgive himself if anything happened to Fatimè.

Lagos, Nigeria.

"Fatimè felt the weight of exhaustion as she yearned to go home and crash. Her hopes, however, were dashed when Sadiq blocked her path.

Ignoring him, she walked towards her car, but he persisted. 'I need to talk to you.'

'I don't think I have anything to say to you, so please leave my way,' Fatimè replied curtly, trying to dismiss him.

Sadiq remained determined, his eyes fixed on her. 'I am not going to take much of your time. It's about what happened.'

Reluctantly, Fatimè gave him a listening ear, expecting an apology.

'I've been digging into the presentation incident,' he began. 'I found crucial information about a phishing attack on your Archivault account.'

'How is that possible?' Fatimè retorted. 'I've always been careful with my login details. If anyone got a hold of it, that would be you.'

Ignoring her accusation, Sadiq explained, 'It was a well-crafted phishing attack. You received an email from the Archivault support team, urging you to update your login details. Does that ring a bell?'

'I think I remember receiving something like that. It seemed legitimate,' Fatimè replied.

'Exactly. That's how they got your login details. The login page was replicated, and they gained access to mess with your presentation files.'

'Okay and?' Fatimè asked. 'I don't understand where this conversation is heading. I think that was already established. The question here is who? Because I don't believe scammers would have any need to include an explicit video in my presentation files. The whole thing seems calculated and personal."

'I was getting to that,' Sadiq said with impatience. 'I traced the email and handed it to our IT department. They returned with a report.' He handed her a file. 'All you need to know is inside there.' With that, he walked away, leaving Fatimè to delve into the report's contents."

Abuja, Nigeria.

Fahad braced himself for the impending nagging and protest from Zahra as he broke the news of his urgent work trip. He couldn't reveal the real reason – that he was going to see Fatimè – if he wanted to return home as her husband. It took a considerable amount of cajoling and convincing, but Zahra finally relented after he promised to be back by tomorrow evening.

As he packed for the trip, Fahad couldn't shake off the worry for Fatimè's well-being. Unbeknownst to Zahra, Madina would be accompanying him, a fact kept hidden for obvious reasons. At the airport, Madina's relieved expression greeted him.

'The flight has been delayed,' she informed him.

Frustration etched on his face, Fahad sighed. 'What did you tell Umma?'

'That I had a conference tomorrow and would be staying at Fatimè's.'

Fahad nodded, motioning for her to sit. His thoughts were consumed by the impending revelation and, most importantly, his concern for Fatimè.

This would be a colossal blow for her – discovering the person she trusted most was a liar or, worse, that she was married to a psychopath. Overwhelming sadness gripped Fahad; it seemed like Fatimè couldn't catch a break.

No words passed between Fahad and Madina because nothing could capture the magnitude of what she had done.

'I am going to make a phone call,' Fahad stated before walking away.

He knew just the person to call, and she picked up on the third ring. 'Engineer...'

'Miss Rukayya, how are you doing?' Fahad greeted.

'Alhamdulillah. How is work? Is there any problem?' Rukayya inquired.

'No, no,' he assured her. 'I just need your help.'

'Okay...'

'I need you to tell me all you know about your ex-husband,' Fahad requested urgently."

Lagos, Nigeria.

The drive home with Henry was a quiet one, Fatimè gazing out the window, her mind a whirlwind of thoughts attempting to make sense of the revelations. Was Sadiq telling the truth? Every piece of information he shared seemed to fit together perfectly. The puzzle pieces formed a clear picture, but the nagging question persisted: Why?

Why would Kamal do something like this? Hacking into a company's system to sabotage her presentation – what was the motive? To embarrass her? Fatimè couldn't comprehend what was happening. Her phone rang, but she ignored it upon seeing Kamal's name on the screen. If he was capable of this, what else was he hiding?

As they arrived home, Henry parked the car, and Fatimè immediately stepped out. Her heart pounded, and everyone and everything suddenly felt like a threat. Henry passed her the keys and bid his goodbyes. Mrs. Simon had sent a text earlier saying she wouldn't be coming in today, so there was no one in the house.

Her phone buzzed again, and she picked it up. 'Fatimè...,' Nafisa called. 'How are you? I've been wanting to call you, wallahi, but I've had no time. Sorry about not being able to meet up the last time.'

'It's fine, Adda,' Fatimè replied. 'I've been caught up with work too.'

'Oh Allah sarki,' Nafisa responded. 'I said let me call to check up on you.'

'That is so sweet of you. Thank you. I hope you are doing well? And the kids?'

'They are all fine. They send their regards.'

Fatimè was about to conclude the call when she remembered something. 'Uhm, Adda, you once mentioned something about my husband looking familiar...'

'Yes, yes,' Nafisa answered. 'I remember him now from our uni. I used to see him on campus. I think he was a year ahead of Furaira and me, but I stopped seeing him after a while. Is something wrong?'

Fatimè's heart skipped a beat. Kamal had told her about dropping out of medical school, but he never mentioned going to the same school as her sister.

'Please check your WhatsApp; I am going to send you something,' Fatimè said.

'Okay.'

Fatimè rushed upstairs and retrieved the picture of her sister, sending it to Nafisa with the caption, 'Do you know this girl?'

'Yes,' Nafisa responded almost immediately. 'That is Safaraah Maitambari. She was in our class.'

'She's Kamal's cousin.'

'Oh haba? What a small world.'

So he did know her sister? Why had he kept it from her? What else was he hiding?"

Fatimè spent the better part of her evening searching her house, desperate for answers.

Kamal's room was her first stop, but she found nothing. If he hid something like this from her, why would he leave anything lying around?

The remaining parts of the house yielded nothing either. She stood at the door of the room by the living room that served as a storage closet and tried her luck.

Everything was neatly arranged, and she skimmed through most of the items, most of which were wedding gifts she hadn't opened yet.

The unopened stroller and crib set tugged at her heartstrings, but she pushed aside her emotions and started opening drawers and cabinets.

Again, she found nothing and let out a frustrated sigh. Maybe there was nothing to find, and she was just wasting her time. The problem was, she didn't even know what she was looking for.

Maybe she should just wait for Kamal to come home, hold her, and tell her everything was a lie.

On the verge of giving up, Fatimè remembered one place she hadn't checked—the study.

As usual, the study was pristine and organized. She checked the shelves and drawers, but all she found were Kamal's work-related materials.

At the far end of the room, she noticed something on the wall—an in-built safe.

How had she never seen that before? Well, to be fair, she hardly spent time in this room; it was mostly used by Kamal.

Walking over to the safe, she realized it had a lock. Of course, it had a lock; it was a safe, after all.

The dilemma now was how to figure out the combination. She went with the usual option first, like his date of birth, but it didn't work. Another try with his ATM pin was unsuccessful. She had one more attempt left and thought hard about it, her frustration evident on her face.

With her last option, she hoped with all her might that it would work—the number equivalent of 'piya.' Miraculously, it did the trick, and the safe opened.

She took a deep breath, knowing she had no idea what she would find inside, but she had to know.

Picking up an envelope, she found a collection of important work documents, contracts, ownership proofs, and certificates.

One document, in particular, caught her attention—an admission letter to an institution. Fatimè swallowed hard as she realized it was Kamal's admission letter to a university.

She kept it aside and discovered a laptop. Who kept a laptop in a safe? She wasn't surprised to find it password-protected.

The dilemma of unlocking the laptop followed, and this time, luck was on her side. The passcode equivalent of 'piya' worked, granting her access to the laptop.

At first, everything seemed normal until she opened the pictures folder. Inside, she found over a hundred pictures of her sister, taken without her knowledge. Fatimè gasped in shock—pictures of Furaira in various places, like at school, walking around, in restaurants, and even at a supermarket.

What the hell was this? Kamal had been stalking her sister?

There were videos, too. Fatimè couldn't believe her eyes. Kamal had been stalking her sister.

But her investigation wasn't over. The next folder she opened left her breathless. Inside, she found pictures of herself in her room and her bathroom—private moments she thought were hidden from prying eyes.

How could this be? She realized with horror that Kamal did not only stalk her sister but her as well.

All this while, he was the one behind the cameras in her room? Her mind raced as she struggled to comprehend the enormity of the betrayal.

This was too much to bear. She slumped to the floor, feeling overwhelmed by the weight of the revelation.

It was no longer just about her; it was about finding out the extent of Kamal's deception. Was Furaira, Piya? Were there secret lovers involved?

Fatimè's mind raced as she considered the implications. The way Kamal had entered her life, was it all a coincidence, or was it a carefully orchestrated plan? The warnings from Nabila, Rukayya's cryptic messages—all the pieces began to fit together.

Had Kamal been responsible for the abortion? She had dismissed Rukayya's overheard conversation as a misunderstanding, but now she couldn't be so sure.

She recalled the conversation as Rukayya had told her:

"You told me it was going to work? You're really incompetent. You ruined my plans!" Kamal's anger reverberated through the room. He didn't wait for a response and cut the call short. Turning around, he saw Rukayya standing by the hallway.

"Why are you up?" he asked. "The doctor said you should get some rest." The air in the room was heavy with tension as Kamal and Rukayya stood on opposite ends of their living room. The evening sun cast long shadows, mirroring the growing distance in their relationship.

Rukayya's eyes flashed with indignation. Kamal's face hardened with frustration. "Who were you talking to? did you try to..."

He scoffed, a bitter laugh escaping his lips. "Are you insane? Is what you're saying even making any sense to you?"

Rukayya's jaw tightened. "Well, I would not put that past you. You can do anything to get me out of the way, including removing anything that would ever tie us together. I've tried, Kamal. I've tried so hard to make this marriage work, but you're always somewhere else. Mentally and emotionally, you're never here with me."

Kamal's eyes flashed with frustration. "You knew what you were getting into, Rukayya. This marriage was never about love. It was about fulfilling obligations, about keeping up appearances."

Tears welled up in Rukayya's eyes, and she refused to let them fall. "I thought maybe, with time, things would change. But you're still stuck in the past, chasing shadows."

His face hardened. "You're exaggerating. I know what I'm doing."

"Do you?" Rukayya shot back. "You're so consumed by this past love that you don't see how it's affecting us. I don't feel safe, Kamal. I don't even recognize the man I married anymore."

Kamal moved closer, his voice low and dangerous. "You knew what you signed up for. This is my journey, my purpose."

Rukayya's frustration reached its peak, and she shouted back, "Your purpose? What about me, Kamal?

Silence hung in the room, heavy and suffocating. Kamal's expression softened momentarily as he looked at the pain etched on Rukayya's face. He opened his mouth to respond, but Rukayya, unable to bear the weight of the argument any longer, turned away and walked towards the door.

"I need some time, Kamal," she said, her voice barely above a whisper. "I need to figure out if I can keep living like this, always second to your past."

Desperation surged within Fatimè. She needed answers. Slowly, she stood up, determined to confront Kamal and demand the truth.

But before that, she checked the safe once more. Inside, she found a box, and when she opened it, she saw a stethoscope.

Her heart constricted at the sight of it. No one had to tell her that it belonged to her sister. It still had Furaira's initials, 'F.F.A.,' engraved on it.

Fatimè remembered how her sister had cried about misplacing the stethoscope—a cherished gift from their father after Furaira passed her JAMB exams.

Next to the stethoscope was a notebook, and Fatimè opened it. On the first page, she saw her sister's name written in Furaira's well-known cursive handwriting: 'Piya.'

As she flipped through the pages, a smile tugged at her lips. In the middle of the notebook, she found a tea recipe that her sister had scribbled.

She felt so foolish to have not clocked Piya was the name of a character in an Indian movie her sister had been obsessed with at some point.

With this discovery, Fatimè couldn't deny the truth any longer. Piya was none other than her beloved sister, Furaira.

Gombe, Nigeria.

Hammadi entered the house with a warm "Salaam" and carefully placed the leather bags he was holding on the center table. The living room embraced him with an inviting ambiance — the scent of Sandalwood and Kajiji wafting through the air, the soft glow of the table lamp casting a cozy warmth. Plush cushions on the sofa welcomed him as he took in the tranquility and comfort.

His wife, Fa'iza, greeted him with a broad smile as she appeared, her advancing pregnancy making her steps slow but graceful.

"Sannu e wartuki." She said and he sealed it with a gentle kiss on her cheek.

"Are you cooking?" Hammadi inquired, raising an eyebrow as he took in the delightful aromas wafting from the kitchen. "You're supposed to be on bed rest, an ananta hala walahi."

Her eyes twinkled mischievously as she pouted, "I was craving indomie," and he chuckled, shaking his head affectionately.

"And you know I can only eat mine..."

He chuckled, shaking his head affectionately. "That's true, you make the meanest indomie. But still, I need you to understand what bed rest means."

"You're talking as if you won't eat it too," Fa'iza teased.

"Of course," Hammadi laughed, "I can never say no."

"Fine, go freshen up. I'll be done by then," she said, dismissing him with a smile.

Hammadi stepped out of the shower to the ringing of his phone, his senses immediately alert. He picked it up and was met with the frantic voice of his sister.

"Hamma..." she cried, her voice trembling, "Can you book me a flight to Gombe today?"

"What? Right now? By this time? Ko fe'i? What is going on?" Hammadi asked, his concern evident.

"I can't tell you much right now," she said, her desperation palpable. "I just need to get out of here."

"Wait. Calm down. I'll get you out of there, but I doubt if I can get a flight by this time. It has to be tomorrow morning. Traveling at this time is risky. Uh, how about I call Mustafa? You can stay at Hajja Dije's place until tomorrow morning?"

"Okay," Fatimè replied.

"Are you hurt? Did something happen? Tell me. Did your husband hit you?" Hammadi's voice was filled with worry.

"No," she said softly, her voice trembling, "I just need to leave this house this minute. I will tell you everything. Just get me out of here."

"Okay. Hang on, I'll call Mustafa right away," Hammadi assured her.

Fa'iza, having witnessed her husband's conversation, saw the worried look on his face when she entered the room. She waited patiently for him to finish his phone call.

"Yes, yes," Hammadi said into the phone. "I have sent you the address, Miyatti. Please keep me updated."

"Ko fe'i?" Fa'iza asked as he hung up.

"I just received a call from Fatimè. She says she needs to leave her house, and I should get her a flight to Gombe. But she wouldn't tell me what happened..."

"Subhanallah. I hope she is okay?" Fa'iza said, her concern mirrored in her eyes. "And she didn't say anything?"

"No, she just kept repeating 'I need to get out of here.' I don't want to think it's what it is because, lord save me if he put a hand on my sister, walahi I would kill him."

"Let's try to think positively," Fa'iza said, her voice filled with empathy. "Also, pray it's not the case. We should find a way to reach her first."

"Yes, I just spoke to Mustafa. He said he'll get to her. I asked her to stay in their house first until I can get her a flight. I doubt there'll be one to Gombe. It has to be Abuja."

"That seems solid. Let's pray she's okay. Do you think we should tell Mami?"

"No, no," Hammadi protested, shaking his head. "You know how she is; she'll just panic. As it is, we don't even know what's happening. I'll just call Mubarak. We'll handle it."

Fa'iza trusted her husband's judgment and focused on saying some prayers for her sister-in-law, hoping fervently that Fatimè would be safe and sound.

Lagos, Nigeria.

As Fatimè anxiously awaited her cousin Mustafa's arrival, her trembling hands hastily stuffed a few clothes into a trolley, desperately gathering the most essential items she could think of. The urgency to escape before Kamal's return gnawed at her, filling her with a deep sense of dread. Thoughts of the impending confrontation with Kamal added to the turmoil within her, and she questioned whether fleeing was the right choice. The PTSD she wrestled with, a constant companion, seemed insignificant compared to the external threat she faced.

Snatching the car keys from the console in the hallway, Fatimè stealthily made her way outside, her heart racing with every step. Her breath caught as she crossed the threshold, but the relief of escaping the confines of their home was short-lived.

Outside, a new terror awaited her – there he stood, Kamal, leaning casually on the car with a smug smile playing on his lips. His mere presence sent shivers down her spine, and a chilling sense of impending danger engulfed her. The shadows cast by the dimly lit surroundings seemed to magnify Kamal's sinister demeanor.

"Where are you going, sunshine?" He taunted, his words dripping with a malevolence that cut through the air, intensifying Fatimè's fear.

Chapter 29

♥

Abuja, Nigeria.

September, 2018.

The soft hum of the air conditioner provided a distant backdrop to the hushed conversation over the phone. Madina fidgeted with the edge of her scarf, her unease evident in the uncertain movements of her fingers.

As she listened, a mixture of emotions played across her face – a delicate dance of loyalty and personal desires. The weight of the request hung heavily in the air, and uncertainty etched lines on her forehead.

"Madina, you have to do this for me," he insisted urgently, his words pressing her to make a choice that seemed impossible. "I need to know what she's up to."

Madina sighed, "I get it, but spying on her feels wrong. What if she finds out? It'll destroy our relationship."

A pregnant pause filled the air before he responded, his voice lowering to a conspiratorial tone. "Remember, this is for you too."

Madina hesitated, her internal struggle reflected in the turmoil of her thoughts. "Fine, but you owe me big for this. And if things go south, you're the one explaining why I invaded her privacy."

After ending the call, Madina took a deep breath, attempting to steel herself for the task ahead. Her mind raced with conflicting emotions, but a resolute determination settled in. She understood the gravity of the situation and set out to plant the cameras in inconspicuous corners of her cousin's room.

The opportunity presented itself seamlessly – Fatimè was out for a doctor's appointment that usually extended for hours. This window of time would afford Madina the chance to carry out her covert mission without detection.

When Fatimè returned, Madina, wearing a mask of feigned innocence, greeted her. "I didn't know you'd be coming today," Fatimè remarked upon seeing her in the room.

"I wanted to check up on you, A jamo?" Madina replied.

"Fine," Fatimè answered, her weariness evident, not wanting to delve into conversation after the exhaustive visit to the doctor. "Do you want to watch a movie? Khalifa sent some to my laptop yesterday."

Madina nodded, grateful for the offered distraction, yet beneath the surface, the conflict within her simmered, a storm of conflicting emotions masked by the façade of normalcy.

Lagos, Nigeria.

30th July, 2018.

When the car finally turned to the corner of Fatimè's street, Madina and Fahad both let out a collective sigh of relief. They had been ensnared in a grueling traffic jam for the past two hours, and Fatimè had become increasingly unreachable as time ticked away.

Originally, they had planned to visit her the next day, but Madina had insisted on making the trip immediately.

As they pulled up in front of Fatimè's gate, they noticed another car parked there. Suspicion immediately raised its head, and Madina and Fahad quickly exited the vehicle. A man was engaged in a conversation with the security guard, and Fahad approached him with a sense of urgency.

"Hamma Musty," Fahad called out as recognition flashed across his face, "What are you doing here?"

Mustafa looked flustered as he responded, "It was Hammadi who called me. He urgently requested me to come and pick up Tims, but when I arrived, the security guard informed me that they had already left. I've been trying to reach her, but her phones are all unavailable."

Fahad turned to Madina, who wore an expression of mounting fear. He then turned back to the security guard, his voice edged with concern, "Do you have any idea where your Oga and Madam went?"

The security guard shook his head, looking perplexed, "No, sir. Oga just returned and asked me to fetch something for him. But when I came back, they had already left."

Madina was frantically dialing Kamal's number, but each call attempt seemed to meet a dead end. Her frustration was palpable as she muttered under her breath, "That bastard."

Fahad voiced the question that loomed in their minds, "Do you think he kidnapped her or something?"

"Kidnap?" Mustafa interjected with alarm, "What's happening here?"

"He's capable of anything," Madina cried out desperately. "We need to find her, Fahad."

Mustafa's phone suddenly buzzed, and he saw that it was a call from Hammadi.

"How's it going?" Hammadi's voice sounded concerned. "Have you picked up Fatimè? Where is she? I can't reach her on her phone."

Mustafa hesitated for a moment, and then Fahad gestured for him to hand over the phone.

"Hamma," Fahad began slowly, "there's a problem."

"What problem? Where's Fatimè?" Panic laced Hammadi's voice.

Fahad took a deep breath and uttered the words that chilled their hearts, "It appears that Fatimè has been kidnapped."

Abuja, Nigeria.

31st July, 2018.

Hajiya Hauwa cradled her face in her hands, her lips silently moving in prayer as she muttered, "Inna lillahi wa inna ilayhi raji'un." Her husband, stood solemnly by the window, engrossed in the phone call he was receiving. Nodding his head in response to what was being said, he finally spoke, "Miyatti," and ended the call. He turned to his distraught wife.

"Abubakar says he has spoken to his contacts, so we have to wait," Alhaji informed her.

"Wait?" Hajiya Hauwa's voice trembled with anxiety as she sprang up from her seated position. "Time is passing, What if something terrible has happened to her?"

Alhaji gently took her trembling hands in his own and offered reassurance, "In sha Allah, she is safe. Let's continue to pray."

Tears streamed down Hajiya Hauwa's face as she lamented, "This is all my fault, wallahi. I can't believe I handed our daughter over to..."

Alhaji interrupted her self-blame, "This is not the time for assigning blame, Jiddu. These events are not within our control."

"But I told you I had a bad feeling, ever since the last time she visited. Something didn't feel right..."

Upstairs, Mubarak, appeared, clutching a set of car keys. His father turned to him with a questioning gaze, "Where are you going? Have you heard any news?"

Mubarak shook his head, his expression a mix of determination and worry. "No, but I'm meeting Hamma at the airport. We'll depart for Lagos from there. I've secured our tickets."

Alhaji nodded in understanding, "Alright. Please keep us updated."

Mubarak moved closer to his mother, seeking to offer comfort, "Please don't cry, Mami. We'll find her, okay?"

Gombe, Nigeria.

"You mean there are no straight flights to Lagos?" Hammadi asked, visibly frustrated, "Okay. Okay. Send me the details kawai."

"What did he say?" Fa'iza said stepping into the room holding a small suitcase, "Ahefti?"

Hammadi let out a frustrated sigh, "No. only Abuja. I'll meet Mubarak then we'll leave from there."

"What of Fahad? Has he called?"

"Still nothing. They have not been able to trace her whereabouts."

"Ya Allah." Fa'iza cried, "What kind of problem is this?"

"I just pray she's okay."

Fa'iza placed her hands on his shoulder, "In sha Allah.

Just finish packing up." He said to her, "Let me warm the car."

Fa'iza moved to speak but he cut her off, "No. you are not coming with me. I don't need to worry about two people please."

Lagos, Nigeria.

The atmosphere in Hajja Dije's house was filled with tension, a tray of tea sat untouched.

"And she was in my house a few weeks ago," Hajja Dije said, "I was even saying I'll make some garin kunu for her."

Fahad's phone rang, and he excused himself. It was Zahra. He braced himself up for the outburst. By now, she was bound to know what was going on. Surprisingly, when he picked up, she was calm, but he still apologized.

When he returned to the sitting room, his aunt was no longer there. Madina sat in silence, pondering every pattern of Kamal's, trying to figure out what he had done to Fatimè or where he had taken her.

Mustafa sat confused; he still did not understand why Fatimè was kidnapped, and most of all, by her husband. He had met Kamal once when they came to visit his mum; the guy looked cool. It had to be a misunderstanding.

Suddenly, Madina got up, "I think I know where she is..."

In the dimly lit corner of the abandoned warehouse, Kamal dragged a rusty chair and settled himself, his gaze fixed intently on Fatimè. The cavernous space echoed with the sounds of renovation work from afar.

Fatimè, trembling with fear, shifted to the far end of the room. She could no longer decipher the intentions hidden behind Kamal's blank eyes.

"Hi..." he had a smile on his face when he handed her, her glasses and she hurriedly put them on. She was still trying to make sense of what was going on.

How did she get here? How long was she out for? Slowly everything came back to her, the laptop, the journal, the phone call with
her brother, and Kamal's appearance.

"You know what is fascinating?" he said, the words slicing through
the air like a chilling wind.

Fatimè remained silent, her body huddled in the corner, a veil of
uncertainty shrouding her.

"Cars," Kamal began, his voice disturbingly calm. "They take us to
different places, work, home, even our deaths. They also take a lot
from us, like your fiancé, your sister..."

Fatimè gulped, her throat dry as she forced out her words. "What
has all this got to do with them?"

Kamal's lips curled into a sinister smile. "Oh, sweet, naïve Fatimè,
Everything, has everything to do with them."

"Is this what all this is about? My sister?" Fatimè's voice quivered
with a mix of anger and disbelief. "You're doing all this for someone
who never mentioned you? I'm pretty sure she had no idea you
existed."

"We could have been something if you didn't ruin it," Kamal
hissed, his eyes narrowing with resentment.

"Ruin what?" Fatimè's incredulity overcame her fear. "Are you
crazy? No, wait, you are crazy. Do you think I set out to kill my sister?
It was an accident! Either of us could have died!" As Fatimè spoke,
the guilt she had carried for so long weighed heavy on her heart.

"But it wasn't you," Kamal muttered, his voice dripping with malice.

"Of course, you think I haven't thought of that?" Fatimè snapped
back, her voice laced with anger. "Do you know how I've lived with

her loss? Please, get out." Fatimè chuckled bitterly at Kamal's absurdity.

"I needed to get back at you with everything I could," Kamal continued, his eyes cold and calculating. "I wanted you to feel the pain of losing someone you loved."

Khalid's memory surged within Fatimè, and despite her unpreparedness, she lunged at Kamal, raining blows upon his chest. "You are despicable! Why not me? It was me you had a score to settle with. Why him? He never did anything to you!" At that moment, the pain of Khalid's death hit her like a sledgehammer, compounded by the revelation of Kamal's deceit. "Why don't you just go ahead and kill me then?" Fatimè cried, her voice filled with despair. "I mean, there's nothing else to live for."

Kamal let out a cold, mocking laugh. "You think if I wanted to kill you, I wouldn't have done that a long time ago? Where's the fun in that?" he taunted, his eyes gleaming with sadistic pleasure. "I prefer to see you in pain, to watch you die inside slowly. To take away every atom of happiness in you."

The events rushed back to Fatimè and she mouthed, "You are the worst of the worst. What did my poor babies do to you? I don't even understand it. You killed your children for the fun of it?"

At the same time, she was not surprised, he was capable of anything. For someone to take his sweet time to get to her. She wondered how someone so sinister was able to infiltrate her life without her getting a whiff of it. One question bugged her, how was he able to get access to her room????

"How did you get those cameras into my room?" she blurted.

"How else?" he answered casually, "It's funny how you think you're some saint when you go around ruining shit for people. You just happen to be there to make people's lives miserable, even the ones closest to you."

Fatimè thought hard about what he was saying, what did he mean by the ones closest to you? - wait, no no no... It couldn't be... nah, he was lying.

He answered just in time, "Yes, you thought it was only me? You're a funny babe."

She felt like a knife had pierced her heart. Madina could not be in on this. It had to be a lie but then she had seen firsthand the lengths Madina went just to keep Fahad to herself, citing Fatimè as a hindrance. Nah, this was the most heartbreaking thing. Everything started to make sense, their meeting was a setup, and everything he had done, was with the help of Madina. She fed him everything. Oh lord.

Fatimè scrutinized Kamal's features, her eyes filled with a mixture of fear and disbelief. Was this the same man she had married? The man who had protected her from harm, whispered sweet nothings in her ear, and kissed her passionately?

"Watching you every day gave me more satisfaction," he added, his voice dripping with malice.

"You've never had any love in your life, and it shows," Fatimè retorted, her voice tinged with pity. "I feel sorry for you because you're sick. You should seek help."

Kamal's smile remained unsettling. "You're cute. It's one of those things that made living with you easy and no, I don't need any help, I just need you. Why do you want to leave me?"

He made a menacing move to touch her, but Fatimè pushed him with every ounce of strength she could muster. "Don't you dare come close to me. You are crazy."

"Crazy about you," Kamal whispered, desperation creeping into his voice. "Can't you see? You're all I have left of her." He knelt before her, his voice quivering. "I loved her. I loved her."

"You call that love?" Fatimè's voice dripped with scorn. "That's an obsession, you sicko. You stalked her and then married her sister for revenge. Who does that?"

"I had to do what I had to do," Kamal insisted, a shadow of vulnerability flickering in his eyes as he spoke of his twisted love for her sister.

Fatimè had been calculating her next move, and as she made a desperate attempt to escape, Kamal proved faster. He seized her legs and flung her to the unforgiving warehouse floor. The impact sent searing pain through her back, and a scream tore from her throat. He pinned her down, her struggles futile against his overwhelming strength, her body already weakened by the lingering effects of the chloroform. Amid her agony, she looked into Kamal's eyes, glimpsing the malevolence within them just before a needle pierced her skin.

Epilogue

♥

G ombe, Nigeria.

December, 2022.

The annual Ardo gathering shifted to a new venue this year, taking place on the ranch. The expansive space had been meticulously adorned, creating an ambiance of liveliness.

Mubarak held his niece in his arms as he approached a cluster of cousins seated on a vibrant carpet spread across the ground. "Inti," he called out to one of them, a warm smile gracing his face. "It looks like you might just gift me this adorable baby of yours. She's too precious, tabarkallah."

Intisar chuckled while her daughter, Amani, waddled over to her side. "Shouldn't you be busy making your babies?" she teased.

Mubarak scoffed, "Ahn ahn, from where to where?"

The banter continued as more cousins joined in. Safiya playfully added, "Yes, mana Hamma Mubarak, it's time for you to give us some nieces and nephews."

Mubarak shook his head, a mischievous glint in his eye. "On wantini yan gite walahi. Toh, your prayers have finally been answered..."

Before he could finish his sentence, they burst into lively chants of "ango."

"Gist us, please..." Mufida eagerly interjected.

Khalifa seized the opportunity to join in. "Her name is Laila..."

However, Mubarak halted him with a playful swat on the back. "Amebo! Is it your gist?"

Fa'iza plopped down onto a chair next to Hammadi, letting out a sigh of exasperation. "Kai. Mi somi walahi. I'm leaving your son for you."

Hammadi raised an eyebrow, a playful smile on his face. "What did he do now?"

Fa'iza rolled her eyes, her frustration giving way to a fond smile. "Do you know how I found him? Covered in mud. That's what I get for dressing him in white clothes."

Hammadi chuckled, offering her comfort. "I told you, let him play abeg. Isn't Hally watching him?"

Fa'iza hesitated before responding, "Yes, but..."

Hammadi interrupted her gently, "But nothing. You like stressing yourself, walahi. Relax." He draped his arm over her shoulder, soothing her.

Fa'iza finally relaxed, finding solace in a plate of cupcakes Hammadi had thoughtfully set aside for her. She swatted his hand away playfully when she noticed a group of their aunts discreetly watching them from a nearby corner.

Hammadi always found her shyness endearing and sometimes intentionally provoked her just to see her reactions.

At a distance, Hajiya Asiya rummaged in her bag, retrieving a piece of kola nut which she bit into. "I don't know what's with my stomach these days. I'll eat something, and the next thing I know, I'm feeling nauseous."

Najma sympathized, saying, "Sannu. It's probably the weather." She then turned to her other sister and said, "Yauwa Jidda, when did you say we were taking those things for Mubarak's wedding?"

"An sa rana ne?" Asiya inquired.

"Not yet," Hajiya Hauwa replied, "We're still finalizing with Baban Mubarak. You know how everything..."

"True, true. Allah hokku sa'a," Hajiya Asiya agreed.

Sa'adatu entered the scene, holding a small basket. "Adda Jidda, here's what you asked for..."

"Miyatti," Hajiya Hauwa acknowledged, taking the basket and rising from her seat. "I'm coming."

She found him on one of the porches, comfortably reclining in a chair, and joined him. "I brought some fura for you. Should I mix it?"

"Yes, please. Thank you, habibty," he responded graciously.

She smiled and began to mix the fura, then handed him the bowl. He took a few spoonfuls and nodded appreciatively. "This is so good..."

"Mhmmm," she replied softly, her gaze shifting to the joyful sight of children running around.

"Are you alright?" he asked after a moment of silence.

"As long as they are all okay, I am okay," she replied, leaning her head on his shoulder.

Abuja, Nigeria.

The timing of the professional exams couldn't have been more perfect for Madina. It provided her with the perfect excuse to avoid showing up at a place where she felt increasingly disconnected.

Most of her hours had been spent rolling aimlessly in bed, her mind wandering far from the books in front of her.

The house was eerily quiet, its usual lively atmosphere muted by the absence of her family members, who had all traveled to Gombe. Only her father remained with her, a constant presence in her now lonely existence.

Lately, her life had settled into a melancholic routine, with work consuming the majority of her waking hours. There seemed to be nothing to look forward to, and a sense of emptiness had gradually taken root.

As she stared at her textbook, her thoughts drifted into the abyss of her sadness. She yearned for something more, something to break the monotony of her existence.

She impulsively picked up her phone and dialed a number, a glimmer of hope flickering in her heart. But, as expected, there was no answer on the other end. She sighed in disappointment and returned her attention to her textbook.

Just then, her phone emitted a notification beep, breaking the silence in the room. She rushed to it with a mixture of anticipation and trepidation. The message contained pictures sent to the family WhatsApp group, and as she began to skim through them, her eyes fixed on a particular image that stirred a complex mix of emotions.

There he was, looking even more handsome than she remembered, the sun casting a gentle, warm glow on his skin as he cradled his 2-year-old son in his arms. A smile played across both of their faces, radiating happiness and contentment. But what caught Madina's attention the most was the subtle curve of her belly, a small but undeniable bump, with his hand tenderly resting on her shoulder.

A pang of longing and regret washed over Madina as she gazed at the photograph. Perhaps, she thought, she should consider offering to become his second wife.

Örebro, Sweden

The sharp contrast in weather fascinated him. Just a year ago, he had been battling the scorching heat of Qatar, and now, he found himself unable to step outside without a jacket in his current location.

Sweden, with its picturesque landscapes and distinct seasons, had become his new home. Living there had been an intriguing experience, with its stunning natural beauty, efficient public services, and the unique charm of its people. The transition from the desert heat to Sweden's refreshing cold had been a stark but welcome change for him.

As he savored a sip of his coffee, he opened his laptop. It was routine for a day like this. An email in his inbox caught his attention, and he paused to read it. Over the past few years, he had received numerous emails like this, but this time, he felt an unusual inclination to entertain the proposition. He finished his coffee, closed the laptop, and decided to leave the house.

The outdoor cafe he chose was a quintessential Swedish spot, with wooden tables and chairs, each adorned with a red-checkered tablecloth. The soft hum of conversation mixed with the occasional clinking of cups and saucers in the crisp air. It was a serene place, perfect for contemplation.

A man at a nearby table, James, noticed his laptop covered in travel stickers from various countries. Intrigued, he struck up a conversation, straight to the point. "Excuse me, I couldn't help but notice your travel stickers on your laptop. They're impressive. Do you do travel photography professionally?"

He smiled, appreciating the directness. "Thank you. Not really; I just do some freelance work in travel photography. What can I help you with?"

James leaned forward, sharing his ideas. "I'm working on a project for a travel magazine, and your style aligns perfectly with what we're looking for. Would you be interested in collaborating?"

He considered the proposal for a moment. "I'd like to know more about the project. Let me think it over, and I'll get back to you soon."

After James left, Kamal leaned back in his chair, his thoughts drifting. He had been observing the woman at the adjacent table for some time now, studying her daily routine. She always arrived at 5 PM, enjoyed her Subway sandwich, and left at 6 PM. Kamal discreetly pulled out his phone and snapped a picture.

Gombe, Nigeria.

The cacophony of voices echoed through the open space of the ranch, filling Fatime's ears. After three years of suffocating silence, she found the noise strangely welcoming. It served as a reminder that she was still alive and that life was continuing despite the turmoil she had endured. Standing on the balcony overlooking the sprawling ranch, she gazed out at the rolling hills and the golden sunset casting its warm glow. The scene held a quiet beauty, a stark contrast to the chaos that had consumed her life.

In the solitude of Aberdeen, she had grown accustomed to the comforting silence her aunt had provided. It had become her refuge, shielding her from the prying eyes and judgmental whispers of others. But it had also allowed them to concoct their narratives, weaving tales of betrayal and heartache to explain her absence.

Stories of her husband absconding to marry another woman or engaging in acts of infidelity had become fodder for gossip. She couldn't help but laugh at the absurdity of it all, for tales were the least of her concerns.

Her mind still struggled to make sense of the fragments of her shattered life. Weeks spent in the hospital had left her physically weakened, her body bearing the scars of her ordeal. But the scars ran much deeper than what met the eye. When her father asked her what she wanted, the only desire that surfaced in her shattered mind was the need to escape. She yearned to be away from everything, to distance herself from the pain and the memories that threatened to consume her.

Her wish was met with little resistance. No one protested, although her mother's tears flowed incessantly. Guilt gnawed at her mother, blaming herself for pushing Fatime into a marriage that had ultimately shattered her spirit. On the other hand, her father berated himself for his perceived carelessness, while her brothers grappled with guilt, blaming themselves for not protecting her. Fatime could only chuckle bitterly, for she had been married to him for over a year. How could she have been so blind? Yet, dwelling on the whys and hows never yielded any answers, only more pain.

There was also the lingering fear of his return, a constant shadow lurking in the recesses of her mind. But Fatime had made the conscious choice to let go. She couldn't allow herself to be consumed by the what-ifs and the fear. Life had dealt her a cruel hand, and she had resolved to move forward and find healing in her way.

Her phone buzzed, breaking her from her thoughts. She glanced at the screen, seeing yet another message that would go unanswered. It was from Madina, her cousin and confidante. But there was nothing more for Madina to say or do. She had done more than enough, and the magnitude of pain and betrayal from someone she had considered a sister was indescribable.

With a heavy sigh, Fatime turned her attention back to the horizon, where the sun was now dipping below the hills, casting long shadows. She had lost the absolute love of her life, and in the process, she had unintentionally inflicted pain on his family. They had believed their son had perished in an accident. She felt a twinge of guilt for Adil, her husband's son, for having a father who was selfish and capable of such terrible deeds. She wondered how Rukayya, his mother, was coping with the aftermath of the revelation.

Her thoughts then drifted to Kamal's mother, a woman shocked to her very core by her son's actions. Kamal had been the perfect actor, skillfully weaving a façade of love and devotion throughout their shared lives. Fatime couldn't help but admire the acting skills he had honed, even as she despised the lies and betrayal that had shattered her world.

A few months ago, Fatime had decided to return home to Gombe. An inexplicable pull drew her to her roots, to the place that held a semblance of familiarity amidst the chaos. Her father had warned everyone not to prod her with questions, and with the unwavering support of her grandmother, she was granted the solitude she craved.

She immersed herself in the quiet routines of the farm, finding solace in the simple tasks of riding horses, taking peaceful strolls, and harvesting the fruits of the land. The farm became her sanctuary, a place where she could find fleeting moments of serenity and tranquility.

His familiar scent announced his presence, and he cleared his throat, making Fatimè turn around.

"Ko gadata upstairs?" he asked. "You are missing the party."

Fatimè smiled. "Just enjoying some alone time. I don't know if I can face everyone at the moment."

"What do you mean? Did you grow two heads?"

Ahmad's question was met with silence. He was used to it. The little time she had spent at their house in Aberdeen was enough. He did more of the talking, and in a way, Fatimè was grateful that he did not treat her like everyone else.

The pity, worry, and all. He talked to her like a normal person, and sometimes he even made her laugh.

"You know it's not your fault, you know? Things happen to people because they are meant to happen, and there is nothing we can do about it. Now stop thinking too much, or you'll shrink and disappear. Who am I going to trouble if that happens?"

Fatimè laughed. "I won't deny myself the pleasure of being a thorn in your life."

Outside, they met everyone setting up for a family photograph. She found her way to the midst of her brothers and parents, who immediately fixed her in the right spot.

Her appearance bore the weight of her pain, though not in a way that made her look horrible. The grief and betrayal had etched itself into her countenance, casting a shadow over her once vibrant features. Her eyes held a depth that spoke of a soul scarred but still searching for healing.

As the sun sank below the horizon, enveloping the world in darkness, Fatime felt a bittersweet farewell welling up within her. This marked not only the end of her story but also a parting with the readers who had followed her journey. The pain and growth she had experienced were woven into the fabric of her existence, shaping her into someone unrecognizable yet undeniably stronger.

As the photographer counted down, she gave her biggest smile. She was grateful to be alive, surrounded by family, and then she took a deep breath, allowing the weight of her burdens to settle for a moment before releasing them into the night. Fatime knew that her journey was far from over and that she still had a long road ahead of her. But for now, she bid farewell to the past, embracing the uncertain future that lay before her and stepping back into the realm of her own life. She carried with her the lessons learned, the scars endured, and the strength forged in the fires of betrayal.

9 781933 121581